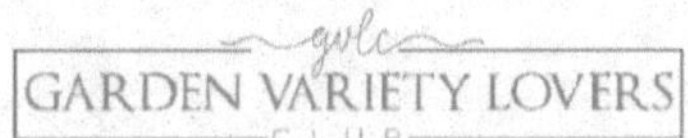

The Coffee Bar on Camellia Court

AUTUMN LAKE BOOK 3

BECKY DOUGHTY

The Coffee Bar on Camellia Court
Autumn Lake Romance Book 3

Copyright 2025 Becky Doughty

Published by BraveHearts Press

Author Information: BeckyDoughty.com

ISBN: 978-1953347824

1

Juno

Poppy sashaying into the shop in good spirits before dawn should have been a good omen.

Juno's day had, indeed, started out so well. Her signature cinnamon rolls and scones had baked to perfection, and she'd had time to make a double batch of syrup for her seasonal lavender honey lattes, which had been this summer's hit. Then Poppy had gotten to work a few minutes early for a change, looking put-together with a genuinely cheerful smile on her face. Five in the morning was tough for most people, but especially for teenagers and young adults. Juno empathized and showed the young woman a little extra grace, mainly because Poppy was an exceptional barista who worked hard to master the craft.

Juno traced her finger along the espresso machine's sleek curves. She'd never forget her first job as a barista fifteen years ago, serving lattes to high school friends in this very shop. Back then, she'd fallen in love with everything—the science of the roast, the chemistry of flavors, the art of the perfect foam.

Now she owned the place.

Then, right around nine AM, Alex Frampton's truck pulled into the small parking lot across the street at Tip-Top Talons. A nail salon, not a pet spa as its name might suggest. In spite of the unfortunate epithet, Sonya and her staff did a fair amount of business, especially during the summer tourist season. Many of Sonya's clients took advantage of Juno being just across the street and became Coffee Bar customers, too.

Tip-Top Talons was open long hours, and Juno appreciated Sonya's strong hands after her own twelve-hour days. The woman was chatty but sensitive to her clients' moods—never making Juno feel bad when she wasn't up for conversation. It was as close to tears as Juno ever came these days.

Today, however, it wasn't tears Juno was fighting back. Instead, she was doing everything she could to not let her gaze wander across the street to where Alex was constructing a small enclosure around the upgraded air conditioner Sonya had gotten installed last week. The unit was enormous and admittedly an eyesore, squatting in the middle of her front flower bed like an industrial wart. According to the heating and air company, however, that had been the best placement for it.

Juno was, of course, glad Sonya was doing something to camouflage the monstrosity. Tip-Top Talons had such a pretty porch bedecked with hanging fern baskets, and lush flowerbeds bordering a small lawn out front, and Juno's customers who sat at the tables in that window often commented on what a cute place it was.

But of all the contractors and handymen in town, did she have to hire Alex Frampton to do the work?

Alex. Big, blonde, and burnished, who wielded his hammer like it was an extension of his arm, his biceps bulging with each mighty swing, the muscles of his back and shoulders rippling beneath his tight t-shirt.

And then there was the woman who was sitting at one of Juno's coveted window tables, staring longingly out the window at him while she sipped on her enormous iced vanilla soy latte with caramel drizzle in the bottom, on the insides of the cup, and on top of the extra nondairy whipped cream, with ten pumps of vanilla syrup instead of the standard six, and an additional six pumps of toffee syrup.

She'd come from Tip-Top Talons, with her shiny long nails and the distinct essence of lacquer that emanated off her when she'd ordered her drink. She'd been sitting there for almost an hour, poring over a gossip magazine like it held the secrets of the ages, mooning over Alex, scrolling on her phone, and shooting dagger eyes at anyone else who so much as noticed Alex gleaming in the rays of sunshine shooting through the puffy clouds overhead.

It was almost like God, himself, felt compelled to shine a spotlight on one of his finest creations.

Juno huffed impatiently, wrung out the rag she'd been rinsing, and started vigorously wiping down the espresso machine. There was a lull in the mid-Saturday morning rush, and by the looks of the machine, it had gone like a workhorse for the last hour or so.

"Sonya's customers have a nice view today," Liz Needham commented dryly from where she sat at the counter, sipping on a large mug of black coffee. She had her back to the window, but Juno didn't have to guess what she was talking about. Or who.

"Yes, and I'm sure they appreciate it. Probably tipping good, too."

Liz chuckled and turned to watch Alex drive a post-hole digger into the soft garden soil. "I bet they are. You should think about putting a tip jar out, too. Or charge to rent a window seat."

The woman in the window must have sensed their attention, because she glared with open hostility in their direction.

"Sheesh, lady," Liz muttered, turning back to roll her eyes at Juno. "Do you know her?"

"She came in with him last Saturday," she said in a low voice. "Dolly. Uh, Payton."

Liz snorted, and in a loud whisper, asked, "Dolly Payton?"

Juno grinned and brought a carafe over to offer her a refill. "No, you nut," she said sotto voce. "Her name is Payton. But I had to use Dolly's name for association so I'd remember."

"A WOOT, I presume?"

"Well, she's not a townie." The locals, primarily living on the south shore, had witnessed dramatic changes to their quiet little town when a travel magazine featured Autumn Lake, calling it "a hidden gem vacation spot." The wild north shore had been cleared for the high-end Carpe Diem Resort, followed by the North Shore housing development with its own amenities catering to the wealthy seasonal residents.

The townies dubbed the tourists WOOTs, or wealthy-out-of-towners, although not everyone who vacationed at the lake booked accommodations at the resort or had a summer home in the North Shore development. There were also those who rented rooms or cottages from the townies, or brought their RVs and boat trailers to the Shady Shores

Campground on the south shore. Juno wasn't sure which category Payton fell under, nor did she care to find out.

What she did know was that Payton was just another in Alex's long line of pretty summer flings. He only dated women he couldn't logistically commit to—summer lakers who'd be gone by fall. Some returned year after year, hoping to pick up where they'd left off, but it never happened. Instead, every summer brought a new conquest clutching his arm and basking in his unrelenting charm.

"Poor thing," Liz said, her thoughts obviously heading in the same direction as Juno's. "Looks like she's flown too close to the sun."

"Yeah. Another summer sizzler." Juno pretended to lick her finger and held it up in Payton's general direction. "Tsssss."

Liz chortled. "Summer sizzler. That's good."

"Thank you," Juno preened. "That one just rolled off the tongue."

"Alex and his summer sizzlers." Liz nodded. "It's got a nice ring to it."

Juno chuckled and turned to the sink to rinse out the rag again. She almost felt sorry for Payton. It wasn't her fault that she'd fallen for Alex. The guy was irresistible with his Viking good looks and easy charm. He had a way of looking at a woman—any woman, Juno conceded—that made her feel singled out. Acknowledged. Special.

"He's doing it on purpose, you know."

"Doing what?" Juno asked over her shoulder, forcing her eyes not to wander toward the window.

Liz gave her a single-eyebrow-lift look and Juno mirrored the sardonic expression back at her. "Oh, you know. The whole shirtless thing. To get your attention."

Of its own accord, her gaze moved to the window just in time to see Alex ball up the shirt he'd just removed, toss it into the open window of his truck, then roll out his shoulders. At her table, Payton let out a dreamy sigh, loud enough to cover Juno's slight inhalation, thank goodness. Juno made a small sound of disgust at the back of her throat, but shrugged. "It's July in Indiana. We're a lake town. Every guy is shirtless today."

"Pastor Darren isn't shirtless."

Juno snorted and shot a look at the fully-dressed man who'd commandeered one of the comfortable reading chairs on the other side of the coffee shop and was engrossed in the day's Courier newspaper. "Yeah, well, Pastor Darren is seventy-two years old and has the good sense to stay indoors where there's air conditioning."

"You know, he could be Thor's younger brother." Liz's tone sounded a little gushy.

"Pastor Darren?" Juno couldn't resist asking.

"Yikes. No." Liz made a face just as Claire Maitland, the proprietress from The Cracked Spine, sank onto a stool beside her. Her long blonde hair was held back from her face by a black velvet ribbon, and she wore a white pinafore apron over a blue dress with a wide checkered border around the bottom of the full skirt. Juno was pretty sure there was some kind of petticoat under it to keep it so poofy.

Claire was always dressing like book characters. Her willowy silhouette and porcelain features were perfectly suited to the costumer's rack that was her closet. If she could figure out how to make it happen, Claire would step into her books and disappear forever.

"Wowzer!" Claire swiveled on her stool so she could openly watch Alex. "Not gonna complain about this morning's entertainment."

"Stop objectifying him, ladies," Juno said, fighting back a grin.

"I'd never objectify Pastor Darren." Liz pressed a palm to her chest in mock offense.

Juno ignored her, and to Claire, said, "And don't you have a bookstore to run?"

"I do," Claire shot back, still ogling Alex while she rifled blindly through her patchwork hobo bag for her wallet. "But I also have a couple of really great employees I pay to hold down the fort while I make a java run for them from my favorite coffee bar. I need three of your lavender honey lattes—two iced, one hot—a salted caramel blended latte, and a breve Americano for me. All mediums, please." She finally turned and grinned at Liz, then Juno. She leaned forward, lowering her voice. "Did you notice the WOOT in the window giving me the evil eye? What's up with that?"

"That's Dolly Payton," Liz said.

"No way." Claire's expression was priceless, her eyes wide, her face lit up with hope. "Dolly Payton? That's awesome!"

"Just Payton," Juno corrected, glaring long-sufferingly at Liz. "Alex's latest summer sizzler. That's what I'm officially calling them from now on, by the way."

Claire clapped delightedly. "Works for me."

"They came in together around this same time last Saturday and he made her introduce herself to me," Juno went on.

"Probably couldn't remember her name," Liz quipped.

"She's been camped out there for more than an hour," Juno continued, a note of genuine pity in her voice now. "I think she's waiting for him, maybe hoping he'll notice her sitting pretty in the window."

"Another summer sizzler," Claire said solemnly. "They burn out so quickly."

The conversation, to outside ears, might have sounded catty, but Alex regularly made light of his short term dalliances. "I'm a summer sunshine guy. Local color. No one expects more from me than that."

Claire cleared her throat and leaned forward over the counter. "Incoming," she muttered out of the side of her mouth.

Sure enough, Payton was making her way to the counter, designer purse swinging. "Could I get an extra large lavender honey latte to go? Extra hot and extra sweet, like me." She glanced over her shoulder at Alex and subconsciously pressed her fingertips to her mouth. "And extra whipped cream on top, too," she added, turning her bold gaze toward the three women at the counter. "I thought my guy out there might need a little pick-me-up."

My guy. Dreamer.

Juno didn't roll her eyes, but it sure took a vat of self-control not to. Liz, however, didn't hold back, but at least she'd turned away so Payton wouldn't see.

"The hot drinks don't come with whipped cream on top," Juno said to the woman. "It immediately dissolves into the drink."

"Fine. Can you put it in a little cup on the side, then?"

Liz's eyes widened. "Like one of those pup cups?" she asked, somehow keeping a straight face.

"Yeah, exactly. But extra. He just loves, loves, loves whipped cream."

"TMI," muttered Liz into her coffee cup before she took a long, slow slurp.

Claire smiled brightly at Payton. "What a nice thing to do," she exclaimed, the slightly higher pitch of her voice the only telltale sign that she, too, was trying to keep her composure. "I hear he likes to read on his lunch hour. You should stop by over at The Cracked Spine and pick him up a book, too." She leaned a little closer to the woman. "He's really into the Outlander Series. Most guys aren't big enough to admit to loving Diana Gabaldon's books, but not Alex Frampton. That man has no shame, whatsoever." The double meaning went right over Payton's head, but it wasn't lost on Liz or Juno, who both had to bite back grins.

Payton gave Claire a bemused frown. "The Cracked Spine? Is that, like, a chiropractor?" Apparently, the whole part about books in general went right over Payton's head, too.

"It's a bookstore," Liz explained when Claire seemed lost for words. She pointed out the window to the shop on the opposite corner. "The books in the window kinda give it away." Claire always had the wildest and most whimsical window displays. Right now, a "flock" of books hung suspended from the ceiling, flying over a lake of books with covers in various shades of blue.

Payton pursed her lips and shook her head. "Um, no," she said, drawing out the words. "It sounds kinda boring. Outlander? Is that like Planet of the Apes or something dumb like that?"

It was Liz who now opened her mouth and closed it, too shocked to speak. No one criticized her big screen ape obsession and lived to tell about it. Claire put a calming hand on her shoulder.

Before either of them could speak, Payton said, "Besides, I want him to spend lunch with me, not with his nose stuck in a book." She pointed at Juno. "Are you going to make that coffee for me?"

A hot, sweet latte in the sweltering heat of mid-July? Really? "Are you sure? Maybe an iced matcha latte? I know he—"

"I know him, too," Payton interrupted. "So please just give me what I ordered, okay?"

Juno pressed her lips together and nodded. She had to admit that Payton probably felt a little fish-out-of-water at that moment, and maybe even ganged up on. The three of them obviously knew each other, and it was probably apparent to Payton that they'd been discussing at least Alex, if not her, too. She nodded and entered the order into her POS tablet. "Coming right up."

"Thank you," Payton said, exasperation making her words breathy. She held out her phone to pay, but Juno shook her head.

"This one's on the house." She wasn't going to charge the woman for an order she knew good and well that no one would drink. Besides, she'd charged Payton for every custom addition she'd requested for her own drink, and the cost had amounted to a ridiculous amount of money; so much, that Juno felt almost ashamed taking anymore from her. And Payton had left a 20% tip on top of it. From the corner of her eye, she saw Liz and Claire exchange glances. She ignored them; she didn't have to explain her business decisions to them.

"Well, thank you," Payton said again, her smile turning genuine, softening her features, making her suddenly look almost lovely, now that the hardness in her eyes had diminished. She turned to look back at Alex, who was now using power tools. "Is he always this..." The blonde gestured vaguely toward the window.

"Helpful?" Liz supplied innocently. "Hardworking? Built like a Greek god?"

Juno shot her friend a warning look, but Liz just grinned.

Payton missed the sarcasm. "Right? You guys know him, don't you? Is he...? He's available, right?" She toyed with a long blonde curl. "We've bumped into each other a few times in the last week, but he's kind of vague about whether he's seeing anyone."

"Alex Frampton? Vague about commitment?" Liz's eyes widened in mock surprise. "I'm shocked. Shocked, I tell you."

The blonde's smile faltered. "What do you mean?"

"Nothing. Ignore her." Claire gave Liz's shoulder a warning push.

But Liz wasn't finished. "You know, I can see that you're different." She paused meaningfully. "Original. So be direct. Go ask him point blank."

"Here you go, Payton." Juno handed over the enormous latte, silently willing Liz to behave. This wasn't high school, and they weren't mean girls. Even if the blonde was about to embark on a mission that probably wouldn't end the way she was imagining.

"Tell Alex we said, 'hi!'" Claire called after her as Payton headed toward the door, the ruffled hem of her short skirt fluttering provocatively as she walked. Even Pastor Darren lowered his newspaper for just a moment when she passed by his chair. Granted, his eyes never strayed to her skirt, but he smiled warmly at her before returning to the news. He really was such a kind man.

They watched through the window as she crossed the street, said something that made Alex grin, and handed him the cup. She held up her phone, and Alex stepped close to her side, draped an arm around her shoulders, then rested his head on top of hers and grinned into the phone camera as Payton took their selfie. He bent and kissed her cheek in thanks, because whatever his faults, Alex Frampton was unfailingly chivalrous, glanced at the label stuck to the side of the cup, then set the coffee on the tailgate of his truck without taking a single sip.

"That's a lot of physical contact from someone who's all sweaty," Claire commented. "Gross."

"Yeah, gross," Liz echoed. The sarcasm was back in her voice. "Eww. Disgusting."

"You guys are too much." Juno grabbed a drink carrier from off a shelf and put the four lattes Claire had ordered into it. "Your Americano is almost ready."

Across the street, Payton was apparently not getting the response she'd expected. She cocked one hip and pointed at her phone. Alex wiped his brow with a bandana from his back pocket, then gestured at the nearly-finished enclosure he'd constructed. He shook his head, smiled sweetly, then tugged on the same blonde curl Payton had been toying with just a few minutes ago.

Liz let out a sympathetic "Oof," then drained the last of her coffee. "Looks like the show's over. I gotta get going, ladies."

Sure enough, Payton's shoulders slumped as Alex walked her to a Jeep SUV in the salon's parking lot. He held the door open for her, waited for her to climb in, then leaned inside.

"Okay," Claire remarked with a chuckle as she spun on her stool. "Not sure I want to see the rest of that scene."

Liz made a gagging sound, then stood up and pushed a couple of bills into the tip jar on the counter.

Juno had already turned away from the window and was busy with Claire's last drink. She didn't want to see it either. She'd been there once, thinking she was different, special, the one who'd...

No. She was not going down that road again.

The sound of screeching tires got her attention. Alex stood on the sidewalk watching as Payton peeled out of the parking lot. When he turned toward the coffee shop window, Juno quickly looked away.

But not before she saw his big old grin.

That man was trouble with a capital T, and Juno Thomas was done with trouble. No matter how good it looked without a shirt on.

2
Alex

Alex watched Payton's Jeep disappear around the corner, guilt churning in his stomach. Why did they always storm off when he wouldn't drop everything at their beck and call? He worked forty-plus hours a week for J&J Contractors, plus any odd jobs he could pick up on the weekends like this AC enclosure for Sonya. He was on schedule if he kept at it, but he'd be heading straight to the St. James' dock from here, having promised Ward to help replace some of the pilings later today.

Even though he enjoyed the tourists who came for the summer months, he was always glad for Labor Day, knowing life in Autumn Lake would return to normal. The pretty women got him in trouble every year—not because he succumbed to the temptations they offered, but because he wasn't good at saying no. He spent too much time dodging ultimatums and sidestepping conflict.

Lately, it seemed that conflict followed him around like a shadow, wrestling with him in his sleep, and biting at his heels in his waking hours.

The latte from Payton sat untouched on his truck's tailgate, mocking him. Alex had set down his drill long enough to thank the woman for the drink, but when he'd turned down her offer of lunch, Payton had pouted, poking out her bottom lip and planting her hands on her hips. She'd probably stamped her foot, too, although he couldn't remember. When he'd ignored the childish display, and picked up his drill to get back to work, she'd then tried to guilt him into it by telling him she'd been patiently waiting all morning just to be with him. "I thought you said you liked spending time with me."

Well, he *had* enjoyed spending time with her that first evening they'd met at Patsy's Pizza. He'd been shooting pool with a couple of friends, she'd come in with some girlfriends, and the two parties had naturally comingled. It had been a good time for all, Alex had thought, and sure, he'd shamelessly flirted with her, but he'd behaved the exact same way toward her two friends, too. Not once, at least in his mind, had he given any of them any indication that he was interested in more than that one evening had entailed.

But last week, she'd hunted him down. Literally. She'd admitted to as much, explaining that she'd asked Will at Patsy's Pizza if he knew how she could get a hold of him, and the dumb kid had told her. Alex couldn't really blame Will, a local high schooler working at the pizza place for the summer. Everyone knew everyone on the south shore, and word of mouth was still considered a failproof method of getting ahold of someone. There was no reason for Will not to share Alex's contact information.

Putting Payton out of his mind, he went back to the white picket enclosure project. He had a few more finishing touches, and if there were no more disruptions, he'd have time to grab a sandwich across the street at Juno's. He'd have to get it to go, but at least he'd get to see her pretty face before he took off.

Movement caught his eye. The Carrols were crossing Camellia Court—Mr. Carrol with his squeaking walker, Mrs. Carrol clutching his arm and chattering away. Like many long-time residents, they'd ignored the crosswalk signal. But coming down Dahlia Drive was a sleek Mazda convertible, driven by a woman in oversized sunglasses who was on her phone, clearly not watching for pedestrians.

"Hey!" Alex shouted, already running, not sure if he was trying to get the Carrols' attention or the woman's. His warning went unheeded by both parties.

The car whizzed past the couple, missing the walker by what seemed like mere centimeters. Mr. Carrol stumbled backwards, dragging his wife with him.

Alex charged into the street. One moment he was on the salon's lawn, the next he was in the crosswalk, one hand bracing the walker, the other around Mrs. Carrol's waist. Mr. Carrol managed to right himself, but Alex stepped in a pothole, his ankle giving out with an unsettling pop. Pain shot up his leg like a hot poker as he went down, pulling Mrs. Carrol on top of him to break her fall.

Then Liz Needham was there, a look of concern on her usually stoic face as she carefully helped Mrs. Carrol up. Alex grunted when the elderly woman bumped his leg. Thank goodness she couldn't weigh more than eighty pounds, he thought, taking slow breaths against the waves of pain that threatened to make him sick.

"Alex? Are—are you hurt?" He'd know that voice anywhere; he didn't even have to open his eyes. But he did. Juno knelt beside him, her hand moving to his shoulder, her dark eyes bright with... fear? Concern? For him, or for the Carrols?.

"Hey," he said, smiling up at her, hoping to quell the worry in her expression. "Give a guy a hand, will you?" His elbow burned where he'd landed on it, and when he shifted, he felt the same searing sensation on his right shoulder. Great. Road rash. Because he'd taken off his shirt.

Juno took his hand, hers soft and strong at the same time, and helped him up. The moment he put weight on his right foot, pain shot through his ankle like a bolt of lightning. But he was up now, and everyone was watching, so he locked his jaw and tried to breathe through it. Maybe if he just stood here long enough, looking casual, they'd all go back to their regular routines. Thank goodness he'd worn his work boots today. They'd give him a little support, at least.

"You're white as a sheet," Juno said quietly, still holding his hand. "And you're crushing my fingers."

He immediately loosened his grip but didn't let go. Couldn't, actually. Her hand might be the only thing keeping him upright.

"I'm fine," he said through clenched teeth. "Just tweaked my ankle a little. Give me a minute." If he could just make it back to his truck...

But the truck might as well have been miles away. He couldn't even shift his weight without the edges of his vision going dark. He didn't want to faint right now, either.

"Whoa, big guy." Juno stepped a little closer to him, studying his face with narrowed eyes. She touched his shoulder with her free hand. "You sure you didn't hit your head?"

"I'm fine," Alex insisted. He *had* to be fine. He couldn't afford not to work. In construction, there was no such thing as sick pay.

To distract both Juno and himself, he released her hand and bent his arm to get a look at his elbow, where a swatch of shredded flesh was just starting to bead with blood. "Ouch."

"Oh, Alex. Yikes. Your back." Claire Maitland stood behind him, and when he glanced over his shoulder at her, she had her hand outstretched, almost like she was going to touch him. He flinched spontaneously; his shoulder blade was starting to sting, sending little zingers of electricity rippling over his skin.

"You sweet, brave boy!" Mrs. Carrol, seemingly none the worse for wear, hovered nearby. "You saved us. You practically jumped in front of that car to rescue us!" Now there were tears in the old woman's eyes and she reached up and cupped his cheek in benediction. "God bless you, dear boy. God bless you." Then she turned to her husband. "Harold, it's that nice Frampton boy."

Mr. Carrol maneuvered his way over, not to be left out of the fray. He lowered himself to the seat of his walker, nodding along with everything his wife said. When he'd caught his breath, he ground out, "Those blasted tourists. Running us down in the middle of the street like that. You okay, Mamie?" He patted his wife's backside affectionately.

"Oh, I'm fine, Harold. But this young man..." Mrs. Carrol frowned, then glanced around her. "Has anyone called the police? An ambulance?"

"No. No ambulance, please," Alex insisted. That was all he needed; an exorbitant and completely unnecessary ambulance bill. If he could get to his truck, he could take himself to urgent care. The thought of that unsettling sound he'd heard—like a snapping stick—made his stomach churn, but surely his ankle was just sprained. It couldn't be broken, that was all there was to it. He'd get home, ice it, and stay off of it all day tomorrow, but he had to be back at work on Monday. "Not for me, at least. Are you two okay?" he asked the couple.

"The police are already here," someone said from out of his line of sight, just as a police cruiser pulled up along the curb outside Juno's cafe. His lights were flashing, but he hadn't bothered running the siren.

When Officer Bobby Wayne stepped out of his car, everyone started talking at once. Bobby raised both hands to quiet the small crowd of onlookers. "Hold up, folks. One at a time, please."

"Did anyone catch that woman?" Juno asked, her voice tight with anger. Her hand was still on Alex's shoulder, and he found himself grateful for the steady pressure. "I can't believe she just kept on driving. She didn't even slow down."

"I got her plate number." Claire's voice radiated calm. "Already called it in."

Bobby nodded. "Yep, we've got a BOLO on her." His experienced gaze swept over Alex, noting the careful way he held himself, the sheen of sweat on his forehead. "You need a chair, Frampton?"

Alex gritted his teeth and grinned. "Nah. I'm good. Catching my breath. Tweaked my ankle, but I probably just need to walk it off."

Bobby nodded slowly, like he didn't exactly believe him, but he turned to the Carrols, anyway. "Let's start with you two. Do you need an ambulance? Would you feel better having a doctor check you over?'

"Oh, no," declared Mrs. Carrol. "We're right as rain, thanks to Alex here." She choked up again and touched Alex's forearm with a trembling hand. "Bless you, dear. Oh my goodness. I'm so sorry—" Then she burst into tears and started shaking like a leaf in a windstorm. Apparently, the shock was wearing off, and the reality of the close call was sinking in.

"Oh dear," Claire said, wrapping an arm around the woman's tiny frame. "Better have First Responders come check them out, okay?" she said to the officer. To Mrs. Carrol, she said, "Can you lean on me so we can get you inside? Or do you want to sit here and wait? We can bring you a chair if you'd like."

"I—I can walk, sweetie. I'm just sha—shaking so badly." She released a quivering breath, then straightened her narrow shoulders and leaned into Claire. "I can walk with your help. Thank you. Honey?" she called out to her husband, trying to look past Claire's shoulder.

"I've got him." Liz had already released the brakes on Mr. Carrol's walker, preparing to wheel him over to the sidewalk in it. "Let's get you two out of the street, shall we?"

The officer nodded his appreciation at the small group of people who headed inside with the Carrols, then turned back to Alex. "Okay. How you doing, man? You don't look so good."

"No, he doesn't," Juno interjected, her chin jutting out stubbornly.

"I'm fine." Alex was getting impatient with all the fuss. He just wanted to get out of the street and off his feet, then figure out what the heck he was going to do about his ankle. He couldn't think with everyone standing around staring at him. He tried to take a casual step, and immediately regretted it. The world tilted alarmingly.

"That's it." Juno's grip tightened on his shoulder. "Bobby, grab hold of his other side and help me get him to the sidewalk." She pointed to the bistro tables outside her cafe. "Then you can take his report while he waits for me to pull my car around."

"I've got a first aid kit in my truck," Alex protested. "Just need to clean up these scrapes and—"

"Alex Frampton, shush." The familiar exasperation in Juno's voice almost made him smile. Almost. "You just saved two people from getting hit by a car. For once in your life, would you please just let someone help you?"

"Yeah, what she said, Frampton." Bobby stepped up to his other side. "You're in no shape to drive yourself."

Alex sized up the officer. He was big dude, taller than Alex by an inch or two, and he spent a lot of his off time at Jimmy's Gym over on Lotus Avenue. He didn't want to lean on Juno, not because he didn't think she could handle it, but because he hated feeling so helpless around her. Around anyone. But Bobby could handle his weight and wouldn't make a big deal out of it, would he?

Clenching his teeth, Alex slung an arm around the guy's broad shoulders and let him half-carry him off the road. By the time Alex dropped gingerly into one of Juno's patio chairs, his stomach was churning from the pain, and he was feeling woozy again. He leaned forward, not quite putting his head between his knees, but close enough that it helped.

"I need my shirt." He didn't lift his head. "And some water, please."

"Here you go, Alex." It was Poppy, the pretty girl who worked for Juno, who had a not-so-secret crush on him. Great. Was his humiliation not yet complete? "Do you need a wet washcloth? I can get you some ice. Or anything else?"

"He's good, Poppy," he heard Juno say, maybe a little impatiently. "I've got it from here. Are Mr. and Mrs. Carrol doing all right?"

"They seem fine to me," Poppy said. "They're inside with a couple of your new lemon blueberry scones—which they love, by the way. They can't stop raving about them, and now half the people in there have ordered one. So woo-hoo for you!"

"Good. Thank you. I'm going to take Alex to urgent care. Can you hold down the fort for me?"

"Sure," Poppy said quickly. "Or I can take him, if you'd rather stay?"

Alex straightened slowly and shot what he hoped was a warning look at Juno. Poppy was legal, sure, but even so, she was way too young for him. Besides, he was in no condition to defend himself if she made any kind of advances toward him. Not that she would—Poppy was a nice girl—but Alex wasn't stupid. He knew how easily a casual interaction could be misconstrued, and Poppy had made it evident on more than one occasion that if he was interested, she was available.

"I've got it from here," Juno repeated, apparently comprehending his wide-eyed response. "But please keep me updated on the Carrols."

A siren sounded in the distance. She turned to Alex. "Are you sure you don't want to go in the ambulance? You're a little green around the gills, you big lug."

He shook his head. "If you'll take me, that would be great. You sure it's not a problem?" He hated pulling her from her work, but him sitting here like a helpless child wasn't getting anyone anywhere fast.

"I'm sure." Juno pointed a finger at him. "Sit tight, and I'll go get my car."

"I can stay with him," Poppy offered eagerly, still lingering close by.

Bobby stepped in, thank goodness. "I'll wait with him. I've got to get his statement," he told Poppy.

Alex pointed across the street. "My keys are in the cup holder. We can take The Beast." To have Juno alone in his truck again? It was a dream come true, although no matter how many times he'd imagined it, none of his wildest dreams had been of her rescuing him.

Juno seemed to shimmer a little... actually, nope. She shuddered. At the thought of riding in The Beast with him? He heard another unsettling pop, this time only in his head. It was the sound of the bubble of hope bursting inside of him.

"That's all right." She pulled her car keys from her pocket. "I'll be right back." She started for the door of the coffee shop, Poppy on her heels, then turned back and said, "I'll grab your shirt and lock your truck for you, too."

3
Juno

Juno took a quick glance around her, narrowing her eyes toward Tip-Top Talon's large front window, but as far as she could tell, no one could see her from where she stood inside the open passenger door of The Beast. Alex had a UV protector screen propped up in his front windshield, which also blocked his view of her from where he sat at one of her patio tables across the street. She hesitated, Alex's rumpled shirt in one hand, his keys in the other. No one would know if she just...

She pressed the shirt to her nose and inhaled. Alex. Under the hint of laundry detergent and sunshine was the unique and still achingly familiar scent of warm flesh, fresh sawdust, and that woodsy cologne he'd worn since high school. The same scent that used to linger in her nostrils after a long drive pressed against his side, inside this very truck.

The Beast smelled the way she remembered, too, and although the truck had definitely aged in the last fifteen years, other than the worn floorboard mats, it didn't look any the worse for wear. The seat cushions were all intact, the steering wheel wasn't peeling or flaking, and the dashboard wasn't faded or cracked. There was a large black toolbox on the floor behind the driver's seat and some scrap lumber in the bed of the truck, but all in all, it looked to Juno like Alex took exceptional care of The Beast.

She'd been surprised to find him still driving the same pickup when she'd returned to Autumn Lake eight years ago. It had been his brother's truck back in high school, but Alex had been given permission—along with death threats if he allowed anything to happen to it—to drive it while Jason was away in the military. Alex must have bought it from Jason at some point, she guessed, and although she wouldn't admit it out loud, she was more than a little pleased the first time she saw Alex pull up outside her coffee shop behind the wheel of The Beast. Surprised, yes, but secretly thrilled at the memories the sight of the two of them stirred up in her.

Enough. "Get it together, Thomas," she muttered, holding the shirt away from her face. She had an injured man waiting, Bobby standing guard, and a coffee shop full of customers watching this little drama unfold, plus whatever clients Sonya had in her treatment chairs at the moment. This was no time for a trip down memory lane.

She shook out the shirt, folded it neatly over her arm, then locked the truck behind her. Back inside her own car, she laid the shirt on the passenger seat, letting her fingertips linger on the collar for an extra moment, then pulled out of Sonya's parking lot and across the street to where Alex and Bobby waited for her.

By the time she'd parked at the curb, Alex was already standing, one hand gripping the back of the chair he'd been sitting in, presumably for balance, since it looked to her like he wasn't putting any weight on his injured ankle. Even from inside her car, she could see the tight lines around his mouth, and the way he was trying—and failing—to hide how much pain he was in. The usually upbeat Officer Bobby was eyeing him with a furrowed brow, concern evident in his expression.

"Typical," Juno muttered under her breath as she got out and circled the car. "Just smile and pretend everything is fine when it clearly isn't." She grabbed his shirt—why had she bothered folding it?—then climbed out of the car. Through the window of the coffee shop, she could see that all her customers were watching her, but she tried to ignore them.

She tossed the shirt at Alex and he just barely caught it with his free hand. "Put that on before you scare away my customers." She hadn't meant to be so... *aggressive* about it, but she was having all sorts of conflicting emotions right now, and she was struggling with how to comport herself. Which irked her fiercely, making her feel even more contrary; she prided herself on her typically steady composure.

Alex, balancing on one foot, said, "I can't. My shoulder's pretty roughed up back there. It's starting to burn something fierce." He draped the t-shirt over his uninjured shoulder and gave her a mischievous look. "Will this work?"

Not completely heartless, Juno nodded tersely. "Of course. Yes. I forgot about the road rash." Glancing over at Bobby, she asked, "Got everything you need from him?"

"We're good," the officer confirmed, but he kept his hand out, prepared to steady his charge if he needed it.

She turned back to Alex. "Okay, Captain America. Can you hobble over to the car or do you need us to carry you?"

"Captain America, hm?" Alex chuckled, but she could hear the strain in his voice. "I can manage," he said, then took a very wobbly step. Bobby was at his side in a flash, and Alex draped his arm over the officer's shoulder, leaning so heavily on the guy they both swayed a little.

"Or not," Juno retorted, moving to Alex's other side. "You big lug. Just ask for help, okay? Or are you too manly for that?"

He flashed her one of his trademark grins. "Juno, you wound me."

Juno snorted. "Uh, nope. Pretty sure you managed that all on your own today." She didn't touch him, but walked beside him just in case an extra hand was needed. This was his road rash side, and she grimaced as she noticed it wasn't just his shoulder blade that was scraped up. His elbow and forearm looked a little like someone had taken a cheese grater to it.

"But you do think I'm manly," he teased.

Juno pressed her lips together, refusing to acknowledge the comment. She gave Bobby a 'let's do this' look, then together, they maneuvered Alex the few feet to her car.

"An Outback, huh? It suits you," Alex said through gritted teeth. He ran a hand over the curve of the doorframe in what seemed like a rather suggestive gesture. "Tough as nails. Practical. And very nice lines." The words were strained, but his eyes still held that familiar gleam of mischief.

"Get in the car, Frampton." And here she'd been just starting to feel sorry for him.

He slid the passenger seat as far back as possible to accommodate his long legs, eased gingerly into the vehicle, then balled his shirt up and tucked it behind him at the base of his spine to keep himself from accidentally leaning back against the seat. Bobby carefully closed the car door, then through the open window, he said to Alex, "Call me and let me know you're okay." Peering past him to Juno, he added, "Make sure he actually goes in. Don't let him talk you into just dropping him off at home."

"I wouldn't—" Alex started.

"You would," Juno and Bobby said in unison.

As she pulled away from the curb, Juno was suddenly acutely aware of how little room there was in the front seat of her car. She'd never thought of her Outback as being cramped for space. She'd hauled coffee and catering supplies all over Autumn Lake and beyond in her little hatchback without once feeling like she needed something bigger. But Alex Frampton, shirtless and bleeding, took up every inch of real estate, at least figuratively. She felt crowded against her door, trapped behind the steering wheel, strapped in place by her seatbelt. *Um, isn't that what seatbelts do?* It was suddenly hard to breathe.

"You don't have to do this," Alex said quietly. He was looking out the window as they drove, his profile tight with discomfort. "I could have called Ward."

"Well, it's your lucky day. You got me, instead." She turned onto Dahlia Drive and headed toward the small urgent care clinic on the other side of town. The closest hospital was Evansville, but the staff at Lakeside Urgent Care was more than equipped to handle Alex's injuries.

"Right." It was only one word, but the nuances packed into that single syllable made Juno's chest tight.

The urgent care waiting room smelled like cleaning chemicals. Juno pulled a small tube of hand sanitizer out of her purse and used it liberally. The handles of the wheelchair they'd let her use to wheel Alex inside the building had been unsettlingly tacky. She sat on the end of a row of seats, his chair parked close, sneaking glances at him while pretending to scroll through her phone. He looked uncomfortable, keeping his injured elbow from bumping the armrest and trying to find a position that didn't aggravate the scrapes on his back.

"I'm sorry about all this," he said, breaking the silence. "You're missing work because of me."

"The shop's in good hands." She tucked her phone away. "Are you in a lot of pain? Do you want me to see how much longer the wait is?" When they'd checked in, the woman at the desk had said it would be a few minutes. That had been at least twenty minutes ago.

"It's okay. I know they'll see me when they can. I just feel ridiculous sitting in this wheelchair." He gestured at himself with his uninjured arm. "Not exactly Captain America's finest hour, is it?"

"Hey," she said, giving him an encouraging smile. "You were amazing out there, Cap. A real hero, especially to the Carrols. They will be telling this story for years to come." She lifted her hands to mime a marquee headline. "Local hero Alex Frampton throws himself in front of a speeding car to save the lives of Harold and Mamie Carrol."

His cheeks warmed a little under her praise and she was glad to see some color. He was awfully pale. "Yeah? What about you?"

"What about me?"

"Do you think I'm a hero?"

Juno met his eyes, seeing past the teasing to something more vulnerable. "You didn't hesitate. Just ran right out there." She nodded. "So yes, Alex. I think you're a hero, too." It was true, at least in this instance. Maybe not back in the day when she'd really needed a hero and he hadn't come through for her. But he'd definitely showed up for the Carrols.

Alex was quiet for a moment, studying her face. "This is nice," he finally said, gesturing with one finger back and forth between them. "We were friends once, weren't we?"

The question caught her off guard. Before she could form a response, he added softly, "I'd like to think we could be again."

"Alexander Frampton?" A nurse stood in the open door of the hallway that led to the exam rooms. When he waved at her and she saw his wheelchair, she crossed the room to them. "Oh, that doesn't look like much fun," she said, her smile sympathetic, if maybe also the tiniest bit flirty. "I'm Katie. I'll wheel you back."

"Do you want to come with me?" Alex asked Juno, something in his voice making her think maybe he wanted her to say 'yes.' She smiled encouragingly, but shook her head.

"I'll be here when you get out. I'm not going anywhere."

"I like the sound of that," he said. Then to the nurse; "You can call me 'Cap.' It's what all my friends call me."

Juno watched him wheel away, her throat tight with unexpected emotion.

Friends. Maybe it wouldn't be the worst thing in the world.

Maybe.

4
Alex

From the passenger seat of Juno's Outback, Alex watched her head into Miller's Pharmacy. Through the storefront windows, he could see old Joe Miller peer out at him, likely making sure it was actually his prescriptions Juno was picking up. Small town life. No chance of someone pulling a fast one here.

The events of the morning had caught up with him. Between his usual insomnia and the adrenaline crash, his whole body felt heavy. He shifted, trying to find a position that didn't aggravate his back or jostle his ankle. He still didn't have a shirt on, and for some reason, he felt absurdly self conscious about it. It had to be the cramped quarters of Juno's car getting to him.

Or just being this close to Juno, period.

He glared down at his bare toes jutting out past the end of the cumbersome black walking boot. He'd just about puked from the pain when the urgent care nurse had pulled first his work boot, then his sock off, but now with his ankle wrapped and cradled in the padded stabilization brace, the nausea had pretty much passed. As ugly as it was, at least the boot meant he wouldn't be completely helpless.

Juno returned, sliding into the driver's seat with a white paper bag. "Antibiotics," she said, peering inside. "Something a little stronger than over the counter stuff for pain, and a cream for your road rash." She held up a tube, then dropped both back in the bag and handed it to him. The unspoken question hung between them: how exactly was he supposed to reach the scrapes on his back?

He wanted to ask her to help. Wanted to ask for so much more than just tending his wounds. The sunlight caught her profile as she pulled away

25

from the curb, and for a dangerous moment, he imagined leaning over and kissing her. The way he used to. He closed his eyes, remembering the way her lips had moved under his, how their breaths had melded into one, their pulses racing along to a matching cadence...

"Alex?" Her voice snapped him back to the present. "You okay?" She patted his forearm where it rested on the console between them. "You were getting a bit of a glazed over look. Don't be passing out on me, you hear?"

"Sorry. Yeah." He blinked heavily. "I think I'm really starting to feel everything now that the adrenaline has completely worn off. Haven't eaten today either. Probably not helping."

"Well, let's get you back to your place, big guy. You can take those pain pills now if you want, but you should probably have something in your stomach first."

The climb to his second-floor apartment was less than graceful. Even with the walking boot, he stumbled twice on the stairs, Juno's steadying hand on his elbow the only thing keeping him upright.

"Straight to bed," she ordered once they were inside, not giving him time to be self-conscious about having her in his space. At least the place was relatively clean; a far cry from the chaos of his drinking days.

He caught himself against the hallway wall and started patting his pants pockets for his phone. "I need to call Ward. Let him know about today."

Juno pointed toward the bedroom at the end of the hall. "Go. You can call him once you're off your feet. I'll fix you something to eat and bring it to you there." She followed closely behind him, then waited while he gingerly lowered himself to the side of the bed. A few years ago, Alex had splurged on a deep mattress and box spring set, which added a good six inches to the height of his bed. He loved the mattress with its extra support, and he couldn't believe what a difference having a good mattress made to the quality of his sleep.

When he *could* sleep, that is.

Juno glanced around the room like she was looking for something. He'd been in a hurry that morning and hadn't bothered picking up in here before he left, but it wasn't too bad, he thought, trying to see it through her eyes. At the foot of the bed was the pair of trainers he'd toed off after the game of hoops at the park last night. The shirt he'd been wearing was on the floor beside them, but he'd peeled off the socks and his shorts in the bathroom and tossed them in the hamper before jumping in the shower. He'd left his closet door open, and there was a jumbled mess of things on the floor of it, but who didn't have a messy closet? At least he'd kind of made his bed. His pillows weren't where they were supposed to be, but he'd pulled the comforter up, even if it was a little crooked.

"Do you have any extra pillows? You're supposed to elevate that leg." She pointed at his foot.

Alex shook his head, but then said, "Maybe the couch cushions?"

Juno nodded. "I'll go grab them. You try to get comfortable, but if you need help, just ask. I'll be right back."

Once again, he wondered how on earth he was going to manage alone for the first day or two. Was he just being a baby? The doctor hadn't seemed to be too concerned, but maybe that was because Juno could instill confidence in anyone. His ankle throbbed and the tenderized skin on his back stung with what felt like jolts of electricity, making his whole body twitch in response. He decided he'd wait until Juno returned with the cushions before he tried to get his leg up on the tall bed; he didn't want to have to move the stupid appendage any more than he absolutely had to.

He'd get the call to Ward out of the way first. Alex fumbled for his phone, but before he could dial Ward's number, it lit up with an incoming call. His thumb hit accept before his brain caught up; and unfortunately, his phone was set to automatically answer to the speaker.

"Alex? Is that you?" Payton's chirpy, little girl voice made him cringe.

He groaned inwardly. Why had he answered? "Hey, Payton."

"Hey, handsome. Can I come over so we can… talk?" The sugar in her tone made his teeth hurt.

"Can't right now, babe," he mumbled, then glanced up as he caught movement in his doorway.

Juno stood there, her arms loaded with sofa cushions, that familiar wall slamming down behind her eyes. Then she bustled into the room, all business, setting the two overstuffed cushions on the bed beside him. "I'll be back with food shortly." And with that, she spun out of the room.

"Juno, wait—"

But she was already gone, her footsteps quick and sharp as she headed down the hall to the kitchen.

"Who is Juno?" Payton. Sheesh. The woman was still on the phone he had pressed to his ear. "What's going on, Alex? You wouldn't have lunch with me, and now you're with *some other woman*? You know, I'd heard the rumors about you, but I didn't believe them. I gave you the benefit of the doubt, and look what you—"

Alex hung up on her. He set the phone face down on his night stand, then carefully maneuvered his leg up onto the bed and shoved one of the cushions Juno had brought in under his calf. He was a back-sleeper, and he knew already that even if he started out lying on his side, he'd roll onto his back soon after falling asleep. "And I thought I had trouble sleeping before," he muttered. He could hear Juno rattling around in the kitchen as he positioned himself so that he could still eat whatever she was whipping up. He'd gone shopping earlier this week, but he was pretty sure she wasn't going to whip out a frozen microwave dinner for him.

He took a deep breath, filling his lungs with as much air as he could, then let it out in a long, slow exhale. As soon as she came back, he'd try to explain about Payton.

Though... explain what, exactly? That Payton meant nothing to him? That he called every woman he went out with 'babe'? That he hadn't meant to lead her on? That she read far more into his actions than he'd intended?

That Alex was exactly the kind of guy Juno thought he was?

Maybe he should pretend to be asleep when she came back with his food.

5
Juno

JUNO POLISHED THE ALREADY gleaming espresso machine, letting the familiar motion center her. The late afternoon rush would hit soon, and she needed to get her head back in the game. Three hours. She'd lost three hours of prime business time playing Florence Nightingale to a man who clearly had other options for care.

Can't right now, babe.

She set the cleaning cloth aside and did a final check of her prep station, making certain canisters were stocked, supplies were accessible, and the glass display case was full. Having things primed and ready at all times helped her feel in control, even when everything else in her life felt like borderline chaos.

"We've had so many compliments on the lavender honey latte today," Poppy said as she pulled espresso shots for an order. Juno could tell her barista was trying to bolster her with her encouraging words. It was one of the things she really appreciated about Poppy; the girl always saw the bright side of things. "Did you change something in the recipe?"

"No changes." Juno eyed glass syrup dispenser. There was less than a third of the bottle left, and that was even with the double batch she'd made that morning. "Looks like we might run out again."

Before she could head back to the kitchen, Poppy piped up again. "Everyone's talking about what happened this morning." Her voice held barely contained curiosity. "Is Alex okay? It was so brave, what he did. Like something right out of a movie," she gushed.

Juno wanted to shake the young woman by the shoulders and tell her to take off her Alex-colored glasses. "He'll be fine," she said with finality. She wasn't going to spend another moment thinking about him. "How are we doing on scones? Will we have enough for this evening, or do I need to make more?"

"We should be fine," she said, peering quickly into the glass case. "We're out of the lemon blueberry ones, but we've got several of the rest of the flavors." Poppy lingered, clearly hoping for more details. "So I heard his foot was broken and that he's in a cast. Maybe he'll let me sign it, you think? And someone also told me that he might have to get skin grafts for his road rash." She looked distraught, her hand pressed to her chest.

Juno sighed and turned to eye the young barista. Might as well give the girl the correct information before the gossip-mongers started making more out of things than what they were. "Poppy, Alex is fine. His ankle, not his foot, is sprained, not broken. He has crutches to use for the first few days until the swelling goes down a little, and he has a walking boot so that when he's comfortable putting weight on it, he can get rid of the crutches. He is *not*," she said sternly, "getting skin grafts for his road rash. I don't know who started that rumor, but you can stop spreading it immediately. His back is going to hurt and get gross and scabby before it heals up, so you'll probably get to see him wandering around without a shirt, but that's nothing new."

"Oh, well, all of that is good, right?" Poppy didn't exactly look apologetic, and Juno thought maybe the girl knew her a little too well. Maybe, just maybe, Poppy had purposely laid it on thick just to get Juno to spill the real details. The little minx.

"That's really good, yes. If the guy had to take a hit for being a hero, then it's best case scenario, all things considered."

Poppy nodded, her eyes wide and innocent. "I bet he could use some meals. Do you think I—we should organize a meal schedule for him?"

Juno was shaking her head before Poppy finished asking the question, but not because she didn't think Alex needed help. It was because Poppy needed to stay clear of the man. There was nothing more endearing than a big, attractive man in need, and after seeing the pitiful contents of his kitchen – frozen packaged foods, lunch meat that had more ingredients than a chemistry lab, and a cupboard full of dorm room staples like ramen and peanut butter and pancake mix – he was inarguably in great need of help. The man ate like a college student and Juno had to resist the urge to purge his kitchen and replace everything with real food.

She could not, in good conscience, let her young barista fall into that kind of a snare. She put her hand on Poppy's shoulder. "Listen. I spoke to Ward when he came to get the truck. Hazel and Penny are going to put together a bunch of healthy easy meals for him. I will contribute sandwiches for a couple of days, and if you'd like to be the one to make them for him, that would be great."

Poppy's eyes lit up. "Okay. I can deliver them, too."

Juno held up a hand to stop her. "Not necessary. Ward is going to pick them up from here on his way to check on him over the next few days," she explained. "Alex is going to be a little grumpy for the first day or two as he gets used to his limitations. Be considerate and put yourself in his position. Would you want visitors if you couldn't take a shower or change your clothes?"

Poppy actually looked like she was seriously considering it, then she twitched her shoulders and grinned. "I could help him shower and change his clothes."

Juno snatched the towel from the counter and playfully swatted it at Poppy. "You are depraved. Now get back to work. You can make his sandwich tomorrow. Roast beef and roasted pepper on sourdough hoagie with the sundried tomato mayo."

"And provolone, right?"

Juno chuckled and nodded. The girl paid attention, and Juno knew it wasn't just to Alex's orders. Poppy was great with all of their customers. She knew people by name, remembered their drinks of choice, was great at suggestions when they didn't know what they wanted, and was adept at upselling a sweet treat with almost every order. Granted, it was hard to say no to her pretty smiling face, but the girl was as genuine as they came, and people liked her for good reason.

"The couple at Table 4 keep looking over here," Juno added with a thrust of her chin in their direction. "Are they waiting for an order?"

"Oh!" Poppy grabbed two tall plastic cups and scooped ice into both. "Yes. Oops. Two cappuccinos for Table 4d coming right up."

The bell above the door chimed and Claire swept in, making a beeline for the counter.

"Hey girl," Juno greeted her. "What are you doing back in here?" Claire rarely made an appearance at Juno's in the afternoons. Business at the bookstore picked up significantly once the day had warmed up enough to send all but the most committed sun-worshippers indoors for a reprieve.

"Can't a girl pay her friend a visit?" Claire asked coyly.

Juno cocked her head and narrowed her eyes at her. Here fishing for an Alex update, Juno was certain. She evaded the question. "And why aren't you sweating in that outfit?" Juno pointed her finger up and down at the gorgeous handmade outfit. Claire sewed all her own costumes. "You're not even dewy."

Claire fluffed her skirts around her knees, layers of crinoline peeking out below the checkered hem of her skirt. "I'm aerated," she quipped.

"You could probably fit one of those little desktop air conditioners under there," Juno teased.

"Now there's an idea." Claire tapped her chin thoughtfully. "I wonder if I could rig up some kind of harness to wear under all of this. Like a Steampunk chastity belt, but instead of a heavy duty lock and key mechanism, a bracket to attach a rechargeable air conditioner. Just plug in and recharge whenever I'm behind the counter."

"You'd have to be careful of the blades, though." Juno went along for the ride, half-believing that Claire was actually contemplating the idea.

"Are you two actually talking about rigging up an air conditioner to wear under a skirt?" Poppy asked, circling around the end of the counter with a tray full of used dishes and trash. "Am I hearing this right?"

Claire nodded, her expression earnest. "Sounds like a great idea, doesn't it?"

Poppy laughed. "You two are wild," she said as she backed through the swinging half-door that led into the kitchen. "I want to be you when I grow up."

Juno shot Claire a lifted brow. "Did she just call us grown-ups?"

"Speaking of grown-ups," her friend segued efficiently. "Give me the scoop on Alex."

Juno let out a sharp "Ha!" then grabbed a cup and saucer and poured a cup of her house roast for Claire. She set it in front of her, followed by a small pitcher of heavy cream, and then pulled out the bar stool they kept shoved under the counter for just such occasions as this. "That man will never grow up."

•❤•❤•❤•❤•❤•

EIGHT YEARS EARLIER...

She stood on the sidewalk, hands on her hips, taking in the storefront before her. The "For Sale" sign was coming down today. Juno could hardly believe it—the little coffee shop where she'd worked as a teenager was now hers. Mr. and Mrs. Bellamy had practically given it away, happy to retire and thrilled that someone who'd once worked for them wanted to revive the struggling business.

"You sure about this, honey?" Mr. Bellamy had asked that morning at the bank when she signed the papers. "Things have changed since that resort went up across the way. Folks have gotten a little highfalutin about their coffee, now that the North Shore folk have brought in their artisanal java boutiques, and our little coffee shop on this side of the lake is hardly holding its own." He was a nice man, but she could hear the bitter note under his carefully worded observation.

Little did Mr. Bellamy know that Juno planned to bring her own artisanal java boutique to the south shore, the heart of the small town of Autumn Lake, but she'd never forget who her customers were. She wanted to make her coffee shop a place where the locals hung out, where people came because it was comfortable and friendly and warm and all the things that made it inviting and inclusive.

This shop was exactly what Juno needed—a place with roots, with history. *Her* history. A place where she could plant herself and grow something lasting.

The sign would be the first thing to go. Faded and outdated, just like the rest of the place. The windows needed washing and one of them sported a spiderweb crack in the corner, so that would have to be replaced as soon as possible. The interior needed a complete overhaul.

But underneath all that, she could see what it could become—what she could make it.

"Well, butter my butt and call me a biscuit." The voice hit her like a physical blow. Deep, familiar, the edges curling with humor. She turned slowly, heart hammering against her ribs.

Alex Frampton stood on the sidewalk just a few feet away, looking like every dream and nightmare she'd had since leaving Autumn Lake almost a decade ago. Broader shoulders, stubbled jaw, same devastating smile. One he knew how to use to his advantage.

"Juniper Bernice Thomas. Never thought I'd see your pretty face again. At least not here in little old Autumn Lake."

Words stuck in her throat. She'd rehearsed this moment in her head a thousand times—cool, composed, indifferent. Instead, she felt sixteen again, breathless and undone by his mere presence.

"Alex," she managed finally. "You're still here."

"I never left," he said, emphasizing the 'I' as if to drive home which of them had been the one to run. But he still smiled, and it seemed genuine, so she wasn't sure if it was a rebuke or just a statement of fact. He gestured at the building. "What's all this?"

"I bought it," she blurted out, unable to completely hide the pride in her tone. "I'm going to reopen the coffee shop."

Something flashed in his eyes—surprise, maybe even admiration. "No kidding? That's... that's great, June-bug."

The old nickname slipped between them, intimate and dangerous. His gaze swept over her, and she felt the heat of it like a physical touch. For a moment, the years fell away, and she remembered how it felt to be the center of his universe.

"You know," he drawled, his eyes traveling back to the store front. He narrowed them in speculation. "I could help," he said, gesturing at the building. "With the renovations. I'm with J&J Contractors and we do good work. We're the best if you want things done right."

Juno was shaking her head. "I'm on a tight budget, Alex. The place passed inspection for the purchase, so most of what I need to do is cosmetic." She lifted one arm and flexed it, then glanced at his bulging biceps and felt ridiculous. But she forged on, hoping he couldn't tell that her cheeks were growing warm. "I'm doing as much of the work as I can myself. If and when I need help, I've got some favors to call in." It wasn't exactly true, but she'd reconnected with Claire Maitland and Liz Needham since returning to Autumn Lake, and both women were over the moon about her plans and had offered to help in any way they could. Liz worked for the local water and sewer company, but she had a plumbing background and had already promised to come in and help with hooking up water lines and filtration systems, and Claire had offered to make window treatments and table cloths and custom aprons for Juno and her staff.

Alex nodded. "Sure, right." Then he flexed, too. Was he mocking her? "I do side jobs. John is cool with it as long as it doesn't take money out of his pocket. I could give you the 'friend' rate."

Hope flickered, treacherous and bright. Maybe he'd changed. Maybe they could—

"Alex! There you are!" A woman burst out of the boating supplies shop and sashayed down the sidewalk. She slipped her arm through his with practiced familiarity—tall, brunette ponytail, with a shockingly bright smile and a white summer dress that showed miles of tanned leg. "You disappeared on me. You promised to help me choose fabric samples for the boat cushions," she pouted, barely acknowledging Juno's presence with a quick glance.

"Anastacia, this is Juno, an old friend," Alex said, not bothering to try to extract his arm from her clutches. "Juno, Anastacia's family has a summer place across the lake."

The woman didn't even smile as her gaze raked up and down Juno, taking in the pale blue Oxford she wore tucked into simple black pants. "Hi," she said, already turning her attention back to Alex. "We need to hurry if we're going to make it back for sunset cocktails."

"We won't be late, babe." The endearment rolled off his tongue with casual ease. "And even if we are, no one will notice."

"Of course, they'll notice." Anastacia insisted.

"And then you'll have everyone's attention, which is just the way you like it," Alex countered, his voice calm and soothing. It seemed to be working; the woman reminded Juno of a cat, the way she practically curled into his side as he spoke. She didn't even seem to notice Alex's irony at her expense.

"You two obviously have some place to be," she interjected, her stomach tight. "And I need to get to work." She made a shooing gesture. "Off with you, now."

Alex shot her an apologetic shrug. "Welcome home. I'll stop by later, maybe we can catch up properly."

"I'm going to be pretty busy for a while," she said with a shake of her head. "And it looks like you are, too."

Ugh. Why had she dropped that last line? The last thing she wanted was for him to think she cared what he did or who with.

Alex grinned. "Yeah, well, I have a well-stocked toolbelt, and I know where you work, June-bug."

Her expression hardened. "Please don't call me that. I'm Juno to my friends. Or you can call me Juniper." To Anastacia, she said, "Nice to meet you, Anastacia. I hope you enjoy your summer here in Autumn Lake."

"Oh, I will," Anastacia cooed, her simpering making Juno clench her jaw in distaste. Then she pushed open the door to her shop, glad she'd already unlocked it, and ducked inside the shadowy interior.

With her back to the cool glass door, Juno felt something harden inside her. The whispers she'd heard around town were true. Alex Frampton had become the summer entertainment for bored vacation women—charming, available, no strings attached.

At least now she knew. Whatever they'd had was long gone, just like the girl she'd been. She was here to build a future, not revisit the past.

And she didn't need Alex Frampton's help to do it.

•♥•♥•♥•♥•♥

PRESENT DAY...

"Earth to Juno." Claire was waving a hand in front of her face. "Where'd you go just now?"

Juno blinked, the memory fading. "Nowhere important."

Claire's eyes softened with understanding. "So tell me how Alex is doing. I heard he's got a broken—"

"He didn't break anything," Juno snipped, cutting her off, followed by a flood of remorse. "Sorry. The gossip in this town is alive and well."

Claire nodded slowly. "It is, yes. But I don't think it's malicious, Juno. People just want to know that their hero is okay."

Their hero. What she wouldn't give to be able to call Alex Frampton her hero.

To be able to call anyone her hero.

Nope. She was her own hero. Always had been. Always would be. She'd learned the hard way a few too many times that depending on anyone but herself was a loser's game.

"Yeah. You're right." She held up the coffee carafe to offer Claire a refill, but her friend shook her head.

"He's all right, then? He didn't say anything to upset you, Juno?"

Juno shook her head. "Of course not. He's a big lug, but he's not intentionally cruel." Then she filled Claire in on the details of Alex's injuries and recovery expectations. "If you want to contribute to meals or anything, give Penny a call. Ward said she and Hazel are going to put together a little meal schedule for the next few days."

Later that night, Juno stood at her upstairs apartment window, watching the last customers leave the shops along Camellia Court. The day's events replayed in her mind, but it was that single word—*babe*—that kept echoing.

Her father had called every woman he knew "babe" too. And her mother had never seemed to mind. Granted, she'd usually been pretty out of it by the time he came home late smelling of cheap perfume and cheaper whiskey. But Juno noticed. She noticed all of it. The pills he brought home with him to tuck into her mother's hand. The crumpled cash falling out of his pockets on good days, the emptiness of his splayed wallet on bad days. The bruises on the inside of her mother's wrists that could only be seen days after they were inflicted. The empty liquor bottles clinking too loudly in the trash bags that Juno snuck out to the neighbor's trash can well after midnight since the trash collector always came early for pickup, and she couldn't risk missing it.

She didn't miss the ramping up of tension, the air practically sizzling with it, in the days before things came to the same end over and over again.

Somehow, her mother was always – *always* – surprised when her father packed them up in the darkest hour of the night to run from his sins, ranting at them to hurry, hurry, hurry. Juno knew to sleep fully clothed, and to keep anything she treasured tucked inside her pillow case; her pillow was often the only thing she was allowed to bring with them, other than the clothes on her back and the shoes on her feet.

Her mother had never learned, but Juno had made a pact not to be like her mother. Not back then, not now. Not ever.

Juno wrapped her arms around herself, fighting off a chill that had nothing to do with the temperature. Some things you couldn't outrun, no matter how far you traveled or how long you stayed away. She might never figure out how to fully get over Alex Frampton, but why was she always – *always* - surprised by the piercing of her heart whenever he proved over and over again that he hadn't changed his ways?

Maybe she was like her mother after all.

6
Alex

ALEX SAT IN HIS truck, parked across the street a block down from Juno's Coffee Bar. He slouched low in his seat, his arms crossed tightly, his flannel just enough to ward off the pre-dawn chill. Through bleary eyes, he watched Juno navigate her morning routine, her silhouette clear through the front windows of the cafe, even with the blinds only half-open. She moved efficiently between the prep stations and the industrial coffee makers, her posture upright, her steps precise and graceful.

He wished he felt as put together as the woman inside the shop looked.

He hadn't slept. Again.

He'd been sitting here for at least half an hour, fighting the urge to rest his forehead against the steering wheel. The pain medication had worn off hours ago, but he'd refused to take another pill. One was enough. One had to be enough. He'd gone down that road before, and he wouldn't—couldn't—travel it again.

His ankle throbbed inside the walking boot. The urgent care doctor had said to stay off of it and keep it elevated for at least three days, and then to only put weight on it to help with balance until the swelling was down.

Well, it had been almost four days now, and Alex was tired of lying around being miserable and feeling sorry for himself. Ward and Penny had been over bringing him dinner the last three days, and they'd tag-teamed bandaging his shoulder last night, hoping he could rest easier, but to no avail. Between the physical discomfort and. of course, the memory of Juno's face when he'd called Payton "babe," sleep had been a lost cause.

Who was he kidding? Sleep had been a lost cause for a whole lot longer than the last couple of days.

Juno was now straightening chairs around tables and nudging small vases of fresh-cut flowers into their proper places. She paused at the door and gazed out, and for a heart-stopping moment, Alex thought she'd seen him. But she must have only seen her reflection in the glass because she just smoothed her apron, glanced at the wristwatch she wore, then headed back. Even with her back to him, he could tell that she was portioning out fresh-ground coffee into the machines for the morning rush. Fresh. Juno wouldn't have it any other way.

Not that he should know her routine so well. What was he doing out here, anyway?

He scrubbed a hand over his face, his palm rasping against three days' worth of stubble. The familiar pressure behind his eyes was building again, that bone-deep exhaustion that made operating any kind of machinery dangerous. That was a lesson he'd not soon forget. It had been in the early hours of a morning just like this, a little over a year ago, when he'd dozed off at the wheel and nearly joined his brother in the afterlife. If Ward hadn't answered the phone that night....

Alex's hands tightened on the steering wheel. He could still hear the screech of metal on metal when he'd hit the guardrail, still feel the sickening lurch as his truck left the road and the jarring jolt as he ended up nose down in the irrigation ditch. He still felt the rush of shame when Ward had pulled over to the side of the road where Alex had been waiting for him, the concern in his friend's eyes as he gave what felt like the third degree. "Are you hurt? Bleeding? Did you hit your head? Let me look at your eyes." He hadn't gone so far as to ask if he could smell his breath—Ward was a better friend than that—but Alex had noticed his flared nostrils, and knew he'd been scenting the air around him for the telltale stench of a man on a bender.

Although he didn't acknowledge Ward's unspoken suspicions, Alex insisted that he didn't need to go to the hospital, nor did he need to report the accident, and that the truck was fine. He just needed help getting it back up on the road. Even with the four-wheel drive, his tires spun in the thick mud in the ditch, and he had no scrap lumber in the truck bed to shove under them for traction.

Ward had finally backed off a little, and with a tow chain and his own 4x4 in gear, they'd managed to get The Beast back up on the road. The truck's front grill had taken the brunt of the abuse, but Alex had assured his friend that it was nothing he couldn't fix with a little Bondo and touch-up paint.

When the proverbial dust had settled and Ward started probing again, Alex had stuck to his story. He'd gone to bed too late, gotten up too early, and hadn't had his coffee yet, but they both knew exactly why he'd been out driving on that country road on that pre-dawn morning.

It had nothing to do with alcohol, although he didn't blame Ward for worrying. But sleep deprivation was its own kind of intoxication, and Alex found himself succumbing to the bad decision-making that came hand in hand with both. Over the years on nights when sleep eluded him, Alex had often made his way out to the cemetery at the edge of town in a vain search for answers for the tragic death of his brother. A death Alex still struggled to come to grips with even after all this time.

Lately, though, instead of the cemetery, Alex found himself parking outside Juno's Coffee Bar in the wee hours of the morning. "Like a stalker," he ground out. How he wished he could just go inside and sit down with a cup of coffee across the counter from her, to talk to her, to listen to her, to just be with her.

But that was just as unlikely to happen as getting answers in a cemetery, wasn't it?

The dash clock clicked to 4:49. In about ten minutes, Juno would unlock the front door and flip the sign to "Open." The early morning crowd would start trickling in - south shore fishermen trying to get a jump on the North Shore tourists, Thad grabbing a to-go cup on his way to open his the bait and tackle shop for them, Dixie May on her way home from working the night shift at the check-in desk of the Carpe Diem Resort, and lately, Ward, who'd been showing up earlier and earlier at Juno's place to pick up coffee and breakfast for the small crew he had helping him finish up the Garden Gate B&B renovation. Tourist season was upon them, and Ward's fiancé, Penny Anderson, and her business partner, Hazel Poleman, were chomping at the bit to put the finishing touches on the place by the end of the month. According to Ward, Penny had already booked their first guests to arrive in less than two weeks, and barring any catastrophes, that barely gave them enough time to let the paint dry.

Of all people, he didn't want Ward St. James to catch him loitering in front of Juno's place. He needed to get out of there.

Alex rolled his shoulders and sat up taller in his seat, then turned the key in the ignition, cringing as The Beast roared to life, the sound echoing off the empty storefronts lining Camellia Court. He shot a quick glance over at the coffee shop, and his heart stuttered in his chest. Through the large plate glass window, Juno had gone completely still, one hand frozen in the act of turning on an antique globe lamp hanging over a set of overstuffed chairs. Even from this distance, he could see the moment recognition hit her. Her head came up, her shoulders drawing back, and she turned slowly to look out toward the street. Although he couldn't make out her expression, he felt the weight of her stare like a physical thing.

He should drive away. Right now.

But he couldn't seem to take his foot off the brake, couldn't seem to look away from her. For a suspended moment, they stayed locked in this strange tableau, him outside in the shadowy dawn, her behind glass and all lit up, almost eighteen years of unspoken words hanging in the space between them.

Then Juno smoothed her hands across the front of her apron and started toward the door.

Alex's foot finally got the message. He threw the truck into drive and was just about to pull away from the curb, when a sharp crack split the quiet like a gunshot.

Juno dropped into a crouch, her instincts sending her straight to the floor. Alex slammed his foot on the brake, and threw The Beast into park, ready to launch himself out of the vehicle to run to her rescue. But even as his heart thundered in his chest, his brain was already processing what he'd actually heard - the distinctive pop of a tire blowout, followed by the scrape-thump-scrape of a car riding on its rim.

A massive cream-colored Buick pulled up to the curb in front of Juno's, listing badly to one side. He immediately recognized the woman behind the wheel - Mrs. Becker, his former high school English teacher. She sat there calmly observing the situation as if she'd had every intention of arriving with such dramatic flair.

Alex released a long, exasperated sigh and bowed his head over his steering wheel. He couldn't drive away now.

He turned off the truck and climbed awkwardly out, lifting a hand in a friendly wave at Mrs. Becker, just in case she hadn't recognized him. He knew he looked pretty rough these days. Their paths met occasionally in the small lake town, and they always greeted each other affectionately. Usually, though, it was in the light of day at the grocery store or a local diner, not on a nearly empty street before the sun was up. Then grabbing his crutches from the back seat, he hobbled across the street toward the front of her car to stand in the beam of the headlights, giving her a clear view of him.

At the same time, Juno emerged from her coffee shop, her back ramrod straight, chin lifted high, a sure sign she was trying to recover her composure. Their eyes met for a fraction of a second before they both looked away.

"Well!" Mrs. Becker's bright, humor-laced words carried through her the window she was rolling down. "I did ask the Lord for a bit of excitement this morning, and hoo-boy, did he deliver!" Her eyes twinkled as she glanced between them, her eyes darting back and forth a few times. "He does work in mysterious ways."

"I'm just glad you're all right, Mrs. Becker," Juno said, her professional voice firmly in place. She circled around the back of the car, Alex noted. He was pretty sure she was keeping as much distance between her and him as possible.

To Alex, she said, "Should you be walking on that foot already?"

Alex frowned at her contrariness. How he wished for the return of the attentive Juno who'd escorted him to Urgent Care and then back to his apartment... until that stupid phone call. Besides, he wasn't walking on his foot. He wasn't walking at all, in fact. At the moment, he was just standing there, letting his booted foot rest on the ground. Other than gravity, he was putting none of his weight on it. He had gotten pretty good with his crutches; he'd had a broken leg back in high school and the muscle memory had come back easily. He started to defend himself, but Juno had already shifted her attention back to Mrs. Becker.

"Let's get you inside," she said to the older woman as she held open the door for her. "I'll put on some tea and then you can sit and watch while Mr. Frampton and I get your tire changed for you."

Mr. Frampton? Alex almost snorted at the formality. And really? She was going to help him change the tire? Sure, he had no doubt Juno Thomas knew exactly how to put on a spare, but there was no way he was going to let her get her hands dirty right before she opened her shop. Sprained ankle or not, he did have his dignity. How he'd get the stupid spare out of the trunk by himself, he had no idea at the moment, but he'd figure it out, even if it meant spraining the other ankle.

"Mr. Frampton?" Mrs. Becker echoed his thoughts with a chuckle. "I haven't heard our Alex called 'Mr. Frampton' since high school, and that was only when he was in trouble." She winked at Alex, who stood a few feet away, giving Juno the space she evidently wanted. "Which, now that I think on it, was rather often, wasn't it?"

Alex grinned good-naturedly at the older woman's ribbing. Mrs. Becker had made it her mission to get to know each of the students who went through her classroom. She learned their strengths and weaknesses, their senses of humor or lack thereof, their habits and quirks, and more. She was the type of teacher who won Teacher of the Year awards, the type students attributed their adult successes to.

"Apparently, I'm still in trouble, according to Juno," he said, then grimaced as he realized how antagonistic the words sounded. *I'm not baiting you*, he tried to convey to her with the crooked grin he sent Juno's way. Alex knew what people—what women—thought of his smile, especially when he looked at them with a slightly sheepish gaze. He'd used "the look" to his advantage on more than one occasion, but at the sight of her narrowed eyes and the grim line of her mouth, Juno wasn't about to be charmed by him.

"I can't imagine why you'd think so," she replied, her tone nonchalant, but the rigid line between her shoulders told him his words had hit close to home.

As if sensing the tension between them, Mrs. Becker pushed open her door and took Juno's proffered hand. "Tea would be lovely, Juno dear." She allowed her to help her from the car, but her sharp eyes didn't miss a thing. "Alex, you look like you could use a cup of coffee. Or tea, if you'd prefer. My car can wait until we all have a little go-juice in our circulatory system." She wriggled her fingers in his direction. "Come on inside with us."

"That's all right," Alex said, digging his heels in. "I'll get started on the tire if you want to leave the keys with me."

Mrs. Becker hesitated, then handed them over. "All righty," she said with a playful wink. "But you know we'll be talking about you in there, don't you? You sure we can't change your mind?"

"On the house," Juno added, barely looking at him, and he could hear the tension in her voice. It bothered him to no end that he was the one that put it there, but he was at a loss as to how to go about mending things between them. He had no idea where to even start.

"Thanks," he said to her. "You know I won't say no to a cup of Juno's Java. I'll take you up on it after I get the tire changed."

Mrs. Becker nodded slowly, but the look on her face told Alex her mind was going a mile a minute behind her bright eyes. "Well, that's fine then. But I need to say that I'm glad to see both of you this morning. The Lord and I have been discussing you two, believe it or not. In fact, I was just over at Hazel's yesterday to see all the work they're doing, and I was telling her how proud I am of you both. I love it when I get to see my former students making such successes of yourselves. And right here in Autumn Lake, too." She patted Juno's arm. "I am so glad you decided to come back here to us, Juno dear."

Juno smiled. "I am, too." She gave the woman a quick side hug before leading her around the back of the car. "I've never wanted to live anywhere else."

Alex remembered her saying the same thing way back in high school. He'd talked non-stop about getting out of Autumn Lake one day, and Juno had talked non-stop about never wanting to leave. It had been one of the few things they'd heartily disagreed on. How ironic it was that Juno had been the one to leave Alex behind.

Alex trailed a good couple of yards behind them, not wanting Juno to feel encroached upon. Once the women were up on the sidewalk, he popped open the trunk and was greatly relieved to find the inside clean as a whistle, a first aid kit and a fleece blanket tucked in behind one wheel well, and a quality hydraulic jack tucked in behind the other. The spare, in good shape, thank goodness, sat in a well beneath the floor mat, not bracketed under the car like some older Buick models, and it was one of those ridiculous lightweight donuts that weren't meant to be driven on for more than a couple of miles. He could do this.

"So tell me, Mrs. Becker, what are you doing here so early?" he heard Juno ask the woman as she led her toward the front door of the shop. Alex was wondering the same thing. Was it even safe for her to be driving in the dark? Granted, the sky was quickly turning from cobalt to ash, the moody clouds overhead letting only a few shafts of early morning amber light tickle the tops of the tree line on the North Shore, but still, the woman had started her journey in the pitch black of the pre-dawn hour.

Alex listened as their voices faded, focusing on the task at hand. He knelt awkwardly beside the flat tire, careful to keep his weight off his bad ankle, and began loosening the lug nuts. His back screamed in protest as the movement pulled at his healing road rash. He gritted his teeth and continued working.

Through the shop window, he could see Mrs. Becker talking animatedly, her hands gesturing, while Juno stood with her arms crossed, nodding occasionally. Every few seconds, Juno's eyes would drift toward the window, toward him, before snapping back to her guest.

What was Mrs. Becker saying in there? And were they talking about him, just like she'd said? Did he really want to know?

7
Juno

JUNO WATCHED ALEX THROUGH the window as he knelt awkwardly beside Mrs. Becker's Buick. Even with the walking boot and crutches, he was stubbornly determined to change that tire himself. Typical. The man didn't know how to accept help, even when he clearly needed it.

"He shouldn't be putting weight on that ankle," she muttered, turning to measure loose tea leaves into the infuser.

"Some lessons we learn the hard way, I suppose," Mrs. Becker said, settling into a chair at a table where she could watch Alex, too. Her eyes, sharp and perceptive as ever, hadn't missed Juno's concerned glance outside. "Though I suspect our Alex has had quite enough hard lessons for one lifetime."

Juno busied herself with the tea preparation, grateful for the familiar routine. Now there was a baited statement if she'd ever heard one, and she wasn't going to bite. If Mrs. Becker wanted to share details about Alex's life, that was all on her. Juno wouldn't be the one to ask.

"You two were so close once." Mrs. Becker's voice was gentle. "Before you left."

Juno poured steaming water over the infuser teapot, releasing the fragrant aroma of Earl Grey into the air. *Before you left.* She wanted to shout "I didn't leave!" but she kept her expression stoic as she loaded a tray with the teapot, a cup and saucer, and a white ceramic single serving cream and sugar set. "That was a long time ago," she finally said as she brought the tray to Mrs. Becker's table.

Outside, Alex set the jack, his movements slow and pained.

"I believe in being direct, Juno," Mrs. Becker continued, watching as Juno set out the tea service on the table in front of her. "So I'll ask plainly. Did you ever meet Jason?"

Juno paused, teapot suspended mid-air. "Alex's brother?"

"Alex's brother." Mrs. Becker confirmed with a nod.

"I never met him, but I feel like I did, the way Alex always talked about him. But he was stationed in Germany back then, and Alex and his parents went there for Christmas the year I was in Autumn Lake." Juno wasn't sure where this conversation was going, but she didn't like the serious look on her guest's face. She glanced at her watch and saw that it was already five. The first of her patrons would be wandering in soon.

Jason was older than Alex by about four years, and Alex thought his big brother hung the moon. Although he had no desire to make a career of the military, which was the route Jason was taking, Alex was all for doing his time defending the country in exchange for a free education and a chance to see a little of the world on the military's dime. And the uniform, he used to joke. "You know how the ladies feel about a guy in uniform." Juno knew it was more than that, though. Jason was Alex's role model, and if Jason had a uniform hanging in his closet, Alex wanted one, too.

As Juno poured tea into Mrs. Becker's cup, she added, "Where is he stationed these days? Do you know?"

Mrs. Becker reached over and laid a soft hand on her forearm. "Honey, Jason took his own life about six months after you left town."

The teapot clattered against the edge of the teacup, and Juno quickly set it down before she spilled the hot liquid, her hands shaking. "What?" The word came out on a breathy gasp.

"I see." Mrs. Becker nodded slowly. "I thought maybe one of your friends might have told you. But then, Claire isn't really a gossip, is she? Nor is that lovely Liz Needham. It's not something people really talk about around here. It completely devastated the Frampton family."

Juno shook her head in confirmation. The others in their Garden Variety Lovers Club had all moved to Autumn Lake sometime over the last decade, so they wouldn't have even known Jason if what Mrs. Becker said was true. But why hadn't Claire ever said anything? "I—I didn't know. No one ever told me."

"I wondered if perhaps... well, I wondered if that might be part of why things have been so strained between you two."

Juno sank into the chair opposite Mrs. Becker, her legs no longer willing to hold her upright. She glanced around at the quiet shop, relieved her usuals were apparently behind schedule this morning. Poppy would be here around six, but until then, Juno was on her own, which wasn't usually a problem at this hour.

Mrs. Becker poured a splash of cream into her tea, then stirred it three times before setting the spoon on the saucer. She picked up the cup and took a careful sip, giving Juno time to compose herself.

"I didn't know," she said again, and suddenly, like watching a movie rewind in her head, she started reeling back the last eight years since she'd been back in Autumn Lake, that fleeting haunted look she'd sometimes catch in Alex's eyes when he sat alone at the end of her bar drinking his milkshake. That devil-may-care image that sometimes felt like a facade. A well-rehearsed one, absolutely, but sometimes she thought she glimpsed cracks in it and wondered what he might be hiding. His summer sizzlers? His career.... "Did—" Juno broke off, suddenly not sure she wanted to know the answer to the question she'd started to ask. She cleared her throat and started again. "Did Alex go into...."

Mrs. Becker was shaking her head. "Alex never went anywhere, Juno. Not the military. Not college. In fact, from what I know, it's only on a rare occasion that he leaves Autumn Lake."

Her words hit Juno like a punch to the gut. She pressed both hands to her stomach. "But he had so many plans," she managed to get out.

"Plans that were sidelined when Jason died," Mrs. Becker said. Then she sighed deeply and added, "It was Alex who found him."

Juno brought her hands up to cover her mouth. *No, no, no.*

"Alex... changed after that," Mrs. Becker continued. "Dropped out of community college. Started drinking. Lost a job or two. For a while, we were all worried he might follow his brother's path."

"I had no idea," Juno whispered. All these years, she'd assumed his playboy reputation, his refusal to commit, was simply who he was. A choice. Not a shield against something so devastating.

"That truck out there? You may already know this, but it was Jason's." Mrs. Becker gestured at The Beast. "Alex kept it running all these years. It's why he's never replaced it, despite having the means to do so now."

Juno swallowed against the lump that had formed in her throat. And she'd had the audacity to think he'd kept it because of her.

"What happened?" Juno whispered, her eyes moving back to Alex where he was still down on his knees beside the tire. Then she reached out and squeezed Mrs. Becker's hand. "Actually, maybe you shouldn't. Not right now. I—I don't think I can bear it right now, and when Alex is done with your tire, he's coming in for coffee, and I don't want—I have customers—I need to...." Her voice trickled out. It was already too much for her to process and she didn't even know the half of it.

"Of course, Juno. Of course. I'm sorry. I chose a dreadful time to discuss this." Mrs. Becker straightened in her chair, then reached into her purse for a notepad and pencil. She flipped open the pad and scribbled something on it, then tore out the page and slid it across the table to Juno. "This is my phone number. You call me whenever you'd like." Her brow furrowed in concern, she watched Juno, as with shaking hands, she folded the slip of paper and tucked it into one of the pockets on her apron. "I don't know why the Lord moved me to speak to you today. It doesn't seem right, now that I think on it, not with that young man here. But like I said earlier, you two have been on my heart and mind almost around the clock the last week or longer. Both of you." The older woman sighed, then turned her gaze to Alex, who was now up and carefully rolling the flat tire toward the back of the car. "I guess I just thought, since you were both here, that God had set this appointment for us."

Juno closed her eyes and pinched the bridge of her nose with her thumb and forefinger. How selfish could she be? *She* couldn't bear it? None of it had happened to her. Alex had borne it all these years, had carried the unfathomable grief of losing his big brother, the trauma of being the one to find him.... "Oh, Alex," she whispered.

Outside, Alex had managed to remove the flat tire and was maneuvering the spare into position. She should go out and offer to help him again. How was he going to lift the flat tire into the trunk on his own? There was nothing wrong with his arms, but the actions he was doing had to be pulling terribly against the wounds on his back.

Turning back to Mrs. Becker, she asked, "Why are you telling me all of this?" It wasn't an impertinent question. She just didn't quite know what she was supposed to do with everything she'd just learned.

Mrs. Becker toyed with the handle of her cup. "Because I've known you both since you were teenagers. And I've watched you circle each other for eight years since you returned, both too stubborn or too scared to bridge whatever gap opened between you."

"We were kids," Juno said reflexively. "What happened back then doesn't matter anymore."

"Doesn't it?" Mrs. Becker's eyes were kind but knowing. "Juno, you sat in my class and heard me say a hundred times that the past may not determine our future, but it certainly informs it. I'm not saying you owe Alex anything. I'm just suggesting that perhaps there's more to his story than you've allowed yourself to hear. Not to drive the point home, but you certainly missed a key element where Jason is concerned. I can't help but wonder if the last decade and a half might have played out differently if you'd know about him all this time."

Juno thought of the way Alex had looked at her in the urgent care waiting room. *We were friends once, weren't we? I'd like to think we could be again.* And she'd been so close to saying yes before he'd called that woman "babe" and confirmed every suspicion she'd harbored.

"Of course it would have," she acknowledged. For one thing, she wouldn't have been so condescending toward him at every opportunity. She wouldn't have judged him so harshly all these years. She might even have been kind to him, to have offered him grace for his behavior, not scorn and disdain. "But I didn't know. No one even bothered to tell me about Jason." Even as the words came out, she could hear how defensive she sounded.

"Did you bother to ask?" Mrs. Becker wasn't chastising her. The look in the older woman's eyes was purely altruistic. "I can't quite grasp why you no longer want to care about Alex, Juno. May I ask what happened between you? Did he do something... did he hurt you?"

Juno shook her head emphatically. "No, Mrs. Becker. At least, not in the way you might be thinking. Alex was the same gentle giant that he is now. He never would have done anything like that."

Mrs. Becker leaned forward, resting one forearm on the table. "But he did hurt you." It was a statement, not a question.

Juno met her teacher's eyes, imploring the woman to understand, and said, "I didn't leave, you know. I didn't abandon him or my friends or this town. My father took us away. After promising it would be different, that we would put down roots here, that we would stay and make Autumn Lake home. In the middle of the night, he packed us up and took us away."

"Oh, honey." Now it was Mrs. Becker's turn to press a hand to her mouth. "I didn't know." After a moment, she asked, "Is it possible that Alex doesn't know, either?"

"Oh, he knows. I wrote to him," Juno continued quietly, feeling somewhat exonerated at her teacher's expression. "When my dad took us away. I wrote to Alex, told him everything about why I had to go. I asked him..." She trailed off, the old pain rising unexpectedly. She shook her head and changed her mind about sharing more. "He never answered. Never even bothered to break up with me. Just... nothing."

Mrs. Becker frowned. "That doesn't sound like Alex."

"Except that it does, if you think about it, Mrs. Becker. He doesn't do conflict. He doesn't push against the grain. It's easier to just go with the flow, right?" Juno pressed her palms flat to the table, then slid her chair back and rose. Out the window she could see Thad just rounding the corner, which meant that Dixie May wouldn't be far behind him coming from the other direction on her way home from her job across the lake. "Look, maybe he had his reasons, and maybe there were good ones. We all do. But that was a long time ago."

"Indeed it was." Mrs. Becker's gaze was thoughtful. "Though I find it curious that neither of you has managed to move on, despite the years between then and now."

"I don't know about that," Juno countered. "Maybe we have moved on, just not in the same direction."

Mrs. Becker waited quietly, her eyes never leaving Juno's, like she expected her to say more.

Finally, Juno reached across the table and touched the woman's shoulder. "Listen, I so appreciate you telling me about Jason. It does change my perspective, and for that I'm grateful. But it looks like Alex is finishing up, and I've got customers on their way in." She gestured out the window, then asked, "I'm going to go put together Ward and Penny's order for you. Would you like more tea while you wait?"

Mrs. Becker shook her head. "I'd better not." She reached out and grabbed Juno's hand. "I'm praying for you."

Before Juno could respond, the bell above the door chimed, and Thad held the door open for Alex as he maneuvered his way inside, crutches awkward in the narrow doorway.

8
Alex

Alex grabbed the crutches he'd leaned against the trunk and hobbled toward the coffee shop door, his ankle throbbing with each hop. Changing Mrs. Becker's tire had been more taxing than he'd anticipated, but he'd managed it, and there was a small satisfaction in that.

"Thad, my good man," he said, just as the owner of the bait shop opened the door and stepped back to let him in ahead of him.

"Morning, Frampton. You've seen better days."

"That I have," Alex said with wry chuckle. "Thanks." He headed into the restroom to wash the brake dust from his hands, then headed toward Mrs. Becker's table, surprised to see Juno slipping away, her expression troubled. Had he interrupted something?

"All done," he announced, setting the Buick keys on the table in front of her. "It's just a donut spare though. You'll need to get it replaced properly today. Do you need help setting that up?"

"My hero," Mrs. Becker beamed. "Thank you for rescuing this damsel in distress." She pointed at the chair that Juno had just vacated. "Now come sit before you fall over."

He hesitated, watching as Juno efficiently handled Thad's order, but when she lingered behind the counter after Thad said his goodbyes, Alex lowered himself gingerly into the chair, careful not to jostle his ankle. The smell of freshly ground coffee filled the air as Juno worked at her espresso machine.

"Extra cream, three sugars," she said, her voice carrying above the whir of the grinder. "Right, Alex?"

His chest tightened with pleasure that she knew exactly how he liked his coffee. "That's right." Sure, she'd remembered Thad's usual order, too, but a 'large black coffee to go and one of your morning specials' was hard to mess up.

When she returned to their table and handed him the coffee, he noticed that she deliberately avoided touching his fingers. His hands were clean, so he couldn't excuse it away; she was maintaining her distance. Not that he could blame her.

He took a cautious sip. The coffee was so good—exactly how he liked it, exactly how she'd always made it for him. "Wow. That's perfect."

"Good. Now do you want to tell me what you were doing parked outside my coffee shop in the dark this morning?"

Alex was taken off guard by the direct question, but he was pleased to note that she sounded more curious than upset. That didn't mean he wanted to explain his presence, though. Maybe he could avoid doing so by making light of it. He cleared his throat. "Hadn't you heard? I'm a small town local hero. I arrived just in time to help Mrs. Becker change her flat." He shifted in his seat to relieve the twinges of discomfort shooting up his leg, but then let out a sharp grunt when he accidentally bumped the brace against the table leg.

"Here," Juno said suddenly, grabbing a chair from another table and swinging it around to face him. "Put your foot up here. You're supposed to be elevating that thing."

"Thank you." He carefully lifted his leg, wincing as he settled his booted foot onto the chair. "So Mrs. Becker," he said with a grin at the older woman. "I know Juno already asked you, but what brought you here so early in the morning?"

"Oh! Well, I'm picking up Ward's breakfast order for his crew out at the Garden Gate," she explained. "Hazel and I are spending the morning out in the garden with Judy. The poor thing is quite distressed by all the activity in the kitchen; it's her favorite room in the house, and she's struggling to process all the changes."

Reality crashed back. Right. "Yeah, he's got my crew working for him this week. Without me. Stupid ankle." He knocked on the frame of the brace in frustration, then asked, "But how did you get recruited? No offense intended, but are they that desperate?"

"Hey now," Mrs. Becker chided, wagging her spoon at him. "I may be retired, but I still come in handy sometimes. I offered to make everyone a breakfast casserole, but I think Hazel let slip that my kitchen skills have something to be desired. Ward insisted that I pick up breakfast from here rather than cooking it myself."

He smiled despite himself. Mrs. Becker had always been able to pull him out of his darker moods, even back in high school.

"Well, no one makes better breakfast sandwiches than Juno," he said, genuinely meaning it. Then quickly added, "Not to say anything against your casserole."

Mrs. Becker's eyes twinkled. "And speaking of kitchen skills, no one is better at installing kitchen cabinets than you, Alex. At least that's what Ward was saying yesterday. They could use your help. Why don't you head on over there with me? I know they'd put you to good use."

He gestured at his ankle. "I'm not much use to anyone right now."

"Nonsense," Mrs. Becker waved dismissively. "Penny was just telling me yesterday how much they miss having you around. Said the place isn't the same without your terrible jokes."

From the corner of his eye, he caught Juno's smile—quickly suppressed, but definitely there. His jokes had always been terrible; he wasn't afraid to admit it. Deliberately so. He shook his head. "Nah. I'm probably going to head back to my place and put my foot up for the rest of the morning. Maybe try to get some sleep," he added. It sounded so good to his ears, even though he knew how unlikely it was. At least the sleep part.

"Right after a cup of sugar and caffeine? Ha." Mrs. Becker wasn't buying it. "And you can put your foot up over at the Garden Gate, too. That way you can still contribute your expertise to the project. Besides, I'd really appreciate you following me over. I'm a little worried about driving on that funny little tire."

Low blow. Mrs. Becker knew exactly what she was doing, playing on his instinct to help. And it was working.

"And Juno," the older woman turned to her, catching her as she started back to the counter.

"Yes?"

"Aren't you bringing lunch by today, too? You should take your break then and join us."

Wait, what? Alex's gaze snapped to Juno, who looked as surprised as he felt. Maybe he'd head to the bed and breakfast after all.

"I don't have that on my calendar," Juno said, frowning slightly.

"Oh. Well, I guess Ward just forgot to put his order in." Mrs. Becker's innocent expression was about as convincing as a politician's apology. "I'm sure he'll call you this morning."

Alex fought the urge to laugh at the transparent matchmaking attempt. Glancing at Juno, he could see she was having the same struggle. For a moment, it felt like they were co-conspirators again, sharing a private joke at someone else's expense. Just like old times.

The moment slipped away as Dixie May pushed through the front door, still in her Carpe Diem uniform. "Hey, gang. What are you all doing up at this ungodly hour?" she asked. "Well, not you, Juno. You have to be up at this ungodly hour or people like me will die."

"Die?" Mrs. Becker echoed, eyebrow raised.

"Yes, Mrs. Becker," Dixie May nodded emphatically. "Literally, not figuratively, die. Dead. Kaput."

Juno looped an arm through Dixie May's and walked with her back to the counter. "Come on. I'll hook up your life-saving IV for you." Over her shoulder, she added, "And I'll get Ward's order for you, too, Mrs. Becker."

As soon as Juno was out of earshot, Mrs. Becker leaned closer to Alex, her voice dropping. "You need to talk to that girl, Alex. Tell her about what you've been through."

His stomach plummeted. "I'm sorry. What?"

"She didn't know about Jason, Alex," Mrs. Becker said gently. "All this time back in Autumn Lake, and no one ever told her."

"That wasn't your story to tell." He fought to keep his voice steady.

"Perhaps not," Mrs. Becker conceded. "But I'm old enough to know that sometimes people need a little push. And you two have been circling each other for eight years now."

"It's not that simple," he said, rubbing his temple where a headache was forming. "I messed things up pretty badly."

"I know." Mrs. Becker's eyes were kind as she nodded. "She told me about the letters."

"Letters?" Alex frowned. "What letters? I don't know about any letters. I'm talking about—" He broke off, stopping himself before he could spill his secret. Now was not the time and place, and not with his old teacher, either. "What *are* you talking about?"

Her expression shifted from understanding to confusion. "The letter she wrote to you explaining her reasons for leaving."

A chill spread through his chest. "I never heard anything from Juno after she left. It was like she disappeared off the face of the earth." His voice trembled just the slightest bit. But before he could press for more details, Juno returned to the table carrying a large carry-out box. Both he and Mrs. Becker fell silent, watching her approach.

"Four breakfast sandwiches, two thermoses of coffee, and a dozen cinnamon rolls," Juno said, patting the side of the box. "Penny's favorite. I'll carry them out to the car for you."

"Perfect," Mrs. Becker beamed, reaching for her purse, and getting to her feet while Alex struggled to do the same. "So we'll see you at lunch time, right?" she pressed.

Juno nodded good-naturedly. "I'll watch for the order."

Alex gathered his crutches, his mind racing. Juno had written to him? For fifteen years, he'd believed she'd simply disappeared without a word, without a backward glance.

"Need a hand with that?" Juno asked, nodding toward his empty coffee cup as he balanced awkwardly on his crutches.

"No," he said, more abruptly than he intended. Then, softening, "I mean, I've got it. Thanks."

He had to talk to her, had to find out about her letter. But not here, not now, with Mrs. Becker watching and customers arriving and his thoughts in chaos. He followed along behind the women, feeling useless while Juno held the door for Mrs. Becker, then for him, her arms full with the food box that he couldn't carry for her.

Standing on the sidewalk, he watched Juno help Mrs. Becker into her car. Juno had written to him. His mind was going a mile a minute. *What had she written?*

At that moment, she lifted her gaze, and their eyes met over the top of Mrs. Becker's car.

Then she smiled. That beautiful June-bug smile that he'd dreamed about for nearly two decades.

9
Juno

JUNO STOOD AT THE window and watched the tail lights of Alex's truck disappear around the corner behind Mrs. Becker's Buick. He'd never actually said why he'd been lurking outside her coffee shop in the dark early morning. The thought sent an uncomfortable shiver down her spine - not of fear exactly, but something deeper, more unsettling.

The Alex Frampton she remembered wouldn't have avoided a direct question like that.

Then again, the Alex she remembered wouldn't have been sitting in his truck watching her through windows before dawn, either.

The bell above the door chimed, making her jump. Claire burst in with her typical dramatic flair, but there was something different about her energy this morning - less theatrical and more... concerned? She hadn't even bothered to style her blonde curls, which were escaping from a messy bun, and she was without her signature Hollywood red lipstick. She was earlier than usual, too.

Claire also started her mornings early at her bookshop, hours before she opened to the public. She once explained to Juno that she liked to think of herself as something of a Miss Clavel from the popular Madeline series. "I'm the last one to leave and the first one to arrive, and I just want to make sure everything is in nice straight lines. Once I do a walk-through of the shop, I can get my coffee, sit down, and start on the other important things. Like bookkeeping," she'd added with a long-suffering sigh.

Claire had a marked flamboyant gene that she expressed in her fashion sense, but her shop was, indeed, run with the same precision of the storybook militant nun. So for her to show up in a bit of a tizzy like this?

"Don't be alarmed," Claire announced, as though reading Juno's mind. She made her way to the counter and planted herself on a stool, not bothering to remove her jacket. "but I've spent the last twenty minutes being a creepy creeper creeping on a creepier creeper." She paused for effect. "I was spying on him spying on you."

Juno's hands stilled on the espresso machine she'd been absently polishing. "What are you talking about?"

"I saw Alex's truck when I got to the shop to do my morning prep. He was just... sitting there. In the dark." Claire's usually playful tone had an edge to it.

Juno didn't know why she even bothered trying to play dumb, but she said nothing.

"I tried calling you," Claire added.

Juno patted her apron pockets. No phone. She must have set it down somewhere during all the hubbub around Mrs. Becker. Maybe she'd been outside helping the old woman out of her car when Claire called. "My phone is in the back," she said, although she knew that wasn't really any kind of response. At least not for someone like Claire. To keep busy, she started making Claire's usual morning drink - a hazelnut latte with an extra espresso shot. The familiar motions helped steady her hands.

"When you didn't answer, I decided to come over and ask you—or Alex— what was going on myself."

When Claire left the statement hanging, Juno prompted, "And?"

"And by the time I put on some makeup, got my coat back on, and walked around from the alley, Alex was driving away, following Mrs. Becker in her car." Claire reached over and plucked a cellophane-wrapped biscotti from a countertop display case. She removed the packaging just as Juno handed her a large to-go cup without a lid so that Claire could appreciate the fancy foam art before she took her first sip. "Which, I have to say, was not the dramatic conclusion I was expecting to my morning of espionage."

Juno chuckled. "It's too early for espionage."

"Apparently, not for Alex," she shot back. "Nor for me. You should have seen me. Well, actually, you couldn't have seen me since I'm so good at espionage. I kept my shop lights off so that I could watch him from the front window. The one with the new design. The silhouette of a girl holding the umbrella made of flowers and the rain clouds—"

"I know the window, Claire," Juno interrupted, taking the biscotti wrapper and dropping it into the trash. "I look at it every day." The Cracked Spine, Claire's eclectic bookshop, was kitty-corner to the coffee shop, and they often waved at each other when they happened to be in their windows at the same time.

"Right. But you didn't know I was there, did you?" Claire wiggled her eyebrows at Juno. "That's because I excel at subterfuge. I'm like a shadow. A wraith. An invisible woman."

Juno snorted. "You are not and will never be an invisible woman, my friend. Not with the way you look." It was true. Claire had an ethereal beauty that made people stop and take a second look. And it seemed so effortless, which made her even more attractive. On top of that, the woman was genuine and kind and the best friend a girl could ever have.

Claire ignored the compliment and took a careful sip of her coffee. She closed her eyes in pleasure. "Perfect," she murmured dreamily. "I don't know how you do it, woman. It's perfect every time."

"That's why you pay me the big bucks," Juno quipped, hoping Claire didn't notice that her cheeks warmed at the memory of Alex saying the same thing.

Claire pushed a couple of dollars across the counter for the biscotti, and Juno reluctantly took the cash for the baked good. Her friend sent so many customers her way, and Juno would have preferred not to charge her for anything, but Claire wouldn't hear of it. She only agreed to accept the first drink of the day as a complimentary one, and only after Juno threatened to not serve her at all if she didn't. A completely empty threat, they both knew, but it did the trick of preserving both their dignities while coming up with a satisfactory compromise for both parties.

"So?"

Juno glanced at the clock again; she kept hoping someone would come in and prevent the rest of this conversation, but no such luck. However, she was nothing if not stubborn. "So?"

"Oh my lands, Juno," Claire said on an exasperated sigh. "Will you please just tell me what went down this morning? I'm dying here, and I have a ton of bookkeeping to do, and you already know that I'll find *any* excuse not to do it. So if you don't want my business to collapse in financial ruin, talk." She cupped a hand around an ear. "I'm listening."

Juno frowned. "You're not going to go away until I tell you, are you?"

"Nope." But her expression grew concerned. "Should I be worried? About you? About him?"

"No," she said quickly. Too quickly. "Mrs. Becker got a flat tire right in front of the shop and he helped her change it."

Claire frowned as she processed that bit of information. Juno could practically see the puzzle pieces in her friend's mind being shuffled around to create this new scenario. Finally, she said, "Well, that explains that loud noise I heard. I had just chalked it up to The Gray Lady." Claire told anyone who would listen that her bookstore was haunted. Sometimes, Juno thought Claire actually believed it, herself. "But honestly, now I'm even more confused. Why on earth was that darling old lady up at this hour and here at your shop before you even opened?"

She dunked her biscotti into her coffee, then shoved a large bite into her mouth before it fell off into her cup. "And that still doesn't explain why Alex was here, too. Half an hour or more before you open. Sitting in the dark. Across the street. From your shop. Watching you." She paused between each sentence fragment. "Like a creeper."

Juno gave her a withering look. "Are you done?"

"Not even close. Not unless you spill the tea. Or the coffee, in this case." Claire's voice softened. "What's going on, Juno?"

"Honestly, I don't know," she admitted. "This isn't the first time I've seen him out there, either. The Beast is hard to miss, even in the dark."

Claire snorted and shook her head. "The Beast. Of course Alex named his truck."

I named it. Juno pressed her lips together, catching the rogue admission before it leaped out, but Claire noticed, and her eyes widened.

"What?"

"What, what?"

"What are you not saying?" Claire demanded. Then her eyes got even larger. "Wait. That's what you called his truck back in high school!" she exclaimed, smacking the countertop with an open palm. "He named his truck after you."

"Gee, thanks," Juno said dryly.

Claire chortled. "Ha! I'm not calling you a beast, silly."

"And it wasn't his truck back then. It was Jason's." Juno watched Claire's face to see what her reaction would be to Jason's name.

Claire nodded solemnly. "I remember." She tipped her head and gave Juno a gentle look. "I think you forget sometimes that I was there back then. I remember how you two were together, before—"

"Before I left?" Juno's voice came out sharper than she intended. She took a deep breath and modulated her tone. Claire knew good and well that Juno hadn't left of her own accord. Her friend didn't mean it that way. "That was a lifetime ago, Claire. We were kids."

Claire's expression didn't change. "Were we, though? You, especially, June-bug, were far older than your years. I could see it in your eyes; you'd lived a lifetime by the time we met."

"Prolonged childhood trauma does not automatically equate to maturity," Juno retorted, but she wasn't really angry at Claire. No, she was remembering how real, how... how *forever* her feelings were for Alex back then, and the shame that welled up in her for being so naive to have given him her heart threatened to overwhelm her if she let herself dwell on it. "We were kids," she repeated. "With kid problems, kid emotions, and kid behaviors. And it's all in the past now."

"But is it? I mean, I still don't know exactly what he did to you all those years ago, but you two are barely on speaking terms, and I know that's mostly your decision." Claire rested her forearms on the counter and wrapped both hands around her cup. "Maybe it's time to forgive him, Juno."

"What makes you think that he's the one who wronged me? What if it was the other way around and I'm the bad guy?" Juno sounded belligerent and antagonistic, even to her own ears, but the emotions bubbled hotly inside her, and she was struggling to keep them in check.

Claire shrugged one shoulder. "Then maybe it's time to forgive yourself." She didn't say it flippantly, but it still stung.

Juno shook her head and turned away, crossing to the display case where she straightened a row of ginger crinkle cookies on a cream platter. "You know, I don't really feel like talking about all of this right now. I'm open for business, remember? But since you're here, and you're obviously not going to let this drop, then let me ask you something."

"Of course."

Juno swallowed hard, then crossed her arms and looked her friend directly in the eye. "Why didn't you tell me about Jason?"

10
Juno

"Jason?" Claire's expression shifted from confusion to surprise. "Alex's brother?" She stared at Juno across the counter. "What about him?"

"His suicide," Juno said, the word still feeling strange in her mouth. "Mrs. Becker told me this morning." When Claire still looked perplexed, she went on impatiently. "That he killed himself, Claire. About six months after I left town. Why didn't you tell me?"

"Oh, Juno." Claire set down her cup, realization dawning. "I thought... I mean, I guess—well, I just thought you knew too. People don't sit around talking about it or anything, but it's not a secret."

"Well, it was to me." Juno turned away, busying herself with wiping down the already spotless counter. "And that Alex found him?"

When Claire didn't respond right away, Juno looked over. Her friend was shaking her head slowly, remembering. "Juno, I'm so sorry. It happened so long ago, and like I said, it's just not a common topic of conversation around here. Everyone was heartbroken about it, and the Framptons were... " She didn't finish the sentence; Juno thought it was because Claire couldn't find a word to describe what it must have been like for them. "Alex was such a wreck. I think everyone was a little worried he'd hurt himself, too."

"What do you mean?"

"Alex went off the rails for a while. Drinking, missing work. Ward practically kept him alive from what I heard. Did you know that Ward took a gap year so he could stick around and make sure Alex survived?"

This was news to Juno, too. "Ward's a good friend."

"He is," Claire agreed. "And he's stuck by Alex through thick and thin, even during the years Ward lived in California." Claire hesitated, then said,

"Alex took it hard when Ward moved so far away. That's when all the summer sizzler stuff started, I think. Like he was afraid to get close to anyone who might stick around."

The pieces were falling into place, creating a picture of Alex that Juno hadn't allowed herself to see before. "I can see why that might happen."

Claire eyed her quizzically. "Does knowing about Jason change the way you feel about Alex?"

"Look," Juno said finally, "I get it. What happened explains a lot about why he is the way he is. Knowing what I know now helps me understand him better. But that doesn't change what happened between us."

"Which was what, exactly?" Claire pressed. "You've never really told me."

Juno squeezed the cloth in her hand. "He really never told you?"

"No. All he ever said was that you left town without even saying goodbye, June-bug. He asked me if I'd heard from you, and I told him you'd written, and that you were okay, but I didn't know what else to say. I figured if you didn't want to talk to him, I wasn't going to go behind your back and do so."

Juno couldn't believe the shop was still so quiet, but right now, she was glad for the reprieve. She threw the bar towel in the sink and leaned back against the counter, pressing her palms to the cool steel on either side of her. "I wrote to him, Claire," she stated, her jaw tight. "The night my dad dragged us away. I told him everything—about my dad and all his addictions. About how scared I was that I'd never see Alex again. I even asked—no, I begged—if he could talk to his parents about letting me live with them so I could finish school here."

Claire frowned. "Wow."

"Yeah, wow. And then nothing. He never responded."

"And he couldn't call because you had no phone."

"Yep. Dad and his paranoia. Do you remember that little green phone I saved up for working here?" She gestured at the shop around them. "He stomped on it right in front of me that night. If Alex tried calling or texting, he'd have found out soon enough that the phone was out of commission. And yes, I told him all about that in the letters, too."

"I don't get it," Claire said, shaking her head. "It really doesn't make sense to me. Juno, he was devastated after you left. He moped around campus like the world was ending. His heart was broken."

Juno clenched and unclenched her jaw. "You know what I think? I think he decided I wasn't worth the trouble. I'd put him on the spot by asking if I could stay with his family, and I think he felt like that was my attempt to tie him down, to force a commitment out of him."

"That doesn't sound like Alex, Juno. And why didn't you ever ask about staying with me? Or Liz?" Claire's tone was gentle, but it was obvious by the look in her eyes that she was a little hurt about it.

Juno looked away, shame making her cheeks warm. "I—I just couldn't. If Alex didn't want to have anything to do with me, then it seemed... I don't know, Claire." She sighed. "I guess I knew you'd keep loving me no matter how long it took for me to get back here, but with Alex so quick to write me off, I wasn't sure I could face him right away."

"Did he have your grandma's address?" Claire asked, but she was grasping at straws, trying to explain away Alex's silence. "And then with Jason—"

Juno cut her off. "I gave him the address in the letters I wrote to him." The old pain surfaced, sharper than she'd expected. "An this was months before Jason died. Don't get me wrong; I feel heartsick about Jason and—and Alex, and I'm actually glad I know now because, like I said, it helps me understand the way he behaves. But it doesn't change the fact that I was out of sight, out of mind with him. It doesn't change the way he is now, and I'm still not interested in being with someone who uses women the way he does."

Claire frowned. "It's not just one-sided, June. Those women aren't exactly victims; they use him, too."

"And he doesn't seem to mind, does he?" She was getting back some of the wind in her sails, and the indignation felt good. Comfortable. Familiar.

The bell above the door chimed as a man in a business suit came in, followed by two women in similar attire. All three of them paused just inside the door and looked around, a bit like they were sizing up the place. Juno felt her hackles rise, but then one of the women smiled and exclaimed, "Wow! This place is delightful."

Claire grinned at Juno, helping to ease the tension a little. "Go take care of your customers. I need to get back to my shop anyway."

Juno grabbed her hand before she could slide off her stool. "Are we good? You and me?" she asked, waving a finger back and forth between them a few times. "This morning has been a little overwhelming, and I don't want you worried that I'm upset at you."

"We're good." Claire scooped up her bag. "But I wish you could find a way to make things good with Alex, too. I think you should talk to him, Juno. Find out what happened with those letters."

Juno nodded slowly. "I'll think about it." She wasn't about to commit to anything more than that, but she wasn't lying. There were days when Alex seemed to be all she thought about. She started toward the other end of the counter to take the newcomers' orders, but all three of them were standing back and reading the menu.

"Welcome to Juno's," she said, giving them a warm smile. "If you have any questions, don't hesitate to ask."

"Give us a minute, please," the man said, returning her smile. "You have so many great options."

Just then, the phone rang. "Juno's Coffee Bar. I'm with another patron right now. Can I call you back or would you like to hold?"

"Hey Juno." Penny Anderson's pretty voice sounded on the other end of the line. "Call me back when you can take our lunch order."

"Will do, Penny."

Claire was carefully sweeping a few crumbs up into a napkin. "What's Penny calling about?"

"They need to place a lunch order; they've got a whole crew over there this week trying to get the kitchen knocked out before the end of the month. They're missing Alex since he's been out of commission the last few days, but he was on his way over there with Mrs. Becker, so hopefully, he's able to help them just by being there with his experience, even if he can't do a lot of the heavy lifting."

Claire gave her a sideways look. "Are you going to deliver it?"

Juno rolled her eyes. "Nope. I'll send Poppy. She'll be ecstatic at the chance to check up on Alex."

"You wouldn't do that to him," Claire chided.

"Alex is a big boy," Juno shot back.

"You know, understanding why someone hurt you and even forgiving them doesn't mean you have to act like it never happened. But it might help you stop letting that hurt control your choices."

"I'm not—" Juno stopped herself. "This isn't about that. Lunch is our busiest time, and I don't like leaving during the rush." She glanced over at the three customers at the counter, but they were still discussing the menu options. Juno came out from behind the counter and gave Claire a hug.

She gently patted Juno's cheek. "You know," she said casually, "both of you were just kids when all this happened. Maybe neither of you had the tools to handle what came your way."

"Maybe." Juno followed her to the door, keeping an eye on the three still at the counter. "But we're not kids anymore."

Claire paused on the threshold, then said, "Exactly my point."

The door closed behind her, leaving Juno alone with those words echoing in her head. She wasn't acting like a child. She was protecting herself. There was a difference.

Wasn't there?

Understanding would certainly help lead to forgiveness, sure. But forgiveness didn't mean she had to invite him back into her life.

11
Alex

ALEX SAT DOWN ON the chair Ward had set out for him. "Yes, please help," he'd agreed wholeheartedly. "But do everything you can from that seat with your weight off that foot."

Alex now stared at the cabinet door he'd just installed. His eyes felt like they'd been rubbed with sandpaper, and no matter how many times he blinked, his vision stayed fuzzy. Was it straight? It wasn't straight. But the level he was using told him it hung perfectly aligned, and it opened and closed like butter, the magnetic touch latch matching up just right. He scooted back to get a broader perspective and squinted.

He'd been working since shortly after leaving Juno's place, fueled by her strong coffee and his desperate need to keep moving, to avoid thinking about how she'd looked at him this morning – wary and defensive, like he was some kind of threat.

"You planning on having a staring contest with that cabinet all morning?" Ward's voice cut through his fog. He leaned against the doorframe of what would soon be the Garden Gate's newly renovated kitchen. "Because I'm pretty sure it's going to win."

Alex summoned up his trademark grin, the one that usually deflected questions and concern. "Just admiring my handiwork. Love this hickory, man. It's gorgeous." He ran a hand over the smooth surface, buying time to collect himself. "Your bride-to-be is going to love you when she sees this."

"My bride-to-be already loves me," Ward said with the confidence of a man who knows what he's worth. "But yeah, she's going to be wowed, that's for sure. She might have picked it out, but there's nothing like seeing it all put together." Penny had been kicked out of the kitchen yesterday

73

when they'd started on the project, because Ward wanted her to be blown away by the end result.

"Where are the ladies today?" Alex asked, hoping Ward would start talking about his fiancé instead of drilling Alex on how he was doing. His friend had been shooting him assessing looks more and more often these days, and although he didn't come right out and ask, Alex got the feeling the questions were coming. Things were always tough for him around the anniversary of Jason's death, but there were other circumstances pressing down on him, and Alex wasn't coping as well as he usually did, and he was well aware that it showed.

Ward eyed Alex quizzically. "You don't know?"

Had Ward already told him and he'd just forgotten? Sheesh. He chuckled and shook his head. "It's your womenfolk, Ward. Why would I know where they are?"

Ward shrugged and crossed his arms. "Oh, I don't know. Maybe because you spoke with one of the said womenfolk just this morning. Early. Right after fixing her blowout."

Alex's hand slipped on the cabinet door, and he had to catch himself against the counter. He covered the fumble by reaching to pick up a drill bit he'd dropped several minutes ago. But when he didn't immediately say anything, Ward went on, his tone droll, almost goading.

"In front of Juno's place. Before dawn. Where you'd been sitting in your truck in the dark for—"

"Right. Mrs. Becker." Alex cut him off. "She needed help with a flat tire," he said, not meeting Ward's eyes.

"And you just happened to be outside Juno's in the dark—"

Alex interrupted him again. "You said that already." He shot his friend a bleary-eyed glare, then began peeling the protective plastic sheeting from another cupboard door. "I was waiting to get my coffee. I like it fresh." Ugh. That sounded weak, even to him.

The silence stretched between them, broken only by the distant sound of hammering from somewhere upstairs where the rest of the crew was working. Alex could feel Ward's steady gaze on him, waiting him out, but Alex had years of practice at avoiding conversations he didn't want to have.

He pointed at the door he'd already hung, and casually asked, "Does that door look straight or do I need to adjust the hinges? Got your level handy?" Then he spotted his own level sitting right in front of him. Playing it cool wasn't working today.

He wasn't fooling his friend, either. "When's the last time you actually slept, Alex?"

"Last night." The lie came automatically to his lips. "Slept like a baby."

"Yeah? What kind of baby? The kind that screams every hour on the hour?"

Alex barked out a laugh. "Nope. The kind that curls up in your arms and dreams of puppy dogs and angel choirs."

"Alex."

"Ward." He matched his friend's serious tone, then grinned again. "Look, I appreciate the concern, but I'm fine."

"You're not fine," Ward contradicted. "You're injured, man. And you're awake before the sun comes up and you're driving around in the middle of the night in a sleep-deprived fog, which I'm having a hard time believing is something your doctor would be chill about—or you're parked outside Juno's place like a stalker—"

"I'm not a stalker—"

"Well, you look like the walking dead." He rubbed his clean-shaven jaw. "And what are you doing parked outside Juno's? Again."

Alex's facade cracked. He turned away, pretending to search his tool belt. How did Ward know? Had Juno seen him—worse, had she complained to Ward? Was she afraid to confront him directly?

He felt exposed, called out, and he bristled inside. "I don't know what you're talking about."

"Right." But Ward moved further into the kitchen, maneuvering around a pile of discarded cardboard and packing materials. "Talk to me, man. What's really going on with you?"

For a dangerous moment, Alex was tempted. The weight of everything he carried pressed down on him until he could barely breathe.

But then he heard footsteps on the stairs, voices getting closer, and just like that, the moment passed. He squared his shoulders and plastered on his easy smile. "The only thing going on with me is that these cabinets aren't going to install themselves." He turned to the guy who'd just pushed through the protective plastic draped across the doorway. "Hey, Harold."

Harold was an electrician who charged by the job, not by the hour, which was fortunate, since his propensity to talk could double the duration of any project. Clients tolerated his elastic timelines due to the quality of his work.

"Looking good in here, boys," Harold said, bracing his feet wide and hooking his thumbs in his toolbelt. He took a deep breath like he was getting ready to launch into a tale, but Alex beat him to it.

"Hey, Harold, did I ever tell you about my great uncle who died in the electric chair?"

Harold's jaw dropped, taking the bait. "Uh, no. Not that I recall."

Alex shook his head slowly. "Yeah, it came as quite a shock."

Ward shot him a disgusted look, but Harold guffawed heartily over the terrible joke. "Hoo-boy. You had me there for a second, Frampton." To Ward, he said, "Boss, I need you to take a look at things upstairs before I close the walls up." Harold was installing dedicated circuits in each of the new guest bathrooms upstairs.

Good. Ward was needed elsewhere, and that meant he'd leave Alex alone. Besides, it was almost lunch time, and Juno would be bringing their lunch orders. He wasn't going to pretend that he wasn't aching to see her again. Then after lunch, he could bail on the day. Maybe he'd go home and take another sleeping pill. Surely, if he was this tired already, a dose of the benzodiazepine would send him into slumber land.

In fact, downing a six-pack of beer and falling asleep in his Lazy Boy in front of a game sounded pretty good to him right now.

The thought came unbidden, and it scared him how tempting having a few drinks was even after years of sobriety. But that's what sleep deprivation did—it made the old solutions seem reasonable again, broke down the barriers between what he knew was right and what his exhausted brain craved. Just a little oblivion. Just a few hours of not thinking, not remembering.

12
Juno

Juno was done in. After the lunch rush, she usually took a break, but there'd been an unexpected afternoon surge, followed by an inventory check that revealed critical shortages she couldn't wait for her weekly suppliers to fill on Tuesday. A late night run to Evansville's supercenter hadn't been in her plans, but Autumn Lake grocers had closed hours ago.

It was now almost midnight, and the streets of her beloved town were quiet at this hour. She'd left two vintage globe lamps on in the coffee shop, a habit from when she'd first reopened the place, and as she drove by the storefront, she smiled at the sight. The low light made the place look warm and inviting even when empty.

She pulled around the back of the shop and into the wide, well-maintained alley in order to park as close to the back door of her kitchen as possible. After a childhood like hers, it was ingrained in Juno to pay attention to her surroundings at all times.

Her headlights illuminated the large blue truck parked near the foot of the stairs that led up to her upstairs apartment.

The Beast.

And The Beast's owner.

It had been a week since she'd last seen Alex, and although she could admit she'd been worried about him, she knew he was in good hands. Penny had been into the coffee shop only yesterday and said Alex was back on the job pretty much full time, and that it looked like they'd be wrapping things up this weekend.

Alex had texted on Saturday, thanking her for the coffee and sandwich, apologizing for being short with Poppy during the lunch delivery. He'd been worried he'd upset her.

But the bubbly Poppy had returned unfazed, gushing about how "amazing" and "what a good sport" Alex was. "He looks tired, but who wouldn't?" she'd declared, hand over her heart.

Juno hadn't gone into detail, but she'd texted back to let Alex know that Poppy was fine, and that she was glad he enjoyed the sandwich. She thanked him for helping with Mrs. Becker, but didn't bother asking why he'd been there. He'd dodged the question when they were face to face; why would he tell her the truth via text?

She'd watched the three little dots dance across the screen for several moments before he simply sent a 'thumbs up' emoji in response. She'd put her phone face-down in the pantry and left the kitchen so she wouldn't be tempted to keep checking it.

When she finally retrieved her phone an hour later, there was nothing more from him.

So what was he doing in her alley now, outside her back door in the middle of the night?

She took her keys from the ignition. She should go inside. She had groceries to put away, a very early morning tomorrow, and a really comfortable bed waiting for her to fall into. Whatever Alex was doing here wasn't her concern, and even if he was here to see her, now was not the time. He could come back during normal waking hours. He could call. He could text her and ask when a good time would be.

But the truck's crooked position, one tire on the curb, made her hesitate. She'd never forgive herself if something was wrong and she didn't check.

Sighing, she retrieved her phone from her pocket, switched on its flashlight, and climbed out.

Alex's silhouette was slumped over the steering wheel. The smell of alcohol wafted from his half-open window, triggering a sickening déjà vu. How many times had she dragged her father, too drunk to stand, from his car and into the house?

"Alex?" He lifted his head, blinking slowly, his eyes unfocused. She shone the light into the cab, then at his face, not even trying to keep the beam out of his eyes.

He squinted and put up a hand to bat away the light. "Juno." Her name came out slurred, barely recognizable. "I... wasn't gonna bother you."

"Are you okay?" A stupid question. He clearly wasn't.

"M'fine." He fumbled with his seatbelt. "Just... needed to see... We need to talk. Maybe tomorrow." He was hardly making any sense at all.

Her chest tightened, anger and concern battling for dominance. "You're drunk."

"Little bit." He attempted a smile that didn't reach his eyes. "Don't worry. Not driving anywhere."

"You drove here," she shot back, anger winning out over worry. He thought this was funny? "How long have you been out here?"

He squinted at the dashboard clock. "Dunno. An hour, maybe? Where ya been?"

Juno sighed, leaning against the truck's door. "Alex, what are you doing? What happened? You can't just..."

"I know," he interrupted, voice suddenly sharp. "I'm screwing up again. That's... that's what I do, right? I mess everything up, and I hurt people."

The raw pain in his voice caught her off guard. Despite his slurred words, it was clear that he was suffering, and it had nothing to do with his ankle.

"I can't—can't do anything right," he continued, voice dropping to a whisper. "Don't deserve anything good anyway."

Juno considered what she'd learned recently—Jason's suicide, Alex's downward spiral, his pattern of dating women who wouldn't stay. He'd been sober for years, yet here he sat, drunk and despairing. This went deeper than just their broken relationship. Something significant must have triggered this relapse.

In the truck, Alex's head was lolling to one side, and he was barely able to keep his eyes open, even though she was no longer shining the light in them. She glanced at her watch. She didn't have the time or energy to take him home tonight. She had too much to do before she could crawl in bed already, and besides, she wasn't sure how smart it would be to leave him alone right now. Not only was he drunk, but he was in a bad frame of mind, too. With a deep sigh, Juno made up her mind.

"Come on," she said, opening the truck door. "You can't stay out here."

He looked up at her, confusion evident on his face. "What?"

"You're coming upstairs. To my place." She reached past him and took his keys from the ignition, then pocketed them. "You need to sleep this off, and I don't trust you enough to leave you alone."

Alex clutched the steering wheel with both hands. "I can sleep here. I won't go anywhere, I promise."

"You are not sleeping out here, you big lug. Now get out and let's go. I don't have all night." She took his elbow and gave it a little tug. "I still have to unload my car, and I'm too tired to fight, so please don't argue with me."

"But... why?" His voice cracked. "Why are you helping me?"

The question hung between them, heavy with their shared history, with all the hurt and misunderstandings and years of avoidance.

"Don't be ridiculous," she said, her tone brusque, but not unkind. "I'm not going to leave you sitting alone in an alley at midnight."

In spite of his attempt to cooperate, it took some effort to get him out of the truck. The walking boot made maneuvering awkward, and being intoxicated didn't help his balance any. By the time they made it up the flight of stairs to her apartment door, he was leaning heavily against her, muttering apologies with each step.

Her home was small but welcoming—a cozy living room connected to an open kitchen, with her bedroom and bath down a short hallway. She guided him to her sofa, where he collapsed with a groan.

"Stay here," she ordered, though he looked incapable of anything else. She returned shortly with a pillow and blanket, as well as the trash can from her bathroom. "If you need to puke and can't make it to the bathroom," she said, setting it on the floor beside him, then pointed down the little hall. "There is a toothbrush and toothpaste on the bathroom counter for you, and I'll get you a water glass, too." He sat there swaying slightly side-to-side, shoulders hunched, chin almost resting on his chest. "I need to go unload a trunk full of groceries. Are you going to be okay while I'm downstairs for the next several minutes?"

Alex nodded slowly. "D'you need any help?"

Juno bit back a laugh. "I'll be fine. Will you?"

"I'll be fine," he assured her. "Sorry."

"Don't be sorry. Be safe." The words came out before she could stop them. On more than one occasion, she'd said the exact same thing to him back in high school. He used to scare her to death with his driving, and when she'd get upset, he'd apologize, and then she'd tell him, "Don't be sorry. Be safe. I don't want to lose you."

Alex held her gaze for a long moment. He was remembering, too. Finally, just like he'd responded back then, he said, "I promise."

When she returned about fifteen minutes later, Alex was stretched out on the sofa, one arm draped over his eyes, the blanket spread haphazardly over him. His booted foot was propped up on one armrest, the other foot planted firmly on the floor, like he was bracing himself for whatever else that might come his way. Juno thought he was asleep, but when she straightened the blanket over his feet, he blinked slowly, focusing his bleary gaze on her.

"Hey," he said as she straightened and took a step back. "I'm sorry. You don't need this."

"No, I don't," she agreed, picking up his nearly-empty water glass and taking it into the kitchen to refill it. "But here we are."

She returned with the glass and set it within reach on the end table near his head. "I hope you don't end up with a crick in your neck. That couch isn't long enough for you, is it?" She eyed his foot on the floor.

Alex gave her a sloppy grin and his eyelids drifted closed again. "If I lift my foot off the floor, everything gets all..." His words trailed off, but he lifted a finger and made a circular motion.

She should go to bed. It was so late, and right now, they both needed sleep. But she also needed answers, and since he was still awake, she'd ask. Come morning, he might have second thoughts about talking, or if nothing else, regrets, and she'd be lucky to get anything out of him except more apologies.

"What happened, Alex?" she asked, sitting on the edge of a chair close by. "Why are you here?"

He didn't open his eyes, but she could see the muscles of his jaw working. Finally, he ground out, "I really messed up."

"What does that mean?" she asked, trying to keep her voice gentle. "I'm not angry that you're here, if that's what you're worried about. In fact, I'm glad you're safe."

Alex didn't speak for so long that she thought he'd fallen asleep. She started to get to her feet.

"You're too nice to me, June-bug." It came out like a moan. "You should hate me."

"I will never hate you, Alex," she returned quietly. Again, she asked, "What happened?"

Alex shook his head, but said nothing, and then she saw a tear squeeze out of the corner of his eye.

"It's okay," she said, touching his shoulder briefly. Why was she pushing him? He was in no shape to have a meaningful conversation. She could give him a little grace and wait for answers. "It's okay," she said again. "We can talk tomorrow. Get some sleep."

Alex swiped at the moisture with the back of his hand, but still didn't open his eyes. "I'm sorry," he apologized yet again. "I'm such a screw up."

"Shh. Enough of that." She moved the trash can a little closer to him and rested her hand on his shoulder again, letting it linger a little longer this time. "I'll be down the hall if you need me, okay?"

As she started to turn away, his hand covered hers—not forcefully, just enough to make her pause. She looked back at him and saw that his eyes were open.

"Thank you," he murmured.

She nodded, then carefully withdrew her hand out from under his. "Get some sleep, Alex. Whatever's going on, we'll figure it out tomorrow."

Later, lying in her own bed, she listened to his soft snores through the wall and wondered what she was doing. After everything, after all these years of keeping her distance, why bring him into her home? Into her private space?

Claire's words from earlier that week echoed in her mind. *Both of you were just kids when all this happened. Maybe neither of you had the tools to handle what came your way.*

Well, like she'd said to her friend, they weren't kids anymore.

And maybe tomorrow, they were finally going to talk—really talk—for the first time since she'd left Autumn Lake all those years ago.

13
Alex

ALEX WOKE TO THE aroma of coffee and baked goods and the worst headache he could remember in years.

He opened his eyes just a crack, disoriented by the unfamiliar ceiling and the light stabbing his eyeballs. As he pulled the blanket higher, its scent caught him by surprise.

Juno.

Then everything came rushing back, making his stomach lurch. He'd been passed out in Juno's apartment.

The letters. Mrs. Becker had refused to elaborate, just patted his arm and insisted he go directly to Juno.

So he had. He'd worked up the courage to come last night after Juno's closed. But her car had been gone, and no one had answered his knock.

He'd waited almost an hour before he'd lost his nerve. Because he wasn't just coming to ask about the letters. He wanted to mend fences, to fix what had gone wrong all those years ago, to bridge the chasm between them. But asking for her honesty meant offering his own, and telling her his secrets risked destroying any bridge they might build.

Back at his apartment, he sat in his parked truck, engine idling. Did he want to endure another eight years of unresolved wounds? Could either of them bear it? What if Mrs. Becker was right—that they'd been circling each other all this time because they both longed for something different?

He harbored no illusions about romance between them. Once he revealed everything to her, there was no way she'd even consider him in that light.

But friendship without this brutal tension? He'd take it in a heartbeat.

In utter frustration over his own indecision, he'd gripped the steering wheel hard and shook it, causing the whole truck to shimmy. He'd revved the engine a few times, even knowing The Beast was loud and obnoxious, then he'd roared out of the parking lot and back down the street the way he'd come.

He'd sit outside and wait for her. Wherever she was, surely, she had to come home, right? And when she did, he'd be waiting. He'd be ready to hear her out, and he'd tell her about Lena. And he'd offer her his friendship, his loyalty. He'd be the kind of man that she could depend on, even if it took him the rest of his life to prove it to her.

So, there he'd sat, his thoughts roiling inside him, the quandary of what to do, how to move forward, of how to become someone different, someone new, churning up his gut.

Then his mind had drifted to the old days and what he used to do on Friday nights. How he'd walk the three blocks from his place to Bill's Tavern, then stumble home hours later, having spent way too much on drinks with his buddies. Or with whatever woman was clinging to his arm that night. Of the way that first sip of cold beer felt sliding down his throat. Of the warmth in his belly when he switched to whiskey.

It was unseasonably cool for a mid-July night, and sitting alone in a dark alley, waiting for the woman he ached for, knowing that after they talked, she'd either hate him even more or agree to be friends and nothing more, all Alex could think about was getting his hands on a bottle of whiskey. Just a shot would do it, a couple of ounces of liquid courage.

In his drinking days, he'd always kept a bottle behind his passenger seat. When he got sober, he'd cleared out every drop of alcohol from his apartment and truck. He even avoided the tavern despite missing their catfish fritters.

But then he'd started wondering—had he checked thoroughly? Was it possible there might be a fugitive bottle still hiding out under that seat?

In moments, he'd begun to fixate on the idea, picturing it in his head, wedged between the brackets that slid the seat back and forth.

It had angered him, that fixation, and, determined to do the right thing, Alex had gotten out to look, intending to toss any findings in Juno's trash.

After some rooting around, his fingers had closed around the familiar weight of a bottle. He'd hardly believed it, having assumed that it had all been twisted, wishful thinking on his part. Somehow, though, one rogue fifth had evaded his cleanout. He'd hesitated, suddenly paranoid—what if Juno had security cameras in the alley? What if she'd been watching him the whole time, deliberately staying away?

Then he'd made the very bad decision to tuck the bottle inside his flannel, clomp back around to the driver's side of his truck, and climb back in to continue waiting for Juno's return.

As time had passed, the comfort the whiskey had offered was too much to resist. He'd just needed a reprieve from the chaos inside his head. One good swallow. Maybe a second.

And then Juno was there, shining a light in his face. On his failure.

Now, in the light of day, shame rolled through him with such force that he clutched his stomach. Three years sober—meetings, milestones, hard-earned chips—all thrown away in one moment of weakness because he was afraid to tell Juno about his demons.

And of all people to witness his downfall, it had to be the one woman he wanted so badly to impress.

Why couldn't he stop messing things up?

When the contents of his stomach stayed where they were, he forced himself to sit up slowly, his head protesting every movement. The events of the previous night came back in fragments. Juno finding him in the truck. Insisting he stay at her place for the night. Helping him up the stairs. The look on her face—not disgust or anger, but something worse, something that brought an overwhelming urge to cover his face and weep like a child: pity.

Besides, he didn't deserve her concern. He certainly didn't deserve her kindness.

"You're such a loser, Frampton," he muttered, pressing the heels of his hands against his eyes.

The room spun as he scooted forward to the edge of the cushion. His injured ankle throbbed inside the walking boot, but it was a minor discomfort compared to the hammer striking his temples. The trash can

Juno had placed beside the couch sat mercifully empty. At least he hadn't disgraced himself further.

Somewhere below, he could hear the gentle hum of the coffee shop in operation. Juno would be down there working, flashing that friendly smile as she served the regulars who depended on her to start their day right. Of course she wasn't up here, dealing with a hungover mess who'd shown up on her doorstep in the middle of the night, uninvited and unwanted. The woman had a business to run, a life of her own to lead.

There was a glass of water on the coffee table, the corner of a folded note tucked under it. In Juno's neat handwriting, he read: *Bathroom's all yours. Towels in the cabinet, a new toothbrush on the counter. Help yourself to anything else you need.*

He picked up the glass of water, his mouth pasty. He had downed half of it when he heard the front door open.

"Oh," Juno said, pausing in her entryway. "You're awake."

She was professional and put-together in her black Juno's Coffee Bar apron, a stark contrast to how he must look. Her eyes swept over him, assessing. There was that pity again.

"I was just coming to check on you," she continued, stepping into the apartment. "How's the head?"

"Not so good." Alex set the glass down carefully. "Juno, I'm so sorry—"

"Hold that thought." She disappeared into the bathroom, returning with a bottle of medication. "Take two of these. Then shower. And brush your teeth. You'll feel more human."

He accepted the pills gratefully. "You should be furious with me."

"Maybe I am," she replied, her expression unreadable. "But right now, I'm more concerned about why you were drinking in your truck in my alley. And after three years sober."

The simple observation—that she knew exactly how long he'd been sober—caught him off guard. It mattered to her?

"I'll go back downstairs and grab you some coffee and something to eat," she continued. "Poppy can handle things for a few minutes while we talk, if you're up to it after your shower."

"You don't have to...." His words faded at her stern expression.

"I know I don't have to." Her tone was matter-of-fact. "Just get that shower. And do it now; I'll be back soon, and I don't have all morning."

After she left, Alex dragged himself to the bathroom, wincing at his reflection in the mirror. Bloodshot eyes, stubble bordering on beard, hair sticking up at odd angles. No wonder she'd looked at him the way she had.

The hot water helped, as did the pain relievers beginning to take effect. By the time he emerged from the bathroom, dressed in his jeans with his dirty shirt flung over one shoulder, the floor beneath his feet had stopped undulating and his stomach seemed to be in a better mood, even if his head wasn't. He was surprised to find that he was actually hungry.

He was so focused on making it back to the couch without falling that he didn't see Juno standing in the middle of the living room until he stood almost directly in front of her.

"You okay?" she asked, stepping back quickly, her eyes darting away from his bare chest. She'd removed her apron and kicked off her shoes at the door, and now only wore a light blue Juno's Coffee Bar polo shirt tucked into form-fitting jeans.

She looked fresh as a daisy, he thought.

"I brought you this." She held up another one of her shop shirts, this one in black. "Yours is... used. I hope it's the right size." She practically tossed it at him, then made a beeline for the kitchen table, saying over her shoulder, "I also brought nourishment."

He'd taken one whiff of his shirt and had opted not to put it back on, so he couldn't be offended by her diplomatic assessment.

Once he'd slipped the clean shirt on and joined her, he took in the tray of coffee fixings and a platter with a couple of pieces of thick toast, a bagel, muffins, and several slices of perfectly fried bacon. Then he noticed the half-empty cup of coffee in front of her. So she'd been waiting for him.

"I was starting to get worried," she confirmed his suspicions. "You were in there a while."

He shot her a wry grin. "Yeah. Sorry to worry you. That might have been the best shower I've had in a long time." He plucked at the front of the shirt. It was snug, but it would do for now. "Thank you," he said, grateful for far more than the shirt and shower.

"You're welcome."

Alex eyed the array of options in front of him, relieved that his stomach wasn't exactly rebelling at the idea of eating. "I don't know where to start."

After a moment, she suggested, "How about why you showed up here drunk in the middle of the night?" Her voice was gentle but firm. "After three years sober," she repeated, driving the point home.

He picked up a piece of lightly buttered toast. The bacon smell was making his mouth water, but he'd better choose carefully, both in what he put in his mouth and what he let out of his mouth. "How did you know about that?"

"Mrs. Becker," she said in her direct way. "When she told me about Jason."

Her expression softened, and she started to reach across the table toward him, but then seemed to change her mind and picked up a muffin, instead. "I didn't know, Alex. No one told me. You could have said something to me, you know." Now she almost looked hurt.

"It's not something I talk about." He wrapped his hands around the warm mug. "It's easier that way."

"Is it?"

"Yes." Then he looked away. "Or maybe it isn't. I don't know. Everything seems harder these days." Wow. Now he was sounding like quite the downer. He met her gaze again. "I'm not making excuses for my behavior, Juno. I messed up bad last night, and I'm sorry you're the one who's stuck dealing with it. With me."

Silence stretched between them, not uncomfortable but heavy with unspoken thoughts. Alex gingerly ate his toast, while through the window, the morning light cast patterns across her kitchen floor. Juno pinched off pieces of her muffin, but didn't really eat much. It was obvious there was a lot going on inside her head.

"I never got any letter from you, Juno." The words came out before he could second-guess himself, and he forced himself to look at her when he said them. He needed her to see the truth in his eyes.

"What?" Her face registered surprise, then confusion.

"The letters you sent after you left. I never got them." He leaned forward.

"Who—" She broke off, then frowned, a suspicious glint in her eyes. "Then how do you know about them?"

"Mrs. Becker."

Juno shook her head. "That meddling woman." But she didn't really sound that upset.

Alex leaned forward, pressing in. "I never got anything from you, Juno. Not a letter, not an email, nothing. My texts went unread, and my thousand calls went straight to voicemail, then your number was disconnected."

Juno's expression shifted, disbelief warring with something else—hope, maybe? She held up three fingers. "I sent you three letters, Alex. To your house. Your parents' house."

He started shaking his head, then thought better of it when the room tilted precariously. "I never got them," he insisted, begging his stomach to settle so he could concentrate on the conversation. The weight of fifteen years of misunderstanding loomed large between them. "All I knew was that you were there one day, and gone the next. No goodbye, no explanation. I thought..." He swallowed hard. "I thought you'd just decided I wasn't worth the trouble."

"I thought the same about you." Her voice was quiet. "When you never answered."

Alex ran a hand through his nearly-dry hair, the smell of her aromatic shampoo he'd used filling his nostrils. "Will you tell me now what they said?" he asked, his voice gravelly with emotion. Would she tell him after all this time? Would her words even be relevant anymore? They'd been teenagers....

Juno looked down at her coffee and said nothing for several moments. Finally, she lifted her gaze to his. "Are you sure you want to know?"

Alex didn't hesitate. "I do."

She pressed her lips together in a thin line, took long breath in through her nose, then began in a flat, almost monotone voice. "I wrote lot of things, Alex. That I was sorry I couldn't tell you before I left. That my dad was making us leave in the middle of the night. Again. That he was making us skip town, to be more precise. I couldn't call or text you or respond to any of yours because he destroyed our phones; said he didn't want anyone to be able to track us."

"Track you?" This all sounded so surreal. Sure, Juno's parents, especially her father, had been oddly detached, uninvolved, to the point where it often seemed to Alex that Juno pretty much took care of herself. But why would he be afraid of being tracked? What had he done?

Juno continued in a more conversational tone, almost like she was telling someone else's story. "My father is an addict. Alcohol, drugs, rolling the dice; any and all of it. Sober, he's an exceptional gambler. Or an exceptional cheater, depending on your perspective. But wasted, he's a sorry excuse for a human being, and when he starts using, that's when things start catching up to him. Back then, that's when things always caught up to us, too. My mother, God bless her, enjoyed the lifestyle he provided while he was winning. Whenever things went belly up, she blindly believed him when he insisted he'd make everything good again, that the downturn had been someone else's fault. My mom also liked her oxy, and since my father kept her supplied with the stuff, she went along with just about anything he said," she added ruefully.

"You're talking in past tense," Alex murmured, his heart racing at her words. "Your parents... are they... gone?"

Juno made a rough sound at the back of her throat, half anger, half pain. "My dad killed my mom a few years after we left Autumn Lake."

14
Alex

AT HIS SHOCKED LOOK, she explained in a droll voice, "He was her supplier, so as far as I'm concerned, he's the reason she's dead. My mom OD'd right after I turned eighteen and moved out. I came by their apartment to check on her and found her sitting in front of the television." Juno's eyes got a far away look, and she almost smiled. "She looked so peaceful. Like she was sleeping." She took a deep breath and let it out in a whoosh, then almost flippantly added, "Maybe if I hadn't been so anxious to fly the coop..."

"Juno." Alex couldn't come up with anything else to say. He thought of the burden of guilt he'd carried all these years about Jason, how even though he knew it was a decision his brother had made, that maybe, just maybe, if Alex had been a better friend to him, been more attentive, more aware, that maybe...

Like Juno, he could never finish that sentence either. Because there was always a 'maybe not' in there somewhere.

"I know," she said, shaking her head. "I know I couldn't have saved her. I think she was escaping just as much as I was. My father wasn't a nice man. He was downright scary, in fact. And the older I got, the meaner he got, probably because he knew he wouldn't be able to control me forever." She took a sip of her coffee. "I didn't want to leave Autumn Lake, Alex." She paused, pressed her lips together like she was trying to decide whether or not to admit something. "I was so scared that night. The next few weeks, months. Dad let it slip on the drive out of town that if whoever was after him caught up to us, we'd be worse than dead."

"I—I didn't know," he whispered, realizing after he said them that they were the exact same words she'd spoken about Jason.

She kept her eyes locked with his, but her hands were trembling. She was trying so hard to be brave. To be vulnerable and brave at the same time. They were two pitiful peas in a pod, weren't they? "I asked in my letters if you thought your parents might let me stay with you. In—in Jason's room while he was gone. So I could finish high school here."

The revelation of all that she'd just said hit him like a physical blow. He brought the heel of his palm to his chest, pressing it against the tightness that wrapped like a tension band around his ribcage. He was finding it hard to breathe. "You wanted to stay? With me?"

She simply nodded.

"I would have moved heaven and earth to make that happen, Juno." He gripped his coffee cup with both hands. "You have to know that."

For a moment, he wasn't sure she'd heard him, but then she nodded again, like she was still debating about whether she should believe him.

"I'm so sorry, Juno. For everything. For all of this. All this time. These misunderstandings between us. I wish I could go back and undo it all, start over." Now it was Alex who reached across the table, not quite touching her. "I would have answered your letters. I would have come for you. I would have chased you to the ends of the earth if I'd known you wanted to stay with me. I would have done anything to help you."

The scope of what they'd lost sat like a heavy raincloud between them. Juno stared at his hand where it sat only inches from hers, palm up. Then she met his eyes again.

"What happened last night, Alex?" Her voice was so quiet, he had to lean forward to make out her words. "Why did you show up here like that?" She graciously didn't say 'plastered' or 'stone-cold drunk,' almost like she was purposefully allowing him to maintain a modicum of dignity.

Alex's stomach clenched, and he let out a slow exhale. This was the part he didn't know how to explain. How did he tell her about the last fifteen years of his life? About Jason. About Lena. About Melissa. About the mess he'd made of everything.

"I didn't come here in that state, Juno. Drunk, I mean." If she wasn't going to say it, he would. It was part of his penance, after all. "I came here to talk, to clear the air between us, and to clear my conscience, I suppose." He sighed and withdrew his hand; she obviously wasn't ready for any physical contact between them.

"So where did the whiskey come from?"

Alex sighed again.

He needed to stop doing that. He sounded like a whiny baby. "I found it stashed under my truck seat from back when I was drinking. I intended to throw it away—" But that wasn't the truth, was it? Hadn't he been more than a little relieved at the thought of that bottle still being there? "Actually, I made the decision to believe the 'just one sip' lie." He said, holding up his index finger. "There's no such thing for an alcoholic."

Juno nodded solemnly. "But why? What happened? Is it just because you found out about the letters?"

Did that mean she believed him when he said he'd never gotten them?

He slowly shook his head. Thankfully, the room stayed where it was. "Learning about the letters gave me the courage to come, but the reason I came here was—is—because I want to fix this broken stuff between us." He gestured between them. "I can't stand it, Juno. I don't want you to hate me—"

"I don't hate you, Alex," she interrupted, sliding her cup to the side so she could rest her forearms on the table in front of her. "I don't know if I like you, exactly, but I don't hate you. I never have."

Alex grimaced. "Well, maybe you don't know me so well anymore. Maybe if you did know the real me, you'd think differently."

Juno narrowed her eyes at him. "And who is that? The real you?"

He opened and closed his mouth three times before he found any words, and even then, they weren't what he'd planned on saying. But once they started, it felt almost impossible to reel them back in. "For a long time after Jason died, I was just... surviving. Going through the motions. The drinking made it easier to pretend everything was fine."

"And the women?" The question wasn't accusatory, just curious.

Alex felt his face warm. "The women." He couldn't deny he had trouble there, too. "Yeah." He let out a snort of disgust; not at the ladies he'd entertained, but at himself for being that kind of guy. "I heard through the grapevine that you all are calling them my 'Summer Sizzlers,'" he said with a sheepish look.

A hint of a smile touched her lips. "You're welcome."

"You came up with that?" He dramatically pressed his hand to his chest. "Ouch."

She shrugged. "If the high heel fits..." She dipped her head toward his booted foot extending out from under the table. "Or the boot. By the way, where are your crutches?"

Alex waved a hand as if to swipe the question out of the air. "I got rid of them several days ago. And yes, I got the all-clear from the doctor." He reached down and rapped his knuckles against the hard plastic frame of the brace. "Just the boot now."

"Well, like I said, 'If the boot fits....'" But then she grew serious. "I don't get it."

Alex waited for her to continue. He didn't want to assume he knew where she was going and stick his booted foot into things. The rest of the conversation was going to be detrimental enough.

"How old are we now? Thirty? What's wrong with growing up? Settling down? I mean, why not make someone a happy woman? You'd have contenders lined up around the block, I'm sure. And I don't mean one of the Summer Sizzlers." She made a soft snorting sound. "I think you just date them because you know good and well that they won't be sticking around long enough for you to have to make a commitment."

For a moment, Alex felt utterly and completely seen. He started to deny it, to toss out a generic deflecting statement, but then stopped. Honesty. He needed to be real. That's what he wanted from Juno, wasn't it? And hadn't she been brutally honest with him? Finally, he nodded, and simply said, "It's easier. No expectations. No disappointments."

"Easier for who?" Juno challenged. "I've seen the way some of these women look at you, Alex. It's not easier for them that you aren't interested in anything more than a summer fling."

He scrubbed his hands through his hair again. This was the most uncomfortable conversation he'd had in a long time, and they were just scratching the surface of the really tough stuff. "You're right. Again. I've been selfish that way. They deserve better."

"But you don't think you deserve better."

The insight, so simple and so devastating, left him momentarily speechless. "How do you do that?" he asked finally. "How is it that you can see through me so easily?"

"Maybe because I've spent years doing the same thing in my own way," she finally admitted. "If we're talking about commitment issues and all." She dabbed at a crumb on the table and brushed it off onto her napkin. "I'm kind of a pro. Keeping everyone at arm's length. Not letting anyone get close enough to hurt me again. In particular, men. I don't have a great track record with the men in my life."

There was no cruelty in her voice, no judgement, either. The honesty of the moment felt fragile, precious. and suddenly, Alex was desperate not to lose it. They'd come so far in the past twelve hours. Surely it would be better to hold off on bringing Lena to the table, at least for now. Juno was talking about men like him. Like her father. Men she couldn't count on. He didn't want to be that anymore.

"I'm sorry about last night," he said, circling back around to the beginning of the conversation, silently berating himself for chickening out. "Breaking my sobriety was a breach of trust. To myself, to God, to you because you knew about it, and to my sobriety group."

"Will it cause trouble with your group?" she asked quietly. "I mean, I know they're supposed to be supportive and all, but judging happens, even when intentions are good."

Alex gave her a wry smile. "I'm not the first in that group to have to return their chips. They'll understand, but they'll also hold my booted toes to the fire." He grew serious. "I mean it, Juno. I'm sorry I let you down last night by being in the condition I was outside your door. It should have never happened."

"Well, thank you for saying as much," she said, nudging the platter of food closer to him. "Although we might not be having this conversation today if it hadn't. Now eat. One piece of toast isn't going to do a big lug like you much good. These are your favorite cinnamon streusel muffins. Or I can make you some eggs if you want protein."

The thought of eggs right then made his stomach clench, and he quickly scooped one of the muffins up and brought it to his nose to clear his thoughts of slimy eggs. He was certain Juno made them perfectly, not slimy at all, but just thinking about them...

Juno's phone pinged from her back pocket. She pulled it out and glanced at the screen. "I have to get back downstairs," she told him as she got to her feet. "We're down one person today, and Poppy and Jared are trying to manage the morning rush on their own."

"Of course," he said, starting to rise, too.

"Sit, Alex," she commanded, then slid an empty chair around so he could prop his foot up on it. "And you should probably still be elevating that leg any chance you get, right?"

But Alex stood anyway. "I should get out of your way. I'll take a couple of these with me, if you don't mind," he said, indicating the tray of baked goods. "What do I owe you for them?"

Juno chuckled and batted the air between them. "Not a dime. They're day-olds, so they sit in the kitchen for staff to eat, and there's no way we are going to get through everything back there today. Tonight, they go in the trash, so take them all."

"Thank you. And thank you for this." He tugged on the collar of the shirt. "And for being nice to me when you didn't have to be."

In her kitchen, she pulled a paper bag from a drawer, returned and emptied the contents of the tray into it, but then just stood there, like she had some unfinished business.

He straightened his shoulders under her direct gaze, hoping what she saw wasn't quite so distasteful to her anymore.

"What are your plans for today?" she asked, surprising him.

"I, uh..." He hadn't thought that far ahead. "I should probably call Ward, let him know I won't be coming over. They're putting the last finishing touches on the new kitchen—curtains and pictures on the wall and stuff—and I told him I'd stop by and help if I got the chance today. But not like this."

"You can't work hung over?" she asked wryly.

"Wouldn't be the first time," he admitted in the same tone. "But no, not..." He gestured vaguely, not sure how to put words to his relapse. "I need to talk to Ward privately about this, not just show up. He'll be able to tell right away; he's seen me this way far too many times."

Juno nodded, understanding in her eyes. "Well, would you like to have dinner tonight? We could talk more."

Once again caught completely off guard, he stammered, "Uh—dinner?"

"Nothing fancy. Just... talking. We've got fifteen years to catch up on, and I have questions. I'm sure you do, too."

Hope, dangerous and fragile, flickered in his chest. He swallowed the lump that had risen in the back of his throat. "I'd like that."

"Good." She gathered their mugs. "Seven o'clock? Trevor is closing tonight, so I'm done downstairs at six."

"Seven sounds perfect. Can I bring anything?"

"Don't you dare." At the door, she paused before exiting. "Alex?"

"Yeah?"

"Whatever's going on, whatever it is that's harder now—you don't have to face it alone. You know that, right?"

The sincerity in her eyes made his throat tight. "I'm starting to."

"Good. I'll see you this evening. Lock up on your way out." She reached over and jangled his keys that hung next to a set of hers on a key rack beside the coat closet door. "Your keys. Be kind to The Beast. He's been through a lot with you, hasn't he?"

Alex thought his keys looked right at home hanging next to hers.

After she left, he stood in the middle of her apartment, feeling more like himself than he had in years. The weight on his shoulders hadn't disappeared, but somehow it felt more manageable.

He hadn't told her everything, about Lena, about Melissa, about the road he'd traveled to get here and the future that loomed in front of him.

But for the first time in a long time, he felt like maybe he could face it, could face himself. He would start again. Take one step. Get through one day sober, then another, and then another.

And today, he'd be having two honest conversations. He'd call Ward now and let him know what had happened. Then he'd call his AA mentor, and turn in his chips at tomorrow night's meeting.

Three honest conversations, he reminded himself, if Juno's invitation for dinner tonight was any indication. He'd find the courage to tell her everything tonight, no matter what it cost him.

15
Juno

THE AFTERNOON LULL IN the coffee shop gave Juno a chance to catch her breath. She'd been running on autopilot most of the day, her thoughts drifting repeatedly to Alex's unexpected appearance on her doorstep last night and this morning's conversation with him. Fifteen years of bitterness and brokenness between them, and suddenly, here they were, planning to have dinner together so they could talk about it all. She could hardly believe it.

She was sitting at the end of the counter going over the day's transactions on her tablet when Alex came limping through the doorway. She smiled at him as he approached, and he lifted a hand in acknowledgement. The walking boot made his gait awkward, but he looked remarkably better than he had this morning—freshly shaven, his hair combed, wearing a clean blue button-down and jeans.

"Hey," he said, sliding onto a stool at the counter.

"The usual?" she asked when he started perusing the chalkboard style menu on the wall behind her. He always did this; read over the whole menu, then ordered the same thing every day.

He nodded, flashing her his grin. "Been thinking about one of your shakes all afternoon."

Alex did love her Decadent Dark Chocolate shakes. They were pretty remarkable, if she did say so herself. She made her own dark chocolate base using maple syrup instead of sugar and an extra-creamy homestyle vanilla ice cream from a local vendor. She served her shakes in pre-chilled Mason jars with the rims dipped in the chocolate sauce, and then she drizzled more of the sauce inside each jar before pouring in the blended shake. Topped with whipped cream and two homemade pirouettes, she finished it off with more chocolate drizzle. Decadent, indeed.

Juno glanced at the clock on the wall. Almost five. "Dinner's in two hours. Don't go ruining your appetite now."

"I would never," he said, his smile reaching his eyes. He rubbed his stomach. "I promise to show up at your door ravenous."

She rolled her eyes but couldn't suppress a smile as she opened the ice cream bin and started dropping scoops into the blender cup. Something had shifted between them, an ease she hadn't felt in his presence in years. Maybe ever.

"Did you get over to the B&B today?" She asked over her shoulder. What she really wanted to know was if he'd talked to Ward yet. Alex seemed in a pretty good mood, all things considered, and she had a feeling that if he hadn't yet done so, he'd still be looking shame-faced. In fact, he probably wouldn't have shown up here.

"Nah. When I called Ward after I got home this morning, he said they were ahead of schedule and told me to take the day off." Alex watched her hands as she prepared the Mason jar. "Said the ladies had everything in hand, and were already talking about kicking him out, too." He chuckled. "In fact, he all but warned me to make myself scarce if I knew what was good for me."

Juno chuckled. "Yeah, Hazel and Penny, when they get their heads together, can be something to contend with." She waited, not wanting to ask if he'd told Ward about his relapse—now was not the time and place—and when Alex met her gaze and nodded, it felt like he was reading her mind.

"Ward snagged a couple of lemonades and met me down on the dock earlier this afternoon." His tone was conversational, but the look in his eyes was solemn as he said, "I caught him up on things."

Juno nodded in acknowledgement, then slid the shake onto the counter in front of him. "Enjoy."

Poppy emerged from the back room with a tray of freshly baked cookies, her eyes lighting up when she spotted Alex. "Alex! I didn't know you were here. How's your ankle doing?"

"Better every day. Thanks for asking."

Juno hid a smile as she collected her tablet and the folder of paperwork she'd been working out of. Poppy's crush on Alex was painfully obvious, but to his credit, he kept things friendly and appropriate.

"So, Poppy," Alex said as Juno tucked the items into a drawer under the counter, then moved to the sink to wash the shake machine paraphernalia. "You seeing anyone these days?"

The young woman's cheeks flushed pink. "No, not at the moment."

"You know, I work with a guy about your age. Ryan. Good guy, hard worker. I think you two might hit it off."

Juno almost dropped the stainless steel tumbler. Was Alex Frampton playing matchmaker?

Poppy, ever the good sport, leaned against the counter. "You should bring him in sometime. I'd love to meet him."

Alex nodded, taking a long sip of his milkshake. "I just might do that."

When Poppy moved to help a customer who'd just walked in, Juno stepped closer to Alex. "Are you actually playing cupid now?"

"Just looking out for Poppy," he said, then lowered his voice, speaking comically from one side of his mouth. "And making sure she knows I'm not available."

The implication behind those words made Juno's heart skip, even though he'd said them in such a lighthearted way. She nodded, biting back her smile. "Good for you. She's a great young woman, and some guy out there will be lucky to get her attention."

"Let's hope I haven't just thrown Ryan to the wolves. Or the wolf." He play-wiped his brow. "She's... intentional with her affections, isn't she? I'd say he'd be lucky to get her attention if he's prepared for the level of attention she gives."

Juno snorted. "Wow. Such insight," she teased.

"I know," he shot back, blowing on his knuckles then rubbing them against his shirt. "Pretty keen for a big lug, aren't I?" He wiggled his eyebrows at her.

Before she could respond, Alex's phone rang. The instant change in his demeanor when he checked the screen sent a frisson of concern racing up her spine. A smile of unadulterated pleasure that quickly turned to what she could only assume was panic. She watched as he pressed the phone to his chest, looked at the screen again, turned it facedown on the counter, then acted like he was going to shove the device back into his pocket.

"Are you going to answer that?" she asked drolly?

Alex glanced at her in surprise, almost as if he'd forgotten she was there, then looked down at the still-ringing phone. "Uh... yeah. Yes." He nearly dropped it trying to hit the button before it went to voicemail. "Hey. Hi. It's Alex."

Juno's brows shot up. Breathy. He sounded *breathy*! Like a nervous schoolgirl. Or like a man hearing from someone he really, really wanted to hear from. Who on earth would elicit that kind of response from Alex Frampton?

Juno busied herself wiping down the shake machine, trying not to eavesdrop but unable to completely tune out his side of the conversation.

"Tonight? Um, wow. Well, I kinda have plans." His voice was low, tension evident in every word. "No, no. Of course I want to see—" He stopped speaking abruptly, like he'd been cut off by whoever it was on the other end of the call. A moment later, he continued. "I wasn't expecting you until next week."

He glanced at Juno, then stood and hobbled toward the door, where he continued the conversation on the sidewalk. Through the window, Juno could see him gesturing, his face a mask of warring emotions.

Her heart skipped a beat. Summer sizzler trouble? But this didn't seem like his usual behavior with the women he dated. This was something different. He looked really upset.

After several minutes, Alex returned, his expression a mixture of frustration and anticipation. He sank back onto the stool, staring at his half-finished milkshake.

"I was about to clear that away," Juno said lightly, trying to ease whatever tension he'd brought back inside with him.

When he didn't respond with his usual banter, she carefully asked, "Everything okay?"

"Yeah, sure," he replied quickly, but clearly it wasn't.

I kinda have plans, he'd said into the phone. Juno squared her shoulders and offered, "Hey, if you need to reschedule tonight, I understand."

Alex shook his head. "That's the problem. I don't want to reschedule dinner with you."

"But?"

He sighed, running a hand through his hair. "I—I'm going to try to work things out, okay?" He pointed a thumb over his shoulder. "I need to go. I have to meet... someone at the book store."

"At Claire's?" Juno frowned, glancing across the street to The Cracked Spine. "Why not just have her come here?"

Alex tensed when she said 'her', but he shook his head. "It's... complicated." He fumbled for his wallet, avoiding her eyes. "I'll be there tonight, Juno. Don't give up on me, okay?"

Warning bells rang in Juno's mind. After their morning of honesty, after what felt like the start of clearing the air between them, here he was, obviously hiding something. "Alex, what's going on?"

"I can't explain right now. I need to go." He placed a ten on the counter and stood. "Can you put the rest of that in the tip jar for me? I'm sorry."

What exactly he was apologizing for, she didn't know, but she didn't care for the way this was all unraveling. She nodded, but said nothing, then watched him leave her shop and cross the street with his uneven gait before he disappeared into the bookshop. A knot of dread formed in her stomach.

She considered calling Claire. Maybe her friend could keep an eye on him, give Juno a heads up on what was going on inside her shop, but immediately dismissed the idea. First of all, she hadn't told anyone that she and Alex were even on speaking terms, so her sudden interest in his behavior would raise alarm bells in her friend, and Claire, being Claire, would start asking questions that Juno wasn't sure she had the answers for. Besides, she wasn't going to spy on him like some jealous teenager. If this was the kind of behavior she was up against, better to know now before she invested any more in whatever might have been between them.

•❤•❤•❤•❤•

SHE'D INTENDED TO LEAVE by six, to let her capable staff do their thing until closing at ten, but she still hadn't heard from Alex. She stuck around, finding one excuse after another to linger, her gaze drifting back to the bookstore time and time again.

By twenty minutes after the hour, Trevor was practically pushing her out the door. "Go home, Boss. Put your feet up. We've got this."

Giving in to his urging and trying very hard *not* to give in to her disappointment, she removed her apron and tossed it into the hamper in the back closet. She pushed through the swinging doors from the kitchen to say goodnight to the two baristas working the front counter... and to get one last look at the bookshop across the street.

At that moment, the door to The Cracked Spine opened, and Alex stepped out, holding it wide for a woman who followed. Tall, slender, expensively dressed, with blonde hair that shone in the fading sunlight. She was stunning in a super model way, and she seemed remarkably comfortable with Alex as she turned on the sidewalk and said something to him, then reached up and patted his cheek affectionately.

Alex still held the door open, and a moment later, a child scampered out of the bookshop after them. A girl, maybe eight or nine years old, with blonde hair streaked with the same caramel highlights as Alex's.

Juno watched, frozen, as the woman leaned up to kiss Alex's cheek, then hugged the child before walking to a sleek silver sports car parked nearby. The little girl slipped her hand into Alex's, tugged hard on it as she wiggled with barely restrained energy, and looked up at him with a smile that was brutally, unmistakably familiar.

Without conscious thought, Juno found herself crossing the street. Alex spotted her approaching, his eyes widening with something like panic.

"Juno." His voice strained. "Hey. I was just getting ready to call you."

She stopped a few feet away, her gaze moving from Alex to the child, who watched her with curious eyes. "Who's your date?" The question came out before she could think better of it.

The little girl giggled. "I'm not his date. I'm his daughter." Then she clapped a hand over her mouth and lifted wide eyes to Alex's face. "Sorry." It was muffled behind her palm.

The world tilted slightly beneath Juno's feet as the child confirmed her suspicions. "Your—your daughter?"

And why was the little girl apologizing for saying so?

16
Juno

ALEX GENTLY SQUEEZED LENA'S shoulder. "It's fine, Lena-bug." Then he swallowed nervously. "Juno, this is Lena. Lena, this is my friend Juno. She owns the coffee shop across the street."

"The one with the chocolate milkshakes?"

"The very same," Alex said, his eyes never leaving Juno's face. "Lena's mom had an emergency, so Lena's hanging out with me tonight."

Juno's mind raced. Alex had a daughter. A daughter he'd never mentioned. Not to anyone, as far as Juno knew, and she'd never seen Alex with Lena, or even the woman who'd just driven off in her fancy sports car—Melissa, was it?—in all the years she'd been back in town. But this child certainly knew him. His favorite milkshake at Juno's? And Melissa clearly had no reservations about leaving Lena with him.

Juno shook her head, trying to realign the pieces of a suddenly complicated puzzle in a way that made sense. Alex had a daughter who looked to be about eight years old, which meant she'd been born right around the time Juno returned to Autumn Lake.

Turning to Lena, she said, "Well, it's nice to meet you, Miss Lena." Her tone was overly bright, and she could hear herself talking too loud, but she couldn't seem to tone it down. "I hope your daddy here is planning on bringing you with him to my place tonight,' she found herself saying, pointing up to her apartment windows. She emphasized the word *daddy* —if he wasn't going to say the word, she would. "I invited him to dinner, and there's plenty of room at my table for three."

Alex looked a bit shell-shocked. "Uh.. yeah. But are you sure?"

"Of course," Juno said, forcing a smile. She checked her watch. Almost seven, and she hadn't prepared anything. "Listen, it's later than I'd planned.

Why don't you two head over to the coffee shop while I get ready. You order anything you want and bring it up with you at seven. Anything you want. I'll call in and let Trevor know. He'll take good care of you." She needed a moment alone to process this revelation.

"Sounds like a plan," Alex said, relief evident in his voice. "We'll be up in a few minutes."

Twenty minutes later, Juno opened her door to find Alex and Lena, arms laden with a large takeout box from the coffee shop. She'd texted Trevor to let them know they were coming.

"Trevor gave us dessert, too," Alex said, as they stepped inside.

"I got a brownie," Lena announced, her eyes taking in the apartment. "I like your yellow walls."

"Thank you," Juno said, finding her manners despite the turmoil inside. "Make yourselves at home. I'll get some plates and drinks."

In the kitchen, she took a deep breath, hands braced against the counter. A daughter.

She'd spent the last twenty minutes trying to sort it all out, but in the end, there was only one scenario that made any sense.

A summer fling that had resulted in a child.

A child who had been on this earth for almost a decade, if Juno was right about her age.

A beautiful, innocent child who deserved better than a father who kept her existence secret.

When she returned to the living room with plates and silverware, Lena was examining the framed photos on Juno's bookshelf.

"Is this your mom?" she asked, pointing to a snapshot of Juno's mother on her wedding day. It was the only picture of her that she had.

"It is," Juno said, setting the plates on the coffee table.

"She's pretty, like you." Lena smiled. "My mommy's pretty too. She used to be a model before she had me."

Juno's eyes flicked to Alex, who was arranging the takeout containers on the table. "Your dad never told me about your mother." The moment the words were out, Juno wished she could take them back. She didn't mind being direct, but using Lena to take passive-aggressive jabs at Alex was beneath her.

Alex winced slightly, but Lena didn't seem to notice. "That's because nobody knows I'm his daughter except Mommy and me." She said it matter-of-factly, as if revealing a mildly interesting bit of trivia rather than a bombshell. "It's our secret, but I think it's a dumb thing to be a secret, don't you, Miss Juno?"

"Lena," Alex began, his tone cautious.

"What?" the girl continued, returning to the coffee table. "Mommy says it's complicated, and I know what complicated means. It means it's hard to understand. But I don't think it's hard to understand. You're my dad. What's so complicated about that?"

Out of the mouths of babes. Juno felt a surge of respect for the child's directness, but it was clear that Alex was trying to hold his head above water right now. Oh, they'd be hashing this one out, that was for sure, but noting the pallor of his face, she took pity on him.

"Let's eat while everything's still warm," she suggested, opening the box and pulling out a grilled cheese sandwich meal for Lena, and two meatball and roasted red pepper sandwiches for her and Alex.

Over dinner, Juno found herself charmed by Lena, despite her lingering anger at Alex. She was bright, articulate, and had her father's easy smile. She talked about her favorite books, her favorite places on the lake, and how she was learning to swim.

"Daddy promised to teach me to fish while I'm here," she said through a bite of sandwich. "He says the best fishing is early in the morning when the lake is still."

"Your dad knows this lake well," Juno agreed. "He's lived here his whole life."

"I wish I could live here too," Lena sighed. "Mommy and me move all the time."

The child's words resonated so personally with Juno, and her heart ached for her. What was wrong with Alex that he would deny Lena the life she so longed for. Even if it was just for the summer, to know she always had a place to come to, a place she could depend on to be there waiting for her. *People* she could depend on to be there waiting for her.

After dinner, Juno put on a movie for Lena while she and Alex cleared the dishes. In the kitchen, with the sound of the film providing cover, she finally confronted him.

"Why on earth are you keeping that remarkable child a secret, Alex?" she asked, her voice low but intense. "And I don't mean just a secret from me. From everyone. Do your parents know about her?"

Alex carried a stack of plates from the table. "They don't," he admitted. "I actually planned on telling you about her tonight."

"Really?" Did she believe him? Did it matter? "Well, that's all fine and dandy but it doesn't change the fact that she thinks she's supposed to be a secret. Your own daughter, Alex." She shook her head in disbelief. "Are you embarrassed by her?"

"What? No! Of course, I'm not embarrassed of her. She's amazing" He glanced over at Lena who was curled under a fuzzy blanket at one end of the sofa he'd slept on only the night before. The adoration on his face was unmistakable, Juno saw.

"Then why does nobody in town know about her? Why the secrecy?" Juno kept her voice down with effort. "What kind of father doesn't acknowledge his own child?"

Alex's jaw tightened. "Melissa wanted—"

"You're blaming Melissa for your decision to not tell anyone you have a daughter?" Her tone had turned scathing now. She snatched the dishes out of his hands and dunked them into the sink she'd just he'd just filled with hot, soapy water.

"You don't understand, Juno. You don't know what this has been like—"

She cut him off again. "Oh, I know good and well what it feels like to have a father who doesn't give a flying flip about you," she shot back. "I know exactly what it feels like to live a secret life, to feel like an inconvenience. Is that how you see her? Is she an inconvenience for your Peter Pan lifestyle?"

"That's enough." His voice was hard. "You don't get to judge me when you don't know the first thing about my relationship with Lena."

"I know you haven't been a real father to her. Standing on the sidelines while she 'moves around' with her mother? Not even telling your parents and friends you have a child?"

"I only learned about Lena three years ago," Alex hissed, his hands gripping the edge of the sink. "When I got a bill from Melissa insisting that if I wanted to meet my child, I'd need to come up with the thousands in back child support I didn't have. I had to prove to her that I was fit enough to be in Lena's life."

Juno stepped back, momentarily silenced. Was that even legal? Or was he telling her a one-sided story to make her feel sorry for him?

"That's when I quit drinking." The anger seemed to drain from his voice. "I had to save every penny to pay for a child I'd never met."

"Oh, so now it's Lena's fault you had to give up your partying?" The words were out before she could stop them, but, seriously? To pay for a child? "You poor baby."

"Are you being deliberately obtuse?" Alex ran a hand through his hair in frustration. "I'm trying to explain—"

"You're trying to justify being a deadbeat dad," Juno cut in.

"Why do you keep cutting me off?" he demanded, crossing his arms. "You ask me a question, and then you don't let me answer."

She jabbed him in the chest, leaving a wet spot on his shirt. "Why are you defending your behavior?"

"Why are you guys fighting?"

They both turned to find Lena standing near the kitchen table, her eyes wide with concern. "Are you fighting about me? Everyone always fights about me."

The wounded look on the little girl's face cut through Juno's anger like a knife. "Oh, sweetie," she said quickly. "We're talking about something we disagree on. I'm sorry if if we worried you."

"It sounded like you were fighting about me," Lena insisted, her lower lip trembling slightly.

Alex moved to his daughter's side, kneeling awkwardly with his booted foot extended. "It's okay, Lena-Bug. You don't need to worry. Juno and I just have some things to work out."

Lena looked unconvinced but nodded. "The movie stopped and I heard you guys."

Juno glanced over at the television and saw that the show had been paused. Lena was obviously a perceptive child. She wondered what other arguments she'd overheard in her short little life.

Alex checked his watch, then turned his wrist so Lena could see the face of the analog timepiece, too. "It's getting late, Lena-Bug. What time does it say?"

Lena studied it for a few seconds, her mouth working as she counted out the minutes. "Eight forty-five," she finally said, a mix of pride and disappointment in her voice. "Does that mean we have to go now?"

Alex nodded. "Your mom wanted you home around nine. It's going to take us about twenty minutes to drive there, so we're going to be a little late, even if we ran out the door right now – and that's not going to happen with this bum leg of mine." He narrowed his eyes at her and squeezed her bicep. "Unless you can carry me...."

That brought a smile to Lena's face. "Daddy, you're being silly. I can't carry you. You're supposed to carry me."

"Right, right," he said, nodding sagely. "I forgot which way that worked. Anyway, even if we sprouted wings and could fly down the stairs right now, we still wouldn't make it all the way around the lake in fifteen minutes. So we better get going. It's time."

"Do we have to?" Lena looked between them. "I like it here. I wish I could stay in Autumn Lake forever." She sighed, the sound too world-weary for someone so young. "Mom said we have to move again so we can live with her boyfriend."

The echo of Juno's own childhood in those words made her heart ache. The constant moving, never having roots, always at the mercy of an adult's whims. Lena was obviously much more privileged than Juno had been at her age, but the longing in her voice, the obvious craving for a place to call home, struck such a nerve inside her.

"Charlie?" Alex asked, his tone neutral. Juno watched his expression, but saw no signs of jealousy, only concern for Lena.

"No," sighed Lena. "It's Daniel now. She really likes him and he has a big house on an island, and there's a pool there," she added, sounding very much like she was repeating something she'd been told.

"I haven't met Daniel," Alex said. "Is he nice to you?"

Lena shrugged one shoulder. "I don't know."

Alex stood, his expression grim. Apparently, this was all news to him, too. "Why don't you get your things together, okay? Your backpack is on the floor by the couch. I'll be there to help you in just a second."

When the girl drifted reluctantly away from them, he turned to Juno. "I'm sorry about how this all went down. I really did intend to talk to you about Lena over dinner, Juno. I'm in over my head, and I could use... some advice. Support. Help," he added a little louder. "Can I come back? Will you still be awake around ten-thirty?"

Juno hesitated, still reeling from everything she'd learned. Part of her wanted to say no, to process all this alone. But Lena was watching them from the doorway, and Juno couldn't bring herself to reject Alex in front of his daughter.

"Okay," she agreed finally. "I'll be here."

After they left, Juno sank onto her sofa, emotionally drained. There was clearly more to this story than she'd assumed, but was she ready to hear it? Could she set aside her personal feelings, which were decidedly opinionated, to be a friend to Alex in his time of need?

"Yes," she said aloud. "You can do this. You're strong. You're capable. People depend on you, Juniper Bernice Thomas, because you're dependable. Be his friend first. That's how it should be anyway."

The self-talk helped, and while she put her little apartment to right for the night, she brewed herself a cup of cinnamon tea, then settled into the corner where Lena had been, and switched the station to something more suitable for someone her age.

When ten-thirty turned to eleven, then eleven-thirty, and there was still no word from Alex, Juno turned off the television, threw off the cozy blanket, and marched into her bathroom to ready herself for bed.

"You're such a fool," she said to her reflection in the mirror above the bathroom sink. "When will you ever learn?"

17
Alex

THE HEADLIGHTS OF THE Beast cut through the darkness as Alex navigated the winding lakeside road. Beside him, Lena chattered away, seemingly unscathed by the tension that had filled Juno's apartment just before they left. His mind kept replaying the confrontation in the kitchen, Juno's accusatory words still ringing in his ears.

What kind of father doesn't acknowledge his own child?

The question hit him where it hurt most. He'd just blindly accepted Melissa's terms, had been willing to take the measly crumbs she'd tossed his way. What kind of a father was he, indeed?

He'd never forget opening the certified mail packet that contained all the proof he'd needed that he had a daughter. The three photos that had accompanied Melissa's letter were of Lena at birth, exactly nine months after he'd spent a summer at the beck and call of Melissa Hayward. There was one of Lena at three, a chubby, blue-eyed toddler that had sent Alex to his parents' place to look at old family albums because of how shockingly alike they looked to his own, and then at six, a ganglier, gap-toothed Lena dressed in a birthday princess dress and wearing what looked to him like a very expensive tiara. When he'd cupped his hand around the child's face to block out her perfectly-styled and bejeweled curls, he'd seen Jason grinning back at him, and he'd broken down and wept like a baby.

Melissa's conditions had been clear. The child was his, but if he wanted to see her, he'd have to pay, but he'd also have to keep their arrangement quiet until they could speak in person, until she could see with her own eyes that he could be trusted to be around Lena.

At the time, Alex hadn't been trustworthy enough to be around anyone, and he'd had no doubt that everyone who knew him would share Melissa's misgivings.

Besides, the amount she was asking for—six years of what she insisted he would have been paying in child support all along—was far beyond the scope of his bank account, and easily more than he made in a year. But Alex, determined to meet the child that was so clearly a part of him—a part of Jason—took the revelation as a call to action, a charge to make some long overdue changes in his life. He quit drinking, worked harder, longer, took on any overtime his boss would give him, and picked up any side jobs he could hustle, sometimes to the point of running on only a few hours of sleep a night for weeks on end.

It took him almost nine months to collect enough to meet Melissa's demands, only to have her put him off. "You said it would take you at least a year," she'd told him over an international phone call. "We're in Paris now and won't be back stateside until May. We should be back around Lena's birthday. Maybe we can arrange something for then." He hadn't wanted to wait another three months, and had offered to come to them in Paris, but she'd only laughed like his suggestion was the silliest thing she'd ever heard and hung up.

At the end of April, Melissa informed him that they were extending their time in Paris until July, when she would return to the United States to spend the summer at her North Shore timeshare. She'd promised to give him dates as soon as she had them, then she sent him a couple of photos of Lena looking very Parisian in a burgundy blazer over a striped shirt and miniskirt, with knee-high boots and black stockings. In one of the photos, she was blowing out the seven candles on a very fancy birthday cake.

He'd stared at the images with such longing, unable to process the flood of emotions coursing through him.

Believing there was nothing he could do but wait, Alex continued to count down the days until Melissa reached out to him again.

At the end of June, at which point Alex had known about Lena for a whole year, Melissa had informed him that they would be arriving in Autumn Lake the first week in July and planned to stay through August.

Then she'd added that if he wanted to meet Lena, she had another set of stipulations.

Alex could come see his daughter at the condo as much as he wanted while they were in town, but Melissa would decide when and if they went public about Lena being his. "I need to see proof that you're a different guy, that you're not going to be a bad influence in Lena's life."

Alex understood her reservations, and in his excitement to finally meet his daughter, he would have agreed to anything.

He'd been so worried that their first meeting would be awkward and uncomfortable, that he wouldn't know what to say or how to act, but the moment he saw the beautiful little girl, a steady stream of tears had begun to roll unchecked down his face. Lena had taken his hand and told him that everything was going to be okay, and then she'd led him through the condo and out into the manicured back yard to a cedarwood swing set. "We can swing until you feel better. That's why I do when I need to cry."

Alex had become quickly enamored with the child, not caring that he couldn't tell anyone about her. Having her be his secret allowed him to get to know her without having to share her with anyone else.

Looking back now, Alex realized that Melissa hadn't been very concerned about being able to trust him with Lena. She was often out of the house whenever he came to visit. Even the au pair, a young woman who'd traveled with them from France, usually disappeared into her own room or left to do whatever it was that wealthy young Parisians did on that side of the lake, leaving him alone with Lena for hours at a time.

When August ended and Melissa and Lena left town with the promise to return the following summer, Alex was shocked to discover how empty his life suddenly felt. How had such a little girl taken up so much space in his heart?

And now, his daughter's surprise arrival in town a week early had been both a delight and consternation. He'd been expecting Melissa and Lena next Wednesday, and he'd had every intention of telling Juno all about her by then, even if it meant breaking his promise to Melissa to keep the child a secret. He wanted there to be no secrets between them from here on out. He'd been only hours away from revealing all, from bringing Juno onboard about Lena's existence... it was almost as if the universe was conspiring against him, throwing all his "fresh start" plans into disarray.

It was obvious that Juno thought he was a deadbeat dad. The scathing in her voice when she'd asked, "Is she an inconvenience for your Peter Pan lifestyle?" still zinged through him every time he thought of it, like touching an electric fence.

She was right. Not about the Peter Pan lifestyle, although it was his fault people assumed as much about him. He certainly didn't go out of his way to change their perception of him, he thought, remembering that he'd intentionally removed his shirt at Tip-Top Talons only a couple of weeks ago, hoping for a better tip from Stacy, but also hoping that Juno would notice. He felt the flush of embarrassment creep up his neck as he thought about how that had backfired on him.

Lena had grown quiet while Alex had been lost in thought, but his attention was drawn back to her when she said, "I like Juno."

Alex glanced in the rearview mirror at his daughter. She had her forehead pressed against the window and was breathing on the glass, then drawing misshapen hearts with her finger before wiping it all away and doing it again. She seemed nervous, agitated, and it unsettled him.

"I like her, too," he said, reaching behind him to squeeze Lena's knee.

She turned from the window and met his gaze in the mirror. "She asks real questions and actually listens to my answers. Most grown-ups don't do that."

"She's good at that," Alex agreed. "It's because she cares about everyone, big or small."

"Does she care about you? I think she was mad at you," Lena observed with the uncomfortable perception of a child who'd spent too much time reading adult tensions.

Alex sighed, his eyes going back to the road. "She's not mad, Lena Bug. She's just... disappointed in me, and she has every right to be."

"Because of me?"

Alex shook his head, but he wouldn't lie to her. "Not because of you. It's because I didn't tell her about you. That's on me; not you. Never you."

Lena was quiet for a moment, watching the dark shapes of trees flash by. "I told Mommy I don't like being a secret. It makes me feel sad."

"It makes me feel sad, too," he admitted.

"Did you tell Mom you didn't like it, too?" she asked quietly.

Another stab of guilt pierced him. He'd been a coward, afraid to rock the proverbial boat that Melissa had set afloat when she'd told him he had a daughter. Why had he never had any of his own demands? Lena was his daughter, too. Didn't fathers have any rights? Why had he never looked into it? He'd just blindly gone along with whatever Melissa demanded.

"I haven't told her before." He cleared his throat, glancing at her again in the mirror. Lena had lowered her chin so he could no longer see her face. "But that's going to change, Lena-bug. I promise. Your mommy and I are going to talk about this stuff while you're here, and we'll make some changes, okay?"

"What changes?"

Alex sighed. He really wanted to do things right, and right now, he felt out of his depth. He should talk to Melissa first, shouldn't he? Hammer out the details with her before he gave Lena any false hopes. Regardless of the details they agreed on, it wouldn't change one thing. "I want to see more of you, Lena."

"I really want to see more of you, too, Daddy." Now she did lift her face so he could see her reflection in the mirror. The lights from the dash were bright enough that even from the back seat, he could see her eyes, glistening with emotion, and he was once again reminded of Jason. "I want to stay here forever with you."

Alex swallowed hard and nodded. "I'd like that more than anything, Lena bug, but your Mommy would miss you so much."

"No, she wouldn't," Lena shot right back, shaking her head hard. "She wouldn't," she repeated more emphatically, crossing her arms.

"Hey, now. That's not true, and you know it."

"Then why does she always leave me with Adeline?" Lena's voice rose, petulant. "She sometimes goes away for lots of days in a row, and when she comes back, she just goes to parties instead of taking care of me. When you come to see me, we do things together. We color, we swing, and read and run, and stuff. Mom doesn't even like swings." She said the last bit as if the concept was unfathomable to her.

Alex knew lots of the children on the North Shore were raised by nannies, that in many circles, it was completely acceptable. But he wouldn't dismiss her feelings by making excuses for Melissa.

"I could stay with you instead of Adeline, and then Mommy wouldn't have to pay any money for me. Mommy says Adeline costs lots and lots of money and that I should be more grateful."

Alex closed his eyes for just a moment, warring with the resentment building inside of him. It was always about money with Melissa, *always,* and the fact that Lena was even aware of it was pretty incriminating.

"If I stayed with you, I'd be infinity times grateful," she added.

Alex wished he had answers for her. Lena had grown up so much since last summer; he'd noticed it with every phone call, but it still caught him by surprise every time he looked at her now that she was here in person. Even so, he hadn't expected these questions, and he wasn't prepared for the sadness in her eyes, the solemnity of this conversation. He reached back, turning his hand palm up, and waited until she put her hand in his. So small, so delicate, so fragile, it was like holding a featherless bird. All he could manage to say was, "I love you, Lena bug."

He heard her deep sigh, but he felt it like a knife to his heart. "I love you, too, Daddy." It was sincere, but she sounded resigned, as if he'd let her down.

Her and everyone else.

Why couldn't he stop messing things up?

They drove in silence for a few minutes, the only sound the steady rumble of The Beast's engine and the occasional swish of tires on the road.

"Mommy's making us leave early this time," Lena said finally, picking up the thread of their earlier conversation at Juno's.

"Whoa. What?" This was news to him. "What do you mean?"

"That's why we came early. Because we have to leave early so we can go with Daniel."

"When?"

"I don't know. She just said early. Maybe next week?" In the rearview mirror, he could see her staring out the window into the darkness.

Well, that was something they'd be talking about at the first opportunity. Tonight. There was no way Melissa was going to take her away again so soon. He didn't like probing Lena for details, but he suddenly felt like it might behoove him to be as well-informed as possible about what was happening in Lena's life. "I'll talk to her about that, I promise."

"Talking won't matter. Daniel has to go to Greece for business, and Mommy said we have to go with him." Then, in a tone that sounded remarkably like Melissa, she added, "It's an opportunity we simply can't pass up."

Alex clenched his jaw, his teeth grinding together in helpless rage. How could Melissa do that to Lena? To him? Hadn't he bent over backwards to be accommodating to her every demand?

"She always says that when she gets a new boyfriend. I asked Charlie why she called him that, and she got mad. I don't even know why."

Alex bit back a comment that would be inappropriate to share with his daughter. At least now he had a good inkling of why Charlie hadn't worked out. His list of discussion topics was growing longer by the second. And he wasn't finished yet. "How do *you* feel about going to Greece?"

Lena sighed dramatically. "I hate Greece. It's greasy. I have to wear sunscreen every single day." She had started kicking the back of the passenger seat, a rhythmic thump-thump-thump.

He paused before asking his next question, not wanting to lead her in any way, but finally said, "And how do you feel about Daniel?"

Thump-thump-thump-thump.

Alex suddenly felt like pulling over so he could look his daughter in the face, but he didn't want to scare her. "Lena-bug?" he prodded gently.

She shrugged one shoulder, a gesture that conveyed far more than words. "He looks at me weird."

18
Alex

LENA MUST HAVE SENSED his tension, because she quickly added, "Not like he's trying to be mean, but like... like he's trying to decide if I'm good enough."

Alex's grip on the wheel tightened until his knuckles were white. "Has he said anything that made you uncomfortable?"

There was that shrug again. "He says I need to learn better manners at the table because I talk too much." Lena's fingers worried the fabric of her dress. "Mommy made me dress up to meet him and she even let me wear makeup."

"Makeup?" Alex couldn't keep the shock from his voice. "You're eight years old."

"Mommy said I needed to look my prettiest. She says appearances matter to Daniel."

Every parental instinct Alex possessed was screaming in alarm. What kind of man criticized an eight-year-old for talking? What kind of mother put makeup on her child to impress a boyfriend?

As they approached the timeshare condos, Alex noticed the darkened windows of Melissa's unit. He checked the dashboard clock: 9:27 PM. Melissa had insisted Alex have Lena home by 9:30 PM, so where was she?

"Looks like your mom's not back yet," he observed, trying to keep his tone neutral. "Do you know where she went tonight?" Why hadn't he thought to ask? She'd said it was an emergency because Adeline had the night off, and if he didn't want Lena to spend the evening with him, that she'd take her over to the resort and put her in the childcare service Carpe Diem offered their patrons.

"Is she with Daniel tonight?" he asked, far too belatedly and of the wrong person. He needed to work on his dad skills, and fast. He did not like the sound of this Daniel guy.

"Prolly," Lena said with the resigned knowledge of a child who'd been through this routine before.

Alex parked in the visitor spot nearest to Melissa's condo. "We can wait in the car until she gets back. Do you want to climb up in the front seat with me?"

Lena unbuckled her seatbelt and leaned forward over the console. "I know the code to let us in," she said, hoisting her backpack up onto her shoulders. "Mommy says I'm independent enough to have it this year."

Alex clenched his jaw to keep from saying something inappropriate, and they both climbed out of the truck.

Lena unlocked the front door of the condo with the practiced ease of someone who did so routinely. Alex followed her inside, flicking on lights as they entered.

The space was immaculate and expensively furnished—white leather furniture, glass tables, abstract art on the walls—all sleek, modern, and utterly impractical for a vacation with a child.

"Are you hungry?" he asked, following Lena into the kitchen. "Did you get enough to eat at Juno's?"

"I'm okay," she said, opening the refrigerator, anyway. Over her shoulder, Alex could see that it was stocked with pre-packaged gourmet meals, green drinks, some exotic fresh fruit, and several bottles of wine. Not a single kid-friendly treat in sight if you didn't count the pineapple, dragon fruit, and kiwis that would require an adult to prep for her.

Lena closed the fridge and trudged into the living room, Alex on her heels. She flopped down on one of the white leather sofas looking completely forlorn.

"Why don't you get ready for bed?" Alex said, his stomach in knots. "It's getting late."

Lena's face fell. "Do I have to? Can we watch TV while we wait for Mommy?"

"Alright," he relented. "One show, then bed."

Her face lit up, and she jumped to her feet and hugged him. "Really?"

"Yes," he said, taking her by the shoulders and steering her toward the hallway. "But first, brush your teeth and put on your pajamas. While you're doing that, I'll find something for us to watch."

"Deal!" Lena darted off and Alex texted Melissa. *We're here. ETA?*

Then he headed into the kitchen to get him and Lena a couple of glasses of water. Was it okay for her to be drinking water this late? Would she wet the bed? "Stop being such a worry-wart," he told himself, then headed back to the living room with the bottom-heavy tumblers on a small tray. He couldn't help thinking of Juno and her tray of delicious treats that morning.

If Melissa didn't get home soon, he'd have to let Juno know that he wouldn't make it back to her place when he'd said. And any later than that was probably too much of an ask. He knew she'd been up well before dawn this morning.

He did not want to cancel on Juno. He needed to talk to her, to explain. He needed an ally, he realized.

He turned on the enormous flat-screen TV mounted on the wall just as Lena came scurrying back into the room, dressed in pink kitten pajamas and fuzzy socks. Tucked under her arm was the large stuffed ladybug he'd sent for her birthday in May. When it took him too long to figure out the remote, she offered to show him how to use it, then she deftly navigated to a streaming service with the expertise of a child raised on digital entertainment.

Alex settled his bulk onto the too-white sofa, feeling out of place among the pristine furnishings. There was an enormous clock on the wall beside the mantle that marked the minutes as they passed. Lena had landed on a cartoon about a gang of heroic dogs and cats, and had curled up in a ball beside him, looking small against the oversized cushions. Her eyelids were already drooping despite her earlier enthusiasm.

Twenty-five minutes later, the episode ended, and Lena's head rested heavily against his arm. Alex thought he should put her in bed, but every time he tried to get up, she shifted and started to wake up.

Fine. He'd let her sleep here on the couch for now. Surely, Melissa would be home soon. He'd carry her to bed then.

He wasn't about to put himself through the torture of another episode of the cartoon, though. He found a nature channel, instead, and settled in to gain some insight into the lifestyles of tropical rainforest birds. A few minutes later, the day started catching up to him, too, and he slouched a little lower so he could rest his head back against the cushions.

The trumpet of an elephant startled him awake, and he rubbed his eyes at the safari scene on the television. Hadn't he just been watching something about the rain forest? Then he glanced at the clock on the wall.

Alex straightened abruptly, making Lena grumble in her sleep beside him. It was almost 11:30 PM, and he'd been asleep for more than an hour.

Juno. He groaned and scrubbed his face with his hands. Even though it was an accident, he'd pulled a no-show. He should have texted or called her an hour ago, but instead, he'd let himself drift off in front of the television.

And now it was too late to call. She'd be in bed already, he had no doubt. The woman had been up since before dawn that morning to open her coffee shop, and he'd already been responsible for depriving her of sleep last night. But he could text.

It took him several attempts to come up with the right words, but finally, he hit send.

I'm so sorry for bailing on you and for not calling earlier. Melissa wasn't back when we got here, so Lena and I decided to watch a little television while we waited for her. We both fell asleep on the couch, and I just woke up. Unfortunately, M still isn't back, so I'm staying here with Lena for now. It's late, so please don't worry about responding. I will call you in the morning.

If she'd even take his call.

He texted Melissa. *Where ARE you?*

When she didn't respond, Alex decided to put Lena to bed. He could try calling Melissa when he didn't have to worry about Lean overhearing, because he had a few choice things he'd like to say to the woman.

He gently lifted the little girl, surprised by how light she felt in his arms, and carried her to her bedroom.

Unlike the rest of the condo, Lena's room showed signs of personality. The walls were still white, but there was a stack of books on the nightstand, and a collection of stuffed animals was lovingly arranged on the bed. The closet door stood half-open, displaying a full array of girls clothing and shoes, and on a desk near the window was a box of crayons and colored pencils and several sketchpads. Still, it lacked the lived-in feeling of a child's sanctuary. No artwork taped to the walls, no toys scattered about. The room was little more than a display in a furniture store.

Alex carefully tucked Lena into bed, pulled the covers up to her chin, and arranged her animals around her again. She didn't stir, exhausted from the evening's excitement. He brushed a strand of hair from her cheek, overwhelmed by a surge of love and protectiveness, then pulled out his phone and snapped a picture of her angelic face.

He leaned over and pressed a kiss to her forehead. "I'm going to fix this," he whispered. "I promise."

Back in the living room, he hit the call button. The phone rang five times and then went to voicemail. "I need to hear from you, Melissa. I'm at your condo with Lena. Where are you?"

Fifteen minutes later, he tried again. Then he also texted. A moment after he hit the send button, his screen showed that she'd read his text. Finally! When she still didn't respond right away, he got up and paced, checking his phone every few minutes.

By midnight, when he wasn't sure whether to be concerned or livid, he sent her a barrage of texts.

Pick up the phone.
Answer your phone.
I know you are seeing my texts.
Melissa, this is NOT cool.
Do I need to call the police?
Call me. I need to know that you're all right.

Except that he wasn't really worried about her, he had to admit. In fact, he was pretty sure she was doing just fine and simply didn't want her lovely evening to end. She knew Lena was safe with him, and he'd told her on many occasions that she didn't have to hurry home when he was with Lena, and more often than not, Melissa took advantage of his offer. So in a way, this was par for the course, wasn't it?

But Alex had wanted more than anything to get back to Juno's to make amends, and now, Melissa's behavior had ruined his chance.

Alex wasn't just angry about his own situation, though. Is that what Lena meant about her leaving her alone with the nanny all the time? What kind of mother stayed out this late without checking on her child? Why hadn't she at least let him know that she was alive, or asked if he was okay to stay a little later than originally planned?

His phone buzzed at 12:23 AM and a text from Melissa popped up on his screen: *Stop blowing up my phone.*

Alex's fingers flew across his keypad: *Where are you?*

The response came quickly this time: *You can go if you need to.*

Alex stared down at her message. What exactly was she suggesting? Before he could think up a clarifying response, another text came through from Melissa.

Is L asleep yet?

That was an easy question: *Of course.*

Then go. I'm just around the corner at the resort. L sleeps like a rock, and the nanny is back by 2.

Shock. Rage. Disbelief. Fear. Each emotion volleyed through him and his hands were shaking. *You leave her alone at night?*

She's a big girl, Alex. The condo has topnotch security. Stop making this a big deal.

He could almost hear Melissa's dismissive tone. The cavalier way she discussed abandoning their daughter made his blood boil.

This IS a big deal. She's EIGHT.

She's mature for her age. She likes her independence.

"Independence?" Alex said aloud, incredulous, hearing in his head how his daughter had used the same word when she'd tapped in the code for the front door. His thoughts circled back to Juno, to what he'd learned about her childhood with unreliable parents. About how she'd been forced to be independent at far too young, to fend for herself. He wouldn't let that happen to Lena.

Get home now or I'm calling the police.

There was a long pause before Melissa replied: *You wouldn't dare.*

Try me. Get. Home. NOW.

He'd let her pull all the strings, call all the shots, and make all the moves, but things were about to change. Just that morning – or was it yesterday morning now? – the last thing Juno had said to him as she headed back downstairs to her cafe was, "Whatever's going on, whatever it is that's harder now—you don't have to face it alone."

Well, he hoped she'd meant it, because he'd love to have Juno back in his life again. But even if she retreated, she was still right. He wasn't alone. He had Ward. He had his parents, even though their relationship had been strained for so many years after Jason's suicide. Grief was an indiscriminate monster that didn't care what kind of destruction it left in its wake, and for so long, Alex simply hadn't known how to make reparations after his years of hard living.

But now, *now* he had Lena. He had a miracle, an angel from heaven, and he knew the moment his parents laid eyes on her, that they, too, would stand behind him, beside him, and support him as he became the kind of father his daughter needed him to be.

Twenty minutes later, Melissa swept into the condo, reeking of expensive perfume and wine. She still looked remarkably put together in her formfitting black dress, her blonde hair perfectly styled despite the late hour, but Alex didn't miss the slight wobble on her stiletto heels.

"You're still here," she said, dropping her clutch on the foyer table before making her way into the kitchen. Her words were slightly slurred.

19
Juno

I'M SORRY FOR BAILING on you and for not calling earlier.

Juno had been staring at Alex's text for nearly twenty minutes, fingers hovering over the key pad, then retreating.

Melissa is MIA, so I'm staying here with Lena for now.

There was no better reason for him to bail on her, was there? Her thumb hesitated over the heart reaction, then drifted away.

It's late, so please don't worry about responding.

What would she even say? *No problem, I completely understand why you'd keep your daughter a secret.* Or maybe: *Don't worry about standing me up, I'm used to it.*

She rolled to her side, the covers tangling around her legs as she gazed out the window at the dark sky. The last twenty-four hours had been quite the rollercoaster, starting with Alex and The Beast parked outside her door, and ending with the revelation that Alex had an eight-year-old daughter with his caramel-streaked hair and easy smile. A bright, articulate little girl who clearly adored him despite only seeing him sporadically.

She closed her eyes, remembering the panicked look on his face when she'd spotted them outside the bookstore. And then Lena's innocent words: *It's our secret, but I think it's a dumb thing to keep secret, don't you, Miss Juno?*

Amen and amen, child.

Juno hated secrets. She knew exactly how heavy secrets could be. She knew the taste of them—like blood in the mouth. She knew the smell of them—like the odor of cheap vodka and fear. She knew the weight of them—like stones in the pockets of a drowning person.

Her thumb hovered over the phone screen again, then she pressed the power button instead. The room plunged into darkness.

It was well after midnight; she was tired, unsettled, emotionally drained, and more than a little disillusioned. Right now was not the time to make decisions about how to handle difficult matters. She set the phone face down on her nightstand. Whatever Alex had to say, whatever explanation he might offer, it could wait until morning. When the sun was up. When they could both see clearly.

How well she knew, from personal experience, that post-midnight decisions were rarely good ones. How many times had her father woken them in the darkest hours, demanding they pack and leave with no explanation? How many terrible choices had she witnessed being made after the sun went down?

The memory surfaced like something dark and bloated rising from the depths, bringing with it the acrid taste of fear in the back of her throat. The beam of a flashlight in her face, her father's voice—urgent, demanding. Not this time. Not again.

FIFTEEN YEARS EARLIER...

JUNO jolted awake in a panic, a blinding light in her eyes, a rush of cold air against her legs as her covers were ripped away.

"Get up. We're leaving." Her father's voice was low, urgent. Not raised—they'd learned years ago that shouting attracted attention.

"Dad, what—"

"No lights. No questions. Grab your pillow and whatever you can fit in a backpack. That's it." He swung the flashlight toward her closet with its crooked door that wouldn't shut. "You got five minutes."

Juno's body responded with practiced efficiency. She didn't bother arguing that he'd promised they'd stay this time, that she had finals next week and a date to the Spring Formal. She'd learned the futility of such protests, and she should have known not to believe his promises. The only thing she should have counted on was that he wouldn't be able to stay away from the bottle or the gaming tables, no matter what he said.

She reached for her pillow, unzipping the lining and shining her phone light inside the case to make certain all her most treasured possessions were there. The only doll she'd managed to keep, her two favorite books, her journal. Her emergency stash of cash from the coffee shop tip jar. She'd been forced to hand over her paychecks as part of her contribution toward rent on the dive apartment they lived in.

She slipped into a pair of jeans, layered on three of her favorite shirts, followed by her dark blue hoodie, then dragged her backpack out of the closet, and began methodically filling it with her toiletries bag, her good work shoes, and a few more items of clothing. She knew better than to toss in her Lakeshore Coffee work shirt; she was never allowed to bring anything with her that might tie them to their past. On the floor by her bed she saw the paperback she'd borrowed from the school library and she shook her head in helpless impotence. The book would become yet another casualty, another debt that would follow her to the next anonymous town.

Juno sat on the edge of her bed and shoved her feet into her high-tops. They were the nicest pair of shoes she'd ever owned, thanks to her after-school job. She had just stood and was taking one last look around the room, when a muffled sob from her parents' bedroom cut through the silence. Juno froze, her hands tightening around the straps of her backpack. Her mother didn't usually complain about their midnight flights, but she'd been sick a lot, lately, and Juno knew she wasn't feeling good. She was also presumably under the influence of the oxy her dad kept supplying her with, which meant her emotions were all over the place.

The sobbing grew louder, followed by a crack like a gunshot, then a crash. Something—or someone—had fallen to the floor.

Juno flung her pack over her shoulder and snatched up her pillow, then hurried to her parents' room, her steps quiet even on the threadbare carpet. The door was ajar, and by the beam of her father's flashlight, she could see her mother crumpled on the floor beside the bed, holding her cheek. A thin trickle of blood ran from her split lip.

Her father stood over her, car keys dangling from one hand. "Get up, Celia. We need to go."

When her mother made no effort to move, Juno made a noise to draw his attention away. He almost looked relieved when he saw her.

"Pack her things," he ordered, tossing another backpack at her feet. "She goes with or without her stuff. Two minutes."

Juno knelt beside her mother, whose eyes were glassy and unfocused. The familiar signs of an oxy high—the constricted pupils, the slack mouth, the faint sheen of sweat despite the chilly air from the open window.

"Mom," she whispered, stroking her mother's hair back from her forehead. "Mom, we have to go."

Her mother's only response was another gurgling sob.

Juno's jaw tightened as she turned to the closet. She'd done this enough times to know what her mother would need. Comfort clothes. The flowered blouse she favored. Underwear. Toothbrush. The prescription bottle from the bedside table that was always close at hand.

Her father returned, standing in the doorway. "Time's up."

"She needs help getting to the car," Juno said, not looking at him as she zipped the bag closed.

"Then help her," he spat, hurrying out of the room.

Juno couldn't shoulder both bags, their pillows, and the cumbersome weight of her mother, too, so she left their pillows on the bed, hoisted both backpacks over one shoulder, then got her other shoulder under her mother's arm, and dragged her to her feet. Celia leaned heavily against her, her head lolling to the side. She continued to weep quietly, and from her peripheral vision, Juno could see a string of blood-tinged saliva dribbling down the front of the nightshirt she still had on.

Juno maneuvered her mother out the back of the apartment and across the small parking lot and to the salvaged Escalade backed into a spot close the dumpster where most folks didn't care to spend too much time. Juno longed for the old sedan they'd driven into Autumn Lake; getting her mother to climb up into the vehicle was a challenging feat.

Juno finally got her strapped in, then she shoved their bags onto the floorboards, and turned to race back inside to grab their pillows.

Her father was just pushing out the back door of the apartment, two large duffels stuffed to capacity, one with its zipper still half undone. Juno didn't like the look on his face, but she hurried back the way she'd come.

"Where you going?" he challenged, stepping in front of her.

"Our pillows," Juno said. "I left them on your bed."

"No time." His voice was flat.

"But I need our pillows—" she protested, panic rising in her chest.

"And I said no time," he snarled. "Get in the car. We gotta get outta here."

"It'll just take a second!" She tried to push past him, but he dropped one of the duffels and caught her arm, his fingers digging into her flesh.

"Now." His voice came out sharp, raw with something that might have been desperation. "Do you have any idea what they'll do to me, or to a pretty girl like you, if they get here before we leave? Get it in the car, Juno."

"Please! It's got all my stuff—" Panic set it. She couldn't just leave it all there in that dumpy place for someone else to find, to paw through. Her small cigar box of pretty stones, feathers, buttons, bottlecaps, and keys, things she'd collected from the different places they'd lived. And her journal, filled with the written treasures of her heart. Notes from Alex that she'd so carefully tucked between the pages, ticket stubs for the movies they'd seen, her first paystub. The secret stash of money she'd been saving.

Her father's face hardened. "Give me your phone."

She took an instinctive step back and pulled the device from her back pocket. "No."

"Juno." Her name was a warning.

She shook her head and pressed her phone to her chest.

"Give me the phone," he roared, his voice echoing off the back wall of the three-story building.

"Let me at least text Alex first," she begged. Tears streamed down her face. She wanted to run, to escape into the night. Her father would never catch her, not if he wanted to get out of town before whoever was after him caught up to him. But she couldn't leave her mother. She just couldn't.

Her father's head swung back and forth as he checked for signs that he'd been heard. "You're going to leave that boy behind," he hissed.

"Daddy, please—"

It came out of nowhere, a backhanded blow across the cheek with enough force to send her staggering. Her phone flew from her grasp, and went scuttling across the pocked and rutted asphalt.

Her father strode over to it, then brought his boot heel down hard again and again.

Juno stood frozen, her palm pressed to her stinging cheek, tears blurring her vision. Her father had never hit her before. Never.

"Get in the car." His voice was now devoid of emotion.

She looked past him to her mother in the backseat of the car, her head resting awkwardly against the window, almost like she was watching their bitter exchange. But Juno knew better. Her mother was probably passed out cold, completely oblivious to the fact that her husband had just assaulted her daughter.

The fetid darkness of the swampy wooded lot behind the apartment was unnerving, and beyond that was the unknown—another town, another fresh start that would only end in disaster again.

Behind her was everything that mattered to her. Alex. Claire. Her job. The place she wanted to call home.

Her father had promised things would be different this time. He'd lied. And he'd keep lying. And if she knew anything about the way evil progressed, he'd keep hitting Juno and her mother, too.

Juno had no choice. She got in the car.

As they drove away from Autumn Lake, Juno watched the lights recede in the side mirror, taking with them the last traces of her childhood. The last of her innocence tucked inside that pillowcase.

PRESENT DAY...

THE STING of phantom pain on her cheek yanked Juno back to the present. She touched her face, half-expecting to find it tender, but there was only smooth skin warmed by tears. She didn't like to cry—it always felt like such an unproductive response to her—so even though there was ough there was no one to witness them, she sat up in bed, and wiped her face with the edge of the sheet.

She hadn't thought about that night in years—had trained herself not to. What purpose did it serve to relive the moment she learned how brutally her trust could be betrayed?

Juno reached for the glass of water on her nightstand and took a slow sip, letting the cool liquid wash away the memory's bitter taste. Her phone still lay face down where she'd left it, Alex's unanswered text waiting on the other side.

Men who made promises, then broke them. Men who kept secrets. Men who left. Why was she drawn to men with darkness in their eyes?

Not that Alex would ever raise a hand to her—she knew that with bone-deep certainty. But hurt came in many forms.

Omission. Deception. Disappointment.

But Alex... well, even the messed up version of Alex that he claimed to be was nothing like her father. Alex apologized for drinking, for being a mess. He asked for help, for forgiveness, and he pursued restitution. Wasn't that why he'd, in such a bumbling, messy way, been outside her door Friday night? Coming to see her because he wanted to fix things?

Alex hadn't lied about Lena, not exactly.

But he'd committed the sin of silence. For years. He may not have known about Lena himself until she'd been five or six years old, but even the child knew she'd been a secret all this time. It was heartbreaking.

Restless, Juno plumped her pillow. She'd accused him of being a terrible father, and he'd tried to explain. Now, hours later in the quiet darkness, she attempted to recall exactly what he'd said.

I only learned about Lena three years ago.

There was more to the story. There had to be. But Juno had been too busy projecting her own childhood wounds onto Alex's situation.

Melissa hadn't let him meet his own daughter until he'd paid up.

But that wasn't the whole picture either. She'd seen that Lena loved her mother, heard her talk about the trips they'd taken, the places they'd lived. She wasn't an obviously neglected child.

The look on Alex's face when he watched Lena talking about books she'd read. The way he'd knelt in front of her, bad ankle and all, to steady her when she was upset. The absolute adoration in his eyes.

And Alex had never gotten her letters. He'd never known how desperate she'd been. He hadn't intentionally turned his back on her when she was in so much pain.

He wasn't Leonard Thomas. He wasn't Juno's father. Alex wasn't a monster, and Juno had to admit that she'd never really it of him.

The realization settled over her like a warm blanket. Alex Frampton, for all his flaws, was trying. He might be fumbling his way through fatherhood, might have made compromises he shouldn't have, but he was there. He showed up. He clearly loved his daughter.

He might be stumbling through rebuilding a relationship with Juno, too, but he'd been the one to show up at her door, to take that first step. A step that, she hated to admit, she might never have taken in his direction.

She let out a self-deprecating snort. Didn't that, on some level, make him the better person?

Juno drew her knees up to her chest and wrapped her arms around them. She'd promised him he didn't have to face things alone. Had she meant it? Or was that just something she'd said to make herself feel better about helping a hungover man in her apartment?

"Whatever's going on, whatever it is that's harder now—you don't have to face it alone."

Her own words echoed back to her, and she realized with startling clarity that she'd meant every syllable. And not because she expected anything in return. No one should have to face their demons alone.

Alex needed a support system and she wanted to be a part of it. She wanted to be his friend, someone he could count on to remind him of how great a guy he was, that he was worthy of good things, of people loving him and standing by him.

With that resolution, Juno felt the knot in her chest begin to loosen. She slid back down under the covers, suddenly aware of how exhausted she was. Tomorrow she'd wake up, go to church, and then wait for Alex's call. She would listen—*really* listen—to what he had to say.

No judgments. No accusations. Just one friend being there for another.

She could set aside her own feelings—the hurt, the attraction, the history—and simply be there.

It would be enough. It had to be.

20
Alex

"Of course, I'm still here." Alex rose from the sofa and followed her, keeping his voice low to avoid waking Lena. "Where else would I be?"

Melissa rolled her eyes. "Well, now I'm here, too, so you can go."

Alex's heart was thumping so hard in his chest, he wondered if she could see it. He'd just had a terrible thought. Had she tried to goad him into leaving Lena alone so that she could somehow use it against him? Use it as an excuse for taking his daughter away from him next week? Surely, she would know that he wouldn't have done anything so horrific.

Then again, it sounded like Melissa did leave the child to fend for herself on a regular basis.

"I'm not playing games, Melissa. I've got questions, and I want some answers."

"Well, I've got a big, soft bed waiting for me, so unless you want to join me there," she said with a suggestive sidelong look, "your questions will have to wait for another time."

Alex smacked his palm flat against the polished dining table top, the sound much louder than he'd intended. It stung, too, but the pain grounded him. "You need to listen to me." He took a step toward her, and when she finally looked over at him, something in his face must have registered, because she straightened her shoulders and lifted her chin in a show of defiance. But he saw the glint of worry in her eyes, even as she tried to hide it.

He needed to back off a little. He didn't want her afraid. He wanted to reason with her, to communicate and collaborate, to come up with a plan that would be mutually beneficial to all three of them, and if she was afraid and defensive, he'd get nowhere.

He wasn't sure they'd get anywhere tonight, anyway, seeing how she swayed on her feet. She reached out to steady herself with a hand on the edge of the counter.

But Alex suddenly found that he wasn't feeling very reasonable right now, either. This woman would have been just fine to leave Lena alone until someone—*anyone*—happened to come home. His stomach clenched at the thought of the child waking up from a bad dream or even just to use the bathroom, to discover that she was completely alone in this mausoleum of home. Or worse, if the wrong person managed to get—

He shook his head hard to rattle loose that train of thought. He couldn't let him mind go there.

"Is this what you do?" he asked. "When the nanny is gone and you can't find a sitter? Do you just put Lena to bed and leave her alone, asleep, while you go out and get..." He gestured a hand up and down at her. "Plastered?"

Melissa glared at him. "Don't be so dramatic. I'm not plastered, and Lena's perfectly capable—"

"She's eight years old!" He struggled to keep his voice down. "Eight, Melissa. She shouldn't be left alone for any reason, awake or asleep."

Melissa let out a scoffing hiss. "Look at you, suddenly Father of the Year." She clung to the edge of the counter as she kicked off her heels, leaving them in the middle of the floor. "Where was all this concern when she was born?"

"I didn't know about her so that I *could* be concerned about her," Alex said through gritted teeth. "Because you withheld that important bit of information from me."

"Like it would have made any difference." She opened the cupboard to take a glass out and filled it with water from the fridge dispenser. "You weren't exactly daddy material."

The accusation stung, partly because it contained more than a grain of truth. Eight years ago, he hadn't been fit for fatherhood. He hadn't been fit for adulthood. He'd been living like an overgrown child. *Like Peter Pan*, he thought wryly.

But that didn't excuse Melissa for not telling him. He'd been desperate for something to live for back then, which was why he'd been so reckless and out of control. Maybe if she'd involved him back then, he would have changed the direction of his life long before he did. Nor did it excuse her from keeping Lena from him for six years, then using her as leverage the way she was now.

"Unfortunately, we can't undo what you did." His voice was almost a snarl. "But this isn't about the past. This is about right now. About you neglecting our daughter while you lure in your next victim." His words were ugly, but it had required a lot of self-control to not spit out what he really wanted to say. The vile things he wanted to call her.

Melissa's eyes narrowed. "Don't you dare judge me. Being a single parent isn't easy, and I've provided Lena with everything she could possibly need."

"Except a parent who spends time with her," Alex shot back.

"I spend time with her!" Melissa retorted, her voice rising, making him think of a child with cookie crumbs all over her face vehemently denying she'd been in the cookie jar.

Ignoring her, he continued. "Except a sense of security. Of safety. Did you know she told me your new boyfriend looks at her 'weird'? That you made her wear makeup to 'impress' him?" He spoke the last question slowly, emphasizing each word.

"Daniel is a successful businessman." Melissa crossed her arms before raking her eyes up and down Alex, taking in his casual attire. "Unlike some, he has standards."

"For an eight-year-old girl?" Alex couldn't keep the disgust from his voice. "And now you're planning to move in with him? How long have you known him, exactly? Weren't you just living in Paris with Charles?"

"My personal life is none of your business," Melissa snapped.

"It is when it affects our daughter. She says you're leaving next week. Were you planning to tell me, or would you have just disappeared again?"

"Don't be so dramatic. I was going to tell you."

"Oh, right. Like you told me when she was born." The bitterness he'd suppressed for years boiled to the surface. He took another step closer, leaned forward slightly, and pointed at her. "You robbed me of six years with my daughter, Melissa, and I'm not going to let that happen anymore."

To his surprise, she slapped his hand away, hard, and called him a vile name. "Get your finger out of my face. You know the arrangement," Melissa said coldly. "You agree to my terms, or you don't get to see her."

"I should have challenged those terms a long time ago, Melissa, and I'm sorry I didn't," Alex admitted, facing his own culpability. "But do you know what I've been researching tonight while you were out till the wee hours, ignoring the fact that you had a child? The parental rights of a father. A simple paternity test is all I need to get the ball rolling."

Melissa let out an ugly sound. "You might want a good attorney, too," she spat out, then added crassly, "Your reputation on this side of the lake doesn't bode well for you, pool boy."

The cruel words hit home. He couldn't undo the things he'd done, either, and now his past was catching up to him.

What a mess he'd made of his life, and the lives of those his messy life had messed with.

But then, that was why he was standing here right now, facing down this woman who had manipulated him into thinking he had no rights of his own as Lena's father, that he was lucky to have what little Melissa doled out to him.

Because he was finished making a mess of things.

He was here to clean up after himself. He was here to set things right. To change the things he could and to let go of the things he couldn't. *Whatever's going on, whatever it is that's harder now—you don't have to face it alone.*

"A good attorney won't be hard to find, and I happen to have a town of people who will vouch for the kind of man I am."

Melissa pushed her way around him and circled the table so that it was now between them. "You really think it's so easy raising a child on your own? You think I haven't had to sacrifice?"

"I have no doubt that it's one of the hardest things a parent will ever do," he shot back. He'd give her that much, although he wasn't sure she'd had to sacrifice much of anything in the process. "But I'm not on my own, Melissa. I have my parents. I have friends, a community of people who know and—and love me." It was the first time he'd ever put that into words, and he was shocked at how true it rang.

A small voice interrupted from the hallway. "You're fighting about me again, aren't you?"

They both turned to see Lena standing in the doorway to the living room, her eyes wide and anxious, her hair mussed from sleep. She clutched her ladybug tight to her chest like a shield.

Alex's heart broke at the resignation in her voice. How many arguments had she overheard between adults who were supposed to protect her?

"Everything is fine, sweetie," Melissa said, her tone instantly switching to saccharine sweetness. "Go back to bed."

"It doesn't sound fine." Lena took a few steps into the room. "It sounds like fighting."

Alex crossed the room and drew her into a hug. "I'm sorry we woke you."

Lena stayed pressed against him for only a moment before stepping back so she could look back and forth between her parents. To Melissa she said, "I don't want to move to Greece, Mom."

Melissa's voice hardened. "Enough, Lena Marie. We've talked about this. Daniel has a beautiful house, and—"

"I don't care about his house." Lena's voice was stronger now, too. "Or the island, or the pool, or any of that. I want to stay here." She glanced at Alex, then back to her mother. "I want to live with Daddy."

"That's impossible," Melissa scoffed.

"Why is it impossible?" Lena pressed. "If I lived with Daddy, you could go wherever you want. You wouldn't have to pay for Adeline. It wouldn't cost you any money if I stayed with him."

Alex held his breath, shocked by Lena's directness but unable to deny the surge of hope her words created.

"You wouldn't have to even think about what to do with me," Lena's voice trembled slightly, but she stood her ground. "Daddy wants me. I want to be with him."

Melissa's expression darkened. "Your father doesn't know the first thing about raising a child."

"He could learn!" Lena's eyes filled with tears. "I could teach him. Please, Mom. I don't like Daniel, and he doesn't like me. I can tell because he looks at me like I don't belong. Well, I belong here. I want to live here. I want Autumn Lake to be my home." Fat teardrops were streaming from her eyes now, and she stood there, trembling like a live wire. "Why can't you be my mommy and stop looking for a new boyfriend everywhere we go?"

The last words seemed to escape before Lena could stop them. Then she brought the ladybug up to cover her face.

For a moment, Melissa looked genuinely stung. Alex, desperate to comfort his daughter, but also wanting to tread carefully in this volatile moment, moved a step closer to Lena.

Melissa's eyes went cold and dark, her back stiffened, and her lip curled into an ugly snarl.

"Fine." She lurched forward, grabbed Lena's arm, and pushed her into Alex.

"Hey!" Alex caught Lena as she stumbled, steadying her against his side with an arm around her shoulders. "That was uncalled for."

"Go ahead." Melissa ground out. "Take her. Keep her for a week and see what it's like having to be responsible for someone else all the time. You'll come crawling back, you'll see. Having a child will change your life, Alex."

Then she snatched the ladybug out of Lena's arms so she could look her daughter in the face. "You want to live with him? Fine. Go live with him. See how you like living on pizza and beer."

"My ladybug!" Lena wailed, her arms reaching out for it.

Melissa poked him in the chest. "You got your wish; she's all yours. I'm going to bed." Then she shoved the ladybug into him, too, and stormed out of the room, listing slightly so that she had to run a hand along the wall to keep her balance. "Get out of my house," she called over her shoulder. "Both of you." Then she disappeared inside her room and pulled the door closed with a resounding crash.

For a moment, the air seemed to echo with Melissa's terrible words.

But then those words stopped sounding quite so terrible, at least to Alex's ears. Did he need her to put it in writing that she was letting him take Lena with him? Was he about to do something stupid by taking his daughter home with him tonight?

Alex looked down at Lena, whose expression wavered between hope and uncertainty. He wouldn't let this moment slip away. He handed her the ladybug and she squeezed it tightly, never taking her eyes off his face.

"Let's get your things, Lena-Bug," he said softly. "Whatever you need for the week."

Lena didn't hesitate. She scampered down the hall ahead of him and started pulling things from her closet. "My suitcase is under the bed," she told him. By the time he pulled it out and opened it on her bed, Lena was efficiently folding her clothes and placing them in piles like she'd done this a hundred times before.

When he realized she didn't exactly need his help, he took her hand to stop her. "I need to let your mother know that we are leaving. Are you okay to keep working in here without me?"

"I'm fine. I pack my own suitcase all the time." She nodded, her messy curls bobbing wildly.

Alex left her room, pulling the door closed behind him. He had no idea if Melissa would even talk to him, but in case she came out of her room swinging, he wanted to keep Lena out of it as much as possible.

He knocked lightly on Melissa's door. "Melissa?"

"Go away."

Alex held his breath. Was it just slurred speech? Or was Melissa crying? "Melissa, can I talk to you a minute? Lena is packing."

"No," came her response.

Feeling slightly creepy, Alex pressed his ear to her door. Sure, enough, Melissa sniffled, then breathed in shakily. She was, indeed, crying.

What should he do? It was too risky to go in her room to offer her comfort, especially since the last time he'd been in there had been for nefarious reasons. He didn't want to give her the wrong impression in any way. But he couldn't just take Lena and leave Melissa alone in there crying, could he?

He squared his shoulders and knocked again. "Can I come in?"

When she didn't answer, he tried the door and found it wasn't locked. He pushed it open a couple of feet, but didn't enter. Melissa sat on the edge of her bed, a wad of tissues in her hand, looking a little more the worse for wear with her smudged makeup and drooping shoulders.

"I told you to go away," she said, but there was very little fight left in her voice. She only glanced briefly at him, then looked down at her hands.

Alex considered his words carefully. "I'm going to go ahead and take Lena home with me tonight so you can get some sleep. I'll have my phone on me and I'll watch for your call if you want to talk in the morning." He paused, partly because he wanted to make sure she was listening to him, but also because he knew she might balk at what he had to say next.

Melissa nodded, but said nothing.

"I'm going to take her to my folks' house for lunch so they can meet their granddaughter. If—" Was he really going to ask? "If you'd like to join us, I know they'd want to meet you, too."

Melissa brought both hands up to cover her face and her shoulders shook as she sobbed quietly into her tissues.

Alex wanted to offer her some comfort, but he wasn't the right person to be her shoulder to cry on, not with her in such a vulnerable state. "You don't have to decide tonight. You don't even have to tell me at all. You can just show up if you decide at the last minute to join us. Mom always serves Sunday lunch at one o'clock sharp." He pulled out his phone and pulled up Melissa's number. "I'm sending you their address now."

Melissa's phone vibrated on the nightstand beside her. She finally lowered her hands, but she didn't look at him.

"Do you want to say goodnight to Lena before we leave?"

She shook her head. "Tell her goodnight for me, okay?"

"I will."

"And that I love her."

"Of course." When she said nothing else, he asked, "Are you going to be okay here alone, Melissa?" She wouldn't do anything to hurt herself, would she? He'd never seen her so despondent, and he didn't know her well enough to know how she managed in situations like this.

"I'll be fine. Adeline will be here in a couple of hours and she'll check on me. She always does," she said. "That girl takes care of both of us."

Alex was glad to hear it. It would be after one by the time he and Lena left, so she'd only be home alone for an hour. But he'd feel better if she didn't look so miserable. "Hey, why don't you go ahead and get ready for bed while we're here. We'll stick around for a few more minutes, if you change your mind and want to see Lena before we go."

Melissa nodded, and he started to pull the door closed, but paused when he heard her say, "Thank you, Alex."

"You're welcome."

Back in Lena's room, Alex asked her to tell him the names of each of her stuffed animals in an attempt to slow her down as she put them into a large yellow duffel. Then he paged through some of her sketchbooks with her before she slipped them into her backpack. On the cover of one book she'd written in careful block letters, 'Daddy.' It was filled with colorful images of him smiling a toothy grin, of the two of them playing, fishing, eating, and even a few with Melissa, too, although usually, she was drawn on the sidelines, sitting on a bench or on her phone. Present, but not engaged. Alex wondered if Melissa had seen the drawings.

When she was completely ready to go, Lena, of her own accord, knocked on her mother's bedroom door. She only waited a moment before opening it and walking in. "I'm going with Daddy, now, Mommy. I love you." From where he sat on Lena's bed, Alex couldn't see inside Melissa's room, but the light was still on, and he could hear her response.

"Love you, too, Lena Marie. I'll call you tomorrow sometime, okay?"

"It's okay. You don't have to," came Lena's response. "I'll be fine with Daddy."

Alex grimaced. Would that set Melissa off?

"Okay," she only said. "Be good."

"I'm always good," Lena replied with a giggle, then she appeared in the hallway again. Before pulling the door closed behind her, she called, "Goodnight, Mommy."

The role reversal scene made Alex's chest tight. His daughter was growing up with far too much responsibility on her shoulders, and he was the only one who could do anything about it.

Things were going to change. Starting now.

As they pulled away from the condo, he glanced at Lena in the rearview mirror. She looked small and a little uncertain, with her ladybug still clutched to her chest.

"You okay, Lena-bug?"

She nodded, then asked in a small voice, "Are you okay?"

Alex pulled over to the curb so he could turn in his seat and look her in the eye. "I'm more than okay, because I'm with you."

"I didn't know Mommy would get so mad." Lena's eyes glistened as they once again filled with tears.

"Hey, now, it's going to be okay." He reached for her hand and gave it a gentle squeeze. "She's more upset at herself than you or me, sweetie. We all just need a good night's sleep, okay?"

Lena nodded and wiped at her eyes with the back of her hand. "You don't mind if I come stay with you? I didn't ask you if it was okay first."

"Not at all," he declared, not needing to fake his enthusiasm. "My apartment isn't fancy like your mom's place. It's small, and I haven't had much time to clean up lately because of my ankle. But we'll make it work, okay?"

A genuine smile spread across Lena's face. "Okay."

As they drove around the lake toward town, Alex's mind homed in on Juno, the way it always did. Even though it had been so late, he couldn't help the disappointment that she hadn't responded to his text. He prayed it was because she was sound asleep, and not because she was choosing to leave him hanging.

He'd call her first thing in the morning. Surely, she would understand.

And then, he'd call his parents.

As they drove through the quiet streets of Autumn Lake, he allowed himself to feel something he hadn't fully experienced in years: hope.

"Are you tired?" he asked as they approached his apartment building.

Lena shook her head. "Not anymore. I'm too excited."

"Me too," Alex admitted. "How about this? Since it's a special night, we can have a little sleepover. Watch movies on the couch until we fall asleep. How does that sound?"

"What's a sleepover?"

The innocent question squeezed his heart. Of course she wouldn't know—when would she have had friends over for such a normal childhood experience, moving from place to place as she had?

"It's when people stay up late together, watching movies, eating snacks, and building pillow forts," he explained. "Doesn't that sound like fun?"

Lena nodded, her eyes round. "Can we build a pillow fort?" she asked, as if doing so ranked right up there with visiting Disneyland.

Alex chuckled. "We can do all of the above."

As they climbed the stairs to his apartment, Lena's hand in his, Alex realized that Melissa had been right about one thing: having a child in his life would change everything.

Alex welcomed that change with open arms.

21
Juno

JUNO SAT IN HER car outside church, fingers tapping on the steering wheel as she watched the last of the congregation filter out into the humid summer morning. Pastor Darren stood at the bottom of the front steps, sending off his parishioners with warm handshakes and smiles. Poor guy; she could see the sheen of sweat on his forehead from here. It was a blazing summer morning, even with the breeze blowing in off the lake.

His sermon today had resonated with her more than she'd expected—how forgiveness wasn't about changing the person who wronged you, but about freeing yourself from the burden of carrying that hurt.

"Forgiveness doesn't guarantee reconciliation," he'd said, his voice carrying through the small sanctuary. "It simply means you're no longer allowing that pain to dictate your future."

She'd thought immediately of Alex, and how the weight had lifted from her shoulders last night when she'd decided to move forward, to be the friend he needed. She felt lighter somehow, as if she'd set down a heavy load she'd been carrying for years.

Turning the key in the ignition, Juno pulled out of the church parking lot and headed toward her coffee shop. The Outback's air conditioning was a blessing against the July heat. She didn't open until one on Sundays—a compromise that allowed her to attend church, enjoy a causal lunch alone or with friends, maybe even a short nap, and still catch the afternoon crowd eager for respite from the summer sun.

As she rounded the corner onto Camellia Court, something caught her eye—a figure slouched in a chair at one of the bistro sets in front of her shop. Even from this distance, even after a decade, there was no mistaking his identity.

Her stomach dropped. Leonard Thomas. Her father.

Thankfully, he hadn't seen her, so Juno pulled into her usual spot behind the shop, her peaceful post-sermon mood evaporating like the morning dew. She took her time gathering her things, mentally steeling herself as she darted up the back stairs that led to her apartment on the second floor. So much for a leisurely lunch and a nap; there was no way she was going to let Leonard Thomas loiter outside her shop for the next two hours without knowing exactly why he was here.

In the bathroom, she pulled her beaded braids into a dark green scrunchy. She washed away her Sunday makeup and applied a much simpler look with a dark plum lip stain, waterproof mascara and some bronze eyeshadow, nothing that would smear or run as the day warmed up and the kitchen got busy.

"Stay calm," she whispered to her reflection, even as her pulse raced and her hands trembled. "He's on your territory. You owe him nothing."

She considered calling the police, just to have someone there in case things got out of hand, but the fact that Leonard was waiting out front and not shlepping around her backdoor made her feel a little less vulnerable.

Besides, she wasn't at all sure she wanted anyone knowing he was in town. She needed to get down there and tell him to go away.

She changed out of her sundress and into her uniform of jeans and a shop polo, then grabbed her keys and headed back out. She'd thought about going in the back door of the shop and watching him through the window for awhile, but the longer she put off speaking to him, the more nervous she was going to get.

With her face a carefully constructed mask of indifference, her shoulders back and her chin high, Juno rounded the building to the front of her shop. Her father turned when he heard her footsteps, and she felt a flicker of bitter satisfaction at the surprise that crossed his face.

"Juno," he said, pushing away from the window where he'd been peering inside, his hands cupped around his face. He'd aged considerably in the years since she'd seen him. His hair was now more gray than black, his face lined and weathered, and his once-imposing frame was now slightly stooped, thinner. But his eyes, dark and unreadable, remained unchanged.

She didn't respond, simply moved past him to unlock the door. "I'm not open until one," she said over her shoulder, her voice impressively steady. "You'll have to come back then if you want coffee."

Leonard stepped forward, not quite crowding her but close enough that she could smell the slight hint of cigarettes clinging to his clothes. "I didn't come for coffee."

Juno turned to face him, one hand on the door. "Then what did you come for?" Her tone was cool, professional. The tone she reserved for difficult customers—polite but distant.

"To see you." Leonard removed his cap, and she was startled to see how thin his hair had become. In some places, she could even see his scalp shining through. "To talk, if you'll hear me out."

Warning bells rang in Juno's mind. In her experience, when Leonard Thomas wanted to talk, trouble wasn't far behind. But standing in the doorway of the business she'd built, in the town she'd reclaimed as her own, she found she wasn't afraid of him anymore. Just wary.

"Five minutes," she said after a long pause. She pushed the door open, the familiar aroma of coffee beans and baked goods a comforting counterpoint to the tension tightening her shoulders. She turned and held the door a little wider, not so much as an invitation but as a statement of control. He was on her turf and she made the rules here.

Leonard crossed the threshold, his gaze sweeping over the warmly lit interior with its polished wood tables and comfortable seating. "Nice place you've got," he said, hands fidgeting with his cap. "Real nice."

"Thank you," Juno replied, not warming to the compliment. She moved behind the counter—a physical barrier between them—and watched as he took in the gleaming espresso machine, the display case currently empty of the pastries she'd put out later.

"Been a long time," he ventured when she offered nothing more.

"At least ten years," Juno agreed, her expression neutral. "What do you want?"

Leonard sighed, the sound heavy with what might have been regret, though Juno knew better than to trust it at face value. He'd always been good at appearing contrite when it suited him.

"I've been sober for almost two years now," he said, meeting her eyes directly. "Working a program. Making amends where I can."

Juno raised an eyebrow, neither confirming nor denying the implied question—would she allow him to make amends to her?

"I know I was a terrible father," he continued when she remained silent. "I—I was a monster. A man ruled by his vices." He paused, swallowing visibly. "And I know I did horrific things to you and your mother."

Juno had to clench her hand into a fist to stop herself from touching her face. How many times had she tended to her mother's split lips and black eyes? Her father rarely left any bruises on Juno, not during the school year, at lease, but how many times had he struck her, his big, open palm cracking against her cheek, the impact sending her lurching backwards? She forced herself to maintain eye contact, refusing to show how much the memories still affected her.

"Is there anyone looking for you?" she asked bluntly.

Leonard blinked, thrown by the direct question. "What?"

"Is there anyone after you?" she clarified, her voice still level. "Are you running from something—or someone—that might follow you here?" The real question hung unspoken between them: *Are you bringing trouble to my doorstep?*

"No," he said, shaking his head firmly. "No, nothing like that. I've been clean, Juno. Honest work, honest living. I would never bring that kind of trouble to you." His eyes, so like her own, held a pleading sincerity that she found herself wanting to believe despite her better judgment.

"I'm—I'm looking for work," he added, twisting his cap in his hands. "Something steady. I've been doing odd jobs, construction mostly, but nothing permanent. Folks are wary about giving a guy like me a real job." He gestured vaguely around the coffee shop. "I could help around here. Clean. Stock. Whatever you need."

Juno nearly laughed at the audacity. After everything, he was asking her for a job? But beneath her indignation, she heard Pastor Darren's barrel-chested voice: *Forgiveness is messy and uncomfortable and it often asks more of us than we think we can give. Forgiveness might even ask us to consider extending second chances, third chances, or more. It's what Christ does for us every time we let him down, and boy oh boy, do we let him down again and again and again, amen?*

She thought of Alex, of how he'd come to her just two nights ago in search of some kind of reconciliation with her, of the way he was trying to forge his way with Lena now.

Of how she'd decided just last night that she would support him in that journey, despite her own misgivings. If she was willing to give Alex a second chance, did that mean she should offer her father one, too?

"Why should I trust you?" she asked, the question surprisingly free of venom. "I've heard this spiel a thousand times before."

Leonard nodded slowly, as if he'd expected this. "True enough." He met her gaze steadily. "I can't prove anything to you with words. Just time and actions. But I'm asking for a chance to try."

Juno crossed her arms and leaned against the counter, weighing her options. Though every instinct screamed against it, she couldn't deny there was a part of her that was curious about what had happened to him over the last decade, what had finally motivated him to get clean, if he really was sober and repentant.

"I've got some time before I open," she said finally. "I was going to make myself a sandwich; you want one, too? Maybe you can give me the rundown of what you've been up to, especially the last few years." She gestured toward the other end of the counter where there were several stools for patrons to use. "Have a seat."

Relief washed over Leonard's face. "A sandwich would be great."

"This isn't a yes," she warned, moving behind the counter. "But I'm willing to listen.""

Leonard nodded, settling cautiously onto a stool as Juno assembled two simple turkey sandwiches. She placed one in front of him along with a glass of water and a bag of kettle chips, then sat down across the bar from him, maintaining a careful distance.

"Two years sober. Tell me about that," She took a bite of her sandwich.

Between bites, Leonard launched into his story, describing rock bottom, a stint in rehab, and the journey through the twelve steps. Juno nodded, made acknowledging noises where appropriate, and asked pointed questions when his narrative grew vague or contradictory. She didn't soften toward him, but she did notice that his hands remained steady, his eyes clear, none of the telltale signs of the addict she remembered.

When they'd finished their sandwiches, Juno brewed a pot of coffee and offered him a couple of her peanut butter cookies. An hour passed as Leonard filled in the gaps of his life. When he finally seemed to run out of things to say, Juno glanced at the clock.

"I should get ready to open." She stood and gathered their dishes.

Leonard rose quickly. "Thank you for listening. And for lunch."

Juno studied him, still undecided. Finally, she spoke.

"I could use someone for custodial work," she said carefully. "Sweeping, mopping floors, cleaning appliances and bathrooms, washing dishes. All the dirty work nobody wants to do."

Leonard's eyes lit up. "I can do that. Any of it. All of it."

"It'd be no more than part time right now," she continued, "but if you're planning on sticking around, it could turn into more. I bought the empty space next door." Her hands full, she jutted her chin toward the west wall. "I've got a crew coming in the fall to get started, and I'm hoping to have it up and running by the end of the year. Business is good." She heard the pride in her voice, and if it had been anyone but her father she was speaking to, she would have been embarrassed. But she wanted him to see what she'd made of herself, how far she'd come in spite of his efforts to crush her.

"You should be proud of yourself," he said, once again looking around at her beloved shop. "I know I am, too."

She leveled a steady gaze at him, refusing to accept his praise. It still meant little more than the air it took to say them. "I pay fair wages, but I expect my employees to show up on time. And sober. You can smoke, but only on your breaks and only out back in the alley. Not out front where the patrons are served." She always set ashtrays out on a few of the tables, but she didn't want him using them. She really didn't want him fraternizing with her patrons at all, at least until she had a better sense of what to expect from him. "The first time you come in here smelling like alcohol or acting erratic, you're done."

Leonard nodded sagely. "That's more than fair."

"If I catch you pocketing a dime that isn't yours, you're gone," she added, her gaze locked with his. "I have worked hard to be where I am, and I will not have you come in here and screw things up for me. I am stretching my neck to give you a chance to prove you're a changed man."

"I won't let you down, Juniper."

"Don't make promises you can't keep," Juno warned. "Just show up and do the work." She paused. "You're staying at the Sleepy Time Motel, right? How are you going to get to work?"

A flash of discomfort crossed his face. "I—I have to check out today. Funds are..." he trailed off, gesturing vaguely.

Of course. He needed money. That's what this was really about.

"I'm not letting you stay with me," she said firmly.

"I wouldn't ask that," Leonard replied quickly. "I was hoping maybe you could front me enough to cover the next couple of weeks until I can find something more permanent."

Juno sighed, calculating figures in her head. She couldn't send him away with nowhere to go, but she wasn't about to set him up indefinitely either.

"I'll pay for ten more nights," she decided.

"That's more than generous," he said with a nod. "More than generous."

"You figure out how to get here. I need you in the mornings between rushes, from nine to noon, five days a week, six days if you're willing." She'd call the Sleepy Time herself to pay for his stay; no chance of him pocketing the money and disappearing.

"I'm willing, Juno." Relief flooded his weathered face. "I won't—"

"Let me down. I know." She moved toward the register. "You start tomorrow. Nine o'clock sharp. We'll see how you do with the basics before I decide what else you can handle."

Leonard nodded, clutching his cap like a lifeline. "I'll be here. Early."

"Good. I'll have Jeffrey show you the ropes. He's our dishwasher and prep guy." Juno picked up her phone. "I'll call the inn now and get you set up. Then I need to start getting this place ready to open."

Leonard took the hint and backed toward the door. "Thank you, Juniper. I mean it. I know I don't deserve this chance."

After he left, Juno leaned against the counter, trying to process what she'd just done. Had she made a terrible mistake? Or was this the beginning of healing something she'd thought broken beyond repair?

Should she tell someone what was going on? Her Garden Variety Lovers Club friends? Or would they think she'd made a big mistake and try to talk her out of it? Maybe she'd better not tell anyone yet. If this all went sideways—*when* it went sideways, because she had a terrible suspicion that it would—she'd rather not have witnesses to her foolishness.

Besides, they'd all find out soon enough. Not only did her peers frequent her shop on a regular basis, but small towns weren't good at keeping secrets.

Juno busied herself with opening preparations, setting up the pastry display case, grinding fresh beans for the three house coffees of the day, wiping down the counter where she'd shared lunch with her father—how weird did that sound? Physical activity helped calm her racing thoughts, but it couldn't completely suppress the worry gnawing at her insides.

By a quarter to one, everything was ready. Juno sat at the counter with a mug of black coffee, staring out the window at the summer sidewalk shimmering with heat. She'd taken a chance on Leonard Thomas—the man who'd stolen her childhood, her security, and nearly her life.

She wondered what Alex would say if he knew. Would he understand, or would he think she was naive? He had his own battle brewing with Melissa over Lena. At least his fight was for something precious—someone worth fighting for. What was Juno fighting for? Closure? Redemption? Or was she simply setting herself up for another devastating blow?

The bell above the door jingled, startling her from her thoughts. Trevor, her Sunday afternoon barista, strolled in with his usual easy smile.

"Hey boss," he greeted her, tying on his apron. "Smells good in here."

Juno lifted her mug. "Got a head start. There's not much left to do, so grab a cup if you'd like." She slid off the stool, grateful for the distraction. "We have a new custodial helper starting tomorrow, by the way. He'll be working mornings after the rush."

Trevor raised an eyebrow, his smile broadening. "Cool. Extra help is always good."

"Thought you'd appreciate the news." Trevor hated to clean the bathrooms, especially the men's. On many occasions, he'd ranted over how disgusting guys could be, not caring that he was decrying his own.

Sunday customers began trickling in—families fresh from church, couples out for afternoon strolls, teens seeking air-conditioned refuge.

As she fell into the familiar rhythm of taking and filling orders, Juno found her anxiety gradually ebbing. This was her domain, her success, built with her own hands and determination. Whatever happened with her father, she would survive it. She'd survived his absence; she would survive his presence.

22
Alex

ALEX ADJUSTED THE REARVIEW mirror for the fourth time, catching a glimpse of Lena in the back seat. She sat perfectly still, hands folded in her lap, the picture of nervous anticipation. She had carefully brushed her hair and slipped a headband on to keep it back from her face, and she wore a pale blue sundress they'd picked out together from the closet of clothes she'd brought with her. The blue matched her eyes—Jason's eyes—and Alex wondered if his mother would notice.

"You okay back there, Lena-bug?" he asked, keeping his tone light.

She nodded, though her small fingers twisted the fabric of her dress. "What if they don't like me?"

"That's not possible," he assured her. "They're going to love you. They already do, and they haven't even met you yet."

"How can they love me if they don't know me?" Her brow furrowed with honest confusion.

Alex considered his answer carefully. "Because you're a part of me, and they love me. And because you're a part of Jason—my brother, your uncle, and their son—and they loved him very much."

"The one who died?" Her voice was small.

"Yes." Alex nodded. She'd asked about the photo of him and Jason he had on his bedroom wall, and they'd talked about her longing for a sibling, and how sad it was that Jason had died before she got to meet him.

Then she brightened. "Will your dog be there?"

The abrupt change of subject made Alex grin. "Ralphy? You bet. He's really my mom's dog. Your grandma's dog."

He heard her whisper in the back seat, like she was tasting the words. "My grandma."

"He'll love you, too, Lena-bug."

She wiggled in her seat, excitement replacing nervousness. "What kind is he?"

"A golden retriever. He's getting old, but he still loves to play fetch."

As they rounded the final curve of the lakeside road that led to his parents' house, Alex felt his own stomach tighten with nerves. He hadn't visited in weeks, making excuses about being busy with work. He hadn't even told them about his mishap until today when he'd spoken to them on the phone, and that was only because he didn't want them to worry when he showed up with the boot on. The truth was more complicated. Things had been hard between them for a long time now. It was hard enough to lose Jason, but then he'd gone off the deep end, too. And even though he'd been clean for all these years—not counting Friday night, he reminded himself with a grimace—Alex still carried the burden of having dragged them through the gutter with him.

Today, however, he was showing up on their doorstep with something good that had come out of that tumultuous time. Something precious. Some*one* precious.

The Frampton home sat on a generous lot with a sloping lawn that led down to the lake. It was a two-story colonial, white with blue shutters, surrounded by mature maples that provided dappled shade. As Alex pulled into the circular driveway, the front door opened, and his parents stepped onto the porch.

Dwight Frampton was tall and lean, with the same sandy hair as Alex, though now it was streaked with silver. Roxanne had a trim figure and carefully styled blonde hair. They stood side by side, their expressions a mixture of curiosity and barely contained emotion.

"Here we go," Alex murmured, putting the truck in park.

By the time he'd helped Lena out of the back seat, Ralphy had bounded across the lawn to greet them, his tail wagging furiously. Lena's initial hesitation melted away as the golden retriever approached, more interested in making friends than maintaining any semblance of dignity.

"Is it okay if I pet him?" she asked, already reaching out.

"Absolutely," Alex assured her. "He loves kids."

As Lena knelt to ruffle Ralphy's fur, Alex looked up to see his parents approaching. His mother's steps faltered slightly at the sight of Lena, her hand rising to her throat.

"Mom, Dad," Alex said, his voice catching despite his best efforts. "I'd like you to meet Lena. My daughter."

Roxanne's eyes filled with tears, but she recovered quickly, kneeling down beside Lena and the dog. "Hello, Lena. I'm—I'm Roxanne, your grandma, and I'm so very happy to meet you."

Lena looked up, momentarily shy again. "Hello," she said quietly. "You have a nice dog."

"Thank you," Roxanne replied, her voice warm, stroking the dog's fur. "Ralphy loves you already, and he's a good judge of character."

Lena leaned in and draped her arms around the dog's neck. "Daddy said he'd love me."

From behind Roxanne, Dwight chuckled, then when Lena stood, he extended his hand to his granddaughter with formal politeness. "It's a pleasure to meet you, young lady."

Lena stood and shook his hand solemnly. "Thank you for having me at your house, um, Mr. Frampton."

Dwight offered his wife a hand and helped her stand. "You can call me Grandpa, if you'd like."

"And I'm Grandma," Roxanne added, touching Lena's shoulder. "We've been waiting to meet you for a very long time."

Lena looked up at Alex, confusion evident in her expression. "But they didn't know about me until today."

Alex winced slightly at her honesty, but Roxanne laughed, a genuine sound of amusement that broke the tension. "We may not have known about you, but we have been waiting for your daddy to give us a grandchild for a very long time," she admitted. "And now that we've met you, we know that you're the one we've been waiting for. We're so happy you're here."

Dwight clapped Alex on the shoulder. "Let's head inside. Lunch is almost ready."

As they made their way toward the house, Ralphy trotting alongside Lena, Alex felt something inside him begin to unwind—a knot of tension he'd carried for so long he'd forgotten it was there.

Inside, the house had changed little over the years. The same comfortable furniture, the same family photos lining the walls, the same faint scent of his mother's lemon potpourri. Lena looked around with undisguised curiosity, taking everything in.

"Would you like a tour, sugar?" Roxanne asked.

Lena nodded eagerly, and Alex watched as his mother took his daughter's hand and led her deeper into the house. Their voices drifted back—Lena asking questions, Roxanne answering with growing warmth.

"That went better than expected," Dwight observed, gesturing for Alex to follow him into the kitchen. "Your mother skipped church this morning to clean the house and make cookies. She's roasted a chicken and baked potatoes, too, enough to feed an army. She'll be sending you two home with more leftovers than you can possibly eat in a month."

"I should have told you sooner," Alex said, guilt tightening his throat. "I should have told you the moment I found out." He'd called them that morning, while waiting for Lena to wake up. It hadn't been an easy conversation, but Alex wouldn't just show up on their doorstep with her unannounced. It didn't take long, though, for surprise to turn to anticipation, and now, he could see in his father's eyes how happy they were to have the chance to get to know their new grandchild.

Dwight shrugged, a gesture so like Alex's own. "You had a lot to figure out." He filled a couple of glasses with iced tea and handed Alex one.

Alex took a long drink, using the moment to collect his thoughts. "I didn't know how to tell you. And honestly, I wasn't sure Melissa would let me be part of Lena's life long-term. I didn't want to get your hopes up."

"And now?"

"Now..." Alex shook his head. "I don't know. Melissa's letting Lena stay with me for a few days, which is a big step." How did he explain the situation he found himself in? "But she's got a new boyfriend who's taking them to his Greek island to live." He shook his head. "Lena doesn't want to go and I think Melissa is hoping if she spends a little time in my Hicksville bachelor pad that Lena will realize how good she's got it with her mom. This Daniel guy can certainly provide her with a lifestyle I never could, even in my wildest dreams."

Dwight's expression darkened. "Can he provide her with a father who loves her? Grandparents? A close-knit community that would embrace her as one of their own?"

"Melissa doesn't even talk to her parents, so Lena's never met them."

From the dining room came the sound of female laughter. Alex peered through the doorway to see Roxanne showing Lena the collection of framed school photos arranged on the sideboard.

"And this one is Alex when he lost his two front teeth," his mother was saying. "He had this adorable whistle when he tried to say anything with an 's' in it."

"Like Mississippi?" Lena giggled, her earlier shyness completely gone. She pointed to another photo. "Is that Jason?"

Roxanne's hand trembled slightly as she picked up the frame. "Yes, that's Jason, Alex's brother. Your uncle."

Lena studied the photograph with intense focus. "He looks like Daddy. And me."

"He does," Roxanne said, her voice thick with emotion. "You have his eyes, exactly the same blue. And his smile."

Alex felt his father's hand on his shoulder, a steady anchor against the sweeping tide of emotion. "She already belongs here, son."

Alex nodded, unable to speak.

Lunch was a surprisingly relaxed affair. Dwight grilled burgers and hot dogs on the patio with a mountain of side dishes Roxanne had prepared. Lena ate with the enthusiastic appetite of childhood, declaring the potato salad "the best thing ever."

After the meal, they moved to the backyard, where Lena and Ralphy chased each other across the grass. Alex sat with his parents on the shaded patio, feeling a peace he hadn't experienced in years.

"She's wonderful, Alex," Roxanne said, watching Lena with undisguised adoration. "Absolutely wonderful."

"I had nothing to do with that," Alex admitted. "Melissa raised her all these years."

"But she has your heart," his mother insisted. "I can see it in the way she looks at the world—curious, open. Just like you were."

Dwight leaned forward in his chair. "You said Melissa is planning to leave the country with Lena."

"I was going to ask you about that," Roxanne interjected. Lena mentioned something about going to Greece soon."

Dwight frowned. "And when will you see her again?"

The question punctured Alex's bubble of contentment. "I need to talk to a lawyer tomorrow. Find out what my options are."

"Good," Dwight nodded. "You'll need someone with experience in family law. I can make a couple calls first thing in the morning." Dwight practiced tax law, but he had connections among his peers.

"In the meantime," Roxanne said, "what does Lena need? School supplies? She'll be starting third grade this fall, won't she?"

Alex shook his head. "As it stands, I only have her for a few days, Mom. A week at the most. They're planning on leaving next week, unless I can figure out how to get a judge to put a hold on that."

Roxanne pressed a hand to her chest. "She can't take her away already. We've just met her!"

Dwight reached over and took his wife's hand. "We'll figure this out," he said, speaking to himself as much to the them. "Together."

The simple declaration—*together*—nearly undid him. For years after Jason's death, Alex had felt isolated in his grief, convinced that his parents blamed him on some level for not saving their firstborn. He'd pushed them away, drowning his guilt in alcohol and meaningless relationships. Now, with three simple words, his father had drawn him back into the fold.

A ball rolled to a stop at Alex's feet, followed moments later by an out-of-breath Lena. "Daddy, throw it for Ralphy," she urged. "He wants to play fetch."

Alex picked up the tennis ball, worn smooth from countless retrieval games. "Like this?" he asked, tossing it gently across the yard. Ralphy bounded after it, ears flapping.

"No, Daddy," Lena giggled. "You have to throw it farther!" She demonstrated with an exaggerated arm movement that sent her nearly off-balance.

Alex chuckled, standing to join her on the lawn. "Let me show you the proper technique."

For the next half hour, they played with Ralphy, the dog's enthusiasm never flagging despite his gray muzzle. Alex's ankle was killing him, but he didn't care. He hobbled around the best he could, letting Lena chase down wildly-thrown balls, but he was secretly glad Ralphy wasn't as energetic as he'd been as a puppy. When Lena flopped down on the grass, declaring herself "too tired to throw anymore," Roxanne appeared with a tray of lemonade and cookies.

"Perfect timing, Grandma," Lena said, the name slipping out naturally now. "I'm starving again."

"Growing children are always hungry," Roxanne replied, clearly delighted with her new role. "And grandmothers are always ready to feed them."

As they settled at the patio table with their treats, Alex excused himself to make a phone call, leaving his daughter in the adoring care of her grandparents. He headed inside and down the hall to his old room, but when he got there, he could hear Lena's giggle and his parents' animated conversation, and he realized he wanted to be right back out there. He didn't want to miss any of his time with Lena, not if there was even the remotest possibility that she'd be gone in a week.

Instead of calling, he texted: *Juno, I have so much to tell you. Lena came home with me last night and we've just had lunch with my parents, who are now in love with their granddaughter. Lena and I are going to have a picnic on my parents' dock tonight. If you can stand the mosquitos, we'd love to have you join us.*

While playing with Ralphy, he and Lena had concocted the plan to hang out with Juno. Lena hadn't been quite ready to leave Ralphy behind for the day, and she'd suggested the picnic idea. When Alex had asked his parents if they could borrow the dock, they'd happily given him the go-ahead.

Alex has just turned around and was heading back through the house when Juno's reply came through: *Wow. That IS a lot. Can't wait to hear all about it. I'd love to have a picnic with you two. Can I bring anything?*

Nope. Mom has more food here than we know what to do with. Just bring yourself. I'll pick you up at 6 at your place.

When he opened the slider, he heard Lena ask, "Can I come back and play with Ralphy again?"

"Absolutely," Roxanne said. "Any time. And maybe next time, we can bake cookies together. Do you like baking?"

Lena's eyes got big and round. "Make cookies? How do you do that? We just buy them."

"I made these," Roxanne said, holding one of her chocolate chip oatmeal cookies up.

"Wow," Lena exclaimed. "I want to learn how to make cookies."

"Well, then we will add that to our list." Roxanne explained to Alex as he rejoined them that Lena had started a list of things she wanted to do with her grandparents while she was here. The list included painting pictures, planting flowers, looking at photo albums, filling the birdfeeders around the yard, going for ice cream at the ice cream shop, and now, making cookies from scratch.

An idea popped into Alex's head. "You up for adding a sleepover to that list, Mom? Me and Lena, both?"

"Yes, yes, yes!" cried an ecstatic Lena. "I had my first sleepover with Daddy last night and we had so much fun."

His mother was nodding emphatically. "You can have a sleepover here any time you like."

"Tonight?" Lena turned beseeching eyes on Alex. "Please, please?"

Alex shrugged and looked at his mother.

"Tonight would be perfect," she said on a happy sigh, and Alex couldn't remember the last time he'd seen his mother looking so pleased. "Lena, would you like to sleep in your daddy's room with him, on the sofa in the living room, or—" Her voice caught for a moment, but she swallowed and went on. "Or would you like to sleep in your Uncle Jason's room?"

"Can Ralphy sleep with me?"

"Of course."

"Then Uncle Jason's room, please. Ralphy and I can have our own sleepover since I don't have my stuffies." Lena suddenly looked concerned, and Alex squeezed her shoulder.

"I'm going to go pick up Juno in a little bit. I'll swing by the apartment and grab some for you, along with your pajamas. You just tell me what you want."

Lena's eyes lit up. "I will make you a list. I like lists."

While Lena headed inside to help Roxanne get the bedrooms ready for them, Dwight turned to Alex. "Son, I want you to know we're proud of you. Stepping up like this for Lena—it's the right thing."

"I'm terrified I'll mess it up," Alex admitted. "I don't know the first thing about being a father."

"None of us do, at first," Dwight said, his expression serious. "We learn as we go. But you've got good instincts, and you've got us to help."

His parents' show of support meant the world to him, and hopefully, after this evening with Juno, he could count on her support, too. He had no doubt that Ward and Penny and the rest of his circle of friends would rally around him, but out of everyone in Autumn Lake, his parents and Juno were the top three people that he wanted on his team.

Dwight and Alex moved inside out of the heat and watched some television while Roxanne and Lena decided now was the perfect time to try their hands at making a batch of cookies. "We're making sugar cookies with sprinkles Daddy!" Lena declared as Roxanne strapped her into a smock apron and doubled the strings around her tiny waist. "Can you believe it?"

An hour later, as Alex was preparing to leave to pick up Juno, his mother and daughter were sitting together in a hammock outside, one they'd made his father drag out of the garage. They'd had a hammock hanging on the porch his whole childhood, but it had been a long time since he'd seen it set up, and it made him happy to see the two of them out there, reading books together. As he watched, his mother's eyes drifted closed, and he thought she must be exhausted trying to keep up with the ball of energy that was Lena, but then he realized that she was just sighing in utter contentment when she put her arms around the child and squeezed her so hard it made Lena giggle.

They'd all missed out on so much. But no more. Maybe they couldn't go back and undo things or start over, but they could start here and now. Today was the first day of their brand new start.

"Hey Mom," he called out the kitchen window. "I'm picking up Juno now and we'll swing by for overnight stuff." He glanced down at the piece of paper in his hand. In her crooked handwriting, his daughter had listed the names of her stuffed animals, not their descriptions, but he'd video chat from his apartment if he had to, and they'd sort it out.

"Sounds good," Roxanne called back, not even lifting her head to look at him. "Lena and I will have your picnic basket ready and waiting."

"Ready and waiting for you love birds," Lena chirped, then broke into a shriek of giggles at her goofy taunt.

"Bye, you goons," he called out, and turned to go just as two arms shot up out of the hammock and waved him off.

Alex climbed in The Beast and shot a text off to Juno to let her know he was on his way. Then he reached over and switched on the radio, pulling up his favorite rock station. He cranked it up, loud, feeling more excited about his future than he had in a very long time.

23
Juno

JUNO STOOD AT HER closet, considering her options. Casual but not sloppy. Comfortable but not frumpy. "Calm down," she muttered. "This is Alex Frampton we're seeing, not the Queen of England." *And* his parents, she reminded herself. It had been a long time since she'd seen Mr. and Mrs. Frampton; not since high school.

She finally settled on a sleeveless turquoise top that showed off her fit arms and a pair of cropped baggy jeans that would allow her to move easily. Alex hadn't mentioned they'd be swimming, so she didn't bother putting on a suit, although the evening was toasty enough that a swim would feel good. She hoped there was some kind of shade on the dock, and that the water was high enough to dangle her feet in. It had been a long time since she'd been at the Frampton's place, and she had no idea what to expect. She slid her feet into a pair of sandals that gave her sore feet good arch support, then twisted her braids into a loose updo, securing it with a decorative clip, and applied a touch of tinted lip balm.

The clock read 5:50 PM. In ten minutes, Alex would arrive to pick her up, and Juno was surprised at how giddy she felt. Her stomach fluttered with a mixture of anticipation and nervousness that reminded her of being sixteen again, and this wasn't even a date. In fact, this little outing was all about Lena, not the two of them.

But it didn't matter. Alex was inviting her into his life, and she was accepting. Things were changing, and she didn't mind in the least.

Her phone chimed with a text from Alex: *Pulling up now.*

She grabbed a light cardigan on her way out in case the evening turned cool. It was the middle of summer, and the sun would be in the sky for a couple more hours, but sometimes the lakeshore breezes could be downright chilly.

She found Alex waiting at the bottom of the stairs, leaning against the railing with an easy smile that made her heart skip.

"Hey," he said, looking up at her. "Sorry I'm early. Lena's excitement is contagious."

Juno glanced at The Beast and saw it was empty. "She stayed behind?" She pulled her door closed behind her, then checked it to be sure it locked. Then she turned and headed down the stairs toward Alex.

"Yep. Couldn't drag her away." As she drew near, he ran a hand through his hair, looking a little nervous, which actually helped her feel more at ease. "She and my mom hit it off immediately. They're baking cookies and making lists of grandmother-granddaughter activities. I've been completely replaced."

Juno laughed. "Already? It's only been one day."

"I know, right? Apparently, I'm just the chauffeur now." His eyes swept over her, and his smile softened. "You look beautiful."

The compliment warmed her cheeks. "Thank you. You clean up pretty well yourself."

Alex wore shorts and a short-sleeved, olive green button-down that he'd left untucked, and he'd trimmed his stubble. He looked healthy and rested, despite the chaos of the past few days.

He offered his arm. "Shall we?"

The simple gesture felt both old-fashioned and intimate. Juno slipped her hand into the crook of his elbow, acutely aware of the solid warmth of him beside her. As they circled the truck to the passenger door, she noticed that he was hobbling a little more than usual. "How's the ankle?"

Alex let out a snort. "Just overdid it trying to keep up with old Ralphy and my eight-year-old daughter."

"Well, you'd better prop that thing up when we get back to your folks' place. You're going to be hurting tomorrow," she warned. "Where are you working?" The Garden Gate Bed and Breakfast was done, and Alex hadn't mentioned J&J's next jobsite. She couldn't wait until they got started on her place; they were scheduled to begin the first week in November.

He held the door for her as she got in, then moved around the hood to his side, his eyes never leaving her face, that grin making her stomach flip-flop. When he'd settled into his seat, he picked up with her question. "I'm taking at least tomorrow off, maybe the next few days. My dad made some calls, and I'm meeting with a family law guy tomorrow."

"Oh, wow. That's great, Alex." She shifted in her seat as the truck roared to life, studying his profile as he pulled The Beast out of the alley and onto the main road. "So tell me about Lena meeting your parents."

Alex beamed. "They fell in love with her instantly. Mom's already planning sleepovers and baking sessions, and Dad's talking about building her a treehouse. It's like..." He paused, searching for words. "It's like she filled a space none of us knew was still empty."

The raw emotion in his voice touched something deep inside Juno. "I'm so happy for you, Alex. For all of you."

"She's sleeping in Jason's room tonight," he said quietly. "With Ralphy."

"And are you sleeping over, too?" Juno teased, hoping to bring things back to more comfortable footing.

"I am." He shot her a sideways grin. "Mom is planning a Belgian waffle and bacon cook-off in the morning. Wouldn't miss it for the world. Get this: Lena has never made a cookie in her life. Until this afternoon, with my mom."

"My goodness," Juno exclaimed. "So much has happened in the last two days. But you haven't told me how you ended up with Lena. Last I knew you were waiting for Melissa to get home last night."

Alex gave her a brief rundown of what had happened the night before, and as Juno listened, she got a new perspective on the situation he'd found himself in. Melissa didn't sound like an evil person, but she certainly didn't sound very motherly, either. "She leaves her alone on a regular basis?"

"Usually not completely alone. Only when the nanny has her days off and Melissa makes plans that she doesn't want to change." He spoke with heavy sarcasm, and Juno nodded slowly.

"I'm glad you're getting an attorney involved, Alex. I have a feeling that things aren't going to get any better as she gets older. An eight-year-old shouldn't have to take care of herself. It's fine that she knows *how* to do things like pack her own suitcase and use a keypad, but it shouldn't be expected of her. She's not old enough to have to fend for herself." Juno knew good and well how scary it was to wake up alone in the dark, especially after falling asleep with a full house. It was the most unsettling thing for a child, and Juno couldn't imagine the sparkly Lena having to grow up so fast. "I'm proud of you."

"Thanks. That means a lot to me." He glanced her way briefly, then back at the road in front of him. "It's been a whirlwind, but a good one, you know? Weird to think that just three days ago, I was sitting in my truck outside your place, wishing I could tell you about her."

"We've come a long way since then."

"We have indeed," he agreed. "Thanks for giving me second chance to explain, Juno. Not everyone would have been so understanding."

"I believe in second chances," she replied, thinking of her father eating a sandwich at her coffee bar just a few hours earlier. "Maybe more than I should."

Something in her tone made Alex look at her again. "Everything okay?"

Juno considered deflecting, but decided against it. If they were going to build something real—friendship or more—honesty had to be part of it.

"My father showed up this morning," she said, her voice steady despite the storm of emotions the memory stirred. "He was waiting for me in front of my shop when I got home from church."

"Your father?" Alex's knuckles whitened on the steering wheel. "What's he doing here?"

Juno snorted. "That's what I asked him, too." She shook her head, still hardly able to believe it. "The one and only Leonard Thomas in the flesh, looking considerably worse for wear but claiming to be sober and wanting to make amends."

Alex was quiet for a moment, processing. "What did you do?"

"Well," Juno hedged. "I kinda gave him a job. Custodial work at the coffee shop."

"You gave him a job," Alex repeated, as if making sure he'd heard correctly. "The man who hit you, who dragged you away from everything you cared about, who—"

"I know what he did, Alex." Juno's voice was sharper than she intended. She took a breath. "Sorry. It's just... it's complicated."

Alex made a visible effort to soften his reaction. "I'm sure it is. I'm not judging, I'm just surprised."

"So am I, honestly." Juno looked out the window at the familiar landscape of Autumn Lake sliding past. "Pastor Darren's sermon this morning was about forgiveness—how it's not about changing the other person, but about freeing yourself. It resonated with me more than I expected, and the timing was eerily providential. I mean, of all things to talk about on the day my father shows up acting all repentant and wanting to reconnect."

Alex nodded slowly. "I get that." He glanced at her. "It means the world to me, reconnecting with you."

The simple admission hung in the air between them, honest and vulnerable. Juno felt her heart expand with hope. "I feel the same way," she said softly.

They drove in comfortable silence for a while, the radio playing quietly in the background. As they turned onto the lakeside road that wound around to the Frampton property, Juno spoke again. "It's a big risk for me, trusting him," she admitted. "I mean, I *don't* trust him, but I feel like I need to give him a second chance, so maybe it's me I'm trying to trust."

Alex reached across the console to take her hand, squeezing it gently. "If you need anything—someone to talk to, a shoulder to cry on, or just a friend to keep an eye on him—I'm here."

"Thank you." Juno squeezed back, grateful for his steadiness.

As they pulled into drive of the Frampton home, Lena burst out of the front door before Alex had even put the truck in park. She raced down the steps and across the lawn, Ralphy loping at her heels.

"Juno!" Lena called, skidding to a stop beside the passenger door. "You're here!."

"Of course I came," Juno replied, climbing out of the truck. "I wouldn't miss a picnic with you two."

Lena beamed up at her, then gestured to the dog. "This is Ralphy. He's my grandma's dog, but he loves me the most now."

"He has excellent taste," Juno said solemnly, crouching to pet the friendly retriever. "It's nice to meet you, Ralphy."

"We're staying overnight with Grandma and Grandpa," Lena announced proudly. "And Ralphy's sleeping in my room with me. It's really Uncle Jason's old room, but I don't think he'll mind."

"I'm sure he wouldn't mind at all," Juno assured her.

"Come on! Grandma made the picnic basket already. It's huge!" Lena grabbed Juno's hand and tugged her toward the house, where Roxanne Frampton stood on the porch holding a wicker basket nearly as large as Lena herself.

"Juno, dear, it's good to see you again." Roxanne's greeting was warm, genuine, if a bit reserved.

"Hello, Mrs. Frampton," Juno replied, suddenly feeling sixteen again, nervous about impressing Alex's mother. "Thank you for letting us use your dock."

"Of course. You're welcome here anytime." She handed the picnic basket to Alex. "We packed everything you might need. Lena helped make the sugar cookies—her first baking experience."

"I used the mixer all by myself," Lena declared, bouncing on her toes.

Dwight Frampton emerged from the house, carrying a blanket and what looked like bug spray. "Good to see you, Juno," he said, handing the items to her. "Been too long."

After a few more minutes of pleasant conversation, Alex turned to Lena. "Okay, Lena-bug, are you ready for our picnic?"

Lena grabbed Roxanne's hand. "I'm having supper with Grandma and Grandpa so you and Juno can have a date."

Juno looked between Alex and his mother. Alex's cheeks reddened. "Uh... it's a picnic, Lena."

"That's what a date is," Lena informed him matter-of-factly. "It's when two people who like each other spend time together. And you do like Juno, right? You said she was pretty and smart and—"

"Hey now," Alex interrupted. He reached over and tugged on one of Lena's curls, then cupped a hand at the side of his mouth, and in a mock whisper said, "That's top secret intel there, missy."

Juno bit back a laugh, touched by Alex's embarrassment and Lena's innocent candor. Roxanne wasn't even trying to hide her amusement.

"Okay!" she said, poking Alex in the arm. "I guess it's just the two of us, then." She wasn't exactly disappointed, if she were being honest.

"Come on, Lena," Roxanne said, taking her granddaughter's hand. "Let's go see if those cookies have cooled enough to decorate."

Lena squealed with delight, her attention successfully diverted. But before she followed Roxanne inside, she darted back to throw her arms around Alex's waist.

"Have fun, Daddy," she said. Then she skipped away, leaving Alex standing there looking like he wanted the ground to swallow him whole.

24
Juno

"SORRY ABOUT THAT," ALEX said, as they started down the path toward the lake.

"Don't be," Juno said, unable to suppress her smile. "She's great."

"She is, isn't she? I still can't believe she's mine." A note of pride rang through his voice.

The dock stretched about twenty feet into the lake, with a covered seating area, complete with a couple of Adirondack chairs and a table between them, at the end. "Chairs or the deck?" Alex asked.

"Let's do the chairs while the sun is still up, then move to the deck."

Alex gave her a sideways look, one brow arched. "Does that mean you're sticking around until after the sun goes down?"

"I didn't come all the way out here just to miss the sunset over the lake," she declared, the flutter in her stomach ramping up at how easy it was to flirt with him now that they were on flirting terms. It made her sad to think of how much fun they'd missed out on having with each other over the years.

"I should warn you," Alex said as he began unpacking the basket and setting out one container after another on the table. "My mother thinks I'm still a growing boy."

Juno laughed, helping him arrange the feast: sandwiches, pasta salad, fresh fruit, cheese and crackers, and at least a dozen sugar cookies decorated with multicolored sprinkles.

"These must be Lena's," Juno said, holding up a cookie with a particularly enthusiastic distribution of rainbow sprinkles.

"Definitely." Alex grinned. "Subtlety is not yet in her repertoire."

As the sun began its slow descent toward the horizon, they migrated to the end of the dock where they spread the blanket on the wooden planks. Alex removed his walking boot and they sat with their legs dangling over the edge of the pier, their feet in the cool lake water. It was exactly as Juno had imagined, the seashell sky above them and its shimmering reflection on the water, the cool breezes cooling their sun-warmed skin, the cicada and crickets starting up their cacophonous choruses all around them, punctuated by the low throttle of bullfrog calls. Conversation flowed easily between them, Juno telling Alex about her plans to expand the coffee shop, and Alex sharing stories from the day with his parents and Lena.

"She asked about you, you know," Alex said, bracing his hands on the deck on either side of him, and leaning forward a little to peer into the water. Then he turned to meet her eyes. "She and Mom were going through old albums and she saw pictures of us. She wanted to know if you were my girlfriend back when we were kids."

Juno's skin tingled, especially where their shoulders touched. His hand was right there between them; what would he do if she covered his with hers? "And what did you tell her?"

"The truth." He didn't look away. "That you were my first love, and that I was an idiot who didn't know how good I had it."

The frank admission caught her off guard. "Alex..."

"I'm not trying to put pressure on you," he assured her quickly, touching her thigh with his pinky. "I just wanted you to know where I stand. After the misunderstandings, the letters, the time that's passed, I feel like we've been given a rare second chance. And I don't want to waste it."

Juno considered his words. Were either of them prepared to jump into this so quickly? Had they given this enough thought? They weren't the same people anymore, and what if the feelings they so obviously both still had were for the people—the children—they'd been fifteen years ago? How would they know if they didn't explore them?

"I don't want to waste it either," she said finally, turning back to him. "But we're not kids anymore, Alex. We both have complicated lives. You're just starting to figure out how to be a father." She hesitated, then added with a wry chuckle, "And I've got Leonard now."

"I know." Alex shifted on the dock beside her, turning to face her. Then he took her hand in both of his. "I know," he said again. He met her gaze and held it, and then in a gentle, sincere voice, said, "But I have a feeling those things might actually be easier if we faced them together."

Juno considered his words. She'd faced all the hard parts of her life completely on her own while growing up. It was called survival. Moving back to Autumn Lake had brought with it a circle of friends, a community that absorbed her with no hesitation, and a sense of no longer being alone in the world. But old habits, old instincts, were hard to break. Inviting someone else into the difficult parts of her life felt both scary and freeing at the same time.

"I might not be very good at this," she admitted. "I'm not really a team player."

Alex chuckled good naturedly. "Well, I think you're very much a team player... as long as you're the team captain."

She poked him in the thigh. "You got that right."

Alex sobered. "I have messed a lot of things up in my life, Juno, but I'm working on changing that. Fixing the mess I've made between you and me is one of my top priorities. I'm not asking for promises from you. Like you said, we both have a lot going on right now." He couldn't squelch the grin when he glanced over his shoulder at his parents' house where his daughter was enjoying an evening with her grandparents for the very first time. "But I want to explore the possibility of us. I want to see where this goes, this second chance we have, and I hope you do, too."

Possibility. It was both less and more than she'd expected—less pressure, more potential. After everything they'd been through, maybe possibility was exactly what they needed.

"I'd like that," she said softly.

With his eyes locked on hers, Alex lifted her hand to his lips and pressed a gentle kiss to her knuckles.

"That makes me very happy," he said simply.

The gesture was so unexpectedly tender that Juno felt herself blushing. The Alex she remembered had been passionate but sometimes careless. He'd grown up, just as she had, and like her, his passions had been tempered by pain. Instead of hardening him, though, this man before her was more deliberate, more thoughtful.

They sat side by side, shoulder to shoulder, just holding hands, and as the conversation shifted to lighter topics, Juno found herself relaxing completely for the first time in days. The weight of her father's unexpected return, the shock of discovering Alex had a daughter—all of it seemed manageable here, with the lake stretching out before them and the easy rhythm of their conversation.

Finally, sensing Alex's growing discomfort, Juno suggested they move to the chairs so he could prop his foot up again. She stood and offered him a hand up.

When he was on his feet, he didn't let go of her hand, but slowly, gently drew her closer, his intention clear in his eyes.

Juno met him halfway. The kiss was gentle at first, almost tentative, a question more than a demand. But when she moved her hand up to his shoulder, he deepened the kiss, one hand sliding up her arm to cup his fingers around the back of her neck.

It felt both familiar and entirely new—the same electricity she remembered from their teenage years, but tempered now by maturity and shared understanding. When they finally broke apart, Juno was slightly breathless.

"I've been wanting to do that for a very, very long time," Alex admitted, his voice husky. "As in, for years now," he added.

"I've been wanting you to," Juno confessed, her hand still resting on his shoulder. "For years now."

They stayed on the dock until the sky darkened and the stars filled the canopy above them. Finally, Alex reluctantly suggested they head back up to the house. "I promised Lena I'd tuck her in."

"Of course," Juno agreed. "I should get home anyway. I've got an early morning tomorrow."

They packed up the remains of their picnic and walked hand in hand back to the house. In the kitchen, Roxanne met them with news that Lena was already bathed and in her pajamas, that Dwight was reading a *Hardy Boys* book to her. "She's quite enamored with the mystery-solving gang.

And can you imagine? That child has no idea who Scooby-Doo and the Gang are! I told her to ask you about them, Alex."

"We'll have to watch *Scooby Doo and the Loch Ness Monster,*" Alex said with a nod. "One of my favorites."

"I think you made me watch that back in the day," Juno exclaimed, a sudden flashback of caber tosses, an old Highland castle, and a red-eyed Loch Ness monster being commandeered by two big Scottish lads. "You'll have to let me watch it with you for old times' sake."

"It's a date," he declared, holding up his hand for a high-five.

Alex headed down the hall to say goodnight to Lena, leaving Juno alone with his mother, who was washing the last of the evening's dishes. As pleasant as Roxanne had been that evening, there was an undercurrent of awkwardness between them, a reservation on Mrs. Frampton's part. She'd felt it as a teenager, but had chalked it up to all of her many insecurities. So to sense it now was unsettling to her. She was no longer that scared, lonely kid in desperate need of a place to belong.

She *did* belong here in Autumn Lake, just as much as the next guy.

But did she belong with Alex? Could she ever really feel like part of the Frampton family? Or would his mother always hold her at a distance?

"I haven't seen Alex this happy in a long time," the older woman observed quietly.

Juno didn't quite know how to respond. She offered, "Lena brings out the best in him."

"You both do," Mrs. Frampton said simply. Before Juno could process this, she added, "He was heart-broken when you left, Juno. And then when Jason... when Jason died... well, I think it was just a lot of loss for him to process on his own."

The words felt censorious, like Mrs. Frampton was somehow accusing Juno for abandoning him. "I—I wish I'd been here for him," she managed to say. "If I'd known, I would have been."

"You couldn't have known, could you?" the older woman replied, and Juno was bemused to hear a note of self-recrimination in her tone. "We knew, though. We knew, and we weren't exactly there for him, either. Granted, we were a little lost ourselves for a while. For a lot more than a while, to tell the truth." She dried her hands on a dishtowel and hung it on the oven door, spending an inordinate amount of time straightening it before turning back to Juno. "I don't think he ever really got over you, no matter how hard he tried."

The frank admission left Juno momentarily speechless. What should she say? *I never got over him either? He's the love of my life? He's the reason I chose to make Autumn Lake home?* But those were all things she should say to Alex first. He deserved to hear them first.

When she couldn't come up with a response, Mrs. Frampton continued. "I'm glad to see you two finding your way back to each other. It does my heart good."

"I... we're taking things slowly," she finally managed.

Alex's mother nodded approvingly. "Slow isn't a bad thing. It gives you time to build something that lasts."

Alex returned then, saving Juno from having to formulate a response. "She wants to say goodnight to you too, Juno," he said.

Touched, and relieved for a reprieve from the uncomfortable conversation with Mrs. Frampton, Juno headed down the hallway to Jason's room. Lena sat cross-legged on the bed, surrounded by the stuffed animals Alex had picked up from his apartment, and with Ralphy curled beside her. She held a framed photo in her hands. Her face lit up when she saw Juno.

"Look at the baby pictures of Daddy and Uncle Jason," she announced, holding up the picture. "They are cuties."

"They sure are," Juno said, sitting carefully on the edge of the bed and studying the picture. Wow. The genes in the Frampton bloodline ran strong. There was no denying that Lena was one of them.

"Grandma says you've known Daddy since you were young like me."

"Well, we met in high school," Juno corrected gently.

Lena considered this. "That's still a really long time." She looked up at Juno earnestly. "Are you going to get married to him?"

Juno bit back a knee-jerk 'No!' response and smiled, unexpectedly moved by the child's question. "We're friends, Lena, which is a really good place to start." She leaned closer and whispered, "Can you keep a secret?"

"I'm very good at keeping secrets," Lena declared. Wasn't that the truth, Juno thought. The child had kept her very existence a secret from the world of Autumn Lake.

"Well," she continued softly, as if relaying a very important message. "Sometimes friends start dating, and sometimes people who are dating end up getting married. In fact, I personally think that's the best way a marriage should happen."

"So you guys are friends. Are you going to date? And then get married?" Lena asked, her tone careful.

Juno studied her, realizing there was more to this question than she'd first assumed. "Well," she began slowly, treading carefully with her words. "Now that Alex has you in his life, I think he'd have to ask you if you were okay with it first."

Lena looked up at her, eyes wide. "Ask me?"

"Of course. If Alex gets married, that person would be marrying you, too, wouldn't she? So you'd better be okay with her!" Juno smoothed a curl, so like her daddy's, away from her face. "You'd better be more than okay with her, in fact. You should probably love her as much as your daddy does, you hear?"

"My mommy never asks me if I like her boyfriends."

Juno fought back the urge to say something cutting about the woman. Instead, she just reached over and hugged Lena. "Well, I know your daddy, and he will always want to know how you feel, no matter what."

"You smell good," Lena said after a few moments of letting herself be held close. "Like coffee and milkshakes."

Juno laughed. "That's about the nicest thing anyone has said to me all day."

Lena yawned widely, then settled back against the pillows. "Goodnight, Juno." Then she wrapped one arm tightly around a large plush ladybug and kissed the top of its head. "G'night, Lena-bug."

Juno heard a sound behind her and turned to see Alex in the doorway, his expression soft and adoring.

"I sent her that ladybug for her birthday," Alex explained as Juno joined him in the hall. "She named it after the name I call her and she told me last night that she always kisses it goodnight and pretends it's me kissing her goodnight."

"Good grief, Alex," Juno said, pressing her palms to her cheeks. "How can you bear it?"

"Right?" he acknowledged. "I don't know how kids can do the whole unconditional love thing. She should loathe me, resent me, or think I'm beneath her. It's really humbling."

They made some small talk in the truck on the way back to Juno's place, but mostly, they spent the fifteen-minute drive in companionable silence, fingers interlaced on the console. The radio played 80's arena rock on a station that, if Juno remembered correctly, had been Alex's favorite even back in high school. "I can't believe you still listen to this stuff."

"It's all part of my arrested development," he declared, shooting her a cocky grin. "And it's inarguably the best music that ever was." He lifted a fist and mock-shouted, "Long live the eighties!"

Juno wouldn't let him come up to her second-floor apartment, but he insisted on getting out of the truck and walking her to the stairs. "You go back to your mom's and get that foot up, you hear?" she ordered, resting a hand on his chest as he stepped in enough to make her feel a little crowded.

"I will."

She didn't back up. "And thank you for the lovely picnic. I had a wonderful time."

"You're welcome." Alex took a step closer, resting his injured leg on the bottom step, then shifting so he could lean against the rail. In what Juno recognized as a well-practiced move, he drew her closer, their joined hands twisted loosely behind her back, his other arm wrapping around her waist.

"Wow," she said drolly. "Smooth move, Don Juan Frampton."

"It worked, though, didn't it?" His voice came out husky, almost gravelly as he closed the space between them.

This time when he kissed her, there was no hesitation. Juno pressed into him, her arms sliding around his neck as his circled her waist. When they finally broke apart, she rested her forehead against his, eyes closed, savoring the moment.

"I should go," Alex murmured, though he made no move to leave.

Reality intruded, but gently. Juno nodded, stepping back reluctantly. "Let me know how it goes with the attorney, will you?"

"I will." He kissed her once more, softly. "Goodnight, Juno."

"Goodnight, Alex."

As Juno watched him walk back to his truck, she felt a peculiar certainty settle over her. Whatever challenges lay ahead—her father's return, Alex's custody battle, their own complicated history—they would face them together. The thought should have terrified her, but instead, it felt right.

25
Alex

ALEX SHIFTED UNCOMFORTABLY IN the booth at Juno's Coffee Bar, his ankle throbbing. He had it elevated on the bench across from him next to Lena, but he'd forgotten to take his pain medication before his appointment with the attorney, and now he was paying for it.

The meeting had gone far better than he could have hoped for—Howard Grantham had assured him that it had been a long time since the days when the courts automatically favored mothers when custody was determined. Based on what Alex had told him, and on what he'd gathered from a conversation with Lena, Alex had good cause to be concerned over the welfare of his daughter. In fact, Howard had filed an emergency motion to prevent Melissa from taking Lena out of the country, and said he thought they might be able to arrange for a preliminary hearing as early as this week.

Alex had called his father from The Beast, and fighting back tears of relief, had thanked him for making the calls that had connected Alex to the right people.

"You're not doing this alone, son. That child is ours, too, and we want what's best for her just as much as you do," his father had said.

Alex had called Melissa twice already today, hoping to discuss things like adults, but she hadn't picked up, and even his text updates about Lena had been met with brief acknowledgments, nothing more.

Lena was going to spend the afternoon with her grandmother so that Alex could head over to the North Shore and talk to Melissa, if she'd agree, but when he texted again to ask if he could come, her response was: *Busy. You wanted time with her. Hope you're having a good time. If you can't handle the responsibility, it's your problem.*

Alex frowned, typing back: Just making sure you're all right. Can I come by so we can talk this afternoon?

Like I said, BUSY. Then she posted a whole string of wine glass emojis. Great. He wasn't sure whether to be disgusted or concerned.

"Is that Mommy?" Lena asked from across the table, looking up from her chocolate milkshake, a foamy mustache on her upper lip.

"Yeah," he said, tucking his phone away so she wouldn't see the emojis. "She's just checking in. She's glad you're having a good time." The half-truth tasted bitter, and he hoped Lena wouldn't ask to speak to her mother; he had no idea what condition Melissa was in, and besides, she still wasn't answering his calls. "How's that milkshake?"

"Amazing," Lena declared, jabbing her straw up and down in the blended drink. "Juno makes the best shakes."

"She sure does." Alex glanced toward the counter where Juno was serving a customer, her movements efficient and graceful. His gaze shifted to the man clearing tables nearby—Leonard Thomas.

They'd come for lunch, beating the rush by only minutes, and Juno hadn't had time to introduce them to her father properly. "But you two already know each other. Go say hi to him, Alex. He'd probably appreciate seeing a familiar face."

Alex, however, had felt a growing sense of unease as he approached the man who was chatting with a customer while wiping down a table close by. When the man straightened and turned to see Alex and Lena coming toward him, Alex hadn't missed the way his eyes had gone cold, steely, dark. For a moment, Alex had felt a strong surge of protectiveness wash over him and he'd had the impulse to shove Lena behind him to keep her out of Leonard's line of sight.

But then the man had nodded in acknowledgement. "Alex. My daughter said you still called Autumn Lake home." His handshake had been firm, his smile wide, but his gaze had been almost wary, almost calculating, when he looked at Alex. There was something about him that set Alex's teeth on edge, a feeling he remembered even back when they'd met the first time.

Back in high school, the first time Alex had picked Juno up from her family's apartment, Leonard had gripped Alex's hand hard, like a challenge, and had made a show of sizing him up. "You dating my daughter, hm?" he'd asked, his chin up, eyes narrowed.

"With your blessing, sir," Alex had returned politely. He'd known even then how to use his good looks and charm to make points with the adults in his life. Leonard, however, hadn't seemed affected in the least by Alex's straight back and fine manners.

"And if I don't give my blessing? You going to break her heart?" Leonard had leaned forward, a threatening glint in his eyes.

"Dad, please," Juno had said, moving to stand closer to her father, like she was prepared to get between them if she needed to.

For several tense moments, Leonard had just stood there squeezing Alex's hand and staring him down, but then he'd finally let go and waved the two of them off. "Get on outta here, boy. And take her with you. I'm a busy man."

"Daddy, why are you looking at Juno's daddy like that?" Lena whispered, following his gaze.

Alex stiffened, caught. "I was just thinking about the first time I met him," he said honestly. "It was a long time ago, and I was wondering if he remembered it, too." Alex watched as Leonard collected dishes from a recently vacated table, his movements quick and efficient. The customers at the next table smiled up at him, and Leonard responded with easy charm, making them laugh with some comment Alex couldn't hear.

"Is he nice?" she asked around a spoonful of whipped cream.

After debating on how to answer, he said, "He seems nice, doesn't he?" But Alex wasn't convinced. There was something performative about Leonard's affability, like he was playing a role.

The bell above the door chimed, and a group of women entered, their laughter preceding them. The cavalry had arrived in the form of Penny Anderson, Liz Needham and her cousin, Candy, Addison Stewart, and Claire Maitland. The Garden Variety Lovers Club, they called themselves, and Alex found himself grinning, his tension easing considerably as the women settled in around a table that had been reserved for them. The group of friends had lunch together at Juno's at least once a week, and now that Addison had left her airport job and was converting the storefront beneath her apartment into a plant and flower shop, all of them worked locally, making it easier for them all to attend.

Alex was glad for these women in Juno's life. Knowing now what he did about her past, he had a feeling that before she'd returned to Autumn Lake, she'd never really known how important friends were. Alex knew he wouldn't have made it through the worst of his times without Ward and guys at J&J keeping him on the right track.

Claire spotted them and hopped up from her seat to come over to their booth. "Well, hello, Lena. Fancy meeting you here," she declared, her gaze darting back and forth between Alex and his daughter. "Do you know this guy?" she asked the child, pointing at Alex.

Lena giggled. "He's my daddy. I'm allowed to tell people now."

Claire's smile faltered for a moment, and Alex grimaced. He assumed Juno would explain the situation to her friends, but he hoped he could get Lena to understand that maybe she didn't need add that last bit on.

"Your daddy, huh?" By now, the rest of the Garden Variety Lovers Club ladies had gathered around and were all grinning like cats in their cream. "Did you know your daddy is a hero?"

"What?" Lena exclaimed, her shocked gaze landing on Alex. "You're a super hero? You never told me that. What can you do?"

Claire reached over and patted Alex's shoulder gently. "He jumped in front of a car to save two precious people from getting run over."

Is that why you broke your foot?" Lena asked, reaching beside her to pat his foot. Then she held up her hand and screwed up her face. "Ew. I just touched your stinky toes. Now my hand is contaminated. Blech." She made a gagging sound that garnered laughter from the group, and Penny pulled a packet of wipes from her purse.

"I always carry wipes with me," she explained. "My mom is kind of a messy eater, and she really doesn't like it when stuff gets on her hands."

"You mommy is messy?" Lena asked, understandably confused by the notion. She let Penny use the wipe on her hands and listened carefully as Penny explained about Jane Anderson's early onset dementia. To Alex's surprise, Lena took it all in stride.

"So she's like my age but in an old lady body?"

"Pretty much," responded Penny, reminding Alex that she'd been an elementary school teacher and was probably well-accustomed to the way kids processed information. "She might even be a little younger than you, so maybe when you meet her, you can be like a big sister to her."

Lena looked delighted at the prospect. "I always wanted a sister."

Alex watched with amusement as his daughter charmed them all, answering their questions with growing confidence. "The apple doesn't fall far from the tree, does it," Claire commented to him in a quiet voice. "She looks just like you; I can't believe I didn't see it the other night."

"Everyone says I look like my daddy," Lena interjected, having overheard. "And like Uncle Jason."

For a moment, the group stilled, but then Alex reached over, scooped a dollop of whipped cream on his finger, and stuck it on her nose.

"You sure do, Lena-bug. The spitting image of him."

"Ew. Spitting is rude."

"You should come sit at our table," Penny declared, reaching a hand to help Lena out of the booth.

"And apparently, we won't take no for an answer," Liz said in her usual dry tone.

Alex decided to take advantage of the impromptu babysitters. "Lena, I'm going to go talk to Juno for a minute, then use the bathroom. Are you okay to stay with these ladies? I promise they won't hurt you."

"You're funny, Daddy. They're Juno's friends; they won't hurt me."

Juno wasn't at the counter, so he ducked into the restroom first, hoping he could catch her in the back hall and maybe sneak in a kiss or two. When he came out again, he could see over the swinging doors that she was still busy in the kitchen. It was the lunch hour, after all, and he'd be lucky to get her alone for even a minute. She usually made a point to join her friends for a break, so if he was at the table with the Garden Variety Lovers Club, he at least get to share her with them.

As he came out of the back hall, his gaze wandered around Juno's café. Echoes of what the place had once been still lingered: on the wall hung the hand-painted sign of the original coffee shop where Juno had first learned her barista skills, two of the bare brick walls had been preserved, along with the chalkboard closet door where folks could write quotes or draw. She'd even preserved the old glass pastry display cabinet, although she'd had to replace a pane of glass and one of the sliding door tracks. It was a warm and welcoming mix of old and new, of vintage and modern, and Alex felt a deep sense of accomplishment on her behalf.

Until his gaze drifted back to Leonard Thomas.

The man was clearing a table near the window, his back to the room. A couple had just left, leaving cash tucked under a saucer. As Leonard gathered the dishes, his hand moved so swiftly Alex almost missed it. The stack of bills disappeared into his front pants pocket, not into the pocket of the apron he wore.

Alex stiffened, his eyes narrowing. Had he really seen what he thought he'd seen?

He watched more carefully as Leonard moved to another table. The same thing happened again. It was a subtle movement, and if Alex hadn't already been suspicious of the guy, he probably wouldn't even have noticed the cash vanishing.

"Alex?" Penny's voice calling him from the large table nearby broke through his concentration. "You okay?"

"Yeah, fine," he said, forcing his attention back to them as he joined the group. He flashed her a sheepish grin. "Just hoping to waylay Juno in the hallway, but no such luck."

Penny's eyes widened. "So, it's true? You two are—" She waved a finger between him and the counter at the front of the shop.

"You've kissed and made up?" Claire suggested, a knowing look in her eyes. Obviously, Juno had already filled at least one of them in.

Alex chuckled. "I'd say it was the other way around. We made up and then kissed." His cheeks warmed but he didn't care. He wanted the whole world to know that one, the most beautiful, most amazing eight-year-old in the world was his daughter, and two, the most beautiful, most amazing woman in the world was his girlfriend again.

"I see you've met the welcoming committee, Lena," Juno said, approaching the table with a tray of drinks and setting one down in front of each of her friends.

"And she's been sucked into our vortex," Claire said, making what was apparently supposed to be a sucking motion with her hands that had everyone at the table laughing.

"Your friends are cool," Lena said from where she sat between Penny and Candy.

"The nicest," Juno agreed. She set a fresh coffee in front of Alex. "How did your meeting go this morning? Is it okay to ask here?"

She tipped her head toward Lena who was once again distracted by something Claire had said to her.

Alex nodded, but kept his voice low. "Better than expected. We filed an emergency motion to prevent Melissa from taking Lena out of the country. There might be a hearing as early as this week."

Relief washed over Juno's face. "That's great news."

"It's just the first step," Alex cautioned, "but yeah, it feels good to be doing something."

"What are you two lovebirds whispering about?" Penny asked, and Lena giggled beside her. "That's what you are, according to this one."

Juno rolled her eyes, then circled the table to poke Lena in the ribs. "Tweet tweet," she said, then to the rest of them, "It's a busy day, guys. I'll have to come back when I bring your orders." She glanced toward the counter where a line was forming.

Alex stood quickly and circled the table to walk with her. He wasn't sure how he'd broach the subject, but he wanted her to be aware of what he'd seen Leonard doing. Before she could duck behind the counter, he caught her arm gently. "I know it's not a great time, but can I talk to you for a minute? In private?"

Concern flickered across her face. "Is something wrong?"

"Not exactly. Just... something I noticed." He nodded discreetly toward Leonard, who was now wiping down tables on the other side of the room.

"Can it wait until tonight?" Juno asked, glancing at the growing line at the register. They were having supper together at Alex's apartment.

"Of course." He released her arm. "Go do your thing. Lena and I have to get going. Thanks for lunch and for the shakes, if we don't see you before we go. You've got a new fan."

As Juno returned to the counter, Alex's gaze once again followed Leonard's movements. The man was good—smooth and practiced in a way that suggested this wasn't his first time skimming tips. Most people wouldn't notice, distracted by conversations or their phones. But Alex was now watching for it, and even though he didn't catch the man at it now, he knew what he'd seen.

"Daddy, I need to go potty. Miss Penny is going to take me, is that okay?" Lena asked, dragging Penny along in her wake.

Alex thanked Penny, then turned back to Leonard. Now would be a perfect opportunity to let the guy know he wasn't fooling anyone. They were in a crowded room so no one would be suspicious, and Leonard couldn't react inappropriately, or, if what Juno had said was true, the man would be fired on the spot. He wasn't going to wait for Juno—he was going to confront her father directly.

He stood, grimacing at the twinge in his ankle, and made his way toward Leonard, who was now refilling napkin holders at the empty tables.

"Mr. Thomas," he said quietly, positioning himself so his back was to the room, blocking the view of their conversation. "Could I have a word?"

Leonard looked up, his expression neutral, his voice smooth. "Of course, young man. Something wrong?"

"Maybe," Alex said, keeping his voice low. He'd decided to simply be direct, the way he thought Juno would be if she were in this situation. "It's about what I just saw. You pocketing tip money from those tables."

For a split second, something cold and calculating flashed in Leonard's eyes before he smoothed it over with a look of confusion. "Excuse me?"

"I saw you pocket bills from at least two tables," Alex said firmly.

Leonard's confusion morphed into understanding, then something like amusement. "Ah, I see the issue." He reached into his pocket and pulled out a several ones and a few fives, even more than what Alex had seen go in there. "My apron pockets are full to overflowing and I didn't want any of this falling out of them as I worked." While Alex watched, Leonard made a show of shuffling things from one pocket to another—napkins, receipts, straw wrappers—then depositing the cash into the now empty pocket. If Alex was guessing, he'd say that Leonard had purposely overfilled his apron so that he could use this very excuse if someone saw what he was doing.

The explanation was reasonable enough, Alex supposed, but something in Leonard's tone—that practiced smoothness—didn't sit right with him.

"So, you'll be putting those in the tip jar now?" Alex pressed.

"Of course." Leonard smiled, a tight expression that didn't reach his eyes. "And no hard feelings about your suspicions. I applaud you for your concern about my daughter's business."

There was a warning in the words, subtle but unmistakable. Alex watched as Leonard sauntered over to the tip jar on the counter and once again made a show of dropping in the bills he withdrew from his pocket.

Alex couldn't help wondering how many tips hadn't made it in the jar that morning. And on his first day working, too.

"Everything okay?" Juno appeared at his elbow, her expression concerned.

Alex hesitated. Should he tell her what he'd seen? Would she believe him over her father, especially when Leonard had such a plausible explanation? The last thing he wanted was to create tension between them just as they were finding their way back to each other.

"Yeah," he said finally. "Just chatting with your dad for old time's sake."

Leonard clapped Alex on the shoulder, his fingers digging into his shoulder blade where Juno couldn't see. "You've got yourself a fine young man here, Juniper."

Juno's gaze moved between them, clearly sensing there was more to the story, but the rush of customers demanded her attention. She nodded slowly. "Yes, Alex is great. I'm glad you two are..." Her voice trailed off and she waved a finger back and forth. "Reconnecting," she finally said. "I'll see you and Lena this evening, Alex." Juno squeezed his arm, her touch lingering. "Say hi to your folks for me."

As Alex collected Lena and headed for the door, he felt Leonard's eyes on him. He turned, meeting the older man's gaze directly. Leonard offered a slight nod, his expression unreadable, before returning to his work.

Outside in the truck, Alex sat for a moment, replaying the encounter in his mind. Leonard's explanation was plausible, but his instincts told him the man was lying, and it twisted Alex's insides to think of what it would do to Juno if his suspicions were true.

"Daddy, can we come back tomorrow?" Lena asked from the backseat.

"We'll see, Lena-bug," Alex said, starting the engine. "Depends on what the day brings." Who knew? Maybe Melissa would get tired of pouting and be willing to talk. Or maybe J&J would need him to come in and give some input on the new jobsite, a kitchen remodel just west of Autumn Lake in a new housing development. It always confounded Alex when folks bought these cookie cutter homes at top dollar, only to remodel everything but the bones, but to each his own. It kept guys like him busy, that was for sure.

As he pulled away from the curb, his thoughts were in turmoil. He hadn't told Juno what he'd seen because he didn't want to upset her without more concrete evidence. But the protective instinct for Lena that had surged through him was now extending to Juno as well.

Leonard Thomas was up to something, Alex was certain. And he was determined to find out what before Juno got hurt.

26
Juno

THE SMELL OF FRESH paint mingled with the scent of the cheeseburger delivery Alex had insisted on ordering after they'd spent three hours painting the walls of what used to be his tiny spare room. They'd had to move out his guitar and monitor, his desk and computer, but the room hadn't been furnished otherwise, so it had been a no-brainer to give the space to Lena.

Juno sat cross-legged on the drop cloth they'd spread across the floor, watching as Alex held Lena up to place glow-in-the-dark stars on the newly painted lavender ceiling.

"Move that way a little," Lena directed, stretching her arm as far as it would go. "That's where the Big Dipper goes."

"You're the expert," Alex replied, adjusting his stance to accommodate her reach. He now only wore his walking boot on the job or when he had to be on his feet for long periods of time, but for around the house, he'd switched to a smaller gel brace. It gave him more mobility, but Juno noticed he how much he still favored that ankle.

"You should sit down," she called over to him. "I can take a turn."

Alex shook his head. "We're on a roll here, aren't we, Lena-bug? Besides, I'm the tallest."

"The tallest." Lena patted his head. "This one goes here." She pressed a star to the ceiling with great concentration, then looked down at Juno. "Do you think it'll look like real stars in the dark?"

"Even better," Juno replied, gathering empty takeout containers into a paper bag. "Because you'll know exactly where to find each constellation."

Lena beamed at her, and Juno felt that now-familiar tug of emotion in her chest. It had been just over two weeks since she'd discovered Alex had a daughter, and already she couldn't imagine her life without Lena in it.

Alex carefully lowered Lena to the ground. The girl immediately darted to the light switch. "Can we turn it off and see?"

"Let's give the stars a few more minutes to set," Juno suggested, knowing they needed longer light exposure if they were going to glow, especially since the room wouldn't be very dark with the sun setting so late. "Why don't we take a break and figure out where your books will go?"

"I have a lot of books now," Lena said with undisguised delight. "Grandma took me to the bookstore, and Claire helped me pick out lots of Nancy Drew books and Hardy Boys books and Cherry Ames books and Trixie Bel... Bel—" She glanced over at the stacks of books on the floor against the wall and pointed at a pile four vintage hardcovers. "Trixie Belden!" she exclaimed. "And Daddy built my shelves all by himself."

"Don't forget about the Scooby Doo books," Alex said with an exaggerated frown. "Those are the most important books, which is why we should put them on the top shelf."

"I think you want them on the top shelf so that *you* can reach them easier," Juno teased.

"Haha," Alex shot back. "I walked right into that one, didn't I?"

"Well, the shelves are beautiful," Juno said, meaning it. The white floating shelves looked professionally done, arranged in a staggered pattern up one wall.

Alex lowered himself to the ground beside Juno and took her hand. She still marveled at how much his touch thrilled her, and she brought his hand up to rub his knuckles against her cheek. He gave her that crooked smile of his, and Juno couldn't help but lean in a little. Even she could see just how besotted he was becoming with her.

"Daddy, you're supposed to be helping me with my books, not making googly eyes at Juno," Lena called from where she was unpacking a box of hardcovers.

Alex laughed, the sound warming Juno from the inside out. "Busted," he murmured, but didn't move away. Instead, he leaned closer and kissed her tenderly on the lips.

"I saw that, too," Lena added with a snort.

"You see everything, don't you, squirt?" Alex released Juno's hand to crawl over to his daughter. "Let's get these books organized, then. How do you want them? By size? Color? Author?"

As they debated the merits of various organizational systems, Juno checked her phone. Three texts from her father, all sent while she'd been painting.

Running low on TP in the supply closet.

Need me to come in early to help unpack the coffee shipment tomorrow?

Found a leak under the sink in the men's bathroom. Fixed it with supplies from the maintenance closet. Hope that's OK.

Juno texted back a quick thanks, but told him not to come in early. She liked the routine of unpacking her coffee shipments, and she preferred to manage her stock personally. She added that she'd see him in the morning, then said goodnight, hoping he'd get the hint and not respond.

Leonard had been working at the coffee shop for nearly two weeks now, and despite her initial reservations, he'd proven himself surprisingly reliable. He showed up early, stayed late when needed, and had started taking initiative with minor repairs around the place. Customers liked him—especially the female tourists who frequented the shop mid-morning. He had a knack for making them giggle.

It was... unsettling, how easily he'd slipped into her life, but that didn't mean she was ready to act like the past hadn't happened. She didn't want to be his only friend in town, and it niggled at her that he tried to engage with her almost every night after work. It felt almost cloying, making him seem needy, and she didn't care for this side of him.

"Earth to Juno," Alex called, breaking into her thoughts.

She put her phone away, forcing a smile. "Sorry. Just checking in with the shop."

"Everything okay?" His eyes narrowed slightly, and she knew he was really asking about Leonard.

"Fine," she said, perhaps a touch too quickly. "Dad fixed a leak in the men's room before he went home this evening."

"I thought he was only working mornings," Alex noted, his tone conversational, but he didn't fool her. She saw the tension in his shoulders.

Alex had crossed paths with Leonard several times over the last two weeks, and while he'd been unfailingly polite, there was a guardedness to his interactions with her father that Juno couldn't ignore. She understood his concern—of course she did—but his persistent watchful regard was beginning to grate on her.

"He's always willing to work extra hours if I have stuff for him to do," she said, keeping her voice light. "He's good with his hands. Always was, even when..."

She trailed off, not wanting to complete the thought in front of Lena, who was arranging books by color to create a rainbow effect on the bottom shelf.

Alex nodded, a muscle working in his jaw. "Well, that's good. Saved you calling a plumber."

The conversation stalled, that invisible barrier rising between them again. Lately, it seemed to happen whenever Leonard came up, which was increasingly often since he'd become a fixture at the coffee shop.

Lena, oblivious to the tension, piped up from her spot on the floor. "Can we check the stars now? Pretty please?"

Grateful for the interruption, Juno nodded. "I think they should be set. Want to do the honors?" She went to the window and drew the drapes, blocking out as much of the setting sunlight as possible, then gestured toward the light switch.

Lena's face was alight with anticipation. "Ready? Three, two, one..." She flipped the switch, plunging the room into shadows.

For a moment, there was silence. Then Lena gasped. "It's perfect! My very own sky!"

As Juno's eyes adjusted, she made out the soft, luminous glow of the stars scattered across the ceiling. Alex had moved to stand beside his daughter, his arm draped around her shoulders as they both gazed up.

"What do you think, Lena-bug?" His voice was soft with wonder.

"I think it's the best room in the whole wide world," Lena whispered back. "I wish Mommy could see it."

Juno met Alex's gaze and tried to give him a silent boost of encouragement.

"I'm sure she'll come see it soon," he told her, ruffling her hair.

Melissa had been understandably livid when she'd learned that her plans to take Lena out of the country had been stalled. She'd not only answered Alex's calls after that, but for a few days, she'd called him incessantly, relentlessly begging him, threatening him, bargaining with him to work with her.

But Alex had stayed firm, partly because by 'working with her,' she'd meant letting her have her way, but also, as he'd expressed to Juno, the more time he spent with Lena, the more he realized how much they needed each other. "I know this sounds selfish, but I'm a much better man when I have someone else to think about other than myself."

Juno had chuckled softly. "Aren't we all?"

And so, two weeks had gone by, and Lena was still staying in Alex's care, while Melissa, supposedly, was frantically rearranging her life and trying to find an attorney who would see things her way. Apparently, she hadn't taken Alex seriously when he'd said he was getting a lawyer, and now she was scrambling.

Over the last week, she'd started video chatting with Lena in the evenings, and sometimes Juno thought it might be a way for Melissa to monopolize Lena's time, now that Alex was back at work fulltime, but Alex didn't mind. He wanted peace between the three of them, and if that meant sharing Lena's attention with Melissa, he was good with it. "She's here with me, and that's what counts," he'd said when Juno had tentatively broached the subject.

Juno marveled at the person she was getting to know, the grown up Alex, a man with a purpose, with goals for his future.

Lena broke away from her father and turned to Juno. "I'm glad you're here," she said, and flung her arms around Juno's waist. The unexpected embrace nearly knocked her off balance, but she recovered quickly, wrapping her arms around the girl and breathing in the scent of paint and the strawberry shampoo they'd picked out together at the store.

Over Lena's head, Juno's eyes met Alex's in the dimness. Something passed between them in that moment—an acknowledgment of what they were building here, the three of them. Something like a family.

The thought should have terrified her. Instead, it filled her with warmth.

Later, after they'd tucked Lena into bed in Alex's room (she'd have to wait another night to sleep in her new room, once the paint smell had dissipated), Juno and Alex slipped outside to sit on his tiny balcony. The night air was warm, humming with the sounds of summer insects. Alex had poured them each a glass of lemonade, and Juno savored the tart sweetness on her tongue.

"How are you doing?" Juno asked softly, watching as Alex tilted his face up to catch the evening breeze.

"I'm okay," he said, not looking at her. "It's Lena I worry about. Though I think having my parents around has helped a lot." Lena spent the days with her grandmother while Alex was at work.

Juno smiled. "Roxanne is a natural grandmother. The way she looks at Lena..."

Alex nodded. "I know." He reached over and took her hand. "Thank you for being part of this. I know it's been a lot, all at once."

"I wouldn't be anywhere else," she replied honestly.

Alex's thumb traced circles on her palm, sending tiny shivers up her arm. "And how are things at the shop? Really?"

Juno took a long sip of her lemonade before answering. "Good. Busy. I've got my dad coming in for a couple of hours in the afternoons now, and he's actually been a big help with the afternoon rush. And the bussing and cleaning. Trevor says it's the cleanest the shop's ever been."

Alex nodded, his expression carefully neutral. "That's great."

"But?" she prompted, unable to keep the edge from her voice.

"No but," he said quickly. Too quickly.

"Alex." She started to pull her hand from his, but he held on, not letting her withdraw. "Just say what you're thinking."

He sighed, rubbing his other hand across his stubbled jaw. "I just want to make sure you're being careful, that's all. I'm glad things seem to be working out with Leonard. I really am."

"I am being careful," Juno countered. "People change, though, you know. He's been clean and sober for two years, now."

"According to him."

"Yes, according to him," she said, heat rising in her cheeks. She tugged her hand free of his and scooted to the edge of her chair, but she resisted the urge to get up and start pacing. "But also according to the way he carries himself, the steadiness of his hands, his clear eyes. I know what to look for, Alex. I grew up with an addict, remember? With that particular addict. People change, and you, of all people, should understand that. Why do you deserve a second chance, but he doesn't?"

The moment the words left her mouth, she regretted them. Alex nodded in agreement, but his injured expression told her that her words had hit home. "I'm not Leonard," he finally said. "And I'm asking for your friendship and affection, not for you to provide for my welfare."

"I'm sorry," she said immediately. "That was unfair of me."

Alex touched her elbow, and said, "Don't be sorry. Be safe."

Juno's cheeks warmed at the familiar words. "I know. I just... I need you to trust my judgment on this. I'm not being naive."

"I do trust your judgment," Alex said. "It's him I don't trust."

Juno leaned back in her chair, trying to quell the defensiveness rising in her chest. She knew Alex's concerns were valid. Even Claire had made a point twice now to ask gently if Juno was sure Leonard wasn't working some angle. Claire hadn't met her father back in high school, but Juno had told her everything after returning to Autumn Lake, and Claire, too, was worried about Leonard's motives for Juno's sake.

"Has he asked you for money?" Claire had inquired, her expression wary. "Beyond his paycheck, I mean?"

"No," Juno had answered truthfully. "He hasn't asked for anything. I pay for his room at the Sleepy Time, but that was my idea." It wasn't the whole truth, though. She'd planned to pay only for the first ten days until he got his first paycheck from her and could foot the bill himself, but he'd told her he'd needed to stock up on a few necessities, and hadn't had enough to cover the room for another week.

Claire had looked unconvinced. "Just be careful, Juno. I know you want to believe he's changed, but..."

But what if he hasn't? The unspoken question lingered between her and Alex now, just as it had with Claire.

"Did you know," Juno said after a long pause, "that he's been attending AA meetings in Evansville? Three afternoons a week, after his shift."

"Is he? Why not attend the one that meets right here in town?" The skepticism in Alex's voice rubbed her the wrong way.

Juno had asked her father the same thing. "He said that group only meets once a week and he still feels like he needs to attend more often." At the time, it had made him sound honorable, acknowledging that he needed accountability like that.

"How's he getting there and back?"

It was a fair question; she'd told Alex her father didn't have a car. "He takes the bus," she said, wondering why she hadn't bothered checking the bus schedule to see if there actually were bus routes that ran at those times.

"Well, I'm glad he's taking the initiative." He still sounded doubtful, but she could tell he was trying to come to middle ground with her.

"You know, I'm trying to give him the benefit of the doubt, to not let the past dictate everything."

Alex reached for her hand again, and this time she let him take it. "I know you are. And I admire that about you, Juno. Your capacity for forgiveness is... it's extraordinary." His eyes searched hers. "I'm just afraid you'll get hurt."

And there it was—the truth beneath his concern. Not judgment, but protection. She felt the last of her irritation dissolve.

"I might," she admitted quietly. "But I'd rather risk that than miss the chance to have him in my life, if he really has changed. That may make me sound naïve, but I have to at least give him a chance, right? Can you try to understand?"

Alex nodded, bringing her hand to his lips and pressing a gentle kiss to her fingers. "I do. And I'll try harder to... to not be such a skeptic."

"Thank you." She leaned toward him, closing the distance between them. When their lips met, she sighed softly, the tenderness of his mouth mingling with the relief of the tension easing between them.

She was learning the different ways he kissed her—playful pecks when Lena was watching, soft brushes of his lips when they parted, and this: deep and languid, as if they had all the time in the world. His hand came up to cup her face, his thumb tracing the line of her cheekbone.

When they finally broke apart, she rested her forehead against his. "I should go," she murmured. "I'm opening tomorrow."

"You always open," he said with a resigned smile. "You know, you could train one of your staff to open so you could have a morning off," he suggested, his voice soft.

"But I don't want a morning off," she countered. "That's my quiet time. Just me and God getting ready to start the day."

"Is God a coffee lover, too?" Alex teased, standing and pulling her to her feet, too.

"God made coffee, so, of course, he loves it."

Later, as Juno drove home through the quiet streets of Autumn Lake, she found herself replaying the evening in her mind. The easy laughter, the way Lena had looked at them both with such open affection, the feel of Alex's arm around her as they checked on the sleeping Lena one more time before Juno left.

It was everything she'd ever wanted, the life she'd dreamed of here in this town she loved. And now it seemed within reach—a business of her own; a man who looked at her like she was precious; a child who was quickly claiming a piece of her heart.

The only discordant note was the wariness in Alex's eyes whenever Leonard's name came up. The same wariness she'd seen in Claire's expression, in her other friends' careful questions about how her father was adjusting.

She knew they were only concerned about her, that they cared about her, and like Alex, didn't want her to get hurt. She understood and appreciated their concerns; she really did.

But she wanted to focus on the good for once, and there was so much good right now. She wanted to stop looking over her shoulder, to stop waiting for the other shoe to fall. She didn't want to entertain the nagging questions that rose unbidden in the quiet moments.

Questions like why Leonard never talked about where he'd been all these years. Why he deflected whenever she asked about his plans for the future. Why sometimes she caught him staring at her with an expression she couldn't quite read.

As she climbed the stairs to her apartment, Juno admitted to herself that she was choosing to wear blinders. Deliberately looking the other way, not asking the hard questions, because she wasn't ready for the answers.

Because she wanted, just for a while, to believe that everything could be this perfect.

She deserved this happiness, didn't she? After everything she'd been through?

Inside her apartment, Juno's phone buzzed with a text from Alex: *Made it home safe?*

She smiled, typing back: *Just walked in. Thanks for the fun evening.*

His response came immediately: *Thanks for painting the stars in Lena's sky. And for hanging the moon in mine.*

Well, she hadn't painted the stars, but she wasn't going to argue semantics. Alex was being romantic, and she was going to let herself bask in it. She smiled, feeling that bloom of love swell inside her. *See you tomorrow?*

Count on it. Good night, June-bug.

The old nickname, once a source of pain, now felt like a gift. She touched the screen lightly, as if she could reach him through it.

For now, she would hold onto this joy. The questions could wait.

Even if, deep down, she knew they shouldn't.

27
Alex

ALEX PUSHED OPEN THE door to Juno's Coffee Bar, the familiar scents and sounds of the cafe welcoming him into the cool interior. From what he could tell, he'd timed his visit perfectly. Only a handful of tables were occupied, mostly by people working on laptops or reading.

His meeting with Howard Grantham had gone better than expected. The attorney's confidence about Alex's custody options had lifted a weight from his shoulders that he hadn't even realized he'd been carrying. For the first time since Melissa had told him about Lena, Alex felt like he had solid ground beneath his feet.

He scanned the coffee shop, relieved not to see Leonard among the staff. The man's presence always cast a shadow over his visits, making it difficult to relax completely. He couldn't shake the feeling that there was something off about Juno's father, something beneath the helpful, charming exterior.

Juno looked up from where she was restocking pastry platters in the display case, and her face brightened. "Hey, you," she called across the counter. "I wasn't expecting you this afternoon."

Alex made his way to his usual spot at the counter, sliding onto a stool and waiting for her to make her way down the counter toward him. "I had some good news I wanted to share."

"Good news is always welcome," Juno said, leaning forward on her elbows. "Does it have something to do with your meeting with your attorney this morning?"

"It does." He smiled at her perceptiveness. "He thinks we have a really strong case for joint custody, both legal and physical. Of course, Melissa will have to be amenable to coparenting with me, because any and all major decisions would need to be made and agreed upon together, for one.

He also thinks I have a good chance of being able to establish myself as Lena's primary residence since Melissa travels so much and doesn't own property other than a stake in the timeshare across the lake. Apparently, her history of moving around so much works in my favor, especially with all the stability I can offer Lena here."

"That's wonderful, Alex." Juno reached across the counter and squeezed his hand. "I'm so happy for you. For both of you."

"It's early days yet," he cautioned, but couldn't quell the optimism in his voice. "We'll have to see how Melissa responds, but Howard seems confident."

Juno glanced at the wall clock, then back at Alex. "I'm due for a break. You want your usual?"

"You know me too well," he admitted with a chuckle.

"Why don't you grab us a spot by the window while I make your shake? We'll have more privacy there."

Alex nodded and stood. "Mind if I use the restroom first?"

"You know where it is."

He made his way toward the back hallway, nodding to Trevor who was restocking the coffee bins. The restroom was small, but like everything in Juno's establishment, impeccably clean. Alex washed his hands, splashed some water on his face, and took a moment to collect his thoughts. He wanted to share everything Howard had told him with Juno, get her perspective on the steps ahead.

As he exited the restroom, he heard a commotion near the front of the shop. Leonard—when had he arrived?—was apologizing profusely to a woman seated at a table near the door. She was middle-aged with a helmet of silver hair, wearing a floral blouse and white pants.

"I'm so terribly sorry, ma'am," Leonard was saying, bending to retrieve a large leather tote bag from the floor. "I didn't see it there."

"It's entirely my fault," the woman replied, flustered. "I shouldn't have left it where someone could trip."

Leonard handed her the bag with a gallant bow. "No harm done."

But as the bag changed hands, Alex saw Leonard's fingers dip inside the open top, emerging with something small that disappeared into his palm before he smoothly pocketed it.

Alex froze. Had he really just witnessed what he thought he had? He watched as Leonard straightened his apron and headed toward the hallway where Alex stood, a placid smile on his face.

The older man nodded as he approached. "Alex. Good to see you."

Without thinking, Alex stepped directly into his path, blocking the way to the utility closet. "What did you just take from that woman's bag?"

Leonard's expression didn't change, but something flickered in his eyes. "Excuse me?"

"I saw you," Alex said, keeping his voice low but firm. "When you handed her bag back, you took something from it."

Leonard's smile tightened. "I don't know what you're talking about. Now, if you'll excuse me, I need to get cleaning supplies."

As he tried to step around Alex, Alex shifted to block him again. "Whatever you took needs to go back to her. Right now."

"Is there a problem?" Juno's voice came from behind him, and Alex turned to see her standing there, a chocolate shake in her hand and confusion on her face.

"Your friend here seems to think I'm a thief," Leonard said, his tone wounded. "Apparently, I stole something from Mrs. Harrison's bag."

Juno looked between them, her brow furrowing. "What's going on, Alex?"

Alex took a deep breath, aware of how this must look. "When he picked up her bag, I saw him take something out of it and put it in his pocket."

Leonard spread his hands, the picture of innocent bewilderment. "That's ridiculous. Why would I do that?"

"I know what I saw," Alex insisted.

Juno set the milkshake down on a nearby shelf. "Dad, did you take something from Mrs. Harrison's bag?"

"Of course not, Juniper." Leonard's voice was firm. "I wouldn't do that to you or your business."

The tension in the hallway was palpable. Alex could see Juno's struggle playing out on her face, wanting to believe her father, not wanting to doubt Alex.

"If you're so sure," Alex pressed, "then empty your pockets."

Leonard's eyes narrowed, but he reached into his pockets and turned them inside out. Keys, a handkerchief, some loose change, and a pack of mints tumbled into his palm. "Satisfied?"

Alex wasn't. He'd *seen* it, plain as day. But if Leonard had taken something, where was it now?

Juno looked troubled. "Alex, are you absolutely sure about what you saw?"

"Yes." He met her eyes, willing her to believe him. "He had his hand inside her bag."

Juno's jaw tightened, and Alex could see her weighing her options. Finally, she sighed. "I need to check this out. I can't just ignore an accusation like this. You two wait right here."

She turned and headed back into the main area of the coffee shop. Alex and Leonard stayed put, a tense silence between them. Juno approached the woman's table, her professional smile firmly in place.

"Mrs. Harrison? I'm so sorry to bother you, but I need to ask you something." Her voice was pitched low, discreet. "Could you please check your bag to make sure nothing is missing? There was a... concern."

Mrs. Harrison looked surprised but obliged, opening her tote and rifling through it. "My wallet is here," she said, pulling it out. "And my keys." She continued her search, producing a tablet, a small makeup bag, and a paperback novel. "Everything seems to be in order."

"You're sure?" Juno pressed gently. "Nothing else that might have been taken?"

Mrs. Harrison gave her a puzzled look. "No, dear. Everything's accounted for."

Juno's shoulders sagged with relief, but her eyes held a hint of embarrassment. "I'm so sorry to have bothered you. Please consider your order on the house today."

"That's not necessary," Mrs. Harrison protested, but Juno insisted.

When she returned to where Alex and Leonard waited, her expression had hardened.

Leonard shrugged, a ghost of smugness crossing his features. "Like I said, I didn't take anything."

Alex felt a swell of frustration. "I know what I saw."

"Apparently not," Leonard countered. "Now, if you'll excuse me, I have work to do." He headed back toward the utility closet, his posture radiating vindication.

Juno watched him go, then turned to Alex. "Come with me."

She led him through the kitchen, past a startled Trevor, and out the back door into the alley behind the coffee shop. The afternoon heat hit them like a wall as the door swung shut behind them.

Juno whirled to face him, her eyes flashing. "What was that about?"

"I told you—"

"No, Alex. I want to know why you're so determined to think the worst of my father." Her voice trembled slightly. "Do you have any idea how humiliating that was? Having to ask Mrs. Harrison to check her bag like that? She's been coming to my shop for years."

"I'm sorry about that," Alex said, genuinely meaning it. "But I know what I saw, Juno. He had his hand in her bag."

"He picked it up to hand it to her!"

"No." Alex shook his head emphatically. "He took something. I don't know where he hid it, but he took something."

Juno crossed her arms. "Why? Why would he do that? He's got a stable job, a place to stay. What would be the point of risking all that to steal from my customers?"

Alex didn't have a good answer, just the certainty of what he'd witnessed. "I don't know. But people with addiction problems don't always make rational choices."

"Why is it so impossible for you to believe that my father has changed? Why doesn't he deserve a second chance?"

"This isn't about second chances," Alex countered, frustration building in his chest. "I'm not questioning his right to start over. I'm telling you what I saw today, with my own eyes."

"What you think you saw," Juno corrected. "Mrs. Harrison has all her belongings."

"That she knows of," Alex pointed out. "Maybe it was something small she hasn't noticed yet. Maybe he dumped it when he realized I was onto him."

Juno ran a hand over her braids, exasperation evident in the gesture. "Do you hear yourself? You sound like you're grasping at straws because you can't admit you might have been wrong."

The accusation stung, and Alex felt his own temper rising. "I'm trying to protect you, Juno."

"I don't need your protection!" She declared. "I need you to trust that I know what I'm doing. That I can make my own decisions about my father."

"Even if those decisions put you at risk? What happens when he's done worse than this and you can't ignore it anymore?" The moment the words left his mouth, Alex knew he'd gone too far.

Juno's eyes widened, then narrowed. "You know what? If my father is going to be in my life—and he is—then you need to find a way to deal with that. And if you can't, well, I don't know. Maybe we're moving too quickly. Maybe we need to take a step back..." She trailed off, leaving the implication hanging between them.

"What are you saying?" Alex's heart pounded uncomfortably in his chest.

"I'm saying that maybe you should focus on fixing your own problems before you start creating trouble for me." She reached for the door handle. "My father isn't going anywhere, Alex. So you need to decide if you can accept that or not."

"Juno—"

But she was already pulling the door open. "I have to get back to work. My break is over."

"Wait, can we talk about this tonight? Can I at least explain—"

"Actually, I don't think that's a good idea." Her voice had lost its heat, replaced by a coolness that was somehow worse. "I think we both need some space to figure out what we want."

And then she was gone, the heavy door closing behind her with a finality that left Alex standing alone in the alley, the taste of an argument he couldn't win bitter on his tongue.

28
Juno

Juno stared at her laptop screen, the electronic banking portal displaying numbers that couldn't possibly be right. She blinked hard, hoping the figures would rearrange themselves into something that made sense. They didn't.

Beneath the current balance, two separate transactions processed through PayQuick, an online payment platform, stood out in stark black text: $16,900 for a refurbished espresso machine, and $26,500 for a company vehicle.

Her heart hammered against her ribs as she clicked on the transaction details. Both had been processed yesterday while she'd been working the lunch rush. And both had been initiated from her mobile banking app.

The room tilted slightly. She knew exactly what had happened. Knew exactly who had done this.

With trembling fingers, she grabbed her phone and called her father. The call went straight to an automated disconnection notice.

She immediately dialed PayQuick's fraud department. After navigating an automated menu and waiting on hold for what felt like hours, a representative finally answered.

"I need to report fraudulent transactions," Juno said, fighting to keep her voice steady. She explained the situation, provided her account information, and described the two transfers.

"I'm sorry, Ms. Thomas," the representative said after placing her on a brief hold, "but both payments have already been processed and the funds were transferred out of our system. There's no way for us to recover them."

"But they were fraudulent," Juno insisted. "I didn't authorize them."

"Were the transfers made from your account? Using your credentials?"

"Yes, but—"

"And you're saying someone else had access to your banking information and authorization codes?"

Juno closed her eyes. "My—my father. He must have gotten my password somehow."

"I understand how distressing this is," the representative said, her voice taking on that practiced sympathy that call center workers perfected. "However, since the transfers were made using your authorized credentials, this would be classified as account compromise rather than system fraud. You'll need to file a police report and work with your bank."

After ending that call, Juno immediately contacted her bank. The conversation followed a similar pattern—initial concern followed by the revelation that the situation was complicated by the fact that the transactions had been properly authenticated. The bank's fraud specialist explained that they would investigate, but recovery of the funds was unlikely if they had already been withdrawn from PayQuick.

Like the PayQuick rep, her bank's fraud specialist also advised her to file a report with the police immediately. "We'll need that report number to proceed with our own investigation."

Juno agreed numbly and hung up. Filing a police report meant publicly acknowledging what her father had done. It meant everyone would know how foolish she'd been.

She sank onto her couch, mind racing. How had he gotten her banking information? The password to her accounts wasn't written down anywhere, and she was always mindful of where her phone was at all times.

Mindful, maybe, but that didn't mean she necessarily kept the thing in sight around the clock.

She suddenly remembered the other day when her father had intercepted her coming out of the supply closet. He had her phone in his hand. He'd seemed surprised to see her, but then handed her the device.

"You might want to keep a better eye on this," he'd told her. "I found it on the shelf over the sink."

She often set it there when washing dishes so she could see if any important texts or calls came in. That day, she'd been summoned to the front to talk to a customer about a catering order, opting to leave the phone behind since she planned to return to finish her load of dishes.

She'd thanked her father for looking out for her and thought nothing more of it.

And then there was the day he'd come bustling out the backdoor to help her unload her trunk of an emergency supply run. He'd gone out to her car for the last load and had returned with her purse along with the box of milk cartons he was carrying. "Don't want this walking off," he'd said, holding it up so she could see. "You left it in your front seat." He'd made a show of tucking it safely under her desk in her tiny office space just off the kitchen. Something about the way he'd behaved had sounded the alarms, but when she checked the contents of her bag, she found everything in place, and had been greatly relieved that her initial suspicion had been unfounded.

But he wouldn't have needed to take anything, would he? Just a quick glance at her driver's license for personal information, a photo of her bank card for the account numbers. And he'd probably watched her tap in her phone's security code to open it up. With that code, he'd have been able to sign onto it and then reset her banking password so that he could access her accounts and have his way with her money.

It had all been a calculated game.

Juno dialed the Sleepy Time Motel, already knowing what they would tell her.

"I'm sorry, Ms. Thomas," the front desk clerk confirmed, "but Mr. Thomas checked out yesterday evening around six."

Of course he had. He'd probably been planning his exit for days, waiting for the right moment.

Juno hung up and stared at the wall. More than forty thousand dollars was just gone. Money she'd been saving for years, setting aside little by little from her profits.

From what she'd gathered, unless she filed that police report, there was little likelihood of her ever seeing her money again. And even if she did turn him in, the only way she'd get any of the money back was if her father hadn't already spent it. Or hidden it. Or gambled it away.

Her stomach turned as the truth sank in. The expansion she'd been planning and preparing for would have to wait. And that was just the financial cost.

The real price was the shame burning through her veins.

Alex had been right. Claire had been right. Everyone who knew and cared about her had been right. Her father hadn't changed. She'd been willfully blind, so desperate to believe in redemption that she'd ignored every warning sign.

She'd defended Leonard to everyone, but especially to Alex, drawing that hard line in the sand. She'd pushed him away because he'd tried to warn her.

And now she couldn't bear to face any of her friends with the truth.

The coffee shop would open in less than an hour. Customers would arrive, expecting their usual cheerful service from her. Somehow, she had to pull herself together and get through the day. No one could know what had happened. Not yet. Maybe not ever.

She wiped her eyes, straightened her shoulders, and got ready for work.

"I JUST WANTED YOU to know," Mrs. Harrison said quietly later that morning, leaning across the counter. "In case it's connected to what happened the other day."

Juno stared at the older woman, her stomach churning. "One of your credit cards was stolen?"

Mrs. Harrison nodded. "The company called me about suspicious charges. Someone maxed it out two days ago—nearly ten thousand dollars. I've filed a fraud report, and the credit card company is handling it, but I just thought you might want to know."

"I'm so sorry," Juno managed, shame washing over her in waves. Her father hadn't just stolen from her; he'd stolen from her customers too. From people who trusted her. How many others had been victimized while she stubbornly defended him?

"It's not your fault, dear," Mrs. Harrison patted her hand, oblivious to the truth of the situation. "These things happen."

But it is my fault, Juno thought as she watched Mrs. Harrison leave. *I brought him here. I gave him access to all of you.*

She headed to her little office and dropped into her chair, sick at heart.

❤ · ❤ · ❤ · ❤ · ❤

THE NEXT MORNING, CLAIRE showed up just as Juno opened up and slid onto one of the stools at the counter. "I've been up for more than an hour already to prep for my big sale this weekend. I need energy. Pep. A pick-me-up that won't make me jittery." Claire's shop didn't open for several more hours, but her early morning visits were routine.

"How about an egg and avocado toast?" Juno suggested, knowing it was one of her friend's favorites.

"Perfect." Claire nodded. "And coffee, of course. I can handle it if I get something in my stomach, I promise."

Juno rolled her eyes but filled a ceramic mug and set it in front of Claire. "I think you might like coffee more than I do," she said, trying to force a lightness into her tone, even though she felt completely and utterly flat.

"So how are things with your dad?" Claire asked, like she'd picked up on Juno's thoughts. "I haven't seen him around the last couple of days."

Juno kept her eyes on the sandwich she was preparing, afraid that if she looked at her friend, Claire would see right through her composure. "He got another job offer. Something with more hours than I can give him."

"Oh?" Claire sounded surprised. "He seemed so... content working here. Where's he working now?

"Out of town," Juno said vaguely. "A construction job."

"Okay." Claire's tone suggested she didn't quite believe this explanation but was willing to let it slide for now. "And how are things with Alex?" She wiggled her brows at Juno. "That's what I really want to know. Are you two getting married yet? You'd better move fast to make up for all that lost time. I'm so glad you two sorted things out. You're perfect for each other, Juno. And now that he has Lena? My goodness, but I love watching him with her. It's like getting to see a whole new side of our Alex, isn't it?"

Juno's hand trembled slightly as she poured the steamed milk. "Wow, you really have had too much caffeine, woman. Slow down."

"Sorry," Claire said, taking a deep breath and blowing it out slowly. "But tell me. You and Alex. And Lena. He and Lena were in The Cracked Spine the other night, but we were packed, and I didn't get a chance to ask him how things were with the custody stuff. Not that I would've asked in front of Lena anyway; don't worry."

Juno held up a hand, not wanting this conversation to go on any longer. "Actually, Claire, I don't really know, either. We're sorta taking a break. Just until he gets things sorted out with Lena, but he really needs to focus on that. Keep things simple for court, you know?" Wow. The lies were just flying out of her mouth today.

"Juno." Claire's eyes grew round, and her voice softened. "What happened? That doesn't sound good."

"Everything is fine," Juno insisted, fanning the hardboiled egg slices over the mashed avocado on a thick slice of multigrain toast. "It's fine," she said again. "It's just while things get sorted out." Ugh. She'd said that already. And Claire wasn't buying it.

Claire studied her for a long moment, then nodded. "Well, if you need to talk, or just want company, call me. Day or night."

Not answering, she set Claire's breakfast in front of her. "Here you go."

She was grateful when a group of men pushed into the shop at that moment. Early morning fishing, she presumed, and they'd likely all just want large black coffees to go. But they gave her an excuse to end the conversation with Claire, so she welcomed them with far more fervor than usual.

TWO DAYS LATER, JUNO sat at her desk, staring at her phone. She'd couldn't put this call off any longer. The news from PayQuick and her bank wasn't good. Without that police report, she'd essentially handed her father $40,000 and sent him on his way.

She dialed J&J Contractors, her heart sinking when John Jensen himself answered.

"John, it's Juno Thomas."

"Juno! Good to hear from you. How can I help you? I was going over your project plans this morning."

"That's actually why I'm calling," she cut in, hating herself for what she had to say next. "I—I need to put the expansion on hold."

A pause. "Is there a problem?" She knew people cancelled on contractors all the time, often last minute, and she hated that she was going to be one of those people. She heard the wariness in his voice.

"I'm so sorry to have to do this." She gripped the phone tighter. "There's been a… financial issue," she finally blurted out. "Someone gained access to my bank accounts and my funds are all but gone."

"Jeez, Juno, I'm sorry to hear that." John's voice filled with genuine concern. "Is there nothing you can do? Doesn't your bank offer fraud protection?"

"Unfortunately, not in this case. The bank is treating it as an account compromise rather than fraud because it was done by someone who supposedly had authority to do so," she said evasively, not wanting to have to explain any of it to anyone. "I will just have to rebuild the fund again." The words were like ashes in her mouth. "I don't know how long it will be, but I'm hoping maybe by next fall?" It was wishful thinking, she knew, but she felt compelled to sound more confident than she felt.

In other words, she was still lying to cover for her mistakes.

"Of course. I'll make a note of it, and you just keep in touch." John hesitated. "You know, Juno, my brother-in-law's on the force, I could talk to him."

"It's being handled," she said quickly. "Thank you, though."

After ending the call, Juno sat in the privacy of her office and listened to the sounds of the busy café just beyond her closed door. Regulars and first-timers, locals and tourist, staff and business contacts… she'd worked so hard for so long to build her dream business. And she'd succeeded. Juno's Coffee Bar was profitable, even during slow months, because her community supported her. Believed in her.

How could she betray their trust by telling anyone what a fool she was?

Her expansion plans were shelved indefinitely. Her father—the man she'd naively given a second chance—had stolen from her and disappeared.

And Alex... Alex had tried to warn her, had seen what she'd refused to see, and she'd pushed him away for it.

The two men in her life were gone, one by his own betrayal, one by her stubborn pride. Her savings were decimated. And she couldn't even seek comfort from her friends because the thought of admitting how thoroughly she'd been deceived was unbearable.

She'd made her bed, and now she had to lie in it. Alone.

Juno wrapped her arms around herself, feeling smaller than she had in years. For the first time since she'd returned to Autumn Lake all those years ago, Juno felt truly, desperately alone.

29
Alex

ALEX WIPED SWEAT FROM his brow as he finished securing the last piece of crown molding. The heat in the attic bedroom of the Petersons' house was stifling, even with the portable fans they'd set up that morning. They were still waiting on the energy-saver window air conditioner that was supposed to be delivered sometime today.

"Looking good, Frampton," his boss said from the doorway. "Meticulous as always."

Alex stepped back to examine his work, checking for any gaps or imperfections. "Thanks. I should be finished up here by the end of the day."

"The Petersons are thrilled. They have been wanting this space finished for a long time." John moved into the room, running a hand along the chair rail that Alex had put up the day before. "It's a shame we had to push back the Coffee Bar project. I know Juno has been chomping at the bit to get that going, too. I was really looking forward to working on that one."

Alex's hands stilled on his tool belt. "What do you mean?" This was news to him, but then, he and Juno hadn't shared more than a few words in the last several days. He texted her a morning greeting each day and she called in the evenings, but then spent most of the phone calls talking to Lena. Juno had told her that she wasn't able to spend her evenings with them right now because her father was in town, and Lena had accepted the explanation without question. It was the truth, wasn't it?

It also felt like a line she was drawing in the sand for Alex. As long as Leonard was in town, in Juno's life, there wasn't room for Alex unless he could set aside his suspicions and accept the man.

But they weren't just suspicions. Alex had seen what he'd seen. So he'd stepped back a bit to give Juno space, hoping and praying that the truth of who Leonard was would be revealed to Juno on her own terms.

"Juno called yesterday to put her expansion on hold." John shook his head in sympathy. "Someone cleaned out her bank account."

The room seemed to tilt slightly beneath Alex's feet. "What?"

"Yeah, she sounded pretty shaken up." John eyed him, his brow furrowed. "Sorry, ma. Figured you already knew."

Alex's mind raced. Had Leonard—? The question seemed to answer itself even as he formed it. Of course he had. Leonard Thomas had played his daughter's heartstrings like a pro. He'd been scamming her all along, Alex was certain, stealing from the tip jar, maybe even from the register, and Alex was certain he'd been stealing from her customers, too, no matter what slight of hand Leonard had used to get away with it the other day. But then, apparently, he'd hit the mother lode with Juno's expansion fund. Alex didn't know how he'd pulled it off, but he had no doubt, whatsoever, that it was Leonard Thomas who'd emptied Juno's bank account.

Then another even more disturbing thought struck him. Was Leonard still working for Juno?

"I hadn't heard," Alex managed to say, the words tasting bitter. "We've both been pretty busy the last few days and haven't had much of a chance to talk."

John raised an eyebrow but didn't press. "Well, I told her to keep in touch about rescheduling. She's hoping for next fall, but she wasn't ready to commit at this point."

Alex nodded mechanically, his thoughts a whirlwind. How much had Leonard taken? How was Juno managing? And why hadn't she told him last night when she called?

The answer to that last question came to him immediately. Pride. The same pride that had made her defend her father so fiercely, that had made her push Alex away rather than consider he might be right.

He knew Juno, even after all these years. She would be suffering alone rather than letting anyone know she'd trusted the wrong man. She would carry the cost of that decision all on her own shoulders, and no one would know the misery she was enduring behind that friendly smile. She'd been that way from the day he'd first met her, which was why he hadn't suspected how horrific her life had been back then.

But back then, he reminded himself, she'd swallowed her pride and reached out to him, only to have him let her down, even if unintentionally, by abandoning her in her time of need.

Was it any wonder that Juno still had trust issues?

The rest of the workday passed in a blur. Alex's hands moved automatically through familiar tasks while his mind circled around Juno. By the time he clocked out and headed to his truck, he'd made a decision.

Their argument didn't matter. His hurt feelings didn't matter. What mattered was that Juno needed help, whether she would admit it or not.

Instead of heading home, Alex drove to The Cracked Spine. The late afternoon light cast long shadows across the street as he parked and made his way to the bookstore's entrance. Through the window, he could see Claire helping an elderly customer select a book, her animated gestures suggesting an enthusiastic recommendation.

He waited until the customer had paid and left before entering, the bell above the door announcing his arrival.

Claire greeted him with a warm smile. "Alex! Where is that lovely daughter of yours?"

"Hey, Claire." He approached the counter, suddenly uncertain how to begin. "Do you have a minute to talk?"

Claire's expression shifted to one of concern as she glanced around the shop. "Sure, let me find Nick so I can let him know to cover for me." The wholesome young man was being chatted up by a group of teenage girls, looking equally flustered and in his element, and it took a few moments for Claire to get his attention.

Nick hustled to the front counter and the girls followed behind him in a tight pack, making Alex think of an amoeba the way they moved.

Claire held the staff breakroom door opened for him. "I don't have any coffee on right now, but there are some sparkling waters in the fridge," she offered. When Alex declined, she gestured at the table and they both sat. "What's going on?"

Alex got right to the point. "It's about Juno."

Claire nodded slowly, like she'd assumed as much. "She told me you two were 'taking a break.'" She made air quotes around the phrase.

"That's one way to put it," Alex said with a humorless laugh. "Did she tell you about her father?"

"Only that he got another job out of town," Claire said slowly, crossing her arms. "But she was being weird about it. Evasive."

Relieved to at least know the guy was no longer working for Juno, Alex took a deep breath. "I think Leonard stole from her. My boss told me today that she's postponed the project because someone emptied her expansion money account."

Claire's eyes widened. "Oh, no," she exclaimed quietly. "She didn't say anything to me. Are—are you sure it was him?"

"No," Alex admitted, but he could tell by Claire's expression that she wasn't surprised by his accusation. "But it adds up. A few days ago, I caught Leonard stealing from a customer's bag at the coffee shop. I confronted Leonard and Juno walked in on it. Juno and I argued about it. She didn't believe me, and since I didn't have proof, other than what I saw, she basically asked me to leave." He ran a hand through his hair. "It wasn't the first time I saw him do something shady, either. I caught him pocketing tips left on the tables, too."

"I knew it. I knew there was something crooked about that guy," Claire muttered, shaking her head.

Alex nodded. "I know. And now you say he's gone, right?"

"Took a construction job out of town," Claire said in a scathing tone. "Like that man has ever lifted a hammer a day in his life."

"Well, apparently, he took Juno's savings with him when he left."

"Why did that man come back here?" Claire smacked her hand on the table. "Hasn't he done enough to her already?"

After a few moments of silence while they both processed the magnitude of the situation, Alex said, "I think she needs help."

"But she's not going to ask for it." Claire finished his thought for him. "You know how she is—stubborn, independent. She'd rather suffer alone than admit what happened."

"Right. But that doesn't change the fact that she needs help," he reiterated. "But I doubt she'd be very happy if I just showed up over there and openly accused her father of stealing from her, since she's not admitting that's what happened, as far as I can tell."

Claire eyed him thoughtfully. "So I take it you have some kind of work-around? A way to help her without her knowing you're doing it?"

"Not me," Alex said. "Or at least, not *just* me. All of us. Her friends. The people who care about her."

Claire's brows went up, but she waited to hear what he had to say.

"Your Garden Variety Lovers Club ladies," Alex began. "I was thinking... maybe we—you ladies—could organize something. A fundraiser of some kind. I think she'd accept it easier if it came from her friends."

Claire tapped her fingers thoughtfully on the table top. "A community event. Something that shows her she's not alone, that Autumn Lake has her back." She frowned. "It's going to have to be a surprise. She'd never agree to it otherwise."

"That's kind of what I was thinking, too," Alex agreed, although a tiny spark of hope was igniting inside of him. Claire was getting on board, and if she commandeered her group of friends into putting on an impromptu event, it might just work.

"You know," Claire said, suddenly sitting up straight in her chair. "Our whole GVLC hasn't gotten together out at the B&B since they opened for business earlier this month. We are due for a lady's night out there, don't you think?"

"That's the idea." Alex grinned, his shoulders relaxing as he watched the wheels turning behind Claire's eyes.

"You leave it to us. We'll get things sorted. A community fundraiser; we can pull that off, no problem." Claire nodded decisively, then cocked her head and studied him for a long moment. "Are you upset at her for siding with her father over you?"

Alex shook his head. "Not even for an instant. She wanted to believe in him, to trust him. She was giving him another chance to be a better man." Alex held her gaze. "I'm glad folks who care about me have given me more than my fair share of second chances."

"And you're proving us right, Alex. I'm proud of you. You've come a long way, Daddy," she said with a teasing smile. Then she reached for her phone. "I'll call an emergency GVLC meeting and get the ball rolling as quickly as possible."

"Thank you."

"Don't thank me yet." Claire's expression was serious. "Juno's going to be furious when she finds out what we're doing."

"I know." And he did. Juno would see it as interference, as a public acknowledgment of her failure. "But she'll know we have her back, even if it kills her to admit it."

"She'll get over it, Alex," Claire said, pushing to her feet. "I have faith in our girl. Besides, it's the right thing to do."

Alex nodded and stood, too, pushing his chair back in place. "I'm glad you agree. Anyway, I need to get going." He couldn't bite back his grin as he added, "I have a daughter to get home to."

"Look at you," Claire said, circling the table to give him a quick hug. "Local town hero. Knight in shining armor. Proud father. What a guy." She stepped back and patted his chest. "I'm glad I know you, Alex Frampton. You're my kind of people."

As Alex walked back to his truck, he felt the weight on his shoulders lighten fractionally. He couldn't fix the damage Leonard had done to Juno's heart, nor could he force Juno to trust him before she was ready. But he could rally the people who loved Juno, who would stand by her, no matter what.

It might cost him any chance of reconciliation with her. Juno might see his involvement as the final betrayal, the ultimate proof that he didn't respect her independence.

He prayed that wouldn't be the case.

He slid behind the wheel of The Beast and sat for a moment, gathering his thoughts. Tomorrow he had a custody meeting with Howard. For whatever reason, Melissa still hadn't demanded that he return Lena to her, for which he was thrilled. He was getting accustomed to thinking about someone besides himself around the clock, and he found it made him want to be a better man all the way around. Not just at home, but with his friends, his work, and even when he was alone. He shaved more often, took better care of his living space, got better sleep, and ate healthier. He wasn't ready to give up his milkshakes yet, but the last few days of skipping the afternoon treat had proved that he could do without just fine.

In fact, it wasn't the chocolate shakes he was missing so badly, but the person who made them for him.

It had been four days since he'd been inside Juno's Coffee Bar, but it felt like an eternity. He eyed her place across the street from The Cracked Spine, and more than anything, he wanted to go in and check on her. But he held back. She needed to come to him on her own terms, he reminded himself. If he pushed, she'd pull away.

His phone beeped and he glanced at the screen to see who had texted. Melissa.

I'm coming to pick Lena up next Friday. Have her things packed and ready when I get there.

A wave of dread washed over him at the sight of those words. What did she have planned? Did he have to just hand Lena over to her mother in ten days without explanation? She wouldn't dare take Lena out of the country, would she? Not with the court order in place. But what if they left the state? What if she disappeared without telling him where they were going? What could he do to prevent her from doing anything she wanted?

In a borderline panic, Alex put his truck in gear and headed for his parents' house. It was too late to call his own attorney, but maybe his dad would have some answers. He couldn't lose Lena again. He wouldn't.

As he passed the coffee shop, a new sense of determination reared up inside of him. He wouldn't lose Juno, either. Come hell or high water, he was going to fight for his girls, his precious ladies. He was going to protect and defend them, be a soft place for them to land, and a strong place for them to hold onto.

He had his work cut out for him, but he was ready to fight this battle, to be the kind of man that both Lena and Juno could count on.

30
Juno

JUNO TUGGED AT THE hem of her cobalt blue blouse, smoothed down her black slacks, and took a deep breath. Her reflection in the rearview mirror looked presentable—professional even. The concealer she'd applied did a decent job hiding the dark circles under her eyes, and the mascara made her look more awake than she felt.

Ten days. Ten days since she'd discovered her father's betrayal, and she still hadn't managed a full night's sleep. Every time she closed her eyes, she saw the bank statement, the transactions that had emptied her account, the culmination of years of saving gone in an instant.

Yet here she was, driving to the Garden Gate B&B for the Garden Variety Lovers Club's monthly gathering. She'd nearly canceled. She'd composed and deleted at least three text messages to Claire with various excuses. In the end, she'd decided that staying home alone with her thoughts would be worse than putting on a brave face for a few hours.

Besides, she owed it to her friends to at least make an appearance. She'd already been dodging Claire's increasingly concerned texts, and Liz and Candy had stopped by the coffee shop twice this week with thinly-veiled attempts to check on her. Then yesterday, Addison had come in with an enormous bouquet of flowers for her. She'd said that someone ordered them, paid for them, then never picked them up, so she'd decided to give them to one of the hardest working women she knew. Addison had set the vase on the end of the counter, and then hugged Juno fiercely. "That's you, my friend!" she'd declared, then added, "I'll see you at the Garden Gate tomorrow, right?"

Even Penny had texted her to make sure she would be there.

They knew something was wrong. They just didn't know what, and Juno intended to keep it that way.

Juno pulled up to the Garden Gate, Mavis Staples's voice rolling like thunder out of her car stereo, singing about there being no time for crying, that there was work to do. She parked her car behind the B&B, noting with surprise the unusually full parking area. There were even cars parked across the gravel road at the St. James's place. What was going on? Was there an event here that she didn't know about? And if so, why hadn't Penny rescheduled their get-together? The six friends could meet any time and anywhere they wanted; there was nothing official about the group, just an excuse to take time out of the busyness of their lives and hang out.

Unease rippled through her as she made her way to the front entrance. The sprawling Craftsman-style home had been beautifully renovated, its wraparound porch adorned with overflowing hanging baskets of petunias and ferns. On any other evening, Juno would have paused to admire Hazel's handiwork, but tonight she was too preoccupied with getting through the next few hours without falling apart.

As she approached the front door, she could hear the hum of many voices within. The door swung open before she could reach for the handle, and Penny stood there, a broad smile lighting up her face, Claire right behind her.

"You're here!" Penny exclaimed, pulling Juno into a quick hug.

"Sorry I'm late," Juno said, forcing a smile.

"Hey woman," Claire greeted her, a sly grin tugging at her lips. "We were getting worried."

"What is going on here tonight?" Juno asked as Claire linked her arm through hers.

Penny gestured for them to follow her inside, and Juno stopped short at the sight before her. The grand foyer and adjacent parlor were filled with people, what seemed like half the town of Autumn Lake. Pastor Darren chatted with Mr. and Mrs. Carrol near the fireplace. Sonya from Tip-Top Talons was listening raptly as John Jenson regaled her with one of his many construction-gone-wrong tales. She saw Trevor, who'd asked for the evening off because of some emergency, over near a buffet table that nearly buckled under the weight of dozens of homemade desserts. Even Mr. and

Mrs. Frampton were there, talking with a group of other couples from church.

Juno did not see Alex or Lena, but she forced herself to stop looking for them. Why on earth would they be at the B&B this evening? Then again, why would any of these people?

Mrs. Becker hurried over and held out her arms for a hug. "Juno dear. It's so good to see you. You are such a treasure to all of us." Then she reached over and patted Claire's hand, winked at Penny, and shuffled off to greet someone else.

"You guys, what's going on?" Juno asked again, confusion giving way to suspicion. "And where are Liz and Candy? Is Addison here yet?"

Penny's smile grew wider. "In the kitchen. Come on."

Before Juno could protest, Claire was guiding her by the arm through the crowd with Penny parting the way in front of them. People smiled and nodded as she passed, a few calling out greetings. Juno returned them automatically, her mind racing to make sense of the gathering.

In the main dining room, a large banner hung across one wall: "Autumn Lake Loves Juno's Coffee Bar." Beneath it was a table lined with donation jars, each labeled with aspects of her planned expansion: "New Equipment," "Contractor Fees," "Furnishings Fund," and more. Every jar had cash and checks in them, and in a basket on the table were what appeared to be greeting cards with her name on them.

Realization dawned, bringing with it a flood of complicated emotions—gratitude, embarrassment, pride, shame, and love. This wasn't a Garden Variety Lovers Club meeting. This was a fundraiser. For her.

Claire squeezed her arm, and when Juno met her gaze, she saw both apprehension and excitement. "Before you say anything—"

"Claire," Juno cut in, her voice low and tight, "what is this?"

"It's your community showing up for you," Claire said simply. "The way you've always shown up for us."

"But how did you—" Juno stuttered to a stop, bamboozled by the overwhelming flood of emotions coursing through her, her eyes stinging from unshed tears. She would not cry; not in front of all these people.

Penny pushed open the door to the kitchen and gestured at Juno and Claire to follow.

In the kitchen were Addison, Candy, and Liz filling more dessert platters to take out to the table. Addison rushed over when they entered and gave Juno a warm hug. "You're here. You're not mad at us, are you?"

"Of course, I am," Juno shot back, her voice husky around the lump in her throat. "I hate you all."

Liz rolled her eyes. "And we hate you, too. See how much?" She waved the spatula she wielded in a gesture meant to encompass the entire event.

Candy dropped a frosted cupcake upside down on the platter she was filling, picked it up, then brought it over to Juno. "Here. Eat this. Cupcakes are magic that way, and I can't serve it now." She practically forced Juno to take it, then licked the frosting off her own fingers before heading to the sink to wash her hands. "Wow. That's tasty frosting."

To give herself time to process, Juno took a too-big bite and chewed slowly. It was a sour cream coffee cake base with a maple frosting; it really was delicious.

When she finally swallowed and accepted the cup of coffee Penny poured for her, she looked around the room at her friends. Her crazy, best-of-intentions friends. She pressed her hand to her heart and thought how very fortunate she was to have these women in her life.

"Thank you," she managed to say, her voice cracking. "I don't know how you found out—yes, I do. It's a small town, isn't it?" She chuckled ruefully. "But thank you for putting this together. I don't hate you."

"We love you, too," Liz shot back, her tone still dry, but there was an uncharacteristic tenderness in the way she looked at Juno.

Claire drew closer. "It was Alex's idea."

"Alex?" The single word came out sharper than Juno intended.

Claire nodded. "He found out from John Jensen when you had to put off your renovation."

Juno clapped a palm to her forehead. What had she been thinking? Of course, Alex would be one of the first to know; he worked for the company. "Why... why would he do this?" she asked quietly, shame and regret radiating through her. "I've been such a jerk to him."

Penny sighed and pulled her into a hug. She was so gentle, so kind, so when she simply asked, "Was it your father? Did he steal from you?" it was almost jarring in its directness.

But that's when the tears started. Tears of grief and shame over what a fool she'd been not to see him as clearly as everyone else had, but also tears of relief at not having to carry the weight of his betrayal alone anymore. Juno pulled away and grabbed a napkin off the counter, pressing it to her eyes carefully so as not to smudge her makeup. Her friends, in an almost synchronized motion, circled around her, huddling close.

"You guys remind me of elephants," Juno sobbed, loving them even more than she had only moments before.

"Elephants," Candy echoed, chuckling, but also sounding slightly offended.

"In the best way," Juno clarified, grinning through her tears. "I saw this show the other night. Sitting all alone in my apartment by myself. Alone."

"By yourself with no one else; yes," Liz clarified. "I think we got it."

Candy hip-checked her cousin, but Liz only laughed.

"This baby elephant was being attacked by a lion," Juno went on, feeling the love and support of her friends in a way she never truly had before. "And all the other elephants circled up around the little guy and ran the lion off."

"Well, if your father walked in right now, I'd run him off," Claire retorted, and the others echoed the sentiment.

Just then, the kitchen door swung open, and Alex entered with Lena, his hand resting protectively on his daughter's shoulder. He cleared his throat. "Sorry to interrupt. Uh... Hazel said you were in here. Lena wanted to say 'hi.'"

"Juno!" The little girl broke away from her father and darted between the women to wrap her arms around Juno's waist in a fierce hug. "I'm so glad I get to see you tonight! Daddy said you were busy with your daddy, but I just missed you so much."

Juno returned the embrace, her throat tight with emotion. "I've missed you too, sweetheart."

She looked up to find Alex still in the doorway, keeping his distance both physically and emotionally. Gone was the easy confidence he usually wore; in its place, an uncertainty that mirrored her own inner turmoil.

Claire observed the silent exchange between them and leaned down to Lena. "Hey sweetie, have you seen the dessert table yet? Mrs. Poleman made those rainbow cupcakes you love so much."

Lena's eyes widened. "Really?" Turning to Alex, she asked, "Daddy, can I go get a rainbow cupcake?"

Claire winked at Juno over Lena's head, then led the girl away, Candy and Addison following closely after them. At the door, Candy stopped and turned back to Liz, who had returned to her stool at the counter and looked like she was just settling in for the duration.

"Get your butt moving, cuz," Candy ordered.

Liz made a big show of being disappointed. "And just when things were starting to get juicy." As she passed by Juno, she leaned in and said in a low voice loud enough for them all to hear, "Good luck, baby elephant." When she approached Alex, who still stood almost blocking the door, she gave him a not-so-gentle shove in Juno's direction, and she followed the others out of the room.

For a long moment, neither Alex nor Juno spoke. Then Juno held out her hand to him, surprising both of them with the gesture. "We need to talk," she said, her voice barely audible. "But not here."

Alex nodded, his fingers closing gently around hers. "Lead the way."

Juno lead him across the kitchen to the back door that opened into Hazel's private garden. The evening air with the breeze off the water was cool after the warmth of the crowded B&B, and the garden was peaceful, illuminated by a few strategically placed solar lights in the borders.

She led him to a stone bench beneath an arch draped a purple clematis, then pulled him down to sit beside her in the intimate space. Only then did she release his hand and turn to face him.

"Did you do this?" she asked, though she already knew the answer.

Alex shook his head. "Your friends pulled this off, not me."

"But it was your idea."

He didn't deny it. "I brought it up to Claire. The rest was all them." He paused, then it was his turn to take her hand. "I didn't know how else to help you, Juno, and I didn't want you to have to deal with the fallout of... of what happened alone."

"You can say it, Alex. My father stole from me. He swindled me out of more than forty thousand dollars, and he stole from some of my customers, too. You were right about Mrs. Harrison. He stole a credit card from her." She heard his intake of breath, but pressed on. "I practically handed him my life savings on a silver platter by letting him back into my life without any evidence that he truly was a changed man."

"It's not such a bad thing, believing in people, Juno," Alex said, reaching up to brush her cheek with his thumb.

Juno took a shaky breath, willing herself not to cry over his tenderness. "I know. I just need to be better about choosing who to believe in. I'm apparently not a very good judge of character, am I?"

"Sure you are," he countered, gesturing back toward the full house. "Look who you have for friends."

"Yes, but as far as the men in my life?" She let out a bitter laugh. "I keep you at arm's length for eight years, but I let him close after eight minutes."

Alex remained silent for so long, Juno wondered if she'd said something wrong. But then he flashed that oh-so-wicked grin at her and said, "So that makes me the one and only man in your life? I think I could get used to that."

"Don't joke about this," she said, trying to remain stern. "I've been an idiot and I'm not done beating myself up yet, so you can't be either."

When his fingers tightened around hers and he started to pull her toward him, she pressed her other hand to his chest. She had to get this out, to say what needed to be said out here in the dark where she could still manage to maintain a little of her dignity. "I'm sorry, Alex. I'm sorry for choosing him over you. For choosing to believe him over everyone. You all knew he was bad news, didn't you?"

It struck her, then, like the last puzzle piece dropping into place, that there was nothing wrong with sometimes needing help, with not always having the answers. Listening to wise council from people who loved her didn't make her weak. In fact, it made her stronger to have her friends and loved ones gathering around her to support her and hold her up. *Just like a pack of elephants,* she thought to herself with a shaky grin.

"Thank you for not giving up on me, even when I pushed you away. For this," she said, waving her free hand at the house the same way he had.

"And thank you for not giving up on me," Alex said, his voice low, gentle, like he was worried she might pull away again.

But tonight, she was leaning in. She was opening her arms and gathering close the people who loved her most. And that meant this very man beside her. The one and only man in her life.

She met his gaze. "I'm tired of being afraid, Alex. I like to think I'm brave, but I'm not. It's all a facade." Her throat tightened as she went on, but she pushed the words out anyway. "I don't want to need anyone, but I—" She broke off and started again. "I need you. I need my friends. I need this community I've grown to love so much."

"Aw, June-bug." Alex pulled her up against his side and she rested her head on his shoulder. "We need you, too, and not just for your stellar coffee."

Juno jabbed him with her elbow.

He let out a dramatic "Oof!" then hauled her closer so she was sitting across his lap, laughing when she let out a surprised little shriek. "I need you, Juniper Thomas," he murmured close to her ear as she wrapped her arms around his neck.

Juno pressed her forehead to his and closed her eyes, relishing in the quiet, intimate moment they were sharing. Was it possible that she, Juno Wrong-Side-of-the-Tracks Thomas could have so much? The unconditional love of a man like Alex, the unfailing friendships of the women who'd circled around her in her time of need? Did she dare to dream that she might actually get her own happily ever after?

And then Alex's hand was cupping her cheek and tipping her face so that he could press his mouth against hers. His lips were soft and warm, a gentle caress that almost made her want to weep with the tenderness of it.

Juno kissed him back with as much courage and faith as she could muster. She kissed him like a promise, with intention and will. With all her heart.

When they finally pulled apart, they were both breathless. Tiny currents of electricity hummed just beneath her skin, making her want to press into him again, but she knew that might not be the wisest idea. They had a whole houseful of family and friends who were probably starting to wonder where they were, and it wouldn't surprise her in the least if one or two of the nosier of the bunch decided to come looking for them.

Juno settled back onto the bench beside him, but stayed close, leaning her back against his side, her head on his shoulder as she peered up at the star-strewn sky. The heaviness of his arm around her was a solid reminder of where she belonged. "So tell me the latest with Lena," she said, her voice low, hoping her question wouldn't dispel the peace of the moment. "And Melissa. What have you heard from her?"

"I thank God every day for my dad connecting me to Howard," Alex told her, his gratitude evident in his tone. She liked the way his chest vibrated against her back when he spoke. "He's working overtime to keep Melissa from taking Lena out of Autumn Lake until the custody case is settled. For now, she's still with me, but only for a few more days. Melissa's coming to pick her up on Friday, and if he can't get the judge to sign the temporary stay, then she could leave town, although she'd have to at least tell me where she'll be."

"Oh wow. Is she still pushing to take her to Greece?"

She felt Alex nod behind her. "She is, but from what I understand, Daniel went on without her, and she's pretty upset right now that I've supposedly thwarted her plans. Those are her words; like I purposely came between her and Daniel."

"You purposely came between Lena and Daniel, is what you did, Alex," Juno countered, straightening up and turning so she could see his face. She kept hold of his hand in her lap. "You are looking out for the best interest of your daughter, and if she can't see that, then you have all the more reason to not compromise. It sounds like a terrible situation for a young girl." Juno felt herself getting worked up. "Sorry. I'm sorry," she said, squeezing his hand. "I just care about her, too. And you."

"I know," Alex said, smiling. "Right now, all I can do is keep track of phone calls and text messages coming and going and wait for Howard to do his thing. I'm doing my best to not let it get to me, for Lena's sake, especially. I don't want her stressing out about this. She tells me every night at bedtime that she misses Melissa, but she still doesn't want to go to Greece. I know she wants me to promise her that I won't let that happen." He paused, like he was trying to decide if he should admit something or not. Then he shrugged one shoulder. "I know I'm not supposed to promise her anything at this point, but I'm not going to let it happen, Juno. And I've told her so."

Juno cupped his face and looked him in the eyes. "Good for you," she said. "Is there anything I can do to help? I could testify about what a great father you are."

"That might help." A small smile touched his lips. "Howard said character witnesses will be important. I've got a growing list of people lining up to do so, but if you want to join the gang, the more the merrier. We can swarm the bench."

"Count me in." She pressed a quick kiss to his lips. "But my name better be at the top of any list you have from here on out, you hear?"

Alex kissed her back, but took his time. "Yes, boss," he said when he pulled back enough to look her in the eyes.

"Hmm," she hummed. "I like the sound of that."

"Me, too," he concurred, pulling her into his side again.

"Alex?" she said after several moments.

"Yes, June-bug?"

"I think we're better together than we are apart. I want to be here for you and Lena, the way you've been here for me."

"I agree," he said softly, pressing a kiss to her temple.

"And speaking of Lena and facing things together," she said, letting a note of resignation seep into her voice. "I think we should probably head back inside and face the music."

"Probably." He sounded equally reluctant.

A small gasp drew their attention to the garden path where Lena stood, a look of absolute delight on her face.

"I knew it!" she exclaimed, bouncing on her toes. "I told Grandma you two were gonna be kissing out here!"

Alex laughed and got to his feet, pulling Juno up with him. "Were you spying on us, Lena-bug?"

"No! Well, maybe a little." She skipped forward, unrepentant. "Claire sent me to find you because people want to see Juno."

Juno stood and opened her arms, and Lena ran into them without hesitation. Over the child's head, she met Alex's gaze, seeing in his eyes the same wonder she felt—that somehow, despite all the missteps and misunderstandings, they'd found their way to this moment, to each other.

"Shall we?" Alex asked, holding out his hand to his daughter.

Lena took it, then grabbed Juno's, and the three of them made their way back inside. Juno felt lighter than she had in days. The road ahead wouldn't be easy, she knew. She still had financial setbacks to overcome, trust to rebuild, fears to face. But she didn't have to do any of it alone. Not anymore.

The people waiting inside, they were her strength, her elephant family. The thought made her want to laugh with joy.

And the man beside her, along with the delightful child he was fighting to protect, offered her a second chance at something she'd thought she'd lost forever.

31
Alex

Alex checked his watch for the third time in less than five minutes. Melissa had texted that she would be there at four o'clock, and she was now almost half an hour late. Was she deliberately keeping him on edge? He wouldn't put it past her.

"She'll be here," Juno said softly from where she sat on the couch with Lena. They were flipping through a photo album that Roxanne had put together, filled with pictures from Lena's first weeks in Autumn Lake. Alex was certain his mother had already taken more photos of Lena than he had seen of himself throughout his entire childhood.

"I know," he replied, trying to keep the tension from his voice. He didn't want Lena to pick up on his anxiety.

Roxanne emerged from the kitchen with a tray of cookies and iced tea for the adults, milk for Lena. "I thought we could use a little something while we wait," she said, setting it on the coffee table. "Lena helped me make these."

"Snickerdoodles," Lena announced proudly. "They're Juno's favorite." She beamed at Juno, who returned her smile with genuine warmth.

Alex watched them together, his heart both full and heavy. In the week since the fundraiser at the Garden Gate, Juno had become a constant presence in their lives. She'd been there for bedtime stories, impromptu picnics at his parents' dock, and quiet evenings sitting close together on the sofa after Lena had gone to sleep. It felt right having her there—like she'd always belonged with them.

And now Melissa was coming to take Lena away. Howard had managed to secure a temporary order preventing her from leaving the state with Lena, but that meant she could take her out of Autumn Lake, which is what she intended to do, according to her last text. She'd already used up her allotted time at the condo, and because she couldn't afford to stay at the resort, she'd told him she'd be taking Lena to a hotel somewhere. She wouldn't tell him where, even though Howard had assured him that she had to, and he was not looking forward to the conversation he'd be having with her when she finally arrived.

It was why Lena and Roxanne were there. In case things got heated, Roxanne would take Lena on a walk and Juno would remain behind as a witness. He would also tell Melissa he was recorded everything, and hopefully, that would dispel the worst of it, but he didn't want to be alone with her for this very important conversation.

Because they still hadn't determined custody, there was nothing he could do to limit how long Melissa kept Lena, either, and that meant he also needed to try to keep things civil so that he could negotiate some details with her.

He felt like he was walking a tightrope without a safety net.

The sound of tires on asphalt outside made Alex's stomach clench. He moved to the window and watched as Melissa's sleek rental car pulled into the driveway. She emerged wearing oversized sunglasses and a flowing maxi dress that couldn't quite hide how much thinner she looked than when he'd last seen her. Or how much more enhanced her cleavage was. He suddenly had a good idea of what she'd been busy doing while he'd been spending these last several weeks with Lena.

"She's here," he announced, turning to the room.

Lena set down the photo album and stood, her small face suddenly solemn. "I don't want to go," she whispered.

Roxanne knelt beside her granddaughter. "It's just for a little while, sweetheart. You'll be back before you know it."

"Your mom misses you," Alex added, crossing to her and resting his hands on her shoulders. "And you've missed her too."

Lena nodded reluctantly. "But what if she tries to take me to Greece?"

"She won't," Alex assured her, hoping his confidence wasn't misplaced. "The judge said you have to stay in Indiana, and your mom knows that."

A knock at the door interrupted them. Alex gave Lena's shoulders a gentle squeeze before going to answer it.

Melissa stood on the porch, her expression unreadable behind her sunglasses. When she removed them, Alex was startled by the puffiness around her eyes. More cosmetic surgery? Or had she been crying?

"You're late," he said, then immediately regretted the accusatory tone.

"Traffic," she replied simply, although the excuse was ridiculous. There was no such thing as traffic in Autumn Lake. Her gaze moved past him to where Lena stood flanked by Roxanne and Juno. Wariness flickered across her face, and Alex couldn't blame her for being worried. The two women looked a little threatening, he had to admit.

"Come in," Alex said, stepping back to allow her entry. "Melissa, this is my mother, Roxanne, and my girlfriend, Juno."

Melissa hesitated for a fraction of a second before walking inside. "Hello, Roxanne," she said with a politeness that sounded rehearsed. "And Juno. You own the coffee shop, right?"

Juno nodded and shook her hand. "Nice to meet you, Melissa."

"Come give mommy a hug," Melissa said to Lena, wobbling a little as she crouched down and opened her arms. Alex almost stepped forward to give her a hand, but he held himself in check.

Lena let out a little whimper and ran into her mother's embrace, throwing her arms around Melissa's neck in a fierce hug.

"Oh, baby. I've missed you so much," Melissa murmured into Lena's ear.

"I missed you so much, too, Mommy," Lena returned, not quite crying, but clearly overwhelmed by her emotions.

They stayed like that for quite some time, rocking side to side a little. The sight of the two of them, so alike and so different, reuniting in such a transparent display of emotions, softened Alex's heart toward the woman who had kept his daughter from him for the first several years of his life.

When Lena finally released her mother and Melissa rose, she lifted her chin in that defiant gesture she seemed to use a lot around him, and asked, "Why are they here?" Her question wasn't accusatory, but it was obvious she hadn't been expecting anyone but Alex and Lena.

"We need to talk," Alex explained. "Just you and me. They're here to keep Lena busy while we work some things out."

"Lena's bags are all packed," Roxanne said, breaking the tense moment. "Would you like something to drink, Melissa? We have iced tea, water, or coffee, if you'd prefer. And your daughter made these delicious cookies, too." She picked up the cookie platter and held it out, and Alex realized his mother was just as nervous about how today would go as he was.

"No, thank you." Melissa shook her head, then rested her hand on Lena's shoulder. "Actually, that's good. I mean, that you have someone to play with for a little bit, Lena." To Alex, she said, "I want to talk to you, too."

Alex hadn't expected this. Juno gave him a subtle nod.

"Of course," he said. "Why don't we go into the kitchen?"

"Lena, honey, come show me which pictures are your favorites," Juno suggested, picking up the stack of photo albums from the couch and leading the girl into her bedroom. Roxanne followed, giving Alex a fierce look that he understood perfectly. His gentle mother wouldn't say it out loud, but if Melissa was here to cause trouble, Roxanne wanted him to know she had his back.

I am a lucky man, he thought as he watched his three favorite ladies head off down his short hallway.

In the kitchen, Melissa leaned against the counter, her arms wrapped around herself in a defensive posture. She looked smaller somehow, more vulnerable than he'd ever seen her.

"You look well," she said after a moment. "Fatherhood suits you."

"Thank you." Alex kept his distance, unsure of her mood or intentions. "I appreciate you saying so. Lena is, well, she's a real miracle, isn't she?" Now he was starting to sound like his mother. "Is everything okay, Melissa? Have you—" He gestured at his eyes, hoping he wouldn't offend her. "Have you been crying?"

She let out a short, humorless laugh. "Crying. Freaking out. Getting work done while I've been stuck in this one-horse town." She pushed a strand of hair behind her ear, and Alex noticed her hand trembling slightly. "I hope Daniel will be pleased with his investment," she added, dipping her chin toward her cleavage.

Alex said nothing, nor did he allow himself to let his eyes wander where she so obviously meant for them to. "I'm sorry you've been upset," he said, and he meant it. "I really want to talk with you about custody. I don't want to fight with you, especially not over Lena. I'd like us to come up with a solution we both can agree on."

Melissa sighed, then moved to the table and dropped bonelessly into a chair. She waited until he took a seat across from her. "I'm not going to fight you for custody, Alex."

The words took a moment to register. "What?"

"I'm not blind," she continued, her voice strained. "I can see how happy she is with you. With all of you." She gestured vaguely toward the living room where she'd met his mother and Juno. "She has a whole village here—grandparents, friends, even a surrogate mother in your coffee shop girlfriend, if I'm reading your lovesick gazes correctly."

"Melissa—"

"No, let me finish." She took a deep breath. "I love Lena. I do. I'm not a bad person, Alex. But I've never been good at motherhood. Not the day-to-day stuff. The routine, the consistency... it's not me."

Alex was stunned into silence, watching as this woman revealed a side of herself he'd never seen. One she probably shared with very few people. If any.

"As you know, Daniel left almost three weeks ago," she continued, her voice barely above a whisper. "I was supposed to go with him—Lena and I, both," she added, as if just remembering her original plans had included her daughter. "But then all this happened with you." She shook her head, but he could see she was more sad than angry. "He had to go. He couldn't wait for me to figure things out."

"I'm sorry," Alex said, and was surprised to find he actually meant it.

Melissa wrapped her arms around herself, the gesture achingly fragile. "I'm afraid if I don't go to him soon, he'll find someone else." She met Alex's gaze directly. "I can't lose him, Alex. I really like him, and I think I could be good for him."

"Melissa," Alex said, leaning forward and resting his forearms on the table. "You're afraid he'll find someone else while you work out custody for your daughter? Is that the kind of man you really want?"

"You don't understand," she said, her voice getting stronger. "Daniel has so much to offer someone like me. I'm not getting any younger, Alex. And he'll marry me, even though I have Lena."

Alex sat back and crossed his arms. "You say that like he thinks Lena is a necessary evil. Extra baggage. Melissa, that's not okay. And I don't even know this guy. I've never met him, and as you already know, I'm not okay with you taking Lena out of the country again. Now that I know I have a say in things, it's not going to happen, Melissa. I'm sorry."

Melissa sighed and looked away, reluctant to meet his gaze. "Look, I need time to figure out what I want, Alex. I want to go to Greece. I want to take some time to just be me for a while. Not a mom, not an aging ex-model." She waved a hand up and down the length of her. "Just me."

Alex pressed his lips together, afraid if he opened his mouth, he'd say the wrong thing. Melissa wasn't going to Greece as Melissa. She was going as an altered version of herself that had been customized to meet what she believed were Daniel's specifications. She was a beautiful woman still, but if all Daniel saw was what his money could pay for, he'd hurt her eventually, because she wouldn't be able to live up to the impossible standards he apparently had.

"And while I need to be in Greece, while I need time to figure things out, Alex, our daughter is too young to worry about all of that."

If Alex had his way, his daughter would never have to worry about any of that. He studied Melissa's face, looking for signs of manipulation or deceit, but found only exhaustion and a kind of defeated acceptance. He took in the more defined angle of her jaw, the new hollows beneath her cheekbones, the obvious fillers in her lips. She believed that her youth and her beauty were the only currency she had.

"I know that Lena needs stability," Melissa continued. "She needs a home, a routine, people who are fully present for her. That's not me. Not right now. Maybe not ever." The admission seemed to cost her something. "I want to sign over primary custody to you."

Alex blinked, certain he'd misheard. "Primary custody?"

"You'd be her primary residence. I'd have visitation rights whenever I'm in town or whenever we can arrange for her to visit me." Melissa's eyes glistened with unshed tears. "I hate myself for not being good at being a mom, especially since Lena is the perfect, *perfect* child. but I can't seem to change that about myself, no matter how hard I try. Maybe this is why I reached out to you in the first place. I just didn't realize it until now. I can't do this parenting thing alone. I don't even think I could do it with help."

The raw honesty in her voice struck him. How much courage had it taken for her to admit that?

"Melissa, you don't have to give up being her mother—"

"I'm not giving her up," she interrupted sharply. "I'm giving her what she needs. What I can't provide on my own." She wiped at her eyes. "I want to be part of her life, Alex. Just... maybe not the center of it."

Alex thought of his own parents, how they'd struggled after Jason's death. How they'd pulled back from him when he'd needed them most. People could love their children deeply and still fail them.

Alex nodded, mulling over everything she said, trying to sort through it all so that he'd be able to share it with his attorney. He wished he'd been recording this all along, but he'd forgotten to take his phone out, and since Melissa was being so agreeable, he wasn't about to stick his foot in it now.

"I just have one stipulation," Melissa said, straightening her shoulders. There went that chin again.

Alex waited, not sure he was going to like the line she was going to draw in the sand between them.

"I don't want to pay child support. I know that's not fair to ask of you, but I don't really have an income, Alex. Not one I can count on."

He didn't bother telling her to get a job.

"I'm the kind of person who needs to be taken care of," she continued, as if that explained it. "My financial situation is determined by the merit of whoever is taking care of me."

Angry for her, that she thought so little of herself, Alex wanted to argue, to tell her she was worth so much more than what men like Daniel had to offer her. But it was clear by the set of her shoulders and the expression on her face that she wasn't there to be talked out of the lifestyle she'd chosen for herself.

She was there because she'd done the right thing. She was there because she wasn't going to make Lena live that lifestyle with her. For that, Alex would be eternally grateful.

"Can we agree on that?" Melissa asked, a hint of her old forthrightness returning. "If so, then I'm ready to settle this out of court. Just us and our attorneys."

He didn't need her money to provide for Lena. Between his job and the support of his parents, Lena would have everything she needed. And if things continued with Juno... well, that was another layer of security for his daughter's future. It was a no-brainer.

"Absolutely," he said, nodding slowly. "I get primary custody, you don't pay child support. But I want everything signed, sealed, and delivered with our attorneys *before* you leave the country."

Melissa nodded, relief washing over her features. "Yes. Of course."

"And I need you to understand up front that Lena will not be leaving the country." He'd seen the Liam Neeson films and there was no way on God's green earth that he was sending his daughter around the globe without him. "And you have to agree to tell me where you'll be at all times when Lena is with you, and if you're going to be late picking her up or dropping her off, I need to know about it *before* it happens."

"I understand," Melissa got in before he continued.

"No last-minute changes or disappearing acts. No ignoring my calls when you have her."

He could tell by her expression that she was beginning to get exasperated. "I get it, Alex. I'll do my best, I promise."

He opened his mouth to challenge her, then thought better of it. As someone who'd made promises and broken them, he understood only too well how important it was for someone to believe in him.

"I promise," she said again, sounding worried now that he might be having second thoughts.

Alex nodded. "Okay. Thank you. I'll hold you to it."

Melissa fidgeted in her seat for a few moments, then said, "I think it might be better if Melissa didn't come with me tonight. I'm heading up to Indianapolis tomorrow morning to see my doctor." She gingerly touched one corner of her mouth. "To get the all clear to travel," she expounded. "I was going to take her with me and spend a few nights up there, but I don't think that's such a good idea."

Neither did Alex, but he wasn't going to say so in case she changed her mind.

"When I get back from Indy, I'd like to have her with me at the resort for a few days, if you're okay with that. Daniel has a room for me there, since my allotted time is up at the condo."

Alex was fine with that. Lena would be just across the lake and a few days would feel like a party to her. Without Daniel there, Melissa could focus solely on Lena for some much needed mother/daughter time.

"I'll be leaving in a week from now. I've already booked my flight." She held up a finger. "Only one ticket, don't worry." She pushed her chair back a little, like she was preparing to leave. "I'll ask my attorney to have everything drawn up by the time I get back in a few days."

"Sounds like a plan," Alex said, his tender heart aching for this lost woman. He cleared his throat, suddenly realizing that he had some things he needed to say to her. "Melissa, thank you. Thank you for trusting me with Lena."

Melissa started to shake her head dismissively, but he held up a hand to stop her.

"This was not an easy decision for you. I can tell. But to me, it shows how much you love our daughter."

Melissa's eyes glistened and she blinked rapidly, but Alex wasn't finished yet.

"I also want to ask your forgiveness."

"For what?" she asked, bemused.

"For what happened between us. For what I did to you all those years ago. I wasn't in a good place back then, and I treated you badly."

Melissa frowned. "That's not how I remember it. You've always been very sweet, Alex."

Now it was his turn to shake his head. "That's not true. I've been selfish and self-serving, and I took advantage of you, and it's past time I took responsibility for my behavior. I'm glad for Lena, Melissa, but I'm sorry I wasn't an honorable man with you. You deserved better. You still do."

Melissa looked away, but not before he saw the tears that trickled from the corners of her eyes. Finally, she whispered, "Thank you."

Alex crossed to the counter and grabbed a roll of paper towels off the counter. He handed them to her and she grimaced. "Sorry," he said. "It's all I've got. A little rough, I know."

Melissa tore one off and gingerly dabbed under her eyes. Then she took a deep breath and asked, "Would you be okay if I took her out for an early dinner right now? There's a little Italian place not too far from here and Lena loves their prosciutto and chicken involtini there."

Involtini? He'd have to look that up if it was something Lena loved.

Melissa grinned at him. "It's essentially a mini stuffed meat roll. It'd be a perfect place for a date night if you ever want to take her out."

"Thank you." Alex was touched by her suggestion. "I'll keep that in mind. Involtini. Got it."

"Anyway, it would just be a couple of hours, but I'd like to explain things to her myself."

A growing respect for her rose in Alex. Despite her flaws, she was trying to do right by their daughter in her own way.

"That's really good of you," he agreed, getting to his feet. "But Melissa? She's going to have questions. Lots of them. And she might be angry or confused."

"I know." Melissa rose, too, and squared her shoulders. She met his gaze with a somber one of her own. "I'll do my best to answer honestly, and I trust that after I'm gone, you'll be kinder than I deserve."

32
Alex

ALEX LED HER DOWN the hall to Lena's bedroom, hoping Lena would be okay with how things had turned out. He knew she was excited for her mother to see her room, and he prayed Melissa would respond with enthusiasm, for Lena's sake.

Lena must have heard their footsteps, because before they could knock on the door, the child opened it and looked up expectantly at them. "Are we going now, Mommy?"

"I wanted to see your room, sweetie." Melissa managed a smile. "And then I thought we could go get something to eat together. Just you and me. Would you like that?"

Lena's eyes lit up. "Can we get hamburgers and fries?"

"I was thinking more along the lines of caprese salad and involtini."

"Yes! Yes! Yes!" Lena bounced up and down on her toes, licking her lips exaggeratedly. Her reaction told Alex that he could learn a lot about his daughter from Melissa if he gave her the chance.

He gestured for Juno and his mother to join him in kitchen, giving Lena time to give her mother a private room tour. "I'll tell you about it in a minute," he said when Juno gave him a demanding look. "Don't worry. It's all good."

Juno and Roxanne exchanged chagrinned glances, but sat down at the table where he and Melissa had talked only moments ago.

Several minutes later, Melissa and Lena emerged from the bedroom and Alex got up to meet them, his mother and Juno following a few steps behind.

"We're gonna go get dinner, Daddy, then we're coming right back, so you don't have to say goodbye yet." Lena hugged him anyway, then Roxanne, and lastly, Juno. She looked up at both women and whispered, "She really liked my room. She loved it, especially the glowy stars."

And then they were off, heading down the stairs and out to where Melissa had parked. He watched from the landing as Melissa helped Lena into the back seat of the Mercedes, glad to see how animated his daughter—no, *their* daughter was. Before getting in herself, Melissa looked back at him and gave a small nod. It felt like an acknowledgment of their agreement, a promise to honor it.

Alex stood there long after they'd left, a strange mixture of emotions churning inside him. Relief that Melissa had agreed to primary custody. Fear that she might change her mind. Worry for Lena and how she would process this transition. And beneath it all, an undercurrent of cautious hope.

"Alex?" Juno's voice pulled him back to the present. She stood beside him, her hand finding his. "Are you okay?"

He nodded, squeezing her fingers. He turned to face Juno and his mother. "Melissa is giving me primary custody of Lena."

Juno's eyes widened. "What? Just like that?"

"Oh, Alex," Roxanne gasped, her eyes filling with tears of relief.

"She'll still have visitation rights, and at least for now, we're going to share legal custody, which essentially means that we both have to agree on big decisions like education and health stuff." He gestured for them to head back to the kitchen. He was suddenly ravenous now that the mess of nerves in his gut had settled. "But Lena will live with me permanently."

"That's fantastic news." Juno searched his face. "This is even more than you'd hoped for!"

"How are you feeling about all of it, honey? You don't think she'll change her mind, do you?" His mother's voice trembled.

"Relieved. Terrified. Grateful. Starving." He opened the fridge and pulled out an enormous container of spaghetti and meat sauce his mother had brought with her. "Are either of you hungry?" It was a little early for dinner, but he didn't care. If he didn't eat something soon, his stomach would start cannibalizing itself. "She's taking Lena for Italian food to talk to her about it."

Roxanne looked up sharply. "She's telling Lena about the custody arrangement? Now?"

"She wanted to explain it herself," Alex said. "I think she's trying to do right by Lena, in her own way."

Roxanne called her husband to let him know to come straight to Alex's from work. "Your father will want to hear everything."

While the spaghetti heated on the stovetop, Alex sliced up a crusty loaf of bread for garlic cheese toast in the broiler, Juno put together a green salad, and his mother set the table. His father showed up just as the toast was coming out of the oven.

During the homecooked fare, Alex filled them in on his conversation with Melissa. He watched them processing it all, their expressions shifting between relief and concern and back again.

"It's good that Lena will have stability," his father said finally. "But I hope Melissa follows through on her promises to visit."

"Yes," agreed Roxanne sagely. "Lena adores her mother, despite everything."

"I think she will," Alex said, wanting to believe it. "She seemed hopeful."

He and Juno exchanged happy smiles, but his mother's expression remained somber. He was just about to ask her if she had any other concerns, when she cleared her throat and set down her fork.

"Alex." Roxanne's voice was strained. She glanced at her husband who gave her a gentle nod.

Now Alex was really starting to worry.

"There's something I need to tell you. To tell you both," she added, turning her gaze to include Juno. "Something I should have come clean about years ago." She wrung her hands in her lap, a gesture so unlike his normally composed mother, and Alex was relieved when his father reached over and covered her hands with his.

"What is it, Mom? What's wrong?"

Roxanne looked to Juno, then back at Alex. "It's about some letters Juno wrote to you." To Juno, she said, "It was years ago, right after you and your family left Autumn Lake."

Alex felt a chill run through him. "What about them?"

"I—" Roxanne's voice cracked. "I never gave them to you."

The room seemed to tilt beneath him, turning his stomach the same way a night of too much drinking did. "Why? Why not?"

His mother's eyes filled with tears. "Leonard Thomas... your father, Juno..."

Dwight picked up when his wife broke off. "Leonard scammed us out of some money just before leaving town. He came to me and told me about a family business he was starting, and he asked me to invest. He talked about how serious you two were about your future together, and thought we might like to be a part of it."

Alex glanced at Juno, whose face had gone ashen. "How—how much?" she asked, her question breathy with anxiety.

His mother must have noticed. "Oh, honey, I'm so sorry. I know this must be such a shock to you, but I'd hoped, now that you know what your father does, that you would perhaps understand."

Juno shook her head, her eyes filling with tears. "But how much? I—I'll pay you back." She tried to pull her hand free of Alex's, but he refused to let go. He would not let her withdraw into herself. What her father did was not her fault, no matter how much she'd conditioned herself to believe it was. He slid his chair around to sit closer to her, even though he knew it might look like he was taking sides with her against his parents.

His father shook his head. "The details don't matter, Juno. We wanted to offer Leonard a good faith gesture; it's not easy moving to a new town and starting over, and with you two having gotten so close, as he pointed out, it seemed like something worth investing in at that time. But then he took the money and we never heard from him again. It wasn't a terrible loss to us financially, and no investment is a hundred percent sound, is it? And because we knew how you felt about Juno, Alex, we decided not to press charges. In hindsight, we should have reported him to the police, maybe saved countless others the same heartache," Dwight added. "But at the time, we thought it best to put it behind us."

Roxanne took a shaky breath. "But I was so angry." She looked at Juno, remorse etched into every line of her face. "And when your letters came, I wanted nothing more to do with your family, nor did I want that for Alex. And so I took them."

"What did you do with them?" Alex asked, angry at his mother's interference, even though he could maybe understand her perspective.

"I put them away, thinking after things cooled a little in regards to Juno's family, maybe after high school when you were old enough to make decisions for yourself, that I would give them to you then. Besides, I was certain your high school romance would fade like most of them do. And then we lost Jason, and for a while, I forgot about them." She turned to Juno and added, "Until you came back to town, Juno."

Alex's whole body tingled at his mother's words. He turned to his father. "Did you know about this?"

Roxanne shook her head, tears now flowing freely. "No, Alex. He knew nothing. I only told him about the letters last week." She looked back and forth between Alex and Juno. "It was all me. What I did was wrong. So terribly wrong, and I'm sorry. To both of you." She reached into her cardigan pocket and withdrew a small bundle of envelopes wrapped in a rubber band. "I've kept them all these years, too ashamed to admit what I'd done. But when you came to our home a few weeks ago, and I saw the way Alex looked at you...." She shook her head, her face a mask of abject misery. "I knew I needed to confess my actions to both of you."

She held out the packet toward them, her hand trembling. "I can only hope that you will forgive me."

"Did... did you read them?" Juno's voice came out a hoarse whisper.

For a moment, Alex thought his mother might not have heard the question, but then she nodded. "I read the first one." She met Juno's eyes. "We couldn't have you live with us, Juno. We would have had to have your parents' permission, and there was no way we were going to engage in any kind of transactions with your father again." To Alex, she said, "And I knew you would fight us on that, Alex. I knew you would push and push for us to change our minds."

Alex stared at the bundle of letters, the familiar slanted script that had become more refined over the years. He wanted to tear them open, to see the proof for himself, evidence that Juno hadn't just abandoned him without a word, even though he already knew it to be true. Glancing at Juno, he saw the same longing in her eyes.

"You had both changed so much by the time you returned to Autumn Lake, Juno. You had your head on your shoulders and you were determined to be a successful member of society," Roxanne said, her voice growing steadier. She dabbed at her eyes with her napkin. "And Alex, you were so lost back then. I thought if I told you about the letters then, it might make things harder for you."

Alex nodded, even though he wanted to rail at her that if she *had* given him the letters then, that maybe he would have been motivated to find his way out of the black hole he'd been in way back then. "I thought Juno walked away without even saying goodbye, Mom. It broke my heart. And Juno thought I didn't care enough to even respond to her, when I would have fought tooth and nail to get her back here. You were right about that, because we weren't just some high school romance. I was completely gutted."

"I know," Roxanne whispered. "I was there, Alex. I know. And I'm so sorry."

The silence that followed was heavy with decades of loss and pain. Juno's fingers intertwined tightly with his, and when he looked at her, he saw not anger, but a reflection of his own grief for what might have been.

"I forgive you," Juno said quietly, looking at Roxanne. The simple words held such power, such grace, that Alex felt his own anger begin to dissolve.

"I do too, Mom," he said after a moment. Hadn't she given him second chances, he reminded himself. And third and fourth chances? Didn't she deserve as much and so much more? He held the letters against his chest. "Thank you for having the courage to give these to us today. I need you and Dad in my life, maybe more now than ever before, now that I have Lena."

Roxanne covered her face with her hands, shoulders shaking with silent sobs. Her husband rose and pulled her to her feet, then wrapped his arms around her as she leaned into his comfort.

Alex rose, too, and circled the table, wrapping his arms around them both, then he felt Juno behind him, circling one arm around his waist, and one around his mother's shoulders. "Group hug," came Roxanne's muffled voice out of the middle of the huddle.

"My elephant family," he thought he heard Juno whisper. Maybe he was mistaken? He'd have to ask her to explain when they were alone again.

Standing with his arms around the people he loved, Alex was overcome by a sense of peace. The past couldn't be undone, but it no longer had the power to define their future. They had all made mistakes, had all failed one another in some way. And yet here they were, finding their way back to each other.

The sound of tires on gravel outside broke the moment. They looked up, startled.

"Could Melissa be back already?" Juno asked, moving to the window. Alex joined her, surprised to see Melissa's rental car pulling up.

A few moments later, the front door of his apartment flew open, and Lena burst in, her face alight with excitement. "Daddy! Guess what? Mommy says I get to live with you forever now! Well, not forever-forever, but like, all the time except when she visits!"

Behind her, Melissa followed more slowly, a bittersweet smile on her face as she watched her daughter's enthusiasm.

"Is that okay?" Lena asked, suddenly uncertain as she looked between the adults. "Mom says it's because you can take better care of me, and she has to travel a lot, and—"

"It's more than okay," Alex assured her, kneeling to her level. "It's wonderful news."

Lena beamed, then turned to include everyone in her joy. "Mom's still gonna visit lots, and maybe someday I can go see her in Paris if she still lives there when I'm old enough. And she says we can talk on the phone every day if I want!"

Alex glanced at Melissa, who stood awkwardly in the doorway. "You're welcome to come in," he offered.

Melissa hesitated, then stepped inside. "Lena wanted to come back and tell everyone the news herself. She was hoping her grandma would still be here." She looked uncertainly at Dwight. "Hi. I'm Melissa. Lena's mother."

"Oh, Melissa, this is my husband, Dwight," Roxanne said, quickly wiping away the last traces of tears. "I'm so glad we got to hear the news from you, Lena-bug," she said to Lena as she opened her arms for a hug.

Alex's father shook Melissa's hand. "Good to meet you, Melissa. Your daughter means the world to us. Thank you for sharing her with us."

Alex felt humbled by his father's kind words toward the woman who had, only days before, been threatening to take Lena away from them.

Then Juno stepped close to Melissa and asked, "Would you like to come in for some coffee and cookies? We still haven't indulged in Lena's snickerdoodles, and I know she'd love for you to try them."

To Alex's surprise, Melissa agreed, and let Juno link arms with her and lead her into the kitchen. With all six of them gathered in the small space, it felt full, but not crowded. He watched as Lena proudly carried her cookie platter around the room, uniting the most important people in her life. Melissa caught his eye over Lena's head, a silent understanding passing between them. They would make this work, for Lena's sake.

He took it all in: his parents with their adoring expressions following Lena's every move, Melissa, almost shy, discovering that she didn't need to impress anyone, and Juno. His beloved, beautiful, second-chance-romance love-of-his-life Juniper Bernice Thomas... soon to be Juniper Bernice Frampton, if he had his way about it.

This was his family now. Unconventional, imperfect, still healing from old wounds. But a family nonetheless.

33
Juno

Juno stepped out of the shop next door to her coffee bar and shook out her arms to release the tension in her shoulders. It was a mess in there, and right now, it was hard for her to see how things were going to come together over the next month. Alex had assured her that the project would take no longer than three weeks, but today, all she could see was the demolition that came before the reconstruction.

"Trust me," Alex had murmured against her ear as he pressed her up against the wall and then kissed her into submission. "I know what I'm doing." He'd taken her to the back of the new space and showed her the carefully draped sign that they were going to hang on the front of the building in the morning: "Juno's Coffee Bar & Bakery." The gold lettering gleamed against the deep espresso brown background and she'd smiled with delight at the sight of it. The addition would nearly double the size of her shop, and by the time they were finished, large windows would run the length of both storefronts, flooding the interior with natural light.

She'd pushed him away. "Don't you have to pick up Lena from school?" she'd asked him, her racing pulse making her breathless. "And I have to get back to work, you big lug."

Her community had shown up *en force* for her, not just with the fundraiser, which had raised an extravagant amount of money, thanks to an anonymous donor who'd paid for J&J's retaining fee. But she was certain that her fellow townies were also making a point to come in more often, to spend more money with each visit, and to leave bigger tips in the tip jar for her hardworking staff.

Because of everyone's efforts, John Jensen had informed her that they would start work in May, and would be finished before the tourist season started in June. "We'll work out the difference if we come up short," he'd told her. "You have a lot of folks around town who want to help out in any way they can, and we won't turn down free labor, as long as we can stay in compliance with the law."

Juno took a deep breath of the fresh afternoon air, then headed inside the coffee bar where her baristas were taking good care of her customers.

She circled the end of the counter and checked the orders to see if there was anything she could do to help.

"We got it covered, boss," Poppy said, nudging her out of the way. "You're supposed to be on your break, aren't you?"

Poppy had become a bit helicopter-mommish since learning about Juno's heartbreak over her father. "My dad left us when I was thirteen. My sister was ten and my brother was four. He just cut and run, so I get it," she'd said, handing Juno a cup of bold roast with a splash of heavy cream one morning last September. "Sometimes people just do things that can't be explained, you know?" She'd fluffed her hair and cocked her head in a sassy pose. "I mean, who would ever leave this, right? Angel Poppy? There is just no logical explanation." She'd made light of the situation, but Juno had recognized the sadness in her young friend's eyes, and she'd hugged her fiercely.

"I'm glad you came to work with me, Angel Poppy. You are one in a million, and don't ever let yourself think otherwise."

Poppy had hugged her back. "The same goes for you, boss. What he did to you wasn't because you're you. It's because he's him. That's what my mom always says."

It had been all she could do not to burst into tears over Poppy's kindness that day, and she'd gained a new respect for the young lady who'd chosen joy over despair.

Juno grabbed a fresh cup of coffee and retreated to her office in the converted walk-in closet just off the kitchen. With the expansion, she'd still be in the heart of things, but her space would be more than twice as large, and she was getting a new desk and a couple of comfortable armchairs so she could hold interviews or have private conversations with her staff and not have to commandeer the break room.

She squeezed in behind her desk and picked up the stack of mail that had been left in her inbox while she'd been next door. She sorted through it, then paused when she came to the envelope addressed in her own handwriting, 'Return to Sender' stamped in red on the front.

It was the third time she'd sent the letter, filling out a new envelope each time, and rather than just throwing it away, her father had scrawled 'Refused' in all caps print, and sent it back. She knew he meant the rejection to sting, and it did.

Juno carefully set the letter on her desk and picked up her coffee cup. She took a slow sip as she stared at the envelope, pondering what her next step should be.

After the Framptons had revealed his crime against them, Juno had changed her mind and reported his theft of her money. She'd received word from the State Correctional Facility that Leonard had been arrested and tried for multiple cases of fraud over the years, including what he'd done to her, and that he'd be serving a minimum of eight years in prison.

Juno had written a letter of forgiveness to him, telling him she believed he could change, that he could be a new man, if that's what he wanted. But now, having had it returned for the third time, she realized that she needed to stop trying to force her father to her will. The letter of forgiveness was more for her benefit than it had ever been for his; it had been a form of catharsis, of taking off the weight of bitterness that had driven her to be such a lone soldier all these years.

"What he did to you wasn't because you're you. It's because he's him." She repeated Poppy's mantra aloud for possibly the hundredth time since hearing it. She was learning to accept that, to accept herself, too.

Her phone buzzed with a text from Alex: *Just picked Lena up from school. Be there in 15. She's practically drooling about her milkshake.*

Juno typed back: *Tell her I've got a special surprise flavor today.*

Alex's reply came quickly: *Now she's kicking the back of my seat. Thanks a lot!*

The weekly milkshake tradition had continued since Lena had officially moved in with Alex.

It had been a bumpy transition at first, with Lena missing her mother and struggling to adjust to school in a regular classroom setting rather than being taught by a tutor.

Alex, too, had discovered that single parenthood was a 24-hour job, seven days a week, and that there was no such thing as time off. His life now revolved around Lena's schedules, Lena's needs, Lena's wants, and Lena's habits, both good and bad. His angelic Lena-bug, he'd quickly learned, had mastered the art of silent treatments and slammed doors, modeled by her mother over the years, he was certain. But in the tiny apartment they shared, her silence was louder than any raised voice.

Then there were her tears. Tears of devastation over a misplaced trinket. Tears of anger over a classmate's unkind words. Tears of remorse that followed the silent treatments and slammed doors. Tears of grief over why Melissa wasn't like other mommies, why she'd rather go live with some guy in France than stay in Autumn Lake to be with her. Those tears, especially, were difficult for Alex, because there was nothing he could do or say to explain Melissa's decisions in a way that would comfort their daughter.

Juno had assured him on multiple occasions that Lena didn't need him to fix everything for her. She needed him to be there for her, to hold her and tell her she was deeply loved.

Melissa had kept her promise to maintain regular contact. She'd been back twice already, once at Thanksgiving, and again just before Christmas, and had spoken with Lena by phone almost daily. She was arriving next Thursday and would spend three weeks in Autumn Lake for Lena's 9th birthday, during which time Lena would stay with her as much as she wanted. To Alex's surprise, Melissa had booked a room at The Garden Gate Bed & Breakfast on the south shore, rather than at the Carpe Diem resort. It was obvious to Alex that she was trying to plug into Lena's new world, and he knew his friends and family would be gracious and welcoming to her, because that was how they were.

In spite of the bumps in the road, Alex had blossomed as a father. He and Lena had made his small upstairs apartment into a home, but having the huge yard and supervised access to the lake at her grandparents' house—plus Ralphy, the dog—gave her lots of room to run around and be a kid. It helped that her grandparents had given her an enormous jungle gym swing set for Christmas, and Lena was looking forward to having a bunch of her new school friends over for her birthday party.

She finished her coffee and headed back to the front of the shop and pulled out her running checklist of tasks, stuff to do when anyone had down time. She'd just started unloading glassware from the steamer when the gentle chime of the door sounded. She turned around to see a very animated Lena, chattering like a mad jaybird as she entered the shop in front of her father, and Alex, nodding like he was listening to her every word. Juno wasn't fooled, though. She saw the glazed over look in his eyes that told her Lena had probably been talking nonstop since the moment she'd gotten into his truck.

Lena spotted her first, breaking away from Alex to rush toward her. "Juno! Daddy said you have a surprise flavor for me!"

"I do," Juno confirmed, accepting the girl's enthusiastic hug. "It's in the kitchen, but you'll have to help me make it."

"Can I?" Lena's eyes widened with delight. "Like, actually help?"

"Your apron's already waiting for you," Juno said, gesturing toward the kitchen.

As Lena darted off, Alex looped an arm around Juno's waist and brought her close for a quick kiss. From her friends' table, she heard Liz call out, "Get a room," and then Candy's reprimand.

Juno took Alex's hand. "Come on. We'd better get back there before your daughter decides to make her own shake unsupervised."

Alex kept his arm around her waist, his warmth a comforting presence. "You doing okay?" he asked, seeming to sense the shift in her mood, but she had long since stopped being surprised by his perceptiveness. Alex was a good judge of character because he paid attention.

"Just been reflecting on everything that's happened this past year. The good and the bad."

"Any word from..." He didn't finish the sentence. He didn't need to.

She shook her head. "No. And I'm not sure there ever will be." She managed a small smile. "I got my letter back again today, and I'm not going to try sending it anymore."

"I'm sorry, June-bug."

"It's okay. I'm okay with it; really." *What he did to you wasn't because you're you. It's because he's him.*

Alex nodded, understanding in his eyes. He'd been there through the entire emotional journey—the anger, the shame, the gradual acceptance that her father's actions weren't her responsibility, and that she couldn't force him to be the man she wanted him to be.

They found Lena with her apron already around her waist, and standing on a step stool by the counter where Juno had set out ingredients for the day's special milkshake creation—strawberries, vanilla bean ice cream, and fresh mint.

"What are we making?" Lena asked eagerly.

"Strawberry-mint dream," Juno replied, joining her at the counter. "It's a spring specialty."

As they worked together, Juno marveled at how natural it felt, this little family they'd created. Alex leaned against the doorframe, watching them with a smile that made Juno's heart skip. She'd caught him looking at her that way more and more lately—with a mixture of tenderness and something deeper, something that spoke of permanence.

Once the milkshakes were blended and poured into mason jars with rims coated in white chocolate spread and dipped in crushed strawberry wafers, they settled at the counter in their usual spot. Alex and Lena each had a shake, while Juno sipped a mild ginger and lemon tea. She'd had enough sugar and caffeine for the day.

She glanced out through the front window and was surprised to see all of her Garden Variety Lovers Club friends gathered out on the sidewalk, their heads together like they were discussing something important. Claire glanced up and waved, but didn't beckon her outside to join them.

Hmmm. The last time her friends had gotten together without her knowing had been for her fundraiser. Surely, they weren't up to something else, were they? Was it possible to die from too much kindness?

Well, whatever they were up to would have to wait. She had a very important young lady and her father to entertain at the moment.

"How was school today?" Juno asked Lena, who was already sporting a whipped cream mustache.

"Good! I got an A on my science project. The one about photosynthesis, remember? And Jesse Draper tried to kiss me at recess, but I told him I'm too young for kissing."

Alex nearly choked on his shake. "He what?"

Lena rolled her eyes dramatically. "Relax, Daddy. I handled it."

Juno bit back a laugh at Alex's stunned face. "Sounds like you did," she agreed, winking at Lena. "Very mature."

Alex shook his head, recovered from his momentary shock. "When did you get so grown up?"

"I'm almost nine," Lena reminded him solemnly. "That's practically a teenager."

This time, Juno couldn't hold back her laughter. "Not quite, sweetheart. You've got a few years to go."

As they chatted, Juno saw Alex and Lena exchange surreptitious side-glances, as if sharing a secret. Twice, Alex reached into his pocket, then seemed to change his mind.

"Okay, what's going on with you two?" she finally asked. "You're being weird."

Lena giggled, eyeing Alex expectantly. He cleared his throat, suddenly looking nervous.

At that moment, her friends bustled inside, then huddled suspiciously in a group by the window instead of coming to the counter to place their orders. They were up to something for sure.

Juno narrowed her eyes at them, but only Liz locked gazes with her, and she shrugged and grinned like she was just along for the ride.

"We, uh, have something for you," Alex said, drawing her attention back to him. He was reaching into his pocket again. This time, he withdrew a small black velvet box, which he and Lena together slid across the counter toward her.

Juno stared at it, her heart pounding. "What's this?"

"Open it," Lena urged, practically bouncing on her stool. And then, unable to contain her excitement, she exclaimed, "Daddy asked me first, just like you said he would, and I said yes. So what are you going to say?"

With trembling fingers, Juno picked up the box and opened it. Inside was an antique-looking band of white gold with a small but brilliant diamond in the center, flanked by tiny sapphires.

"It was my grandmother's," Alex said quietly. "Mom gave it to me to give to you. With her blessing."

Juno looked up at him, her vision blurring with tears. "Alex..."

He reached across the counter to take her hand. "I love you, Juniper Thomas. I've loved you as long as I've known you. I never stopped loving you, even when I thought I'd lost you forever." His voice was steady, though his eyes betrayed his nerves. "You're the best thing that's ever happened to me—"

"To us," Lena interjected, reaching over to add her hand to theirs.

"To us," Alex amended. "Will you marry me?"

"Marry us, Dad," Lena corrected again. "Remember?"

Juno was aware of Trevor and Poppy frozen in place down near the register, of Claire and Penny, of Addison and Liz and Candy, still loitering at the back of the room, but with their full attention on her. Of the handful of regular customers who had gone silent, all watching the scene unfold.

But in that moment, all she could see was Alex and Lena, looking at her with matching hopeful expressions.

"Yes," she whispered, and then louder, "Yes, of course I will."

The shop erupted in applause as Alex slid from his stool and drew her around the corner so that he slip the ring onto her finger. It fit perfectly, as if it had been made for her.

"I love you," she murmured as he pulled her close.

"I love you too, June-bug," he replied, the old nickname a term of endearment rather than a reminder of what they'd lost.

Lena wiggled her way between them, wrapping her arms around them both. "We're going to be a real family now," she declared, her face alight with joy.

Juno bent to kiss the top of her head. "We already are, sweetheart."

And it was true. Somewhere along the way, through all the pain and misunderstandings and second chances, they had found their way back to each other.

As Alex pulled them both closer, Juno caught sight of her friends moving in to circle around them, their faces alight with happiness for her.

"My elephant family," she declared, fighting back tears of joy. "I love you all so much."

♥ · ♥ · ♥ · ♥ · ♥

Isn't it remarkable how hard it can be to ask for help? And how rewarding it can be when we finally realize we're better together? I hope you found Juno and Alex's journeys toward forgiveness, second chances, and new beginnings both inspiring and satisfying. It's always a pleasure to have you read along as we walk with these characters through life-altering events and see them through to the other side where hope and love prevail.

There are more Autumn Lake Romances!
Visit me at **BeckyDoughty.com** and **subscribe to my mailing list** so you'll be the first to know when another book releases.

~ ~ ~

**The Renovation on Hollyhock Hill
Autumn Lake Romance Book 4**

MISS SUNSHINE MEETS MR. Grumpy in this heartwarming story of renovation, redemption, and second chances.

Candy Needham has rebuilt her life from the ground up after a devastating TV scandal nearly destroyed her career. Now establishing her own renovation business in Autumn Lake, she's determined to prove she's more than just a pretty face with a toolbelt. The lakeside house on Hollyhock Hill is the perfect showcase project... until she finds a brooding squatter claiming ownership.

Jonathan Burkhardt has spent the last several months doing penance on the Appalachian Trail, carrying his father's ashes and his own heavy guilt. He wants nothing more than peace and quiet to figure out his next steps. The house his estranged aunt offers him—his father's childhood home—seems like the perfect refuge... until he's awakened by a tiny blonde wielding a great big hammer and threatening to call the police.

Maeve Lewis, Jonathan's aunt and Candy's benefactor, considers the mix-up providential, and comes up with a less than ideal solution. Forced to work together on the renovation, Candy's sunshine optimism clashes with Jonathan's thundercloud pessimism at every turn. As walls come down in the old house, so do the barriers around their hearts, but their unresolved histories threaten to derail not just the renovation, but any chance of a future together.

The Renovation on Hollyhock Hill is a touching story about honoring the past while building a future, finding strength in vulnerability, and discovering that sometimes the most beautiful transformations require tearing everything down to the studs first. With her trademark warmth and wisdom, Becky Doughty crafts another heartfelt story about healing, hope, and the transformative power of love.

Keep reading for an excerpt from **The Renovation on Hollyhock Hill.**

From the Author

Excerpt: The Renovation on Hollyhock Hill

1 – CANDY

~ ~ ~

"Good morning, Hearth Breakers! It's Candy Needham coming to you on a fabulous Monday morning, and folks, it's Demolition Day!" Candy beamed at her phone mounted on the dashboard as she pulled into the driveway of the charming two-story house on Hollyhock Hill. She put her SUV in park and reached for her framing hammer from the passenger side floorboard. Holding it aloft in front of the camera, she asked, "Are you ready? I know I am!"

She took a moment to appreciate the lake house's potential. The home had that classic character that made her heart flutter—natural wood trim, tall windows, and a wide, welcoming porch that wrapped around the front. Sure, the flaking paint on the eaves and the overgrown garden beds showed signs of neglect, but she could already envision how stunning it would look once she worked her magic.

It was perfect showcase material, Candy thought, the butterflies in her stomach doing a happy dance. After working so hard to salvage her reputation, this project could be the cornerstone she needed.

She unclipped the phone from the dash and slid out of the car, trying not to jostle her camera too much. "I can't wait to show you the transformation we're about to begin." She panned slowly to capture the house and the property it sat on. "This beauty has so much potential hiding under her dated façade. We're going to honor all that gorgeous character while bringing in some modern touches."

She flipped the camera back to herself, the early morning sunlight glistening on the lake behind her. "Wait until you see the floors, you guys. I think there might be original hardwood underneath the decades old Berber carpet!"

Candy ended the recording and posted it to her social media accounts, resisting the urge to watch for that first heart or thumbs up. Her follower count had been steadily climbing back since the TV scandal a couple of years ago, but she still had a long way to go. Every like, every comment felt like a small victory in reclaiming her reputation from the ashes.

After tucking her phone away, she grabbed her tool bag from the floorboard behind her seat and headed toward the house. The owner, Maeve Lewis, had given her the keys to the castle, so to speak, and had granted Candy carte blanche to renovate to her heart's content. Although the property had once been Maeve's family home, it had been a summer rental for years, and had slowly become too much for the older woman to manage. Having decided it was time to sell, Maeve had assured Candy that she had no compulsion to be involved in what was going on. "Do with it what you would if you were the owner," she'd told her.

For Candy, who'd been living under the dark cloud of the fallout of her DIY home improvement show scandal, Maeve accepting her offer had been nothing short of a miracle. A full renovation would bring the home up to modern standards in order to fetch the best price on the market, and would also allow Candy to showcase her talents to potential clients. It was the perfect way to launch her new renovation and restoration company.

She pulled out her phone, fluffed her blonde ponytail, straightened her "Hearth & Home Renovations" t-shirt, and hit record.

"Let's take a little tour before we start tearing things out," she said, keeping her voice upbeat as she pushed open the front door. It creaked a little, sending a shiver of excitement up her spine. "That's the sound of a warm welcome from a house like this one," she said, panning her camera around the foyer. Inside, the air was musty with disuse, but sunlight streamed through the tall windows that faced the lake, illuminating the home's beautiful bones.

"Hello?" she called, her voice echoing. To the camera she said with a chuckle, "Just in case the critters haven't heard I'm coming."

She wandered through the open plan downstairs, careful not to move too quickly, lest she make her viewers seasick. "Check out these gorgeous crown moldings. And look at that fireplace with the original stone surround!"

She continued her tour into the kitchen, with its avocado green appliances and worn linoleum. "This kitchen is going to be our biggest transformation. I'm thinking glass paned upper cabinets with low watt lighting inside to display the contents, a butcher block island, a farm sink with granite countertops in—" She stopped abruptly, her ears picking up a sound from upstairs. A thump, followed by what sounded like... growling?

Candy froze, her pulse racing. Great. Was she going to have to deal with a crazy raccoon or an angry possum today? She'd been kidding when she'd joked about the critters a moment ago, but the idea of actually coming face-to-face with an animal who might see her as a threat was not appealing to her.

Putting on a brave face, Candy grinned into the phone. "Did you guys hear that?" She pointed toward the stairs. "I think we might have a visitor to oust. Maybe I'll have to add wildlife removal to my list of renovation services."

She wasn't afraid of mice or spiders; she'd had to accept them as part of her career choice. But something larger? *Please let it be a squirrel that's more afraid of me than I am of it,* she prayed silently, not wanting her viewers to pick up on her trepidation. She squared her shoulders and started toward the stairs, her camera facing outward. "Let's investigate, shall we? This house has been empty for quite some time, after all."

She climbed the stairs, still narrating quietly. "All three bedrooms are on the second floor. Two share a Jack and Jill bathroom between them, but the largest bedroom has an en suite bathroom with an enormous claw-foot tub. We're keeping that fabulous tub, but the rest of it needs a major overhaul. I'll show you that in a minute, but first—" She approached the first of the smaller rooms where the soft growls seemed to originate. "Let's see what's making that noise, shall we?"

Was it growling? The sounds were almost... rhythmic.

Wait. Was that—could it be snoring?

A flicker of unease passed through her, but she dismissed it. This was Autumn Lake, not Chicago. Animals snored, too, right? At least, her dog, Chipper, did.

Surely, it wasn't a squatter. She'd just been in the place two days ago, and there'd been no evidence of anyone but herself in the house.

The sound stopped. She held her breath and listened again. Was the creature on the other side of that door holding its breath and listening for her, too?

She grabbed the hammer she'd tucked into her tool belt and gripped it at the base of the handle, giving her swing an extra sixteen inches if push came to shove. Being barely five-feet-two, she'd take it.

She flipped the camera to herself and whispered, "Let's do this."

She raised her hammer boldly and stepped closer to the door. She pressed her ear to it. Something rustled inside, then let out a snort.

Her heart was pounding in her ribcage. Was she being stupid? Should she call the police? Should she be recording this?

Why, yes. Yes, she should be recording this. All of it. This was her renovation site. If some stray—or squatter, heaven forbid—had broken in, they needed to leave. Now.

She flipped the camera again so she'd capture footage of whatever was in that room and rapped a knuckle on the door. "Hello?" she called, hoping with all her might that no one would answer.

When there was no other sound, she tapped the door with her boot. It wasn't latched and drifted partially open. She stepped back, daring only to peer into the six-inch gap, but she couldn't see anything except the far wall of the room where an empty bookshelf stood.

"Hello?" she called again, louder this time. "Is someone there?" She nudged the door open the rest of the way.

The room was dim, curtains drawn against the morning light. As her eyes adjusted, Candy started violently, the phone jerking in her hand.

A large shape was sprawled on the twin bed under the window. Not an animal, but a human form in a sleeping bag, a shaggy head of dark hair protruding from the opening, facing away from her toward the wall. A large, filthy backpack rested against the foot of the bed, alongside a pair of well-worn, even filthier boots.

Her heart thrashed around inside her ribcage. "Hey!" she shouted, instinctively raising the hammer higher. "This is private property!" Her voice came out with much more authority than she felt.

The figure grunted and rolled over. A bearded, disheveled man glared at her through slitted eyes from across the room. He was clearly displeased at being awakened, but she didn't back down.

Well, she didn't run screaming, which was what she *wanted* to do, but she did back up so that she was outside the room. "I don't know who you are, but you need to leave right now."

He closed his eyes and burrowed back into the sleeping bag.

"I said, wake up!" Candy flipped the light switch on the wall on and off several times, hoping the flickering would irritate him even through his closed eyes. "You're trespassing! I have you on camera right now, and thousands of my followers are seeing this. I'm calling the police!"

That got his attention. The man pushed himself up into a sitting position, the sleeping bag slipping down around his waist to reveal a threadbare t-shirt that might have been white at one time. In spite of his broad shoulders, the shirt hung on his slender frame.

Candy's grip on her phone tightened. If everything worked out, this would make for some potentially viral footage. If things got ugly, she'd have evidence to turn in to the police. *If you survive,* a small voice in her head whispered. The guy was definitely hostile.

"Lady," he growled, his voice rough with sleep. "You're the one who's trespassing. Since you let yourself in, you obviously know where the door iso you can let yourself out again." Then he flopped back down and turned his back to her, drawing the sleeping bag up over his head as if to shut out both the morning light *and* her.

"Buddy! Hey!" She raised her voice. His dismissive tone sent an ever ready spark of anger through her. She'd dealt with enough condescending men in her career to recognize the type.

"I'm not your buddy," came the muffled retort.

"I don't care who you are, but you need to leave," she repeated, growing angrier by the second. "Now."

He flipped back the top of the sleeping bag but didn't roll over to look at her. "This is my house," was all he said before drawing the cover up over his head again.

"No, it's not." Sheesh. Was she arguing with a squatter over ownership of the house? On camera? He was making her look like a fool.

"That's it," she said. "I'm calling the police." She stopped filming and dialed 911 on speaker so that he could hear just how serious she was.

The phone rang twice, then was answered by a calm male voice. "9-1-1. What is your emergency?"

The man in the bed sat bolt upright and threw back the covers again. "Is this some kind of a joke? Who are you?" He pulled his legs from the covers and pushed to his feet, causing Candy to take another step back. She also raised her hammer again. The man snorted with derision. "You planning to club me with that thing?"

Candy straightened her shoulders defiantly and brought the phone a little closer to her mouth. "I'm at 1432 Hollyhock Hill and there's an intruder here. I need the police."

The operator paused a moment, then asked, "Ma'am, are you safe? Are you in the home with the intruder?"

Candy shot a challenging look at the man who now stood in the middle of the room in only his t-shirt and boxers. "Am I safe?" she asked him, refusing to look away. All the important bits were fully covered, and since he didn't seem to be embarrassed by his state of dishabille, then she refused to let him think it bothered her. Besides, what if he lunged at her the moment she turned her back on him?

"Ma'am?" The operator spoke more urgently. "Do you know the intruder?"

"No, I most certainly do not," Candy exclaimed. "Please send the police as quickly as possible." She gave the dispatcher her name and promised to stay on the line with him until the police showed up.

The man was shaking his head, his tangled hair and beard wild from sleep, giving off major irritated sasquatch vibes. "Idiot," he snarled, turning away from her. As if suddenly remembering that he was only in his underclothes, he reached for the backpack and withdrew a pair of cargo pants with holes in both knees and one back pocket nearly torn off.

"Did you just call me an idiot?" Candy demanded, offended by his belligerence. And now she was sounding belligerent, too. Great.

"Nope," the guy grunted, his back to her as he unceremoniously stepped into his pants. He was almost gaunt, Candy noticed. She could practically count his ribs through the thin fabric of his shirt as he bent forward to root around in his pack again. He stumbled a little when he straightened, but placed a hand on the wall to steady himself.

He looked like he needed to eat something. Was he sick?

Oh, no, no, no. Don't start feeling sorry for him, Candace Needham. He just called you an idiot.

Because in spite of his denial, he certainly hadn't called himself an idiot, had he? Obviously, this guy was gunning for a fight, hoping to get a reaction out of her.

"Ms. Needham?" It was the dispatcher trying to get her attention. "I'm advising you to remove yourself from the situation while you wait for the police. You should get out of the house, maybe into your car and lock the doors."

But Candy wasn't about to give up ground. Sure, she was being stubborn, but after sizing up her opponent, she figured she could take him. She was armed with a hammer, after all.

Besides, she was finished with men dictating her every move.

"Thank you," was all she said in response, but she did acknowledge to herself that she didn't have to loiter in the doorway and stare at the guy. She moved to the top of the stairs where she could see the front door below, while still keeping an eye on the open bedroom door just a few feet down the hall. "So much for a smooth first day on this project," she muttered under her breath.

The man didn't emerge from the room, which was almost more unnerving than if he'd tried to flee, especially with the police coming. Either he was completely delusional and truly thought he owned the place, or he was the most confident squatter in Indiana history.

Within ten minutes, a police cruiser pulled up outside. Candy hurried downstairs to meet Officer Wayne, a clean-cut man in his mid-thirties, and a familiar face to most of the Autumn Lake locals.

"Hey, Bobby," Candy greeted him, holding the door open. She said goodbye to the dispatcher on the phone and hung up. "He's upstairs. Unless he's crawled out a window. I have no clue how he even got in."

The officer eyed the hammer she still clutched in one hand.

"Oh," Candy said, flushing under his questioning gaze. "Yeah. Effective, don't you think?" She shoved the thing back into her toolbelt like she was holstering a gun.

"Why are you still in the house?" Bobby asked, scanning the large open floor plan beyond her. "Why didn't you wait in your car for me?"

Candy drew herself up, trying to look taller. "He didn't seem that dangerous."

"And you could tell that by looking?" Bobby frowned. "Was he armed?"

"He was sleeping," she shot back, not appreciating what sounded to her like a condescending tone.

"I know a lot of guys who sleep with their weapons."

Candy took a deep, steadying breath. She would not fight with Bobby Wayne. Not today. She had a renovation to tackle, and the sooner she could get both men out of the house, the better. She'd put herself on a strict schedule, having already posted her Open House weekend online and in the local Courier newspaper, and this was not the kind of delay she'd accounted for.

Instead, she waved a hand toward the staircase. "Will you please go deal with him? I'm not the one trespassing, remember?"

Bobby was a good cop. He was a good guy in general. Candy knew he wasn't belittling her, that she was just being defensive, and so she conceded a little ground to him. "I'll wait down here."

Bobby nodded, grim-faced. "Good idea. I'll go take a look."

"Holler if you need me," she added, as he started up the stairs.

Bobby shot her a long-suffering glare over his shoulder, and Candy fluttered her fingers at him, grimacing in acknowledgement that maybe that might have been a little much.

~ ~ ~

Read the rest of Candy's story in The Renovation on Hollyhock Hill: Autumn Lake Romance Book 4